KETHA'S DAUGHTER

Suzanne Francis is a captivating author. Her writing
pulls you from the realm of reality and places you
into the world of imagination so smoothly that
you may not know you have arrived there.
Dianna Doles Petry, Sage Fire Reviews

Ms. Francis paints her setting with specific, colorful
details that completely drew me into the land of Yrth
and its ongoing civil war. I recommend it highly.
Dandelion, Long and Short Romance Reviews

Suzanne Francis, author of the "Song of the Arkafina"
Series, is one of the best small press authors. Suzanne
delivers an exceptional, unforgettable story every
time. Her worlds are filled with colorful details and
captivating characters that kept me turning the pages.
Pat Bertram, author of *A Spark of Heavenly Fire* and
More Deaths Than One, from Second Wind Publishing

Also by Suzanne Francis

Heart of Hythea
Dawnmaid
Beyond the Gyre

KETHA'S DAUGHTER

Suzanne Francis

Published by
Bladud Books

For my parents —
Bob and Christine,
with a world of love.

First published in 2008 by Mushroom eBooks

This Edition published in 2009 by Bladud Books,
an imprint of Mushroom Publishing, Bath, BA1 4EB
United Kingdom
www.bladudbooks.com

ISBN 978-1-84319-809-3

Printed and bound by Lightning Source

Contents

Prologue

Geya sits before her silver mirror, outside of time and space.

One sister appears before her. Her beautiful, moonlit eyes are troubled. I joined with my vessel and healed her husband, as you said to, Geya. You were right. He is not the son of Shiqaba.

Geya sighs. Is he one of us?

No.

Then who is he?

Dai! He is Dai, Geya. After everything he said to us about leaving the humans alone, he goes and becomes one!

Geya is angry. He has betrayed us for the last time! Carry a message to Raven. She will deal with this.

Moonlight shakes her lovely head in horror. You would give Dai over to Keth Dirane? Geya, you know what she will do to him. His end will not be a pleasant one. Even if he is a traitor, he is still our brother Amaranthine.

He *was* Amaranthine, you mean. Now he is only a man. But when he is reborn he will truly be one of us, Moonlight. He will be a traitor no longer.

But my vessel loves him. You would take her husband from her?

Now Dai has became human he could die at any time, and Death would feel no remorse, so why should I?

I wonder though...

What, Moonlight?

Why he decided to become human. Perhaps he has some plan to stop the Angellus. Perhaps we should not interfere.

He is the one who has meddled. She was meant to marry the son of Shiqaba. Only Moera knows what difference it may make to this turn of the Gyre.

The Numen might know.

You are right, Moonlight. I will go to her.

1

Lutyond's Leviathan

An old woman sits by a fireplace, and rattles a skin pouch filled with round stones, worn smooth by the action of the waves on the beach. She closes her eyes and places her hand inside, then stares at the stone she retrieves. It has been carefully incised with a stylized ice-berg symbol.

Turning to her companion, who also sits close to the warmth of the fire, she says — Look, Hieronymus, it is Lutyond's Leviathan.* That means Raven is on the move at last.

~~~~~~~~~~

"No! I am not going and that is final. You cannot make me, Mother, and you know it. So why do you continue to argue?" Gwenn Benet angrily stamped her booted foot and glared at her mother.

Katkin sighed. The girl was right — she could not force Gwenn to do anything she did not want to do. She tried to reason with her stubborn daughter. "Listen, Gwenn. I have been Queen for sixteen years, far longer than I originally thought I would have to keep the position. Beaumarais does not need me any-more. The country is at peace with all her neighbors and trade is more profitable than ever. What is more, your father..."

Gwenn interrupted sarcastically, "My what? Call him Jacq. He means nothing to me."

The Queen gave her an angry glance. "Jacq, then. I promised him many years ago I would not stay in the City any longer than I had to. I know he is weary of being the Queen's consort, Gwenn. He does not complain, but I see the unhappiness in his eyes. It is time for us to move to the country and go back to the life he loves best. He has been more than patient."

"And you expect me to give up being a Princess, and go and live in some disgusting... hovel in the back of beyond just so you

---

* For more information on the use and meanings of the runes, see Appendix I.

can make him happy? Why should I? I like it here in the Citadel, with Jessamine and the rest of my friends." Gwenn's stormy expression left Katkin little doubt her carefully rehearsed arguments had fallen on deaf ears.

"Acorn is not a hovel. You saw that for yourself when we rode out there last week. When I instructed my men to rebuild the house your father... I mean, Jacq, and I used to live in, I told them to expand and refurbish it. They even added indoor plumbing."

Gwenn gave her mother a withering look. "Indoor plumbing? My Gods, Mother, get a grip on yourself. Why did you not have Tintaren Manor rebuilt instead? That might be a decent place to live."

"Tintaren Manor burned down long ago, and I don't have any desire to live in my family's old mansion anyway. My father made his fortune by exploiting the cottars who worked for us. How would it look if I retired and took up residence there? It is out of the question. Anyway, I have already had Acorn rebuilt as a surprise for Jacq, and I intend to tell him tomorrow at your birthday banquet. I know he will be pleased."

"Are you planning to tell him any other secrets?" Gwenn said poisonously. "I know one which would not please him at all."

Katkin took a deep breath, determined to keep her temper in check now Gwenn had begun her favorite game. She said, firmly, "That is in the past and it needs to stay there."

"Oh yes, my Mother, and it will, as long as I get what I want. And what I want is to stay here in St. Valery." Gwenn looked at her mother and Katkin felt a sudden urge to slap the sneer from her face. Still, she did nothing.

"If you could stay here and go to school, as I did in my younger days, then I would not mind. Since you have managed to get yourself thrown out of every educational institution in St. Valery that is not possible. What happened at the last one? Beating up the headmaster, was it not?"

Gwenn's sneer turned into a pout. "Because I threatened to slice up that awful François Besson after he tried to kiss me, the headmaster took my sword away and told me to go to my room. Faugh! I challenged him to a duel and he laughed at me. I had to crush him; my honor was at stake."

"You have been listening to too many of Jacq's tales. Young

ladies are not supposed to behave like warriors. What am I going to do with you?"

"You are not going to do anything with me. I don't have to listen to you. Ketha says..."

Katkin felt her grip on her temper slipping. "Leave that venomous snake out of this conversation. None of this would have happened if not for her."

"What do you mean, Mother? Ketha is my best friend in the whole world. She has given me powers you can only dream of."

"She has made you quarrelsome and unkind and I rue the day I ever let you near her. But that, too, is in the past and I cannot change it. Now listen to me, and listen well. You are going to leave St. Valery and move to the country with me and Jacq, and that is final." Katkin held her daughter's intense blue eyes in a challenging stare.

"No! Stop ordering me about or I *will* tell him the truth." Gwenn gave a satisfied smile, sure this threat, which had served her so well in the past, would come to her defense again. This time her mother surprised her.

"Go ahead and tell him," Katkin said bitterly. I have lived with that secret for sixteen years. I am too tired to fight any more."

She thought back to the day long ago when Gwenn had come to her, full of questions, carrying a braid of blond and chestnut hair carefully twined together and tied with a ribbon. Katkin had hidden it away in the bottom of a locked chest in her personal dressing room, and she had no doubt the troublemaking Keth Dirane had sent the girl to find it. The blond hair woven into the braid belonged to Captain Tomas de Vigny — Gwenn's true father. Katkin had once allowed him to make love to her, in return for a visit with her incarcerated husband, Jacq Benet. Unbeknownst to her, Tomas later made the braid — using a lock of her hair wound together with his — as a memento of the assignation that created Gwenn. Jacq knew nothing of Gwenn's true parentage, of course. Katkin had sworn on the heart of the Goddess Lalluna she would never tell him, on the day Tomas de Vigny died.

"Fine, maybe I will!" Gwenn snapped back. "Then you will be sorry."

"So will you, one day," Katkin spoke quietly now, with regret. "Jacq loves you so much. I only wish he felt as proud of Tristan as he does of you."

"Of course he is proud of me. Even if he is not my real father, I am still the true heir of the *Dinrhydan**, the greatest swordsman in the history of Beaumarais. That baby Tristan cannot come close. Ketha made me strong, and Jacq taught me the ways of the warrior. There is no man who could vanquish me now."

Katkin wearily shook her head. "Such skills belong to a different time. Now the world is at peace. When will you understand that?"

"Ketha speaks of a place where the accomplishments of the warrior are still valued, and someday soon I am going there. I will have such power, no-one will tell me what to do, ever again." She gave her mother a meaningful glance. "I will make you pay dearly for all your lies." With this, she turned and ran from the room. Katkin watched her go. After brushing the tears from her eyes, she called for her equerry to ready her pony, Alys.

As Gwenn strode through the Citadel passages on her way to the blacksmith's shop, Ketha's voice echoed hollowly in her mind. "Are you going to tell him our secret? You said you would." She sounded hopeful. As Gwenn stepped on to the grassy parade fields, she paused to admire a detachment of Queen's Guard practicing close order drilling. She spoke out loud, though there was no-one near her.

"No, of course not. I love Jacq, even if he is not my real father. He is the only one who understands me. Not like her. I hate my mother!"

"You told your mother he meant nothing to you." Ketha's disappointment sounded plainly in her voice.

"I just said that to make her angry." Gwenn sighed. "I suppose I will actually have to do as she says this time."

"When are you going to learn, my dear? You must not allow your mother to dictate to you. That is not the way to freedom, child. Make her pay, Gwenn, as you threatened. Let us leave tonight, and make our way north. You can make new friends there, friends with real power. Later we can come back and crush her, as you have always wanted. Then we can have Jacq all to ourselves."

---

* Gwenn's stepfather, Jacq Benet, earned the name "Dinrhydan" in the War of the Rising. It means "true heart" in the old tongue of Yr, which is closely related to the present-day language of the Firaithi.

Gwenn listened to this in surprise. Had she always wanted to crush her mother? If Ketha said so, she supposed it had to be true.

She came in to the blacksmith shop and greeted her stepfather cheerfully. Jacq grinned at her as he hammered a red-hot horseshoe. Gwenn had been helping in the smithy since she was just a little thing, barely big enough to lift the heavy metal implements. Now she watched with interest, ready with the tongs to plunge the finished shoe into the cold water. Jacq nodded to her when it was ready and the shoe joined the others in the bucket with a brief hiss of boiling water and steam.

Jacq labored at the Citadel ironworks several days a week, making horseshoes or other handcrafted metal implements as needed. Of course, as the Queen's consort, he did not really have to work at all, but it made him feel useful to be making things with his hands. He felt very proud of his famous wife, who had saved the City from certain annihilation when she became the Avatar of Lalluna. Though she had been terribly maimed in her efforts to heal Hythea, the volcano Goddess, and now had only one arm, Jacq still thought her as beautiful as the day they met. Then she had been six years old and he ten. He had never loved another woman, could not even imagine it, until his little girl had been born and stolen his heart. Of course, he loved his son Tristan as well, but the boy could not compete with Gwenn, who shared Jacq's fascination with sword fighting.

They toiled together in companionable silence for a few moments and then she asked, "Do you have any swords to work on today, Jacq?"

He shook his head and she sighed regretfully. This use of his first name no longer troubled him, for she had been calling him that a few years now, for some reason he could not fathom. Katkin had assured him their daughter was just going through a phase and would grow out of it — but she had not.

"Are you almost finished?" she asked him eagerly. "Let's go practice for a while. I think I almost had you yesterday, you know. If only I had done a half turn to the left instead of the right, you would have been at my mercy."

"Of course we can. And you may turn whichever way takes your fancy today," he added drily. Jacq smiled and placed his sledgehammer with the other tools on the rack above the work-bench. Though he had more work to do, he always made time for Gwenn and her sword fighting lessons. He began teaching her the day she showed an interest in his long, two-handed sword, d'angwir,* when she was six years old. Over her mother's strenuous objections, he had forged a tiny blunt-tipped metal blade for her. She had taken to swordplay with such determination and skill he continued to make her weapons as she grew and they spent many hours a week practicing. Other than tumbling, it was her only interest. Certainly, school had not held her attention, but that did not bother Jacq at all.

"But wait a moment. I have something to give you first."

He walked back to a dark corner of the smithy, behind the big forge, and returned with a long, bulky object wrapped in a dirty cloth. This present had taken him six months to make, and in it he had placed all the love and pride he felt in his heart for his warrior daughter.

Gwenn looked baffled as he handed over the bundle. He said, "I know your birthday isn't until tomorrow, but I want you to open this now, in private." Jacq smiled and shrugged sheepishly. "Your mother wouldn't understand, and I did not want there to be an argument at the banquet."

She unwrapped his present eagerly and gasped at the contents. There, in her hands, lay the most beautifully worked sword she had ever seen. Her stepfather had executed every detail impeccably, from the finely shaped damascened steel blade, to the wrist guard made of twisted gold and silver wire with inset jewels. Gwenn held it up to the light, a look of wonder on her face as she admired the detailed engraving that flashed with glints of fire from the forge.

"Oh, Papa, it is a most magnificent sword! Did you truly make it just for me?"

Jacq smiled happily and nodded — pleased he had shocked his daughter back into calling him by his title again. She held it before her and executed some rapid slashes. The perfectly balanced weapon performed just like a living extension of her arm.

Gwenn gave a whoop of sheer delight. "Come on, let's go and

_____

* Jacq's sword was christened "truth bearer" in the old tongue.

practice, right now! You had better watch out. Now you have given me this, I think I might be able to vanquish you at last, my Papa."

He handed her a matching scabbard and baldric, crafted with equally loving attention, and said, "First we must consecrate your new blade and give it a name. It might take you some time to think of the right one, and you should not use it until then. Today you should use your old sword."

She shook her head decisively. "I already know what name I want. My sword shall be called keth'fell."

"Keth'fell? Are you sure?" Jacq thought the name, which meant "death crow" in the old tongue, seemed a strange one for her to choose.

"I am sure. What do I have to do to consecrate my sword?" She waited impatiently as Jacq explained she must draw her own blood with the sword and smear it onto the blade.

"Then you must repeat the name of the sword three times and call upon the Goddess to protect you from harm. Will you do the bloodletting yourself, or do you want me to do it for you?"

Gwenn seemed unsure, so he took her hand in his huge rough one. "Ready?" he asked, and gave her a worried look.

She nodded confidently and said, "Do it, Papa." He drew the edge of the blade across her palm, making a shallow cut that bled freely. Gwenn blinked once or twice but did not make a sound. Jacq looked on proudly as she dabbed the puddle of blood in her left hand with her fingertips and anointed the blade.

"Now say keth'fell three times and call on Lalluna," he instructed her.

Gwenn did as he said, but instead of petitioning her mother's Goddess, the peaceful Lalluna, for protection, she silently prayed to Keth Dirane. Ketha's voice came to her in her mind, saying, "Of course I will always protect you Gwenn."

Once they finished the ceremony, Gwenn followed Jacq out of the smithy into the bright spring sunshine. She chattered exuberantly about her new sword as they made their way across the parade field towards the special fighting apparatus Jacq had built for them. It consisted of many individual platforms on several levels, with connecting stairs, ramps, and swinging bridges. Jacq spent a few moments rearranging the platforms into an unfamiliar configuration as Gwenn happily did back flips, cart-wheels and somersaults on the grass. Her bright blond hair flashed in the sun.

Jacq placed his own sword with the blade pointing diagonally towards the ground. Gwenn joined him on the platform and crossed his sword with her own. She felt a shiver of pure delight when she saw that keth'fell was the equal of her father's mighty weapon, d'angwir. He locked eyes with her, grey into blue, and forgot he looked upon his daughter. Now she was only his oppo-nent, and he focused completely on her. He held up his hand, and barked, "En garde!" Gwenn nodded and the fight began.

Their lessons almost always drew a crowd. Passing Guardsmen stopped to watch the Dinrhydan's magnificent skill with d'angwir, as he fought off charge after tireless charge from Gwenn. Though Jacq had seen his fortieth birthday this year, he still moved with the easy grace of a dancer as he ran backwards up a flight of steps and then jumped down to the lower platform. Gwenn executed a front somersault and landed before him. She swung in a vicious arc and Jacq ducked quickly to avoid losing his head. He thrust forward and she did a one handed back flip, the landing perfectly balanced. The crowd before them cheered, but neither heard the cries. Only the flashing of swords and the movement of the oppo-nent's body occupied the fighter's attention. Neither gave or asked the other for quarter.

The contest continued for thirty minutes, until Jacq's face dripped with sweat and his breathing became ragged. Gwenn watched him carefully, waiting for the moment when he would tire and drop his guard for a split second. Never had she felt so invincible. Keth'fell made her into the warrior she had always dreamt she would be. Whirling sideways, she sent Jacq staggering with a swift kick, and watched triumphantly as he fell backwards. In a split second, she had hooked his wrist guard with the point of keth'fell and disarmed him. He gazed up at her in surprise. Her eyes hardened, and she touched the wickedly sharp tip of her sword to the hollow of his throat below the Adam's apple. Seeing the pulse beating in his neck gave her a curious thrill of power. The crowd below her murmured in consternation. Jacq lay very still, resting on his elbows, and his heart hammered as he waited for Gwenn to release him.

9

"Why don't you finish him?" Ketha hissed to her. "Now is your chance to prove you are mightier than the Dinrhydan."

Gwenn backed away, shaking her head, and dropped her sword. She cried out, "No! Not him. I won't do it."

Jacq stared at his daughter. "Who are you talking to?" he asked her.

She hung her head in embarrassment. "No-one, Papa. I just got confused for a moment." Gwenn held out her hand and helped him to rise.

He picked up keth'fell and handed it to her carefully, saying with a smile, "Well, I guess the time had to come, my daughter. You are the victor today, and I could not be more proud of you. Happy birthday, sweetheart." He gathered her up into his arms for an embrace, and Gwenn put her head on his broad shoulder, and managed to wipe her eyes surreptitiously on his already soaked shirt. As a true shield maiden, she did not want to be seen crying like a little girl.

After a moment, she said, "If I am a warrior truly worthy of respect, it is because of you, my Papa. Thank you for keth'fell and all your patient lessons. I will never forget this day. I love you, Papa Bear."

Jacq smiled and unashamedly wiped the tears from his own eyes. She had not called him that since she was a little girl. "I love you, too, Goldilocks."

The crowd around the platform broke up now that the show had ended. Father and daughter walked back towards the Citadel tower, arm in arm, animatedly discussing the finer points of the battle.

Fourteen-year-old Tristan Dinrhydan Benet watched them approach from his bedroom window. As it always did at these moments, his mind festered with jealousy and rage. His father and Gwenn had something special that Tristan knew in his heart he could never share. He had practiced and practiced with his sword, but it was clear he would never be his sister's equal in that department. Papa would always love her more. Turning away from the window in disgust, Tristan went to find his mother to tell her Gwenn had been fighting again. If he could get his sister into trouble, it might make him feel a little better.

Gwenn met him coming down the stairs. "Hello, little Shrimp. Where are you going with such a stormy face?" she taunted him.

"None of your business, Longshanks. Get out of my way." Gwenn towered over Tristan, and could easily best him in any physical contest, from racing to wrestling. He took some comfort in the fact he excelled at school. But though his father pretended to take pride in this, Tristan could tell it did not impress him nearly as much as his sister's dazzling swordsmanship.

Gwenn stepped aside saying, "Go on, Brat. Run to Mummy and tell her I have been practicing with Jacq." She smirked at Tristan when she saw by his expression that her guess had hit the mark.

He gave her a black look, and then noticed the sword she wore strapped to her back with the baldric Jacq had made for her. "Holy Goddess! Where did that come from? Did you steal it?"

She gave him a haughty look. "Of course I did not steal keth'fell. Papa made her for me, as a present for my sixteenth birthday." Gwenn produced the weapon with a ringing flourish and showed it off to her brother.

Though Tristan tried hard not to look impressed, his jealousy showed plainly on his face. He said, "Mother will not be pleased. You know she hates it when you and Father fight. The last time the surgeon had to stitch him up, she shouted at him for ages afterwards. Both of you are going to be in trouble now."

Gwenn laughed in his face. "I don't give a damn what she thinks. Soon, I will bring her to her knees and make her beg me for her very life. She will be the one in trouble, not me."

He looked at his sister with wide, shocked eyes. "You should not talk that way! Our mother is the Queen, remember? Such threats are treason. It is my duty as a citizen of the realm to tell her what you said. They will send the Guard for you."

"Tell her. I don't care. No-one can catch me where I am going," Gwenn said smugly.

"Are you leaving?" This unexpected news made him feel happier than he had for some time.

"Yes I am, and don't go running to Mummy with that piece of news. If you do, I'll cut your heart out and feed it to the cat for dinner." She glared at her brother.

Tristan smiled cunningly at her. "Don't worry, big sister, your secret is safe with me. Where are you going?"

"I am not telling you, little boy. But when I come back, you had

11

better watch out. All of you." She said nothing else, just brushed past him up the stairs. Tristan watched her go, and he could not hide his hopeful expression.

Gwenn went into her bedroom and lay down on the ornately worked metal canopy bed her stepfather had made for her long ago. "A bed fit for a princess," he had laughingly said to her, on her eighth birthday.

Back then, she had been happy, for she had not known about her mother's lies. Reaching under her pillow, she removed a pearl-handled dagger and studied it closely. It had once belonged to her real father, Tomas de Vigny. Gwenn had kept at her mother for ages until she gave her the knife, saying it was the only thing of Tomas' she owned. Besides the hair, of course, but Katkin had refused to give her that. Tomas had been Jacq's sworn enemy. Gwenn still did not understand how her mother could have done such a terrible thing to her beloved Papa, and she hated her for lying to them both.

Ketha's voice rang in her head. "The sooner you leave here, the sooner you can make her pay."

"He is supposed to be coming back here to St. Valery," Gwenn said earnestly. "I want to see him before we depart. Jessamine told me he sent a letter."

"We cannot wait forever. He is months late already. We need to go *now* so we can make our way north in good weather. Perhaps we will meet him on the way."

"Do you think so? Could you find him, in all this wide Yrth?"

Ketha cackled. "Of course I can find him. Am I not a Goddess? But you must not tell him your real name or your destination. He might try to stop you, or come back here to warn the others."

"But Ketha, I..."

"No! Heed me, or I will punish you. Do you understand?" Ketha's voice was harsh, and Gwenn knew this was no idle threat. Her hand instinctively strayed to a long ragged scar on her upper thigh.

"Very well. I will do as you say." Gwenn heaved a sigh and stood up.

"That is better. Now start packing. We leave tonight, after the moon sets."

Gwenn moved slowly around her bedroom. Though she had been saying for months she could not wait for the day she could leave home, now the moment was at hand she felt curiously reluctant. She examined her collection of stuffed animals on the shelf, next to the books optimistically given to her by her mother that she had never even opened. There were prizes for tumbling pinned to the walls, and pictures she had painted as a child. Her first little sword, that Jacq had made her all those years ago, had pride of place over the mantle piece. She ran her fingers along the dulled edge regretfully. Her eyes filled with tears as she recalled his proud expression today after she had defeated him.

Ketha said, "What is this? I thought you were a shield maiden. You cannot afford to be sentimental. You want power, do you not? And freedom? Jacq has taught you everything he knows. He can be of no more use to us. Now we must move forward and find a race of warriors for you to command. That has always been your dream, has it not?"

Gwenn wiped her eyes and nodded. Ketha was right, as usual. She began stuffing some old clothes into a leather shoulder bag while looking with distaste at the beautiful dresses her mother had bought for her. She left them untouched on their hangers in the armoire, along with the dainty slippers and luxurious stockings. At least her mother would never force her to wear such things again. She pulled on her over-the-knee leather boots, and placed the dagger into the top of the right one. Suddenly, she remembered she could not slip away until it was dark, and that meant dressing for dinner. Gwenn felt sure another meeting with her stepfather would make her change her mind about leaving all together.

With a look of grim determination, she placed the scabbard and baldric belonging to keth'fell over her head, and shouldered her bag. After creeping along the deserted hallway, she went to her mother's dressing room, reached into the back of her wardrobe, and pulled out a small wooden coffer. Deftly, she picked the lock with a hairpin and removed the keepsake that had once belonged to her real father. Underneath it, she saw a curious amulet. With a sly smile, she placed it around her neck. She snapped the chest shut again, placed it back in the wardrobe and went back to her own room. After hastily rolling up one of the woolen blankets from her bed, she tied it with some rarely used hair ribbons.

Although her room stood on the third floor of the Citadel tower, Gwenn often exited through the window to avoid whatever tedious duty her mother wanted to impose on her. She scanned the parade field below. The mess hall bell had just rung, and all the Guardsmen were inside having dinner. Gwenn stepped over the sill and found a good handhold on the ivy clinging to the brickwork. After one long last look at her bedroom, she swiftly climbed down the wall and left her old life behind.

Chapter Two

Orlinir Flow

The Numen sits quietly by her fireplace, in an old rocking chair. Hieronymus stays with her, as he always does.

As he makes a little sound, she looks towards the door. Someone coming eh, Hieronymus? Who might it be?

Hieronymus blinks his golden eyes at the Numen.

~~~~~~~~~

Arkady Svalbarad rode south, down a rutted and little used track. He urged his horse forward at the best speed the tired beast could manage. Ajax lifted her proud head and neighed, her chestnut flanks glossy with sweat in the late afternoon sun. The sand dunes on either side of the track sent up wobbling waves of heated air and blocked the cooling breeze from the ocean. Arkady retrieved a water skin from his saddle and took a long drink, and poured a little of the water over his head in a vain effort to keep cool. The heat of the southern summer bothered him now, though as a boy he had labored outside for hours on hotter days than this. But it was many years since his wanderings had taken him this close to the land of his birth.

Arkady had been traveling for many months — still he rode easily in the saddle. Once he had learned everything he could at the university in St. Ekaterina, he had taken the road as his companion and teacher. For four years he had been an itinerant scholar, and had seen much. Now, he felt called by his homeland, Beaumarais, and the desire to see his family again. He had written, ages ago, to say he was coming, but spring storms in the Gulf of Angar'et made it impossible to get passage down the coast on a trading vessel. But Arkady was nothing if not patient, and he bided his time on the coast working as a fisherman's jack, hauling in nets and checking lobster pots. Such hard physical labor contented him, for his mind could roam freely where it desired, while at the end of the day his body was pleasantly ready for food and sleep.

Ajax stopped, having spied a patch of tempting looking grass off to the side of the track. "All right, girl," he said, lightheartedly. "I am ready for a break too. How about if we set up camp, here, in this shady spot?" He dismounted in the lee of a high dune and stroked Ajax's ears fondly. "Tomorrow we will rise before the sun, and make up the lost time in the cool hours of the early morning."

In the distance he heard the whistling cries of sea birds, a familiar sound after so many days aboard ship. Arkady smiled ruefully, remembering how long it had taken him to get his sea legs. The blond sailors of the Dalvolk had laughed at him as he spent unhappy hours those first few days at sea with his head over the side of their wooden, two-masted Knar* ship, his face pale and sweaty. Nevertheless, they quickly befriended him once they found he could speak their tongue. Arkady helped them make trades as they made their way down the coast, for he spoke five different languages well, and had a smattering of others. In the end they had been sorry to see him go, but he politely refused their offer of a full time position on the boat, wanting only to feel the steady land under his feet as he made his way home on Ajax.

He still had some distance to cover, another two weeks at least, before he would see the familiar high purple hills marking the boundary of Beaumarais. Then he would truly be home. The thought pleased him. His four brothers, all older than he, had wives and children, some born since he left on his travels. His younger sister would be a teenager now. Arkady liked children, and doted on his nieces and nephews. But he had no wife or child of his own, for the road had become his mistress, and he was satisfied with that.

His last teacher, Dawa Tinley, of the mountainous country of T'Shang, had taught him much about satisfaction and illusory yearnings. He had learned more from that wizened little man in a single year than all of his illustrious professors in St. Ekaterina taught him in his four years as a student there. All the hours spent sitting completely still, trying to silence the incessant chatter in his mind, had eventually paid off. Dawa had sent him on

---

* Wide-bodied vessel used for hauling cargo short distances along the coastline.

his way, saying laughingly he could teach him no more, and why did he not find a student of his own?

Arkady sat now on the warm sand, with his legs crossed and his hands resting lightly on his knees. Hunger fretted away inside him, but he ignored it, intent on having an hour's meditation before giving way to his desire for food. Now, in the shade of the dune, he could feel a cool breeze, and he removed his sodden shirt, throwing it over the oat grass nodding in front of him. It would be dry by the time he finished his meditation. The sunlight, still bright in the late afternoon, made a red haze in front of his closed eyes. Arkady focused on the redness and began to repeat his mantra. Soon he slipped into a deep state of relaxation, and there were no more thoughts of hunger or home. Just the endless rushing sound of the blood in his ears, like the pounding waves of time in the universe. Arkady did not notice when a small sea bird passed almost right in front of him on the sand, hunting for tiny insects. The bird paused, completely unaware of the motionless figure before it. A second later, it flew away, frightened by the girl that had appeared from behind the nearest dune.

She stood and watched Arkady for a long time. His stillness confused her and she wondered if he slept, though she had never heard of anyone sleeping sitting up like that. Stepping softly back, she found a pebble and tossed it carefully. It hit him on the thigh. The girl ducked quickly out of sight behind a low hummock of sand and grass. Nothing happened. The man before her remained as unmoving and silent as a rock. Frustrated, she threw a larger pebble a little bit harder and was rewarded.

Arkady felt the pebble hit his leg, and unhurriedly brought himself back into the present moment. He felt no distress at this sudden interruption of his meditation. It seemed obvious someone was trying hard to gain his attention. He did not rise, just sat quietly, thinking perhaps some child was playing a game with him. A few seconds later, he heard a hastily smothered giggle from behind the dune. He saw blond hair mixed in with the strands of oat grass, just on the other side of the mound in front of him. A little girl then, perhaps belonging to one of the Dalvolk. But what was she doing here, five miles from the coast?

He spoke to her in their language, "Don't be afraid, little one. Come out and say hello to me."

She did not answer right away and Arkady wondered if she could be lost or frightened. Moving cautiously, he rose, and walked over to where he thought she was hiding in the grass. He saw only a depression in the sand and a trail of blurry footprints leading off between two larger dunes to his right. Arkady scratched his head, wondering if he should pursue the girl, or go back to his meditation. He called out once more, and received no reply. Hunger finally persuaded him to give up on both and he turned away.

Presently, a song drifted over the oat grass towards him. Arkady listened with growing interest, for the tune was a familiar one, and the words were in the patois of Beaumarais, his homeland.

Intrigued, he followed the girl's singing along a winding path between the dunes. He had no doubt she meant the song as an invitation, for the words were too apropos to be a coincidence:

Where do you travel, where do you go?
Clever little bird, take me along.
Fly up high, fly down low,
Clever little bird, sing me a song.
I would travel too — I would like to go,
If I had wings to fly like you,
Fly up high, fly down low,
Clever little bird, up to the blue.

The path rounded a corner and he came upon the yellow-haired girl. She sang as she knelt before a small fire tending two skinned and gutted rabbits on a spit. Arkady stopped, not wishing to alarm her. He said reassuringly, "Don't be afraid. I won't hurt you."

She laughed merrily. "Why would I be afraid of you, pretty man?"

Her unexpectedly confident reply confused him. Obviously this was no young girl, wandering the dunes. Arkady studied her face. He thought her sixteen or perhaps seventeen years old. She had the bluest eyes he had ever seen, fringed with very dark lashes, despite her blond hair. They were set wide apart above her high cheekbones. Her nose was straight and fine, though not overly small, and nicely balanced by a generous mouth and strong jaw line.

He asked her, "Are you lost? Where are your companions?"

"I am not lost, nor do I have companions. But I have these rabbits and I would share them with you in return for a tale or two. Will you stay and sup with me?" He looked down at her in surprise. She acted as though she had been waiting for him to arrive.

Her eyes studied him with shameless curiosity as she asked, "How old are you? Your chest looks like a black bear but you have hair like a grandfather." Arkady had inherited prematurely grey hair from his father. He had begun to go grey in his late teens and now his hair was almost completely silver. After his year in T'Shang, he had taken to wearing it in braids, woven with colored yarn and bits of turquoise. With his high cheekbones and light hazel eyes, it made him look quite exotic.

He said, smiling, "I am twenty-seven, and not yet a grandfather." Then, prompted by her brazenness, he asked, "How old are you?"

"Eighteen," she lied.

Arkady looked at her skeptically. "You should not be out here alone. The Fynära raiders use these dunes to stage attacks on the coastal villages. I would hate to think what would happen if they caught you. Have you not heard of them?"

She shrugged non-committally, so he told her what he knew of the Fynära*.

The young woman, who had remained squatting by the fire during his talk, abruptly rose to her feet. She moved with agile grace. Arkady stepped back in surprise. He was tall, just over six feet, but this girl stood taller still, and her shoulders were broad and obviously well muscled. She was dressed in a linen tunic, leggings tied with thongs of leather, and boots. Across her back she carried a long sword on a baldric. He suddenly found the tip at his throat.

But if she meant to frighten him, she was disappointed. Death held no sway over Arkady, for Dawa Tinley had taught him of the endless wheel of existence. He stood still, waiting to see what unexpected thing she might do next.

"I am not afraid of the Fynära," she said harshly. "When we

---

* For more on the history of the Fynära, see Appendix III.

meet it is they who will fear." Slowly she lowered the sword and put it back in the scabbard. Her blue eyes gazed at him fearlessly, and he could see the flicker of interest there. Immediately embarrassed, he remembered he had left his shirt drying by his meditation spot and excused himself to retrieve it. Her merry laughter followed him back down the track.

Arkady returned a moment later, dressed, and leading Ajax by her halter. He said, "I would be pleased to share your food, Miss, and I have many tales I can tell in return." He paused, looking a little discomfited. "But I still don't know your name."

"Do you not? Then I will tell you. But first you must tell me your name, and where you are bound," she replied.

"My name is Arkady Svalbarad and I am going home to the City of Isle St. Valery in Beaumarais. Is that where you are from?"

She glanced away over the dunes before speaking and Arkady felt sure that whatever she answered him would not be the truth. "My name is Krikka, and I go now to my father's homeland, Danica."

Now he knew she was lying. Still, he smiled at her, determined to play along with her game. "Krikka is an unusual name for a girl, is it not?" In the language of the Dalvolk, her name meant "crow."

She smiled back. Her very white teeth and sharp canines made the grin look feral, like an animal baring its fangs. Krikka said softly, "Oh, but I am a most unusual girl, Kadya."

"I can see that." Then he gaped at her, taken aback by the realization she had just spoken his childhood nickname. No-one, except his family, ever addressed him as Kadya. "Why did you call me that?" he asked her suspiciously. "Have we met somewhere before?" Her face did look vaguely familiar, but Arkady was positive he would have remembered seeing her, because of her height.

She shook her head. "Krikka knew another Arkady, long ago, and Kadya was his name too. I just got confused. But you don't mind, do you, if I call you that? It seems to fit." Arkady smiled and said he did not mind at all. She turned away from him and produced a long pearl-handled dagger from the top of her boot. The sun picked out the gold highlights in her hair as she squatted before the fire and tested the meat. "The rabbits are cooked. Are you ready to eat?"

Nodding, he turned to his pack, and retrieved his tin plate and a small knife. He was hungry, and the rabbit smelled good, though it had been a year since he had last eaten any flesh. That was another thing he learned from his teacher in T'Shang — respect for all living creatures. But Dawa had also impressed upon him the importance of kindness to others, and that meant accepting any gift without complaint or reservation. So he ate the rabbit with pleasure and shared what food he had in return. There was a little blue-veined cheese left over from the last port the Dalvolk ship had visited, and he offered it to her along with some ship's biscuit. She sniffed it suspiciously and tried a small bite. Her eyes went wide and she quickly consumed what he gave her and asked for more. Arkady looked at her in amusement. He had never met anyone who appeared to be such a curious mixture of innocence and menace.

"Who caught the rabbits? Was it you?"

She seemed offended at this. "Of course it was me. I told you I have no companions, did I not? I set a snare by their burrow and waited patiently. Later, when I saw you sleeping in the dunes I thought to share them with you. Why do you ask so many questions?"

He laughed. "You ask plenty yourself. But why should I not want to know about you? You must admit it is a little unusual to meet a girl in the middle of nowhere who looks like a shield maiden out of one of the old tales. I am just curious about you. And I was not sleeping, not at all. I was meditating, and that is a very different thing."

She sniffed derisively. "It looked like sleeping to me. But now, what of the tale you promised me in return for dinner? Tell me of the places you have seen."

Arkady smiled and settled back on his blanket. The long light of the late summer evening gave the oat grass a quality of sharp relief against the darkening sky. Everything, including the girl who sat next to him on the blanket, seemed bathed in a golden aura. He began his tale this way: "I left my home in Beaumarais when I was eighteen years old, and headed north. My father's family lives in St. Ekaterina, in the principality of Ruboralis, and I wanted very much to meet them. I also wanted to study languages at the University there."

She interrupted him, asking, "You wanted to go to school? No-one made you go?" This struck her as funny and Arkady had to wait until her fit of giggling had passed before he continued.

"Yes, I liked going to school, as strange as it sounds, and I was pleased to have the opportunity. The University in St. Ekaterina is very famous. I studied there for four years, and I lived with my grandparents. They have a big house on Karador Prospekt."

"How big?"

"Thirty or forty rooms. I don't think I ever went into all of them."

"My house is much bigger than that!" she boasted.

Arkady peered at her with sudden interest. "And where is this house, girl who calls herself Krikka?"

She smiled and shrugged, embarrassed at almost being caught out. "You are telling me the tale. Please continue."

"St. Ekaterina has many beautiful palaces and churches. On winter days, when I did not have to go to school, I used to walk all over the city. I talked to as many people as I could, to practice the language and learn about the culture. It is very different than my home. St. Ekaterina is much bigger, for one thing. Almost seventy-five thousand people live there. There were so many interesting things to do. Sometimes, my grandmother, Irina, and I used to go to the symphony at the Victory Palace."

Krikka wanted to know what a symphony was and he patiently explained. She listened with rapt concentration. Everything he told her about St. Ekaterina seemed to interest her and she asked many questions.

He continued, "One day, my grandfather Nicolai took me to the open market in Gueroi Square. I saw things from all over Yr for sale in the stalls. We were passing by a quiet corner of the market and an amazing painting caught my eye — of a beautiful woman, with green skin. Many other bright colors filled in the background. I went to have a closer look and asked the stall keeper where he had gotten it from. He was a small dark-skinned man with curious almond-shaped eyes. He told me it came from his home, T'Shang."

Her eyes went wide. "Where is that?"

"A country full of the biggest mountains and the bluest skies you have ever seen, far to the east of here. All at once I was struck with a desire to go there. Over the next few weeks I found out everything I could about it. There was not much to discover, for T'Shang has been closed to foreigners for many years."

"What about the green woman?"

"I found out about her too, after I bought the painting. Her name is Hana, and she is a Goddess of the East. Would you like to see?"

She nodded her head enthusiastically. Arkady rose and went to his saddlebag. He retrieved a rolled-up length of heavy silk and spread it out on the ground in front of the fire. Though the sun had sunk almost completely below the horizon and shadows crept over the dunes, the colors still shone luminously. The girl stared at the picture for a long time without speaking. She said softly, "Your Goddess has a very kind face. I would like to know her. But some Goddesses are not so nice."

Arkady gave her a curious glance but she said no more. He carefully rolled up the painting and replaced it in the bag. Then, in the gathering darkness, he went on with his tale. Krikka rose and threw more wood on the fire so that it blazed up in a rising ribbon of sparks.

He said, "I finished my studies at the University and started on my journey to find the lost country of T'Shang. My grandparents did not want me to go because I did not even have a proper map, only a book I had stolen from the library. It took me many weeks and months of riding to the east to reach the mountains. When I arrived there, I found that I had to wait for summer so I could cross the high passes. I spent my time learning to speak the language of the people I found myself with. They were yak herders and lived in tents of skin they could take down and move with them as they followed the animals from winter pasture to summer meadow. At first, they were shy with me, but once I could speak their tongue, I found them to be kind and very warm-hearted. When I could, I went up into the mountains and came down into T'Shang. It is the most beautiful place I have ever seen. I stayed there a year, in a village called Khalama, and I learned many things."

"What sort of things?"

"Like meditation. What you saw me doing this afternoon."

"Sleeping?"

23

He laughed. "Not sleeping. I told you already. I was awake."

"Why did you not move when I threw the stone at you?" She looked at him in confusion and he smiled.

"It is hard to explain. I close my mind to the things outside in the world and listen to what is inside."

She nodded her head as if she understood perfectly. "I do that too, sometimes." Then, thinking perhaps she had given too much away, she rapidly changed the subject. "Where is your weapon? I would like to see it."

He smiled and shook his head. "I have none, only the little clasp knife you saw me eat with."

"How did you travel so far without a sword? Did you not fear to meet bandits on your way?" she asked, clearly amazed at his admission.

"I learned a few things about fighting without weapons in T'Shang. Only in self-defense, of course."

This caused her to howl with laughter. "You could not defend yourself against me without a weapon! I would make short work of you."

"Let us put that to the test, if you are willing?"

She shrugged and said carelessly, "All right, but don't blame me if you get hurt." Standing abruptly, she drew the dagger from her boot and assumed a fighting stance.

He stood more slowly and brushed the sand off his breeches, saying, "We should move further away from the fire. Otherwise you might get burned when you fall." She raised an eyebrow at this and took a couple of steps backwards, toward the darkened dunes. Then she lunged towards him, as swiftly as a snake. The dagger flashed in the firelight.

Arkady sidestepped rapidly, caught her behind the thigh with his knee and pushed her down into the sand. She looked very surprised, and scrambled to her feet immediately. Another quick lunge brought the same result. This time she stood up more slowly and thoughtfully circled him, the dagger held loosely in her hand. She feinted several times and watched his reaction carefully. Arkady knew he would not be able to use the same move on her again. When she thrust the dagger at him he caught her by the wrist and twisted hard. With a cry of pain, she dropped the weapon and Arkady kicked it away across the sand. Now she furiously threw herself forward and tackled him. He let her momentum carry him backwards and flipped her neatly over his body so that she landed hard on her back. She lay there, panting, as he rose and brushed the sand off his clothes.

Arkady stood above her and offered his hand. "Have you seen enough?" he asked.

She reached for his outstretched hand and then quickly kicked out, catching him on the shin with her boot. Arkady felt his legs go out from under him and he landed awkwardly on the sand next to her. Krikka dropped on his midsection and drove the air from his lungs in an explosive rush. He rolled over and tried to extricate himself from her grasp, but she had her legs around him in a scissor lock. Arkady could not believe how strong she was. Obviously, she did not intend to give up without a prolonged battle.

After trying once more to gain the upper hand, he suddenly found himself on top of her. She stopped struggling immediately and looked up at him, her eyes glinting with fire in the dim light. Her hair spread out on the sand like a golden halo around her face. Abruptly, desire raced through him, setting fire to every nerve before settling like a blazing inferno in his belly. A second later she fastened her mouth to his with such abandon he could hardly breathe.

The disciplined part of his mind told him in no uncertain terms to stop at once. He barely knew her, or anything about her — not even her real name. Those thoughts were obliterated by the drumbeat of wanting that pounded in his temples and groin.

He was half-disappointed and half-relieved when, a moment later, she tore her lips from his and rolled out from under his body. She stood and walked back over to the fire without speaking. Slowly she turned back to face him and pulled her tunic off over her head. The firelight gilded her smooth skin and flickered on the shapely curve of her breasts.

"Krikka, what do you...?" Arkady began, uncertainly, but she was already bending to unlace her breeches.

When she had finished undressing, she stood before him silently — waiting... breathing. Her form was breathtaking, taut and finely muscled, like a long-distance runner. Arkady knew then he had long passed the point of no return. He stood and shed his own clothes as quickly as he could and fell with her onto the blanket next to the fire.

The prolonged and intense lovemaking that followed made all of his other sexual experiences seem arid and clumsy. They coupled almost immediately in a torrent of passion that spent itself quickly, and hardly diminished the hunger they felt for each other. Twice more he took her, as her nails raked his back and she sank her teeth into his shoulder like a wild animal, before he felt he had satisfied her desire and his own.

Later, resting on the blanket, the night breeze cooled the sweat on her skin and she shivered in his arms. The fire had died down to glowing red ash and he could barely see the outline of her face in the darkness. Arkady whispered, "Who are you? Will you not tell me your real name, my beautiful crow girl?"

She turned to face him and her voice sounded bleak. "I cannot, dear Kadya. She would be angry with me."

"Who would be angry?"

"Ketha. I must do as she says." She sighed deeply. "Sometimes I wish I did not have to."

Arkady rolled onto his side and rested his head on his hand so he could see her face more closely. He said, "I don't know much about you, but I can see you are in some kind of trouble. You don't have to tell me anything else if you don't want to. Let me help you. We can both ride from here right now on Ajax, and by tomorrow we can be far away from this place. Trust me, I will make sure, whoever this Ketha is, she cannot find you."

She shook her head miserably. "Ketha will always find me. There is nothing you can do to stop her."

He begged her, "Please, I want you to stay with me. What hold does Ketha have on you? Will you not say?"

"Don't ask any more questions!" she cried in frustration. "We have so little time to be together before she returns. There is only one thing you can do for me this night." He could not see the tears clinging to her lashes but he tasted them as she turned her face to his and sought his mouth once again.

Afterwards, utterly spent, Arkady fought a losing battle to try and stay awake. But as her fingers lightly stroked the hair on his belly, he felt his eyes closing, and forced them open again. He knew instinctively she would be gone when he awoke, so he whispered,

"Don't go, Krikka. Please don't leave me." She said nothing in return, just waited patiently for him to fall asleep. Then she rose very cautiously and dressed herself. She located the pearl-handled dagger in the sand and shoved it back down into her boot.

Ajax rested quietly in the lee of a dune and made no sound as Krikka saddled her. The girl carefully unpacked the rest of Arkady's food and the water skin and left it by the fire. She placed the rolled silk painting of Hana next to it. Krikka wore a periapt tied with a leather thong around her neck — a withered crow's foot clutching a green crystal. Thoughtfully, she slipped it over her head and dropped it on top of the painting. She walked slowly back to where Arkady slept on the blanket and said, very quietly, "Farewell, Uncle."

A large black crow flew down and landed on her back. For a few seconds it looked as though the girl had sprouted a pair of black wings, and then the crow disappeared. Krikka bit her lip so the pain would not make her cry out. Then she led Ajax away through the dunes and headed north towards the coast and the Fynära.

"What took you so long?" Ketha croaked angrily. "I told you we should have just killed him and taken the horse. We could have been miles away by now."

"I am sorry, Ketha. You promised me I could see him before we left. I don't want him to die because I care about him. Do you understand?"

The battle crow laughed harshly. "He will die soon enough, when the Fynära pay a visit to Beaumarais, my pretty girl. Ketha will have plenty of carrion to feast on then."

When Arkady woke the next day, the sun was already high in the sky. As soon as he saw the pile of things she had left, he did not bother to look further for Krikka or Ajax. Spying the crow's foot, he picked it up and gazed at it for a long moment. Krikka's face came back to him, and her eyes. As blue as the skies of T'Shang. He shivered slightly, thinking of their feverish encounter of the night before. If she hadn't stolen his horse, he might have thought it all some wild, fey dream. As he placed the charm around his neck, Arkady wondered if he would ever see her again. He shouldered the satchel that held the food and his water skin and turned away from the ashes of last night's fire, sighing deeply. It would be a long, slow walk to Beaumarais.

Chapter Three

The Wild Horses of Grandfather Ods

She listens and makes a face. Geya it is. I don't like her much, do you?

Hieronymus blinks and stretches. Exactly. She is not to be trusted, that one. Too wrapped up in the human sphere. Wants their worship, always wants more power. But what does she want with me, eh Hieronymus?

~~~~~~~~~~

Gwenn Benet pushed the horse she had stolen from Arkady as hard as she dared, but Ajax continued to be skittish and hard to handle. All animals behaved this way when they sensed the presence of Keth Dirane inside her. She had found it easy enough to hide the existence of the Goddess from most of her friends and family, but animals possessed far more intuition. Her mother knew the truth, of course, for she had been able to ask Lalluna why her daughter talked to herself constantly.

She spoke to Ketha now as they rode along the coast, searching for the abandoned village the battle crow insisted her aerial surveys had shown lay somewhere close by. The Fynära used the empty houses to store supplies for their frequent raids on the coast, and Ketha planned for them to wait there until the raiders visited again. The weather had been good for several weeks, just right for a quick boat journey from the island of Starruthe to the coast of Secuny. Ketha knew the movements of the raiders well, for she had followed them for years in her crow form, always assured of a good meal when they finished their work.

"How much further do we have to ride? I am getting tired of trying to make this stupid horse go in a straight line," Gwenn complained.

Ajax shied again at the sound of her voice, and Gwenn kicked her viciously. The horse was hungry and thirsty too, for they had found no fresh water in days, and Ketha would not let her have any of the meager amount left in the water skin. Gwenn had stolen three other horses on her journey north with Ketha and all had died of neglect or run away. It seemed likely this one would not last much longer either.

"Stop being such a baby. Look there, the path to the village is just through the dunes," Ketha chided her.

Gwenn turned her balky horse down the track winding off to her left, away from the ceaseless sound of the ocean. They made their way inland for a mile and came upon the ruins of a settlement. The raiders had burned most of the houses and kidnapped or killed all the occupants long ago, but a few structures remained undamaged. Gwenn kicked open one of the doors and found a cache of food and water, and some hay for Ajax.

"Now you have something to eat, child, I must go and find something for myself. I always take care of you, remember? No-one else loves you as much as Ketha, not even your so-called father." Gwenn nodded in agreement, her eyes vacant.

When Ketha spoke from inside her, Gwenn found almost everything she said to be perfectly reasonable. Only when she took her bird form and left to seek some carrion, did the girl entertain any doubts about the Goddess who had been her constant companion since birth. She stiffened in pain as Ketha withdrew from her body, and sighed in relief as the big, black crow flew off in search of some dead thing to eat.

She unsaddled Ajax and gave her some water from a stone cistern just inside the door. The horse drank deeply and then attacked the pile of hay in the corner of the stone cottage. Her new mistress watched her thoughtfully, while she chewed on some stale ship's biscuit taken from one of the barrels stacked in the room, after soaking it in a cup of water to make it palatable.

She recalled the conversation in which Arkady had proudly told her about Ajax.

"That is a beautiful horse you have, Kadya."

"Thank you. She came from Ruboralis. Did you know the finest horses in Yr are foaled there? Expensive, too. I worked very hard to pay for her. Truly, she is my most prized possession."

Gwenn was surprised by this. "Even more so than the pretty picture of the green lady?"

"Of course," he replied laughingly. "That painting can't save the *soles of my boots the way Ajax does. And I can talk to her, as well. She is good company, Krikka."*

Now that Gwenn had taken Ajax away, she wondered if he would ever forgive her for it.

She wrapped her arms around herself to ward off the chill evening breeze and thought again of their meeting. Normally, Ketha's presence in her mind chased such thoughts away immediately, but now she was gone, Gwenn could allow herself to remember the ecstasy of their frantic sexual encounter.

His gallant offer came back to her...

We can both ride away from here right now on Ajax and by tomorrow we can be far away from this place. Trust me, I will make sure, whoever this Ketha is, she cannot find you.

Gwenn fervently wished this was true, but she knew otherwise. No doubt the Goddess would have made her kill Kadya, just as she had killed his father. She only hoped he would be gone from Beaumarais before she returned with the Fynära.

After Ajax finished eating, Gwenn led her outside and removed her saddle and bridle. Sighing deeply, she slapped the horse's rump and sent her galloping into the dunes.

When the battle crow returned and had entered Gwenn's body, she asked her sharply about the horse. Gwenn said carefully, "She ran away, like the other ones. What an ungrateful beast!"

But she could not fool Ketha so easily. "You let her run, you wicked girl! I will punish you right now for your deceitfulness." Gwenn looked on in horror as her right hand moved down towards the boot that held the dagger. As hard as she tried, she could not control her arm. Her uncooperative fingers grasped the hilt and raised the weapon high over her trembling thigh.

Gwenn's eyes filled with tears, "I am so sorry. Please, don't make me do it. I swear I will behave from now on."

Ketha cackled madly, "That is right, little girl, beg for mercy. Not that it will do you any good, my dear. Now feel the wrath of Keth Dirane, and remember, next time, to be obedient to me!"

Gwenn cried out as the blade flashed downwards and pierced the skin of her thigh, and drove deep into the muscle. She dropped the dagger and fell to the dusty floor, writhing in pain, as Ketha's laughter echoed inside her mind.

"Be thankful I did not punish you any worse for your lying

ways. Now get up and stop whining. The raiders are on their way. I saw their long boat from the air, less than a day's sailing from here. You must be fit and ready to fight their leader when they arrive."

Gwenn sat up and stanched the flow of blood from her thigh with her palm. She knew from long experience that such cuts mended quickly, for the force of the Goddess gave her body healing ability far beyond an ordinary mortal. By tomorrow there would be nothing left but a jagged, red scar to join the collection of many others.

The next morning, as Gwenn stared into the rising sun, Ketha's voice droned in her head, telling her of the Fynära and their customs. "A long boat christened *Fire Drake*, rowed by thirty men, is on her way here. Gunnar Strong Arm is her Captain. He fights with an axe as well as a sword. You must challenge him to a contest of strength and will in front of the rest of his crew, and humiliate him utterly. Otherwise they will not accept you as their leader. Do you understand?"

"What sort of contest? Why can I not just kill him?"

"His men will not follow you unless you can show cunning as well as skill with a sword, Gwenn. These men do not respect women. To them they are only good for two things — sport or childbearing. You must teach them otherwise."

Gwenn nodded, and said confidently, "I have a plan."

"The Fynära come. We should go down to the beach and meet the boat when they bring it in," the battle crow urged her. Gwenn walked down to the shore, her pace unhurried. Though she was about to face her first real combat, she felt no fear. Ketha had promised her protection, and she had keth'fell and all the skill her father had given her.

The waves lapped quietly in the stillness of early morning, disturbed only by the occasional raucous calls of the gulls. Gwenn stood on the sand, like a figure carved from stone, and keth'fell shone in the rising sun. She watched the *Fire Drake* approach, the oars on each side moving in perfect unison. The dragon figurehead, painted the color of blood, skimmed towards the beach, until the shallow keel scraped on the shingle and the oars came to rest. Cries issued from aboard the boat, for the men had seen the maid waiting on shore. They piled out, wading through the breaking waves until they stood before her. She did not move or speak.

Gunnar Strong Arm stepped forward. He was tall and flaxen-haired, like all of the Fynära, and wore a black tunic and breeches. An iron helmet with a nose guard protected his head, and he carried a sword in his hand and an axe hanging from his wide leather belt. He had forked and braided his long, red-blond beard. Gwenn judged him to be about twenty-five years old. He wore no chain mail, for the raiders did not expect to meet enemies at this landing place. They had killed or taken all the local residents long ago.

He addressed his men, saying only, "Touch her not. She is mine."

Gwenn laughed at him and said, "Am I, indeed? You will have to catch me first, man of the North. I am Sif, of the Golden Hair, and if you would take me, you must prove yourself faster than a jackrabbit and have the courage to run alone. Do you accept my challenge?"

The leader of the Fynära hesitated, and narrowed his bright blue eyes. If this golden-haired maid belonged to the Skyrene*, as she claimed to, he did not want any part of her. When the Gods paid a visit to Yrth, it meant nothing but peril for the mortals whom they encountered. Nevertheless, since she had issued the challenge in front of his men, he had no choice. He would have to chase her or lose face. If she were a Goddess, he would no doubt come to regret his decision, but if only a maid, well then... he would enjoy himself very much after he caught her.

Gunnar grinned wickedly at the girl, and boasted, "Run, little Sif, if that is who you really be, for when Gunnar catches you, he will split you wide open with his sword and cut off all your pretty golden hair to sell at the market in Thalheim."

Gwenn stuck out her tongue at him, then turned and ran for the nearest dune. She scaled straight up the side and stopped at the top to look down on the leader of the Fynära, still standing on the beach below. Lifting her shirt, she exposed her breasts to him and laughed jubilantly when he broke into a furious run, as his men cheered him on. In an instant she had cart-wheeled down the back side of the dune, and began running down a winding path between the clumps of sea grass. She could hear Gunnar's

---

* The Fynäran pantheon.

footsteps behind her, and his heavy breathing. Gwenn ran for fifteen minutes, keeping just far enough ahead of her pursuer to be tantalizing, before she judged him to be winded enough to be easy prey. Her own breathing remained effortless and she barely broke a sweat.

On the far side of a dune that screened her from Gunnar, Gwenn stopped and drew keth'fell from the scabbard strapped to her back. She stood loose-limbed and relaxed as her pursuer rounded the sand hill and drew up short, panting heavily. He stared at her silently, and fingered his own sword.

Gwenn said softly, "Would you fight me now, Man of the North? Know I will slay you. Yet your death could be avoided."

Gunnar growled sullenly, "What other choice do I have, Sif? A warrior of the Fynära lives and dies by his deeds of valor. My men expect me to return with your golden hair in my fist. I would rather die at your hand than go back without it. Prepare to perish, unless you be one of the Immortals."

After these words he charged towards her, and Gwenn watched him come. When he was almost upon her, she sidestepped adroitly. His intended slash with the sword went wide. As his momentum carried him past, she kicked him roundly on the rump and sent him sprawling face down on to the sand. As he started to rise, she put her sword tip to his throat. Gunnar dropped his own sword and lay back heavily, pretending to capitulate. His left hand had already unfastened the axe from his belt. With a fierce cry, he swept it in an arc and tried to cut Gwenn's legs out from under her. She jumped straight up in the air and came down directly on his groin. He screamed in pain and rolled onto his side, cursing her roundly. Gwenn picked up the axe and his sword and threw them into the long grass.

"Go ahead, girl, kill him. Then you can carry his head back to the beach. That should impress the rest of his men," Ketha urged.

Gwenn disagreed. "He can be more use to us alive. I plan to use him to convince the crew to follow me."

The Fynäran leader rose stiffly to his knees and stayed there. He said harshly, "Why don't you finish me off, Sif? Now that a female has defeated me, my life is over. I have no heavenly reward to look forward to."

She knelt so she could peer into his eyes. "Gunnar Strong Arm, I do not wish to kill you."

He looked at her disdainfully. "You would show me mercy? I do not want it."

She smiled, and her pale beauty pierced his anger. "Yes, Gunnar. I would have you as my right hand, and together we can lead the Fynära to greater glory than they have ever seen. There are rich fields of blood and fire, ours for the taking, where a man can earn his place in Skyre* a hundred times over. Would you rather go to your death?"

Gunnar stared thoughtfully at her for many moments before bowing his head. "No, Lady Goddess. If I die now, I would be among the women in Hel, instead of in the glorious hall of Skyre drinking and feasting with the other warriors. I will serve you instead, for as long as you have need."

Gwenn reached out and touched the silver talisman he wore around his neck. "Very well. Now you must swear fealty to me, on Lutyond's anchor. But before you do, you must know the truth. I am no Goddess, just a woman, mortal like you, but a warrior all the same. My name is Gwenn, and I am called the Faircrow."

He stared at her in surprise and she wondered if he was now reconsidering his decision to help her. She stood and walked over to where his sword and axe lay in the grass and picked them up. With a smile, she offered the weapons to him, saying, "Do you wish to try and defeat me again? I promise you, the result will be the same."

The raider shook his head. "I still believe you are a Goddess, whatever you say your name is. No mortal could have defeated the mighty Gunnar Strong Arm with such ease. If you wish to hide in the form of a human woman, so be it. I pledge my oath on the Mariner's anchor to serve you."

She gave him her hand and he stood. They gazed at each other without speaking for a good minute. His filthy blond hair hung in lank, greasy locks around his face. Uncomfortably aware of the powerful odor of his unwashed body, Gwenn stepped back a pace and asked, "Who amongst the crew can we trust?"

Gunnar removed his helmet and scratched idly at a flea in his

---

* Heaven—home to the departed warrior. Eternal land of feasting, across the bridge of Atenfy.

hair. "Most of the men are true warriors, but there are a few whose loyalty I question. Jürn is their leader. I have seen them whispering in the bows when they think I am busy at the steering oar."

"Do you believe this Jürn wishes to usurp you?"

He grunted in agreement.

Gwenn gave him her most feral smile. "Then he shall die. Wait here for me and hide yourself in the long grass when I return. You shall watch as the Faircrow does her work." She turned and ran swiftly back towards the beach. Gunnar watched her go, shaking his head in astonishment. The ways of the Skyrene were puzzling, but not to be questioned.

Gunnar's men restlessly milled about on the sand, waiting for the return of their leader. Gwenn approached them fearlessly, but she kept keth'fell ready in her hand. The sun had climbed well above the horizon now and a stiff wind came off the ocean. When the remaining raiders saw her returning without Gunnar, they murmured in consternation. Several men made to approach her, and she raised keth'fell defensively, saying, "Hold, raiders, or I shall slay you all, as I have slain Gunnar Strong Arm."

One of the Fynära, an older man with a jaggedly scarred face, said dismissively, "She lies. There is no blood on her sword. It is a trick. Let's get her."

Gwenn cursed herself inwardly for forgetting this most obvious of details. She quickly tried to distract their attention. "I said hold, Men of the North. Is there one among you with the name of Jürn?"

A very unsavory-looking raider stepped forward and said, "I am he."

She grinned at him. "Before Gunnar died he spoke your name. I think he meant you were to replace him as leader. So now I shall issue my challenge to you. Do you accept? Or does the death of your Captain strike fear in your puny heart?"

Jürn clenched his fists in anger. "Be silent, impudent woman. I am no coward. Just because you have slain that fool Gunnar Strong Arm does not mean you will do the same to me. You would be no harder to catch than the rabbit I had for dinner last week." Most of the others shook their heads in disgust and walked away from him. It showed no wisdom to mock the Skyrene.

"Come then, Jürn. Would you like to bring a few friends

along? Perhaps you will catch this little bunny for your supper tonight." Her taunting had the desired effect. Jürn issued a quick command and three other raiders — Axel, Stig and Dagfinn, smartly stepped forward. Gwenn turned and ran into the dunes, and the four men followed, cursing noisily as she quickly outdistanced the swiftest of them. After slowing her pace so that they could keep up, she led them on a merry dance through the dunes, and called back insults when she thought they might be flagging. Eventually, by a roundabout route, they arrived back at the place where Gunnar Strong Arm lay hidden in the long grass.

Gwenn stopped and faced the four men. She bent and placed her hands on her knees, pretending the chase had winded her. Jürn stepped forward triumphantly, and gloated, "Now you are mine, little rabbit." The others crowded around him and he said harshly, "Get back, you lot. I'll take her alone."

She said softly, "I can see why Gunnar was frightened of you. You caught me ever so easily."

He snorted derisively. "You saved me the trouble of killing the old fool myself. My men and I had already planned to take over the ship. Though the rest are loyal to Strong Arm, they will have no choice but to follow me, especially when I return bearing that pretty scalp of yours." He laughed and moved towards her, flexing his fingers wide.

From his position in the long grass behind the dune, Gunnar mouthed a curse. He admired Gwenn's cunning in getting Jürn to admit the truth, but he wondered if the girl had bitten off a little too much by bringing all four of the rebels at once. His muscles tensed, and he put his hand on his axe ready to leap to her aid, if necessary. He saw Jürn attack, and then the Faircrow executed a piece of sword work so dazzlingly expert Gunnar had to smother a gasp. Within seconds, Jürn lay dead on the ground, neatly filleted.

His three companions decided to rush her all at once, and Gunnar once again made ready to offer his aid. She did not need it. Gwenn did a neat front flip and landed squarely in their midst, catching all three off guard. With a sweeping turn, she beheaded one of the attackers, and gutted another.

With a frightened cry, the last man, Stig, turned and ran blindly back towards the beach, shouting, "Help! Help! She is a fiend. Don't let her get me."

Gwenn took off after him. Within a minute, a strangled scream indicated she had caught up with her prey. Gunnar watched her approach, whistling cheerfully and dragging the unlucky fourth member of the conspiracy by his hair across the sand. She dumped his body with the rest and wiped her bloody hands on the grass.

"Now, you have no more enemies among the crew, Gunnar. The rest will follow you?" Gwenn gave him a questioning glance.

He nodded, and asked with admiration, "How did you get that lot to come after you?"

She laughed. "I told them you were dead. Now you must go and show them otherwise."

"Will you come with me, Gwenn Faircrow? You are our leader now." He stood before her and bowed his head.

"You still command the *Fire Drake* and her crew. I only wish to join them, for the present. I have much to learn of your ways. But you have pledged your loyalty to me and I will not forget that, Strong Arm. Someday soon, it will be required."

She pulled the dagger from her boot and held it out to him. "There is a task you must complete before we leave."

"Why do you offer me your knife?" he asked nervously.

"You said you could not return to your men without my hair in your fist. So cut it."

He quickly backed away, waving his hands in panic. "I do not want your golden hair, Sif. You may keep it." Her blue eyes stared directly into his and he licked his lips nervously.

"You have sworn to be loyal to me," she said earnestly. "I give you my golden hair as a remembrance of your pledge. In that way we become as one warrior, and we will be invincible. Do you understand?"

He nodded respectfully. "You are wise and merciful, beyond your young years. I know not how you gained such wisdom, or the ability to fight like Nung the demon, but I am glad I have become your ally and not your enemy. Otherwise I know I would lie gutted, as they do, like dead fish on the sand." He watched silently as she knelt before him and held up her hair. With trembling hands, he cut it carefully, and in a moment held a large handful of spun gold curls.

Gwenn laughed and flipped her shorn locks back. "Much

cooler this way, anyhow. Now, let's go." She chatted casually about planned raids to Gunnar as they made their way back to the beach. He walked beside her, and wondered if he dreamed, for he still could not quite believe such a maid existed in the living world.

Ketha, who had remained silent during all the chasing and fighting, now spoke in Gwenn's mind, "You have done well, my dear. I am proud of you. Remember though, you cannot trust these Northmen. They would sell their own grandmothers as slaves for the right price. We will need to remain vigilant, until we weed out all the troublemakers. But do not fear, child, for Ketha will keep watch over you. She never sleeps."

Gwenn said nothing in return. She did not want her companion to wonder who she talked to.

When they reached the last dune before the strand, Gwenn said, "I will wait here, Gunnar. Go and speak to the men and tell them I will be joining the crew." She flopped down on the sand and began carefully cleaning her sword with a rag from her pack. With a curt nod, he left her to it.

When the remaining Fynära caught sight of Gunnar approaching on the path from the dunes, they immediately formed a close group and drew weapons. Arvid Scar Brow, the older raider who had questioned Gwenn, stepped forward. He raised his sword threateningly and said, "Stop right there, and say whether you be spirit or flesh, Gunnar Strong Arm. Has the girl bewitched you?"

Gunnar regarded him seriously. "I am as I have ever been, Arvid. You and I have been shipmates for nigh on ten years. Why do you now raise your sword against me?"

Arvid glared at him suspiciously. "The Goddess, Sif, told us she killed you."

He grinned back at his first mate and said, "She lied. We wanted to find out who among the crew was disloyal. Now Jürn and his friends are dead by her hand. I have seen her fight, Arvid. She is amazing — even faster than Keld Thunder Blade."

The raider called Keld snorted in disbelief.

Arvid fingered the ornately worked silver dragon brooch holding his shirt closed at the neck. After stepping back so he could look the Captain over carefully, he decided he did not look bewitched. He caught sight of the golden hair Gunnar still clutched in his fist. The first mate's eyes lit up. He said admiringly, "You took a prize from the maid? That was a mighty deed if she is as great a warrior as you say."

"I took it with her permission. As a guild piece between us. Now she wishes to join the crew of the *Fire Drake* and I have agreed."

The others gasped in shock. Had their Captain gone mad? The other men of the crew clustered around Arvid and Keld and held a whispered discussion.

Keld, a shorter, stocky man with a very muscular frame, stepped forward. "You say she wields a sword better than I? I say you lie, Gunnar Strong Arm. No man has ever bested Keld Thunder Blade in a fight and no woman has ever even tried. Let her come forward. I challenge the maid to combat, right now. If she wins, we will allow her to join us. If not, I will slay her before your very eyes and Arvid will lead us henceforth, for we will follow you no longer."

His Captain spoke quietly. "You don't want to challenge her. Believe me, she will slaughter you where you stand. I cannot afford to lose any more men."

"What are you afraid of?" Keld said scornfully. "That I'll slice open that pretty face of hers? What were you two doing in the dunes, anyway? Having a poke?" He laughed crudely and Gunnar balled his fists. He charged at Keld, and the two men fell down on the sand in a furious wrestling match.

Gwenn came running and stopped the fight with a cry. She drew keth'fell and said, "Let him come to me. I will soon show Keld the error of his ways."

The men formed a circle in the sand and Keld brandished both his sword and his long-hafted axe. His fierce expression left no doubt he meant to kill her if he could. Gwenn looked at him and laughed blithely, saying to Gunnar, "Do you want him alive or dead?"

As Keld scoffed in derision, Gunnar said, "Alive, for he is a good man, and I would be sorry to lose him, even if he is acting the fool right now."

She shrugged and said, "As you wish, Strong Arm." Then to Keld, very coolly, "Shall we begin?"

Keld glared at her as she stood relaxed and fearless before

him. She held keth'fell diagonally across her body, and waited for him to approach. He feinted with his sword, to get her to move left, and hurled his axe directly at her head, hoping in this way to bring the fight to an immediate end. Gwenn's reflexive somersault took him completely by surprise and the axe whistled harmlessly over her, scattering the watching raiders behind them. She came up immediately in front of him and stabbed his shoulder lightly with the point of keth'fell. The men in the circle murmured in surprise, for they saw she could have ended the battle right then had she so desired. This minor wound enraged Keld and he slashed across her body with a lightning movement, but not quick enough to touch Gwenn, for she had already flipped backwards and away.

He ran after her, crying, "Stand still and fight me, wench!"

She did as he requested, lest any of the others might think she was cheating. They engaged in a ten-minute exchange of heavy blows, their swords ringing with each clash. The men cheered both combatants, for they appreciated a good fight. The blistering attack continued and Gwenn began to tire a little. Keld's blows remained viciously punishing, and she wondered how much longer he could keep up the pace. She crossed swords with him again and they strove against one other, pushing as hard as they could. Gwenn tried to hook her leg around his, to pull him over, but he knew this trick and kicked her foot away. Her strength evenly matched his, a fact not lost on the watching raiders, and it seemed as though the contest might go on for some time.

"Submit," he growled at her, through gritted teeth. "Submit and I will let you live."

Gwenn only laughed, but as he lunged at her again, she wondered seriously if her rash promise to take him alive might lead to her defeat by this relentless Northman. Following a sudden inspiration, she threw herself down on the ground and rolled forward. It had the desired effect. As she bowled into his legs, Keld went down hard and she twisted his wrist as he fell. He dropped his weapon with a cry and lay back in the sand. Gwenn picked up his sword and stood over him triumphantly. The other raiders crowded around her, and offered their congratulations on a magnificent battle.

Keld, still on the ground, boiled with anger at his defeat and resulting loss of face. Moving his hand slowly downwards, he managed to retrieve his dagger from the holder on his belt without attracting any attention. He sank the knife deep into Gwenn's thigh before she had a chance to react.

"Take that, bitch!" he crowed triumphantly.

Gwenn screamed in pain. Before any of the others could react she kicked Keld solidly in the face with her boot. He fell back again, knocked out cold. Rage overtook Gwenn. She lifted Keld up bodily and threw him into the ocean, and he landed with a resounding splash, before sinking out of sight under the waves. None of the other men dared go to his aid.

She turned back towards the assembled raiders and cried harshly, "Do any of you others wish to challenge the Faircrow? I am ready to fight you all, one at a time or all at once. Come on!" She stood before them, panting wildly, keth'fell ready in her hand. The blood poured from the stab wound in her thigh, and she scrunched up the material of her breeches with her left hand to try and stem the flow.

Gunnar moved towards her, his hands spread wide, saying softly, "Easy, Gwenn. No-one else wants to fight you. Now you must rest, and let me treat your leg wound. You have proved yourself worthy of the Fynära this day."

She lowered her sword and allowed him to lead her towards the storehouse. On the way she could not help wondering if her Papa Bear would be proud if he could see her now. The sound of Ketha's raucous laughter inside her head drowned out any other thoughts.

Chapter Four

Feathers of Fyn

Well, Geya. What is it this time?

~~~~~~~~~~

After a weary week of walking, Arkady came across a group of wandering horse traders on their way to Beaumarais. The Firaithi Kindreds called nowhere home — except their brightly decorated caravans. No-one, even among the very wise, knew from whence they originated, but their dark coloration set them apart from the rest of the residents of Yr. The Firaithi kept very much to themselves, spoke their own obscure tongue and never stayed in one place for very long. As a result, they were feared by the settled peoples and sometimes even persecuted. Nevertheless, their fine horses were a desirable commodity and Beaumarais opened its borders to them once a year for the trading fair.

When the Firaithi passed him on the road, the hungry and dispirited Arkady called out to them, "*Amma, shenti,*" words he was fairly sure meant 'stop, friend' in their language.

He knew only a little Firai, but his greeting was intelligible enough to bring the column of caravans to a halt. An older man, with long black hair, silvered at the temples and braided with many ribbons, rode back towards him and dismounted. He framed a question in Firai, speaking rapidly.

Arkady smiled and shook his head, understanding nothing, and asked him, "Do you speak Maraison?"

The Firaithi man answered slowly, with a strong accent, but his words were perfectly understandable. He said gruffly, "What do you want with us, Gruagá? The Firaithi do not offer aid to lost travelers. I am Grigor Adaryi, the Tane of this Kindred and I have spoken." The old man meant to be unfriendly, for Gruagá meant "white devil" in Firai. Arkady looked at him, trying to decide how best to convince the Tane to at least give him something to eat.

He said, "I am hungry, Tane, for another Gruagá stole my horse seven days ago, and I have run out of food. I have no money, but I will work for the kindred if you let me ride with you as far as Beaumarais." As he spoke of Krikka, his hand unconsciously strayed to the crow's foot talisman he still wore. Grigor saw it and his eyes narrowed.

"Where did you get that fetish? Have you dealings with the Battle Crow? Speak quickly or I will slay you." The old man glared at Arkady fiercely and drew the curved sword from his belt.

"The Gruagá who stole my horse wore this charm. She left it behind. I don't know anything about a battle crow."

"She? A woman gave you Keth Dirane's claw?"

Arkady asked him sharply, "Did you say her name was Ketha?"

The old man nodded briefly. "Keth Dirane. She is an evil creature — a demon who feasts on human flesh. I am astonished to see you alive if you have had dealings with her, Gruagá. Are you a man or of the race of Gods?"

Arkady shrugged. "I am no God, just a man like any other, yet the girl I saw in the dunes north of Secuny did me no harm."

He paused, remembering their encounter. Krikka resembled no other woman he had ever met, and not just because of her size and strength. But could she have been a Goddess? He did not think so. She seemed too young and inexperienced, for all her brave talk. Yet it was obvious Krikka knew Keth Dirane, and feared her greatly. Arkady, who had thought of little else since the girl abandoned him in the dunes and rode away on Ajax, suddenly became very afraid for his erstwhile lover.

His mind snapped back to the present as Grigor asked, "What is your name? Though we seldom offer aid to strangers, I would hear the tale of your meeting with the girl who gave you this talisman. You will ride with us and share our fire tonight."

"My name is Arkady Svalbarad, and I would be honored to ride with your kindred, Grigor Adaryi." He added a word of thanks in Firai, "*Lesna*", and the old man gave him a grudging smile.

He said, "If all men took the time to address us with respect, as you do, Arkadios, they would find the Firaithi more welcoming." He called out a sharp command and a younger man rode forward from the line of caravans. "This is my son, Huw. He also speaks your tongue."

Huw, who had the same dark hair as his father, also arranged in brightly woven ribbon braids, must have been in his mid-thirties. The elder Firaithi spoke to him in their tongue. He dismounted and held out his hand in greeting. Arkady shook it warmly and smiled. Huw said, "Welcome, Arkadios. I have a spare horse tied to the back of my caravan. Will you ride with me? We have a little distance yet to cover before we set up camp for the night."

He followed Huw, who led his horse back towards a small, neatly painted caravan. A darkly beautiful woman sat in the driver's seat, wearing leather breeches and an off-the-shoulder peasant blouse, embroidered with bright designs. She gazed down at Arkady, obviously intrigued. Huw introduced her. "My sister Eira, Arkadios."

Arkady smiled at her and said, "Tsmare onat shalomir,*" which was the proper reply to an introduction. Eira nodded but said nothing in return. He couldn't help feeling that he had seen her somewhere before. Her face seemed very familiar — intimately so. Arkady opened his mouth, ready to ask if she had ever traveled to St. Ekaterina, then belatedly wondered why she had not returned his greeting.

Huw smiled at her. "Please do not be offended, Arkadios. She cannot speak, my sister, but she would give you greeting if she could."

"Of course, I understand." Arkady wondered why the woman could not talk, but he decided it would be rude to ask her brother in front of her, so he smiled again and followed Huw around the back of the caravan. A roan horse, with brightly colored cloth braided into her mane and tail, waited there.

"This horse, Ylene, will not take a saddle or bit. Only the Gruagán use such things to make an unhappy beast do their bidding. Can you ride without them?" Huw looked at him appraisingly and Arkady could tell quite a lot of respect rode on the answer to this simple question.

Fortunately, he had learned to ride bareback in T'Shang. He nodded to Huw, who untied the roan mare and handed the trace

_____
* The moon gives you greeting.

44

to him. Arkady used the back of the caravan as a step, and slid on to the blanket covering her back, which immediately tried to shift sideways under him. He patted the mare and spoke softly to her whilst trying to find a comfortable riding position. Huw supervised briefly and then climbed on his own horse, apparently satisfied Arkady knew what he was doing.

Grigor called out a command and the line of caravans slowly started forward. Arkady rode next to Huw but did not try to make conversation. It had been many months since he had last ridden bareback and he needed all his concentration to keep the roan mare moving in a straight line, using only his knees to give her commands.

After a few moments, when it became clear that Ylene was prepared to be docile and obliging, Arkady relaxed and studied the countryside around him. Thistles and gorse grew in profusion on either side of the road as it wound through a wide river valley, between two ranges of distant hills. Only wild goats lived here, for the soil was too thin and stony for cultivation. The sun beat down relentlessly and Arkady wiped the sweat from his forehead with his shirt.

Presently, Huw asked, "Where were you heading when you hailed us? Back to Beaumarais?"

Arkady nodded. "I have been away for many years and I have had no news of my homeland for quite some time. I don't even know who leads the country any more."

Huw said, "The Prime Minister is a man named Philip Tremayne. We have had only a few dealings with him over the past year, but the borders of your land have become much more difficult to cross since he took office."

"The man he replaced — Nicholas Reynard. What do you know of him?" Arkady forced his voice to sound disinterested.

The Firaithi spoke regretfully. "He was a great man. Always honest and fair in all his dealings with the Kindred."

Arkady gave him a piercing glance. "Was?"

"Yes, Arkadios. Nicholas Reynard died last year in an accident." Then, noticing his companion's distressed expression, he asked, "Did you know him?"

Arkady sighed and looked away. "He is my father. I have had no tidings of his death. Can you tell me what happened?"

Huw looked stricken. "I am very sorry you had to learn of your father's passing in this way. I will tell you what I know, though it is not much, I am afraid. Your father and a man called the Dinrhydan were on a hunting trip when the accident occurred."

"Jacq shot my father?" Huw gazed at him in confusion, so he explained, "The Dinrhydan is my half-brother, Jacq. We have the same mother but different fathers. Is that what happened?"

Huw shook his head. "No, it was a girl who shot Nicholas. The daughter of your brother Jacq. I think her name is... Gwenn."

Arkady took in this information silently. Though it did not seem possible, his father had been dead for a year and he hadn't known. He wondered how his mother, Elisabeth, had coped with this distressing event. And what of his niece, Gwenn? The last time he had seen her she must have been seven or eight years old. Now she was old enough to go out hunting with Jacq and his father? That did not seem possible either. The slow pace of the caravan suddenly disturbed him, and Arkady thought perhaps he ought to ask Huw if he could take Ylene and ride ahead to St. Valery.

After further reflection, he decided against this.

The wheel of life for his father had turned a year ago and nothing Arkady did would change it. Huw would probably refuse his request anyway. The Firaithi were notoriously distrustful of strangers. Arkady resolved he would spend his time with the kindred wisely, trying to learn more of the language and culture of this reclusive people. He would deal with his father's death at the proper time — when he arrived in Beaumarais.

Huw regarded him worriedly and Arkady spoke to reassure him. "I have been gone for eight years, Huw, and part of the time I was far from any means of communication. In my heart, I have always known there might be bad news waiting for me when I arrived home. My father saw his seventieth year, and he accomplished many good things in his life. I am sorry I did not get to see him once more before he died, but my grief does not extend beyond that. Please do not regret telling me this news."

Huw asked curiously, "Where did your journeys take you? You are like no other Gruagá I have ever met. I see in your eyes death holds no sway over your soul, and you ride like one of us. Are you descended from the Firaithi?"

"I thank you for the compliment, but my father's family comes from the far north — St. Ekaterina, in Ruboralis. He came to St. Valery as a young man."

"How is it you bear a different name? I might have guessed the connection if you had said your last name was Reynard, for now I see you resemble Nicholas."

Arkady explained, "My father changed his name to Reynard soon after the start of the Cottar Rebellion. Originally, he was an officer in the King's Guard. He wanted to fight for the cottars so he allowed his superiors to think he had perished in a fire. Then he took a new last name and formed the Rising. After the fighting ended, my father became Prime Minister as part of the peace agreement brokered by the Goddess Lalluna. Though I am proud of my father and what he accomplished as Nicholas Reynard, I wanted to go back to his real name and I did so at age twelve." Arkady did not go into the real reason he had changed his name — his classmates at St. Valery's School for Boys had insisted on treating him deferentially because of his famous father.

Huw said, "We Firaithi mostly avoided Beaumarais during the War of the Rising. Much blood was shed, and both sides mistrusted the Kindreds. But your beautiful Queen eventually brought peace. Now we are welcomed for the horse trading fair, but I think we are still disliked by most people of your country."

"Have you met the Queen, Huw?" Arkady asked. "I am sure she would treat you respectfully. She is married to my brother Jacq. Do you know of her role in saving the City? I felt a little afraid of her when I was younger, because she used to be the winged Avatar of Lalluna."

Huw stared at him, shaking his head. "For a man with such high born family, Arkadios, you are very humble."

Arkady smiled inwardly at this, thinking back on his impoverished childhood. His whole family would have starved if his brother Jacq had not gotten a blacksmithing apprenticeship at the Citadel. Arkady had not even owned a pair of shoes until his father, Nicholas, became Prime Minister.

Huw's voice interrupted his thoughts, "I did get to meet the Queen, at a trading fair. She came looking for a replacement for her favorite pony, who had just died of old age."

"Brinna?"

47

Huw nodded. "Yes, Brinna. She missed her very much. I helped her to select a new pony. It took several days and I talked much with her, but not of her brave deeds in saving St. Valery. She was too modest to speak of that. But I already knew of her exploits. Who in Yr has not heard tales of the one-armed Avatar of Lalluna? I thought her very brave, and kind. Like you, she could have been Firaithi. In different circumstances, I might have..." Huw paused, studying the distant hills before saying, "Your family is quite extraordinary." He sighed and said nothing else.

Grigor rode up to join them and held a hurried conversation with his son. Huw translated for Arkady. "My father says the forward scouts have reported a group of men waiting at the border of Mardon, just ahead. They bear arms, and it looks as though they mean to prevent us from crossing on our way to Beaumarais. We will leave the caravans here with the women and children. You must remain with them, for there will be fighting."

Arkady asked, "Do any amongst you speak Mard? Perhaps if you tell them you intend to pass through quickly, they will leave you alone."

Huw shook his head.

"I will go with you and communicate for the Kindred, if you will allow it. I can speak their language."

Grigor asked, "How is it you know Mard? Are you one of them?" He seemed very suspicious.

Huw spoke in Firai, "We can trust this man. I will vouch for him before the Elders. He is the son of Reynard, my Patre."

The Tane looked at Arkady with new respect. "The son of Reynard? Very well, you may ride with us. But you must say nothing without speaking to me first. Do you understand?"

Arkady nodded nervously, wondering what he had just let himself in for. He urged Ylene forward and rode with Huw and his father up the line of caravans. Once they reached the head of the line, a lot of other Firaithi men joined them. Arkady said in a low voice to Grigor, "Tane, it might look less threatening if you and I and Huw ride to the border alone. If there is trouble the others can join us."

Grigor nodded and told the others to wait at a bend in the road beyond the sight of the waiting Mardonne. But he would not leave his weapon behind, though Arkady urged him to. He said unwaveringly, "We are the Firaithi, Arkadios, and bow before no man."

About twenty men of the Mardonne waited for them at the border, marked by a shingly ford in a wide stream. They had armed themselves with clubs and a few swords. Arkady and the Firaithi rode to the water's edge and stopped. The two groups eyed one other for a tense moment before Grigor said, "Ask them why they block the road."

Arkady greeted the Mardonne in their tongue and relayed Grigor's question. A burly, dark-haired man answered while swinging his club suggestively. "What business do you have with us, Firaithi excrement?"

Arkady kept his expression carefully controlled and loosely translated the man's reply to Grigor. The Firaithi said, "Tell him we wish to pass through on our way to Beaumarais and will travel their lands as quickly as we are able."

This Arkady did, and the man said in return, "We will have no thieving darkies on our soil, even for an hour. Tell your friends to clear off, White-hair."

"He says they do not wish us to pass, even if we go quickly. What would you have me say in return?"

Grigor frowned and turned to Huw. Huw shrugged. "We must ford the Sharm River here, Patre — there is no other way across with the caravans. I will call the others."

Arkady, anxious to avoid bloodshed if possible, suggested, "Why not camp on this side of the border tonight? Perhaps they will grow tired of waiting and go home. We could leave early tomorrow morning."

Huw shook his head, but surprisingly the elder Firaithi agreed with Arkady. The three men turned their horses and rode away. The men of the Mardonne gazed in confusion at their unexpected retreat. Grigor gave the order for the caravans to circle close to a grove of trees off to the side of the road. He sent some men to collect water from the Sharm as the women gathered firewood. Later, after the Firaithi had set up camp and built a large bonfire, Arkady sat quietly with Huw, while the younger children exuberantly chased fireflies in the summer twilight. He watched as Eira silently supervised the other women as they put together a stew of lentils and some greens and tubers gathered from the stony roadside. Her hands deftly signed her wishes, and the others spoke in reply. Occasionally her dark eyes would flash in his direction and she would favor him with a small, secretive smile, but only if her brother was not paying attention. Each time she did this, Arkady was reminded of someone... but who?

He decided he must find out more about her. Arkady said softly to Huw, "Please forgive my curiosity, but why is Eira mute? She seems to hear and understand when people talk to her."

Huw looked over at his sister and answered curtly, "She has been that way since she was a child." Arkady could tell by his expression that there was much more to the story, but he did not know how to break through Huw's reticence.

Grigor joined them by the fire. "Come, break fast with us now. I would hear more of your journey, and of the girl who gave you the crow's foot."

Eira handed Arkady a bowl of the stew and a hunk of hard, unleavened bread. When he said "*lesna*" to her, she touched his chin with the tips of her fingers. He finished the food quickly, for he had had nothing else to eat all day. She refilled his bowl before squatting before the fire to eat her own portion, well away from the men.

Arkady softly told Huw and Grigor of his journey to T'Shang and some much-edited details of his meeting with Krikka.

"You have walked the paths of our ancestors," Huw said in surprise. "No wonder I thought you one of us! Is that where you learned to ride?"

The two men asked many other questions and Arkady answered them willingly. Even though it was obvious the Firaithi had some legend or tale featuring Ketha, they would not share it with him in return. Arkady hoped he might eventually win their trust so he did not press them for details. Shortly thereafter, Huw announced he intended to turn in for the evening.

After bidding Huw and Grigor good night, Arkady unrolled his blanket by the fire. He sat down with his legs crossed, and prepared to do his evening meditation. The stars above him blazed into a million pinpricks of light as the Firaithi camp settled down for the night. Soon it was silent, except for the conversational pop and crackle of the dying fire. The heat settled into his bones as he thought back on the unpromising start of his day, and its unlikely conclusion. He let his eyelids sink as he began to repeat his mantra:

Hana Hana sen mejum.

He had only just begun when a faint click made him open his eyes again.

He noticed Eira stepping quietly from the back of the caravan closest to him. She stared provocatively at Arkady, and slowly walked away from the fire, towards the darkened trees. Her bare feet made no sound on the soft ground. The smoldering look she gave him over her shoulder left little doubt as to her inclination.

After a moment of indecision, Arkady rose and followed her. Her footprints, shining in the dew-soaked grass, led him towards the riverbank.

The leader of the Mardonne stood just inside the band of trees and watched with interest as the woman approached his hiding place. The five men with him muttered with feral glee at the prospect of the degradations they could visit upon her. When she was within easy reach, the leader grabbed her and covered her mouth with his hand. She struggled violently, but could not cry out. The men crowded around, trying to rip her clothing off.

Their leader said, in a furious whisper, "Get your hands off her! She is mine. The rest of you can have what is left when I am finished. Now stand guard while I..."

He said nothing else. A stone came whistling out of the darkness and struck him solidly on the temple, killing him instantly. As he crashed to the ground, his companions rushed blindly forward, swords and knives at the ready.

Arkady hurried into the forest, another round river stone ready in his hand. "Run, Eira!" he cried. She took off as four of the five remaining men surrounded Arkady, intent on revenge for their fallen leader. The remaining Mardonne went after Eira and caught her before she could raise the alarm in the camp. He dragged her back into the cover of the trees.

The second in command hissed, "I want him alive so we can take him back over the border with us. He will be begging for death before we have finished with him."

Two of the men lunged towards Arkady. He clubbed one down efficiently with the stone and flipped the other to the ground. The other two were on him before he could recover his balance and he cried out in pain as a knife blade deeply pierced the flesh of his shoulder.

Arkady felt a powerful rage welling up inside him. He did not fear death, but how could he leave Eira to suffer at their hands? Obeying a sudden compulsion, he closed his eyes and drew on his centre. The Mardonne holding him felt Arkady's body stiffen and quickly grow very hot. He let go of his prisoner with a cry.

Now free to move, Arkady placed his hands a few inches apart in front of his belly. Eira and the others watched in astonishment as he formed a glowing red fireball between his outstretched fingers and threw it straight at his nearest assailant. The man burst into brilliant sheets of flame and ran screaming towards the river. The others broke and fled in terror, dragging the body of their leader with them. Arkady let them go, for Eira had fainted. He knelt beside her and shook her gently as the culprits melted away into the woods, leaving nothing behind except for the streaming wound on Arkady's shoulder.

But the cries of the burned man had roused the camp. Within minutes five men of the Firaithi surrounded Arkady as he bent over the fallen woman.

"Pig!" one said angrily, as the others pulled him away.

"Wait," Arkady cried, but he did not know the words in Firai to make them understand. "I didn't hurt her..." One of his captors cuffed him soundly across the cheek.

They bound Arkady between the ends of two caravans. Now he stood before Grigor, Huw, and the other Elders in a hastily assembled gathering. Huw stepped forward and spat in his face. "Gruagá filth! We trusted you and this is how you repay us. How could you do this, Arkadios? To my own sister!"

Arkady merely shook his head unhappily. He knew his situation was dire. Even if Eira regained consciousness in time, she could tell no-one what actually happened. He struggled to explain from behind his gag.

"Don't pretend you are innocent," Huw said. "I saw the way you were staring at her all evening. Take off his shirt, Padarn." Another of the Firaithi ripped off Arkady's bloody shirt, wrenching his wounded shoulder so badly his head swam and he thought he might faint from the pain. Huw said, "Bring Eira. She should watch as we cut out his heart and show it to him before he dies." He waited as the others brought his sister forward into the firelight. She tugged at his arm in supplication but he threw off her hand angrily, and drew a curved dagger from his belt. He stared into the hazel eyes of the Gruagá but saw no hatred or guilt — his unwavering gaze held only deep sadness. Huw paused, now filled with uncertainty. He said, "Arkadios, I..."

Eira turned and ran.

Grigor commanded him harshly, "Finish him, Huw. The maggot deserves to die for what he tried to do to Eira." Shaking his head, Huw raised the dagger. Arkady closed his eyes and prepared his soul for the turning of the wheel. Just before Huw struck, a woman's voice, speaking urgently, echoed through the darkness.

"*Amma! Amma!*"

Grigor and Huw both whirled so that they could see who had spoken. Eira stood before them, weeping, and in her trembling hands she held the rolled up painting of Hana.

"Eira," Huw cried in disbelief. "You spoke! You spoke to me..."

The men stared in disbelief as she let the piece of silk fall open. The light from the fire burnished the brilliantly colored silks, and highlighted the gentle expression on Hana's face. "The Un-Named One," said Huw, hoarsely. Eira nodded and glided forward like a sleepwalker. She touched the talisman resting on Arkady's bare chest. She said haltingly, "Do not... slay him, my brother. He saved me from evil men. He is... the Seed Bearer."

With a cry, Huw dropped the dagger and tore the gag from Arkady's mouth. He said in a trembling voice, "Is this true? Did you save my sister?" Arkady hadn't understood what she said. Now he nodded and Huw fell to his knees and covered his face in shame.

Eira continued, "Six men of the Mardonne were hiding in the trees. They accosted me, Patre. He killed two of them. The rest ran away. He saved my life." Grigor, almost overcome with shock at the sound of his daughter's voice, could hardly take in what she said. The other Firaithi crowded around her with questions, but she ignored them. Walking forward, she cut the ropes binding her rescuer and said, "I cannot thank you enough for risking your life for me. Please permit me to bandage your wounds, Arkadios."

He understood only the word *lesna,* but it was enough.

Grigor stared down at Huw and said harshly, in Maraison, "There is a judgment to be passed first, on my son Huw, who has falsely accused another man of a terrible crime. The penalty for this transgression is death, Arkadios, and as the wronged man, you will carry out the execution. Now." He picked up the dagger and held it out to Arkady. Huw stayed on his knees with his head down and said nothing in his own defense.

Arkady refused it. "No, Grigor. Though I respect the customs of your people, I cannot do this. Huw has not harmed me. Let him go free."

The Tane replied, "He cannot be spared, for it is our Law. If you will not kill him, then one of us must." He spoke sharply to Padarn and handed him the dagger.

Arkady begged him. "Is there no way to stop this? I don't want his death."

"No, for he is not your kin. Only the ties of blood may override the Law."

Arkady nodded wearily, understanding now what he must do. He took the dagger from Padarn and moved to stand by Huw, who gazed up at him in mute acceptance. Arkady bent low so he could catch Huw's hand up in his own. Taking the dagger, he quickly drew it across Huw's open palm, leaving a gash that bled copiously. Huw gasped in shock. Before any of the others could intervene, Arkady did the same to his own palm and then tightly grasped the Firaithi's hand, so the blood flowing from the wounds would mingle.

"Now you will release my brother, Patre, for we share the same blood."

Grigor stared at Arkady for a long moment, his expression unreadable. Finally, he said, "So be it. Arkadios, brother of Huw Adaryi, has claimed the right of kindred. I am Grigor and I have spoken." Huw rose to his feet unsteadily, shaking his head at this wholly unexpected deliverance. Then he put his arms around Arkady and held him up as his new brother abruptly passed out from blood loss and shock.

Chapter Five

The Mariner's Abode

Geya can feel the Numen's disapproval, so she replies defensively. Can't I just come and visit sometimes? I don't want anything except to sit at your feet and hear your wisdom.

After a short humorless laugh, she says dryly, You do amuse me, little one. What do you wish to know?

~~~~~~~~~~

When Arkady awoke, he found himself lying in a strange, cupboard-like bed, inside one of the caravans of the Firaithi. He stared up at the low ceiling, decorated with painted green flowers, and wondered how long he had been sleeping. Eira sat in a chair next to him, and she gave a relieved smile when she saw his eyes open. "Welcome back, Arkadios," she said. It took a moment for him to realize she had addressed him in a language he understood.

Arkady gazed at her in surprise. "You speak my tongue, Eira? Yesterday you could not speak at all."

She laughed. "Does it not please you to hear me talk?"

"I am very glad you can. Will you tell me how it happened?"

"That terrible night, when I saw the crow's foot you wore around your neck, I unexpectedly found my voice again. Hana spoke to me, as she did on the day I lost it. She told me to fetch the painting and show it to Huw. So I did. I had to save you."

Arkady gave her a piercing glance. "That picture of Hana — it looks just like *you*, Eira. Why is that?"

Eira looked at her hands and said nothing. After a moment she began, "Arkadios, I..."

She stopped and shook her head in distress. "I am sorry you had to suffer so for my foolish behavior. Why did you follow me, anyway? Were you going to make love to me?"

"I followed to protect you, not for any other reason. Though

55

you are very beautiful, I should tell you, my heart belongs to another woman." Arkady blinked in surprise as he heard himself saying this to Eira. Until then, he had not realized it, but now he knew it to be true.

Eira said sadly, "In payment for your protection, my kinsmen falsely accused you of rape. Are you going to tell Huw I tried to seduce you?"

"What you did was between you and me, and is no-one else's business."

She sighed. "You might have died, my brother."

He shrugged and grimaced at the pain that shot through his shoulder. "I am not afraid of death."

She stared at him intently. "Who are you, truly? Say not that you are just a man, Arkadios, for I saw you call upon the secret fire that destroyed our enemy. Hana told me you are the Seed Bearer. What does that mean?"

"I don't know. Nor do I have any idea how I made the fire that blossomed in my hands. I *am* just a man, Eira." He paused nervously. "Did you tell anyone else what you saw?" He hoped she had not. The Firaithi might think him some demon if they found out. Until he could understand himself what terrible rage had called up the fire that formed between his fingers, he wanted no-one else to know of it.

Eira said, "No, of course not. It is our secret. A secret shared between you and me and Hana. Like this conversation we are having now." She leaned forward and muttered earnestly, "Do not forget that she watches and waits for the coming storm. She knows that Keth Dirane is but a messenger flying on the wings of an evil wind. Your child — the Dawnmaid — will join the battle against the fell demons of blackness. You must know that the wind does not change direction by chance." She smiled at him softly. "Now I must go and tell Huw you have awoken. He has been anxious to know of your condition. Farewell for now."

Arkady wanted to ask her a thousand questions, but she would say no more, so he thanked her and said, "Now that Huw and I have become brothers, I would be honored if you would call me Kadya, as my other sister does." She nodded and left him.

He struggled into a semi-sitting position, touched his shoulder gingerly, and found Eira had wrapped it in a thick bandage.

His hand, too, had been bandaged securely. Sitting upright made him feel so dizzy and nauseous that he had to lie back down almost immediately. He hoped that the Firaithi would find it in their hearts to care for him until he recovered enough strength to travel back to Beaumarais.

Arkady needn't have worried. Huw greeted him with delight. "I came as soon as Eira told me you had woken, my brother. How do you feel?"

"A bit sore and dizzy. How long did I stay out for?"

"You have been unconscious for two days. After your collapse at the judgment, our sister Eira cared for you with her own hands, sitting by your side without sleep until you awoke just now."

"I have been awake for a little while. Eira and I have been talking."

Huw's expression showed plain disbelief. "How did you do that? Our sister does not speak Maraison, and you do not know that much Firai, do you?"

He shook his head. "But I spoke with her. I swear it. I don't understand."

"Neither do I, Arkadios, but there is a way to find out. I will fetch her."

When Eira returned with Huw, Arkady looked at her imploringly and said in Maraison, "Tell him, my sister, you understand what I say."

Eira turned to Huw and uttered a questioning burst of Firai. She seemed genuinely confused. Arkady listened, completely mystified. Had he dreamed the conversation with the girl? Then he remembered her words to him just before she left the caravan:

A secret shared between you and me and Hana. Like this conversation we are having now.

Eira gave him a meaningful look and left them alone. Arkady stared silently at Huw's hand, which bore an identical bandage to his own. Huw followed his eyes and spoke sadly. "There are no words to say how sorry I am about what happened. You risked your life for my sister. That we falsely accused you of harming her brings great shame upon the Firaithi and to me most of all. I hope someday you will be able to forgive us, my brother."

"There is no need for forgiveness between kin. The wind does not change direction by chance." He paused, astonished Eira's words had come back to him so readily. Shaking his head, he continued, "I am very glad you and I have become brothers. I feel in my heart we met for some purpose that is yet to be revealed."

Huw nodded. "I feel the same. You came bearing the crow's foot fetish, and Eira says the Un-Named One has spoken to her of you."

"Will you tell me now of the fetish and what it means to the Kindreds? Perhaps it will help me to make sense of what has happened."

Huw said, "Yes, of course. Now you are one of us, Arkadios, you must know the truth."

Arkady interrupted him briefly. "Now you must call me Kadya, as my other brothers do."

"Very well, Kadya, it shall be as you ask. The legend of the crow's foot has been passed down through many generations of the Kindreds. It says a man will come bearing the sign of Keth Dirane and death will follow him, for he carries within him both the Seed and the Secret Flame." Arkady paled at this, but Huw, intent on his story, did not notice. "His child, the Dawnmaid, will redeem the Firaithi. The legend does not say anything more, but for all the years we have wandered, persecuted and mistrusted by the Gruagán, we have harbored a secret hope that one day we will be allowed to settle in a land of our own. Does that help you understand?"

Arkady sighed regretfully. "I wish it did. More than anything, I would like to find the woman who gave me this talisman. Somehow she is involved with Keth Dirane, and I fear she is in grave danger."

Huw gave him a long look. "Do you love this woman? If so, you should take great care. Anyone who has dealings with Ketha is perilous."

He nodded. "Yes, I do care for her, though I knew her less than a day. I have not been able to forget her, as much as I have tried. Perhaps our meeting in the dunes was also fated."

Speaking of Krikka made him unhappily aware he had no idea where she was or when he might see her again.

"What is the answer to this riddle, Kadya?"

"I do not know. Perhaps Katkin can help me, once I return to Beaumarais. She knows more about the ways of Goddesses than anyone else I can think of."

Once Arkady had recovered enough strength to travel, the caravans set off towards the Sharm River ford. Huw and Grigor rode at the front of the line. The forward scouts reported no activity at the border with Mardon so they crossed the river with care and proceeded on their way to Beaumarais. In all the days they spent crossing the territory, they did not see a single person and Huw wondered at this. But news of the flame-conjuring demon riding with the Firaithi had spread throughout Mardon, and no man would approach them.

The Firaithi traveled even more slowly than usual, for Eira begged Grigor not to hurry on the rutted back roads he knew best. She pointed out that the constant jolting would cause her patient pain and slow his healing. Arkady lay on his back for almost a week before she allowed him to rise and take a few shaky steps, supported by Huw.

"Back to bed with you!" she chided playfully, but Arkady demurred, wanting to watch and learn as much as he could about the Firaithi.

Now he sat outside by the back door of the caravan, enjoying the scents of the sultry morning air. The sun felt good on his face after his long confinement. The camp bustled with activity and he studied everything with interest. The women busied themselves with domestic chores, and lines of clean washing sprang up like flocks of fluttering egrets. Even the children collected firewood or wild mushrooms and herbs for the nighttime meal. Every Firaithi, from the youngest toddler to the eldest Kymatre*, worked hard for the Kindred. Much food had to be gathered, for the Firaithi ate no animal flesh.

When Huw stopped by to see how he was feeling, Arkady asked curiously, "How do you manage to feed yourselves without remaining in one place long enough to grow vegetables?"

Huw smiled. "There are many things to eat in the wild for he who knows where to look. We teach our little ones from a very young age to identify edible plants and tubers. Of course, we cannot gather everything we need, so we make trades along the way, for dried pulses and grains. There are certain farmers that we trust, who know us well, and they grow the things we require."

---

* Grandmother

"Still," insisted Arkady. "It must be very difficult — always traveling like this. Do your young people not grow tired of your rootless existence?"

"Of course, some do," admitted Huw. "Perhaps two or three each year decide to leave the Kindreds and make their way in the world of the Gruagán. But we raise our young ones to honor asparitus, so most come back to us after a few years."

"Asparitus? What is that?"

Huw stared thoughtfully at his sister Eira's neatly painted caravan. "I don't know a word in Maraison that means the same thing. Asparitus is our way of life. It means to tread gently on the Yrth, to use as little as we are able, and put back as much as we can." He frowned. "We have very little, compared to the Gruagán in their fancy houses. They think of us as impoverished tinkers and thieves, when they think of us at all. But truly, Kadya, few of us would give up our place here amongst the Kindreds for all the gold of the Gruagán. Asparitus is all the treasure we need. Do you understand, my brother?"

"Of course," he said, but inwardly he marveled at their ability to thrive in such a harsh and uncompromising world. In some ways, the Firaithi appeared very like the yak herders he had once wintered with, and he wondered at Huw's comment about their ancestry. Certainly, the small and wiry build of most of the Firaithi matched the people of T'Shang. Then there was the confusing business of their secret worship of the Goddess Hana. Arkady had given much thought to Eira's mysterious words during his enforced rest and he found himself no closer to understanding them. He was more determined than ever to learn the language so he could ask her about their conversation.

To this end, he begged Huw to teach him as many words of Firai as he could.

His new brother obliged him willingly, and they spent many hours studying together. The Firaithi had no written language, so Arkady used his linguistic training to create a simple alphabet he could use to transliterate the words he learned. Huw watched him with interest. He and Padarn, the horse master, could read and write Maraison, for they needed to make trades at the fair. No other of the Kindred possessed this skill.

After three long weeks of bumpy travel, Arkady at last saw the familiar purple hills of his home in the distance. He asked Huw what the Firaithi planned to do when they reached Beaumarais.

"We go to the fairgrounds east of the villages known as the Three Sisters. There we will set up camp and wait for the day of the summer solstice. The people of St. Valery will come to trade and buy horses for a week after that. Once the fair is over, we will pack up our caravans and head for Spanja. Your country will only allow us to stay for a month, no more."

Huw paused to pick an apple from a wildly twisted tree standing off to the side of the road. Arkady's horse, Ylene, scooted sideways towards the tempting pile of windfall fruit lying underneath. He tried to control her, without success, for he still felt weakened from his injury. Eira had only allowed him to travel by horseback for the first time that day. Huw laughed as Ylene almost took Arkady off her back by charging head down into the lower branches. Arkady swore colorfully in several languages and dismounted. Huw raised his hand, brought the caravans to a halt, and announced they would be taking a break.

Eira rushed from the front to see what caused the stop. Arkady explained in broken Firai and she asked laughingly, "Who is the boss, my brother, you or the horse? Be firm!"

The three of them walked up to the line of waiting caravans, and Eira set about making some tea. She handed the men some flat bread for lunch, with fresh goat's milk cheese.

Huw announced with a grin, "I think we will make the Three Sister's camp by nightfall, unless Ylene and Kadya have another disagreement."

Arkady smiled back, but his heart lurched at the thought of seeing his family again.

Later, now bone-tired from his first day on horseback since his injury, Arkady sat quietly by the fire as the others around him murmured in Firai. They talked of the coming fair and the various horses they hoped to sell for a good price. He listened with interest, pleased that he could now understand some of their conversation.

After the talk died down, Grigor went to his caravan and came back with a curiously shaped three-stringed bowed instrument. After Padarn produced a drum and Huw a flute, they sat down by the Tane. Arkady listened with pleasure as father and son broke into a rousing dance tune, with Padarn keeping up a rapid-fire rhythm on the skin drum. Eira and some of the other women began whirling around the fire while clapping their hands along with the beat. One stopped in front of Arkady and smilingly held out her hand. He joined in the dance happily, trying hard to follow the complicated steps, until he was out of breath and aching.

Eira looked at him with concern and ordered, in simple Firai, "Sit down!"

Grigor now played a slow, mournful tune, and the flute provided a haunting counterpoint. The music went on for some time, until the moon set. One by one, the Firaithi melted away into the darkness, until only Arkady and Eira were left by the fire. She took his hand and squeezed it affectionately. He sighed, wishing his command of the language would allow him to question her about their conversation the first day he woke up in the caravan.

She said, "Kadya, there is something I must show you."

Arkady gazed at her in confusion. Why could he now understand what she said? Suddenly, the answer dawned on him. She spoke the language of Hana — T'Shanga.

Eira continued softly, "But first, I want to thank you for giving me back my voice. Our meeting was a blessed one by the moon. I will miss you when you go back to St. Valery tomorrow. I hope we will meet again, but I think it may not be in this life. Hana tells me the wheel will turn for many in the years to come."

Eira took three dark red octahedral stones from the pouch hanging from her kirtle. After chanting a rhyme in Firai, she tossed them one by one onto the sandy soil by the fire. Arkady waited with impatience as she picked up each one and studied the symbol incised on the uppermost facet.

"What do they say to you, Eira?" he asked anxiously.

He took no comfort from her words. "The stones say you will suffer greatly, my brother, before the Dawnmaid comes to bring us deliverance. I tell you of this suffering not to frighten you, but so you may know it will happen, and will eventually come to an end."

"What can the stones tell you of the girl I met in the dunes?" he asked urgently. "Where is she now? What hold does Keth Dirane have on her?"

Eira spoke regretfully. "I do not know the answers to your

questions about this girl. The legend says that the mother of the Dawnmaid will be one of the Kindreds. You, yourself, must find her, for you are the Seed Bearer. The battle crow will try everything in her power to stop you, but you must not fail. Otherwise how can true Dawn return to this world?"

Arkady sat back abruptly, realizing for the first time she meant he was to father the Dawnmaid. He felt profound disappointment. The girl he knew as Krikka could not be the mother, for she was not of the Firaithi. His feelings for her had blossomed so quickly he assumed he and Krikka must somehow be linked by the prophecy. How could he unravel this mystery?

Eira squeezed his hand and left him alone by the dying embers of the fire. He stared for a long time at the flames, but they gave him no answers.

The next morning, Arkady mounted Ylene carefully and waved good-bye to Eira and Grigor.

Grigor said gruffly, "Be careful with that horse, Arkadios. We do not often give our best steeds to a Grua..." He stopped himself and gave a sheepish grin. "I meant — to one of our own, who is leaving the Kindred. Farewell."

Eira called, "Tsmare an fyr arterre.*"

Huw rode alongside, on his horse Alun, and together they took the Queen's Road east to the Yoke. Arkady wanted to find his brother Jacq at the Citadel, and Huw planned to see Queen Katrione Arkafina, to discuss the coming horse fair. As the brothers trotted along they chatted in a combination of Firai and Maraison.

"You have learned far more of our tongue than I would have thought possible in such a short time, my brother."

"It is mostly due to your patient lessons, Huw," Arkady said gratefully. "But thank you for the compliment."

As they crossed the bridge over the Ariane River, Huw pointed and said, "Look, there is your City on her peninsula. She is beautiful in the sunlight, is she not?"

Arkady sighed and gazed into the distance to where the Mere shimmered in the morning sun. He could see St. Valery too, and

---

* May the moon light your way home.

her high walls shone white. The battlements of the Citadel, with their flag-topped towers, brought back poignant memories of home. Arkady lowered his eyes and did not answer Huw's question. They rode on in silence, as the road wound through the verdant trees of St. Valery's Acre. A pair of playful red squirrels leapt from branch to branch, high above their heads.

Huw watched them for a moment and then asked softly, "Are you troubled about meeting your family again? After eight years they will be very surprised to see you, I think." Huw looked across to him and Arkady nodded in agreement.

"I am looking forward to seeing them, but I am little bit afraid too. My father's death happened a year ago, but my grief is very new. I hope they will understand." As he spoke, they passed through the last of the trees and drew up to the Yoke, the land bridge to the City. The gate stood wide open. The guard waved a desultory hand and stepped aside to let Arkady pass.

But when Huw attempted to follow, the guard stepped in front of Alun and stood at attention. "State your name and your business, Firaithi." His voice dripped contempt.

"You just waved me through," Arkady interjected quickly. "Why can he not come with me?"

"This does not concern you. Proceed onto the Yoke," the guard said curtly.

"It does concern me, Guardsman, because this man is my brother. Now please explain to me why I am allowed to cross into the City while he is not." He glared at the guard and Huw put a hand on his arm.

"Do not let this trouble you, Kadya," he said, quietly. "I am used to answering their questions." He sat up straighter in his saddle and said proudly, "I am Huw Adaryi of the Firaithi Kindred Chandrathi. I seek an audience with Queen Katrione Arkafina, to discuss business related to the Horse Trading Fair."

The Guard looked distinctly skeptical. "I will have to send a runner to the Citadel to see if the Queen has any appointments remaining for today. It may take several hours. You might as well come back later."

Arkady could not believe his own home city, St. Valery, could be so unwelcoming to a stranger. He spoke firmly to the guard. "He is not going to come back later. We are crossing right now."

The guard raised his sword and called for reinforcements. Three other men joined him at the gate. "If you do not clear the entrance to the gate immediately we will arrest you both."

Huw said anxiously, "I don't want any trouble. You go ahead into the City, and I will join you when I can, my brother."

The guards moved in to separate the two men. Arkady dismounted from Ylene, and struggled briefly with them. He found himself tightly restrained. The guards pulled Huw off his horse and dragged him inside the gatehouse, out if sight of the passersby. They threw him face down on the ground and one of the guards viciously kicked him in the back. Arkady looked on in horror. How could this be happening to Huw? He fought against the guard holding him, but the man had his arm pinned firmly behind his back and every motion brought excruciating pain to his injured shoulder.

A deep booming voice interrupted the guards as they continued to kick Huw, who had rolled into a ball on the ground in an effort to protect himself. A very tall man stepped from behind the inner gate. "What are you doing? Let that darky alone."

Arkady abruptly stopped struggling, for he recognized the voice. He called out, "Jacq, thank the Gods. It is me. Your brother, Arkady."

Jacq stepped closer, peering intently, and broke into a broad smile. He rushed towards his youngest brother. "Kadya! What on Yrth? I hardly recognize you. Your hair is different." He frowned darkly at the guard and roared, "Get your hands off him at once."

The guardsman let go of Arkady's arm, and stepped back a pace. "I am sorry, Dinrhydan, but this man ignored a direct instruction to leave the gate area. We were just following orders. He defended this Firaithi pig, and we had to restrain him."

Huw groaned weakly and Arkady quickly knelt by him on the cobblestones. "My Gods, Huw, are you hurt?"

Before he could answer, Jacq asked, "Who is this man? Why are you traveling with a darky?" Arkady noted the suspicious tone in his brother's voice, but decided to ignore it.

Arkady helped Huw to his feet. He said, through teeth gritted in pain, "Broken rib, I think. I had better ride back to the camp and have it seen to."

"No, Huw. You will never make it back to St. Lisane like that.

Come with me now to the Citadel. Katkin, that is... the Queen, is a healer. She can help you."

Jacq said quietly, "Maybe it would be better to let him go back to his own kind. Kat's awfully busy today, and I don't know..." He scratched his head, and it was obvious the whole situation made him very uncomfortable. Arkady felt his temper rising and fought to control it. His own brother wanted to send the injured man away.

Arkady, his tone clipped, asked, "His own kind? Listen to me, Jacq. If he goes, I go too. This man is my blood brother Huw Adaryi, son of a Firaithi Tane. They took me in when I had no food and no horse. I owe him a great deal."

Jacq laughed and slapped Arkady on the back. "Simmer down, little brother. Of course, if he is a friend of yours, we would welcome him into the City. I am sorry about the fracas, but we cannot be too careful these days. There are a lot of undesirables about, you know, and we try to keep them out of St. Valery." He held his huge hand out to Huw, and said, "I am Jacq Benet, Queen Katrione's consort."

Huw shook Jacq's hand and said politely, "I am honored to meet the husband of the Queen. I had hoped to see her today about the trading fair."

His voice sounded strained and it was obvious the broken rib caused him great discomfort. Arkady helped him slowly mount Alun, and they joined the stream of people crossing the Yoke towards the City.

Though Arkady desperately wanted to question Jacq about his father Nicholas' death, he knew the crowded and noisy Yoke would not be the proper place. He waited until they had entered the quiet confines of the Citadel and then he said, "I know what happened to my father. Huw told me about the accident. How is mother doing?"

Jacq suddenly looked very unhappy. "Gods, it was such a surprise to see you again, I forgot you did not know, Kadya. I should have told you right away." He sighed, shaking his head. "Mother died soon after your father's accident. She just seemed to fade away without him. We tried to contact you, but Nicholas' family in St. Ekaterina said you had gone on a long journey east. Since I have to be the bearer of bad news, you may as well know we lost Thad as well, in the measles epidemic two years ago."

Huw, who rode almost bent double, with one arm curled protectively around his middle, said, "I am so sorry, my brother. This homecoming has not been a happy one for you."

Arkady sat silently for a few moments, trying to take all Jacq's news in. His parents were dead, and one of his brothers. So much had happened, but what did he expect? He blinked hard, and the tears in his eyes spilled over and ran down his cheeks. Jacq, riding beside him, reached over and patted him sympathetically while shedding tears of his own. Seeing this, Arkady decided he must keep his grief private. It would not be fair to put everyone through the pain of these losses once more. He wiped his eyes and adopted the most serene expression he could manage.

They rode now across the wide green expanse of the parade field, and past the blacksmith's shop. The passing soldiers stared at them curiously. Firaithi were not commonly allowed in the Citadel, and to see one riding with the Dinrhydan was very unusual indeed. Someone must have alerted the Queen's personal guard, for in a moment she came running out of the tower doors, and breathlessly caught up with them as they dismounted by the stables.

"Kadya! It really is you. One of the guards recognized you, but I thought he must have made a mistake." She hurried to embrace him, and looked closely at his face. She said unhappily, "I see Jacq has told you all the news. I am sorry." He nodded, and tried once again to swallow his grief. At his side, Katkin saw Huw sway alarmingly, and she said, "This man is unwell. Lay him on the ground at once." She called over a waiting guardsman and gave him instructions to fetch a stretcher.

Huw said weakly, "Please don't trouble yourself on my account, your Majesty. I can walk."

She whirled in surprise and knelt down at his side. "Huw? My Goddess, what on Yrth happened?" Huw, not wishing to cause further embarrassment, said nothing as she pressed gently on his chest to determine the extent of the injury. Arkady noticed the flicker of anger in Jacq's eyes as she took the Firaithi's hand in her own and squeezed it.

Jacq said casually, "He got in a little tangle with the guards at the gate. Luckily, I came along before it became too serious." She glared up at him angrily.

"A little tangle, Jacq? He has two broken ribs. I want a full investigation into this matter, and I want to talk to the Captain in charge of the gate detail personally. The guards have no business roughing up visitors to the City. What on Yrth must Kadya be thinking of us?"

Arkady said carefully, "It was just a misunderstanding, Katkin. Please don't let it trouble you." He sighed, thinking that thus far, his long-awaited visit had been nothing but a disaster.

"No, Kadya," she said, bitterly. "It was much more than a misunderstanding. What happened to our friend Huw is a small demonstration of how small-minded this City has become."

Jacq said, "Kat, that is enough..." and the warning in his voice was clear.

Arkady could see that he and Huw had stumbled into some longstanding dispute between the Queen and her husband. At that moment, the guards arrived with a stretcher and Katkin instructed the men, "Take him to the double guest room within my private quarters. Be quick now, but go carefully. He has suffered enough at our hands already!"

Katkin no longer had the Gift of healing from the Goddess Lalluna, for that had been lost when she became pregnant with Gwenn. But she still had nine years of medical training at the Infirmarie, and was a fully qualified physician. Though she had only one hand, she wore a cunningly crafted prosthesis made for her by her husband. With it, she was able to bandage Huw's broken ribs adroitly. She offered him some tincture of opium for pain and was somewhat surprised when he refused. He asked for tea instead. As soon as he was resting comfortably, she left him alone.

Arkady went looking for Jacq after he had unpacked his small bag in another opulent guest room. He wandered aimlessly through the winding corridors, until he came to a long banqueting hall. Many formally posed portraits hung on the creamy plaster walls. One in particular caught his eye and he moved over to study it more closely.

He shook his head in disbelief. The life-size painting portrayed a beautiful flaxen-haired girl sitting by a weathered gravestone, under a spreading oak. Though she was dressed very formally, in a high-necked gown of cerulean blue to match her eyes, he did not doubt her identity. The girl in the picture was Krikka, his mysterious lover in the dunes.

Chapter Six

Dead Man's Lick

Geya takes a deep breath, to keep her voice steady. The Numen has far more power than she, for now anyway, and Geya knows she cannot afford to antagonize the old woman too much. Nevertheless, she swears to herself that one day she will depose the Numen, and rise to take her place. Then the Amaranthine will rule, instead of skulking in the lesser pellicula, as they do now.

But she does not wish the Numen to know her plans, so she says sweetly, I have come to ask you of Dai, Numen. Has he come to you with any new scheme to defeat the Angellus?

~~~~~~~~~~

"Beautiful, isn't she?"

Arkady jumped. He had not even heard his brother Jacq approaching — such was his astonishment at finding a portrait of Krikka in this unlikely place. He asked, a bit too casually, "Who is that, Jacq? Her face seems very familiar."

Jacq looked baffled and asked, "You don't recognize her? Ah well, I suppose she must have been just a little girl when you left on your travels." Arkady's heart jumped, and a horrible sensation suddenly clawed at his insides. A second later, his brother confirmed his worst fear. Jacq said proudly, "That is your niece, Gwenn. We had her portrait painted last year, when she turned fifteen. She did not want to get dressed up like that, but she agreed after Kat let her pose next to some old gravestone."

It took every shred of Arkady's self-control not to let his brother see what effect this identification had on him. He took a deep shaky breath, and stuck his hands in his pockets to hide their trembling. *Gwenn. His niece...* Maybe there was some mistake — had he misidentified the girl in the picture? He clung to this hope like a drowning man. Arkady tried to speak normally, but his voice came out in a hoarse whisper. He asked, "Is she here now? I would very much like to see her again. She has grown up so much."

Jacq's face fell as he said forlornly, "No, I am afraid not. She ran away a couple of months ago, on the day before her sixteenth birthday. It isn't the first time, and I keep hoping she will come back. Apparently, she headed northwest, towards the coast. We have people out looking, but there has been no sign of her for the last several weeks."

Somehow, with a superhuman effort, Arkady managed to say, "I am sorry, my brother. You must be very worried about her."

His brother smiled, but his eyes were sad. "I am not worried. Gwenn can take of herself. I just miss her, that is all."

The certainty Krikka and Gwenn were one and the same hit Arkady like a blow to the abdomen, and a wave of nausea filled his mouth with sand. He knew he must get away from Jacq somehow, before his composure evaporated all together. But his brother kept talking, relentlessly. Arkady hardly heard what he said. He kept his eyes locked on the picture of Gwenn, and the memory of their night together threatened to overwhelm him — he had made love to his sixteen-year-old niece, not once but four times, in the fire-lit dunes of Secuny.

"What have you heard about the accident that killed your father? Did you know Gwenn was involved?" Jacq looked at him questioningly, and Arkady could only nod silently. "We went hunting, and somehow she became separated from us. Something frightened her, and she fired the matchlock blindly into some trees. The shot hit your father and he died." Noticing Arkady's stricken expression at last, Jacq said, "I don't think he felt any pain, my brother. It was over very quickly. Gwenn was devastated by the accident. I wish she could tell you herself."

Arkady nodded despairingly again. He could not even look at his brother anymore. What could he say now?

I am sorry to have to tell you this big brother, but I made love to your daughter several times, just a few weeks ago...

No, he could not tell Jacq. He had never been particularly close to his eldest brother. Jacq had left home when Arkady was only three years old. Of course, he loved him, but they had nothing at all in common except their mother. He wished now, more than ever, she still lived. Somehow, in her calm way, she would be able to tell him what to do — how to make everything right again. But her wheel had turned last year and now he had this appalling secret knowledge to deal with all alone. He had to tell someone, did he not? What if Gwenn came back? She might already have his child growing inside her. This terrible thought could not be borne. He had to leave, right now, or break down completely in front of Jacq.

Arkady mumbled, "Have to go now. Need to check on Huw..." and walked from the room as quickly as he could. Jacq scratched his head in confusion and watched him go.

Once he found himself alone in the corridor, Arkady put his hand in front of his mouth to stifle a sob. All the painful events of this impossible day, from Huw's beating to Jacq's news about the deaths of his mother and brother, were mere pinpricks compared to the unspeakable reality facing him now. He stumbled along brokenly, without seeing or hearing anything, for many minutes. Finally, he found himself outside, in a tiny, walled garden. The sun shone brightly, as if nothing had ever been wrong with the world. Swallows swooped here and there, catching insects. The clouds in the sky, the roses in the carefully manicured beds, the fountain with its playful spray of water — all were an affront to the demon-infested darkness now ruling Arkady Svalbarad's world. How could such things as light and air still exist? He sank down onto a stone bench, and let his despair take him completely.

"Kadya? Are you all right? Jacq sent me to find you. He said you seemed upset." Katkin's voice penetrated the veil of blackness inside him and he opened his eyes.

She stood in front of him with the sun high above her. For a second her chestnut hair became a halo of gold, and he could easily see now how much Gwenn resembled her mother. Arkady gave a strangled sob and covered his face with his hands. He should have known, somehow. Why did he not recognize the girl in the dunes as his own kin? Why did she not tell him? She knew perfectly well who *he* was and yet she had allowed him to take her.

Katkin sat down beside him, and she took his hand. She could not hide the concern in her voice. "My Goddess, what is it? Look, if you are worried about Huw, he is going to be all right. I just went to check on him and he is resting comfortably."

She peered at him and Arkady shook his head, saying numbly, "Not Huw."

"Then what is troubling you, my brother? If you are in some kind of difficulty you must tell me, and I will do everything I can to help you."

Arkady looked at her, and his red-rimmed eyes were wild with grief and despair. "You cannot help me. Not now."

Though his expression frightened her, she forced her voice to remain calm. She said, "Tell me anyway, Arkady. You need to confide in someone, or you will go mad."

He grasped her hand tightly. "I don't know what to say — how to tell you. I have done something terrible. Beyond terrible..."

Her voice held nothing but gentle sympathy. "Just start at the beginning."

He took a very deep breath, and said sorrowfully, "I met a girl. In Secuny, by the dunes. She offered me some food. Then we... Oh Gods, how can I say this?" Katkin squeezed his hand encouragingly, and somehow he made himself continue. "She wanted me to, I swear it, Katkin. I did not force myself on her. I never would have..." His voice trailed off and he began to cry once more.

Katkin looked at him in confusion. There did not seem to be anything particularly upsetting about his story. Obviously, there must be more to it than a simple tryst in the dunes. She waited patiently beside him until he could speak again.

He went on hoarsely, "I should have recognized her. She looks just like you, Kat. But she lied about her name, and I had not seen either of you in eight years. I did not make the connection until I saw the picture in the banquet hall. Jacq told me, just now. That is why I ran away from him. Do you understand?" He let go of her hand and covered his face.

Suddenly she did understand, and her eyes went wide with shock. "It was Gwenn? The girl in the dunes was Gwenn? Is she all right?"

He nodded and kept his face covered. He did not want to see the horror in her eyes, now she knew what he had done with her daughter. Only birdsong broke the silence. The heady perfume of the roses filled the air. Arkady waited despondently for Katkin to vent her anger and disgust on him.

She said softly, "Look at me, Kadya."

He could not.

As gently as she could she pulled his hands away from his face and said again, "Look at me." Her eyes held nothing but sorrow and pity. She whispered, "You haven't done anything wrong, Kadya. This is all my fault. Now I must try to put it right."

Arkady could not believe what he was hearing. He snarled at her, "Your fault? How in the Gods' names could it be your fault? Why are you not enraged? Did you not understand me? I made love to your daughter." His desperation made him angry, and he could stay still no longer. He stood up and paced before her.

She stood too, and caught his arm. He clung to her as she wrapped him in a warm embrace. The anger inside him died, to be replaced with a tiny flicker of promise. Was it possible, somehow, she did not hate him for what he had done? She whispered in his ear, "Listen to me, Kadya. We need to talk more on this, urgently, but not now. Will you wait here, while I fetch some horses?"

He nodded, and his expression held a dawning hope as he wiped the tears from his eyes. Katkin smiled at him, and said, "That is better. I will return as quickly as I may." She hurried away towards the stables.

A little while later she returned, riding Alys and leading Ylene by her halter. Four mounted guardsmen followed at a distance. Arkady looked at them questioningly and she shrugged.

"My personal guard. I cannot leave the Citadel without them. But they will not disturb us. Come, ride with me."

She said nothing else until they had crossed the Yoke and passed into St. Valery's Acre. Katkin guided Alys along a well-worn path through the forest that covered part of the western lakeshore. As they continued, the path narrowed until it turned into hardly more than a game trail winding through the undergrowth. Alys seemed to be familiar with the route, and Ylene followed her without difficulty, though the trees grew closer together as they progressed into the deepest part of the Acre.

They came at last to a high wall built of fieldstone, with an arched opening secured by a sturdy wooden door. The four guardsmen, long familiar with the routine, dismounted without any instruction from the Queen. Katkin removed a key from her pocket and handed it to one of the guards. He unlocked the door and went inside the walled compound.

A moment later he returned, saying, "All clear, your Majesty."

Katkin and Arkady rode through, ducking carefully to avoid the stone arch above their heads. The guard closed the door behind them. Though Arkady now had a thousand questions, he did not speak. He could see the wall surrounded a grassy dell with a huge oak tree in the middle. The tree sheltered a lonely but carefully tended grave, graced with a stone statue of winged Lalluna. Arkady experienced a fractured moment of déjà vu, until he remembered the setting for Gwenn's portrait. She had obviously posed for the painter underneath this very tree.

His sister-in-law jumped down from Alys, sat on the bench, and patted the seat beside her. Arkady dismounted and let Ylene stray free on the long turf. He joined Katkin on the bench and asked, "What is this place, Kat? Why have you brought me here?"

She sighed and said, "You were afraid to tell me about Gwenn because you thought I would be angry with you. I have something to tell you too, and I am equally afraid. So, I brought you here to try and explain something I did sixteen years ago, that I have kept hidden all this time. I could not let you make a scene in the courtyard garden, in case Jacq saw you."

Arkady stared at her, unsure what she meant. "Go on," he said, evenly.

Katkin took his hand and he saw her eyes fill with tears. She spoke in a trembling voice. "The man buried in this grave is Gwenn's real father."

He looked at her in disbelief. "Jacq is not Gwenn's father? Does he know that?"

"Her father made me swear I would never tell him. But Gwenn knows the truth."

The realization, when it arrived, made him giddy with relief. "Then Gwenn and I are not related by blood! Is that what you wanted to tell me?" She nodded and he caught her up in an impulsive embrace. The crushing darkness lifted from his heart, and he felt as though he could breathe again. As he released her, he asked, "Why on Yrth did you think I might be angry at you?"

"Why would you not be? I became pregnant with another man's child after I married your brother." She glared at him defiantly, and waited for his response.

Arkady rubbed his face in confusion. "Tell me the whole story. I know you well enough to know that whatever you did, you must have had a good reason for it."

"I thought I did at the time, but I have had many second thoughts since." Looking at the gravestone thoughtfully, she continued, "Do you remember when the Guard arrested Jacq at the Temple, the day I had to rescue Roseberry from the Maitress of the Unity? You must have been about eleven at the time."

He nodded.

"The men of the Fourth Company took him to the Citadel. Their leader was a man named Tomas de Vigny."

Arkady interrupted her, saying, "I heard Jacq speak of him with loathing, many times. He called him the scum of the Yrth — his worst enemy."

Katkin blinked hard several times and said, "Tomas is Gwenn's father."

His voice rose and he could not control it. "You gave yourself to that devil? Jacq's torturer? My Gods, Kat, how could you do that?"

She said sadly, "I knew you would be angry." Arkady stood and walked away from her, to try and hide his agitation. "I was alone, Kadya. My parents were dead. Willow, my sister, had gone away without as much as a goodbye. Tomas and I had been friends, once upon a time, when I saved him from drowning and healed his leg. He loved me, but I chose Jacq over him, and he wanted revenge. But I had no-one else to turn to, so I asked for his help."

Arkady turned to look at her. "Did he rape you?" He did not wait for her answer, but said with certainty, "Of course, that must be what happened. You have no need to feel shame over that, my sister." His relief dissolved rapidly as she shook her head.

She said dully, "He did not force me. I gave myself to him freely, in return for a visit with Jacq. I thought they were going to execute him the next day, and I wanted to see him so I could tell him goodbye. At the time, it seemed like a small price to pay."

Arkady tried to hold on to his anger at her betrayal, but found he could not. Would he have behaved any differently? He sat down beside Katkin and took her hand, saying apologetically, "I should not have shouted at you. Please tell me the rest of the story. How is it Tomas de Vigny came to be buried here?"

She wiped her eyes with the hem of her sleeve. "When Jacq's

comrades in the Rising freed him the same night, the Guard issued a warrant for my arrest. Tomas helped me escape from the City and left me here in the Acre. When I met up with Jacq the next morning he had gone mad with the pain from his injuries. He challenged me to a sword fight, and Tomas had to intervene to save my life. He shot Jacq in the shoulder. I tried to heal him, and that is when I found out about my pregnancy, for my Gift had gone."

Arkady said in wonder, "I never heard any of this before. I guess my parents thought I was too young to know the truth."

"Jacq was dying and I could not help him. I begged Lalluna to do something, but she said she could not, because Death had already come for him." She stopped talking, and stared, through tear-filled eyes, at the blurred outline of the weathered gravestone.

"What happened then?" Arkady asked her softly.

"After making me swear I would never tell Jacq the truth about Gwenn, Tomas shot himself as he sat under this tree — so Death would take him instead of Jacq. He saved my husband's life, because he wanted me to be happy and Gwenn to have a loving father. After Tomas' suicide, Lalluna and I were able to join together and heal Jacq. Later he and I managed to escape to your father's headquarters in St. Germain. You probably know the rest of the story."

Katkin stood and walked over to the gravestone, then squatted before it so she could sweep aside the tangle of vines that covered the inscription. "When I became Queen, I had Tomas buried properly. His men never found him, you see, and his bones were still here under the oak tree. After what he did for Jacq, I thought he deserved to have a proper resting place."

"But why is his grave surrounded by a wall? It seems too isolated to need protection from vandals."

"I come here often when my heart is troubled, to talk to Tomas about Gwenn. I feel his spirit still lingers here somehow, and he is a friend to me now, in a way he never could be while he lived. I have had many such talks with him since she came into the world. I cannot tell anyone else the truth about her. That is why I had my men build the wall, so I could be alone here, and still be safe."

"What on Yrth do you mean? Is there something wrong with Gwenn?" She could hear the deep concern in his voice, and knew then he was in love with her daughter. Katkin walked back to the bench and sat down again.

"Yes there is, and that is my fault too, Kadya. Before Lalluna entered my body to heal Jacq, she warned me the child I bore could be at risk. But I would not listen, because I wanted Jacq to be well again and I did not care about the consequences."

He asked in frustration, "What consequences?"

"When Lalluna crossed the heavenly plane, something else entered at the same time and settled into my child. An evil demon, named Keth Dirane."

Arkady's eyes went wide. "You think Ketha lives inside Gwenn's body? How can you be so sure?"

"At first I was not sure at all, but I could not ignore the signs. Gwenn talked to herself all the time as a child, but I told myself she had an imaginary friend and so I let my fears rest. Then she started to grow and grow, and still I said to myself that Tomas, her father, was tall, and that she takes after him. It was only after she began speaking to her imaginary friend in a different language that I truly began to worry. Her behavior further deteriorated once she became a teenager. She became cruel, Kadya, and cared for nothing but battle and conquest. Finally, three years ago, I went to the Temple and called on Lalluna. She told me about Keth Dirane."

Arkady sat silently beside her, and shivered as he remembered Gwenn's words as she lay with him on the blanket.

Ketha will always find me. We have so little time to be together before she returns...

"Does Jacq know about this?" he asked.

"I tried to tell him once, but he would not believe me. He loves Gwenn more than anything, and always defends her. Even now, after she has been thrown out of every school in St. Valery for fighting and disobedience. 'Youthful high spirits', he calls it. Of course, she worshipped Jacq as well. The mighty warrior, Dinrhydan. He taught her everything he knows about swordsmanship and that is a great deal, believe me. On the day before her sixteenth birthday he gave her a weapon he forged himself in the smithy at the Citadel." Her voice grew bitter. "Tris told me that. Jacq meant to keep it from me because he knew I would be angry. Keth Dirane made her strong, but your brother armed her and made her dangerous." Kat-kin looked at Arkady and her green eyes shone intensely. "Please listen carefully to me, Kadya, and believe what I say. She is *very* dangerous, and full of hatred. And she despises me most of all."

"Why? You are her mother. How can she hate you?"

"Because I lied about Jacq being her real father. Once she found out the truth, she never forgave me. She blackmailed me for years to get whatever she wanted. Gwenn made my life hell to punish me for what I had done to her beloved Papa." Katkin started to cry again, and Arkady patted her shoulder sympathetically.

"It must have been hard to keep all this pain to yourself for so long. But now you have confided in me, you have no need to be anxious. I will be leaving soon, and I will not tell Jacq anything."

She gazed at him doubtfully. "You are in love with her, are you not?"

He turned to face her and she could tell her question startled him. He nodded reluctantly. Katkin said, "So you are going to try and find her again."

Again, he nodded.

"What will happen if you succeed in freeing her from Ketha's grip? Eventually the two of you will end up back here. Then there can be no more secrets."

He shrugged. "The Yrth is a big place. I won't bring her back here if you don't want me to."

She sighed and accepted this. "So what will you do now?"

"Kat, there is a Firaithi prophecy I learned about on my travels with them. Somehow, I am a part of it, and I must talk to Gwenn and find out where she got this..." He pulled the amulet out from under his shirt and showed it to Katkin.

She was very surprised. "I can tell you that. The crow's foot peri-apt you wear belonged to my grandmother, Neirin Mare. Gwenn must have stolen it from my keepsake chest before she left."

"Your grandmother? How did she get something so sacred to the Firaithi? The prophecy is a secret known only to the Kin-dreds. They only told me after I became Huw's blood brother."

"I will tell you another secret. My mother, Anwen, was Firaithi. My father met her at a horse fair long ago and took her away from the kindred of Anandi. Her father, Ifan Mare, was their Tane. The du Chesnes kept it quiet, of course, because it would have caused

78

a scandal in the sort of society we lived in, and my mother had such a light complexion, no-one ever suspected."

Arkady's eyes lit up. He said, wonderingly, "Then she *is* the one the prophecy talks about. Eira said she had to be one of the Kindreds. I though it must not be Gwenn, but it is."

Katkin looked confused and asked, "What are you talking about? Why did Gwenn give you the talisman anyway? Did she say where she was going?"

He rubbed his chin pensively. "To Danica, the home of her father's people. But nowhere specific."

"How on Yrth did she meet up with you?"

"I don't know. But it seems obvious to me now she must have deliberately waited in Secuny for me to ride by. As I said, she offered me some food, and we talked a lot about my travels. She would tell me nothing about herself, not even her real name." He shifted uncomfortably and said, "I already told you what happened after that. Maybe she planned for us to do that too, I just don't know anymore. Anyway, after I went to sleep, she stole my horse and rode away without saying goodbye. But she left me some food and water, and this amulet as well."

"If Gwenn wanted you, she would figure out a way to make it happen." Katkin smiled ruefully. "She can be very determined when she wants something. Ketha must have helped her locate you and then left to look for something to eat. Otherwise, I doubt you would have found her so welcoming."

"I thought she seemed frightened and unsure. But even though I begged her to stay with me, she would not. I wish I could have..." His voice was filled with desperation. "Somehow, I have to help her. You understand, don't you? I must find her again." He clutched at Katkin's hand and she nodded.

"Yes, Kadya. I understand. But I am not so sure that you do. Ketha can make Gwenn do anything. She might kill you, as she killed Nicholas. You do know about that, don't you?"

Arkady looked worried. "Jacq said my father's death was an accident, that Gwenn was frightened and fired blindly."

Katkin spoke forcefully. "Have you not been listening to me? I told you, he always defends her. The truth is Gwenn has never been frightened of anything in her whole life, except Ketha. When she shot him, I have absolutely no doubt it was deliberate."

Chapter Seven

The Grasping Hands of Old Mother Cinnus

The Numen gives her a sharp look. If he did, it would be between him and me. No business of yours, Geya.

Geya makes an impatient sound and says petulantly, You must tell me Dai's plans, Numen. He has chosen to become human this turn of the gyre, and his foolish action might ruin all my delicate arrangements. I deserve to know what he is up to.

~~~~~~~~~~

After Gwenn joined the crew of the Fynäran raider ship *Fire Drake*, they continued down the coast to the next inhabited village. The residents had little worth stealing, but they took what there was, and burned several houses. Gunnar watched over Gwenn carefully, but she acquitted herself so well he soon ceased to worry about her. Though his crew now fought short-handed, she more than made up for the men she had killed.

Several of the men had tried, mischievously, in the first few days, to catch her unawares at night. But Ketha never slept, and could warn Gwenn of any danger.

After she injured two more men, one seriously, Gunnar said to the others, "No-one is to approach the Faircrow without my permission. Keep away from her — or else." He knew he could not afford to lose any more of his crew to her sword, keth'fell. But it was not long before the others learned to respect the strength and valor of the blond shield maiden who had become their newest shipmate.

Gwenn had taken the black clothing from one of the dead Fynära — the unfortunate Stig, and with her short hair and slim, muscular build, she easily passed for a lad. Other than her disconcerting habit of washing every day, she was soon indistinguishable from any other of the crew.

After they pillaged and torched several more villages, the raiders headed back towards Starruthe. The ship groaned with the spoils from their forays, and Gunnar knew he would be in for high praise when they reached home. Thoughtfully, he fingered the lock of blond hair that he kept in the leather pouch that hung from his neck. His alliance with the maid who called herself Gwenn Faircrow had been an auspicious one so far. Now he watched from the rudder as she took her turn at the oars. Though no-one doubted her skill with a sword, she had needed to learn a great deal about rowing. There was a lot of good-natured cursing before she had managed to keep a steady rhythm with the other men. She looked up and gave him a smile and Gunnar nodded briefly to her. It would not do for the others to see him showing any hint of favoritism to the girl.

Gwenn rowed steadily for two hours, until Arvid came up to replace her. She stood and stretched away her stiffness before walking back to the stern, where Gunnar still stood at the steering oar. "How much longer until we get back to Starruthe, Captain?" she asked him eagerly.

He shrugged. "If we can pick up a favorable wind we might be back tomorrow. Though we have left the coast behind, we still have a lot of open water yet to cover. A hundred leagues or more. What is your hurry, anyway? What do you plan to do when we arrive?"

"I don't know yet. First, I have to find lodgings, I suppose." She gazed at him with her wide sky blue eyes and asked, "Do you have a woman, Gunnar?"

This question, asked with such direct innocence from his newest crewmember, made him distinctly uncomfortable. In a gruff voice, he teased, "Why do you ask? Are you applying for the position?" He figured humor would be the best way to hide his discomfort. The truth was Gunnar could not quite sort out what he thought about Gwenn, but he did not want her to know that.

She seemed not to notice the jest, for she answered his question quite seriously. "No, I don't think I ought to do that. The rest of the men might not like it. I just wondered if maybe I could stay with you for a while. Do you think I could?"

Somehow, he did not think his men would think much of *that* arrangement, either, however innocent it might be. He shook his head and replied, "I am sure we can find a place for you to stay when we get into Einar."

"How do we share out the spoil? I am going to need something to trade for some proper clothes." Gwenn had scrubbed and scrubbed Stig's tunic and breeches but they still smelled terrible.

"The spoil belongs to our Magnus,* Per Drake's Son. He will share it out as he sees fit. In the past, he has not been overly generous with me and my crewmen, but we have never brought back such a haul as this before. I think he will be very impressed with you, Gwenn Faircrow. I am sure you will have enough payment for some clothes, if that is what you wish." He looked at her in bemusement. Obviously, he had other plans for his own share of the loot.

"He had better be impressed. I plan to ask him for enough men and supplies to set up a permanent camp on the coast of Secuny, close to the ruined village where we first met."

"What?" Gunnar's explosive reply made several heads among the rowing crew snap up, and he quickly lowered his voice to a furious whisper. "You cannot be serious, Gwenn. Per Drake's Son will never agree to such a scheme. It is far too risky."

She frowned at him and said obstinately, "Why is it too risky? All these little raids you do on the coastal villages will never amount to much. We need a base closer to the true heart of Yr. From there we will be able to stage boats and go far inland on the waterways. There are uncounted riches in Mardon and Beaumarais, Captain. Cathedrals, museums and treasuries just waiting for our swords to liberate. They do not fear the Fynära, for you have left them alone until now. Their defenses are lax. We can fly through like a storm from the east, and leave nothing but ruin in our wake."

Her words stirred him. He stroked his beard thoughtfully. "There is something in what you say, Faircrow. I believe you are right. But how do you plan to convince our Magnus? He knows nothing of your skill as a warrior. Why would he agree to let you lead such an expedition?"

Gwenn's blue eyes were bright. "I will challenge him and fight his best warriors, one at a time or all together. It is all the same to me. I will not be defeated. Eventually, he will have to give in."

Such confidence seemed uncanny to Gunnar, and he looked askance at her. "How can you be so sure you will not lose? You said you were but a mortal, like me."

She smiled her feral smile. "Because I have a secret weapon

---

* The Lord of a Fynäran settlement.

— and it never fails me." Though he gave her a questioning glance, Gwenn would say no more.

The wind picked up and the men hoisted the square woolen sail. Gwenn watched the water slip by under the hull of the long boat, as Ketha told her more of the customs of the Fynära. "The Magnus, Per Drake's Son, is very rich and well-respected because of his generosity. He will hold a huge feast for all the returning raiders, and of course he will invite the crew of the *Fire Drake*. Once there, you can issue your challenge to the Magnus. You may have to fight many men before he is convinced, so go get some rest now. We don't know what the morrow may bring, my dear." Gwenn nodded obediently and took out her blanket. She rolled herself up by the mastfish, out of the way of the rowers, and drifted off to sleep, with Ketha's words still ringing in her ears.

The early morning mist clung to Gwenn's hair and made her shiver. She groaned and tried to wrap the blanket more tightly around her as Gunnar kicked her roughly. "Get up, girl. We will be in the harbor soon and I need you to row."

Sighing, she rose and folded up the blanket carefully before returning it to the iron bound wooden chest that had once belonged to Stig. She sat down on top of it and began rowing, carefully keeping time with the others. Through the mist, she saw the masts of other ships, both longboats and the wider, heavier merchant vessels called knar. Gunnar shouted instructions from the helm, as the crew brought the boat into the harbor to an empty jetty and tied her up.

He stepped forward and said shortly, "Well, Faircrow. Welcome to Einar. Now get moving and help shift the spoils."

Gwenn gazed about her with interest. The early morning sun lit the wharves, and in the distance she could see the thatched roofs of many warehouses. Seabirds swooped and shrieked overhead. The town spread out all around the natural harbor, and she could see it was well fortified by a high wall with a log palisade on top.

The men who hurried forward to help unload the cargo were not at all typical of the Fynära. Gwenn saw many with dark hair and skin, and she asked, "Where do all those small men come from?"

"They are thralls," Gunnar replied. "They belong to our Magnus, Per. We captured most of them in raids to the south, on the coast of Spanja. He keeps the best and sells the rest on to Haba traders. Now stop gawking and get to work!" Though Gunnar had sworn loyalty to Gwenn, as long as he remained her Captain he intended to act the part.

A tall, grey-haired man approached the *Fire Drake's* jetty, and the thralls parted respectfully to let him pass. "That is Per Drake's Son," Gunnar whispered to Gwenn. His clothes and regal bearing easily set him apart from the rest of those present. His trousers were dyed a rich green color, and he wore a bright blue fur-lined cape with many embroidered decorations. An ornate silver brooch, of two dragons entwined, fastened his linen undershirt at the neck. He smiled when he saw the amount of cargo on the boat, and stopped to admire a silver platter looted from a church in southern Secuny.

"Don't tell him about me yet," she hissed at Gunnar.

Gunnar looked askance at her and scratched his head. "Why not? I thought you wanted to talk about your plan. You certainly won't get anywhere with him by being shy."

Gwenn busied herself with the stolen goods and tried to look inconspicuous. "I don't want any trouble here at the docks. I'd rather talk to him later." she replied, and hurried away to the stern as Per approached Gunnar.

Per slapped him on the back and said, "Looks like you had a very good trip, Strong Arm. But aren't you a few men short?"

Gunnar stared over Per's left shoulder and tried to make his voice sound unruffled. "We had a little trouble in Celeste. I lost five men."

Per did a quick survey. "I only count four missing."

"Um... Well, I found an extra crewman. Also in Celeste." Gunnar looked at Per nervously. That sort of thing just did not happen on raiding trips and he wondered what the Magnus would say.

"Who is this new man? I want to meet him." Per studied the men on the boat, and tried to pick out the unfamiliar face. Fortunately, Gwenn had her back turned.

Gunnar said pointedly, "I think he is onshore already. Have you seen this work of art we picked up in Scarfinda?" He took Per's arm and dragged him over to an ornamental enameled screen propped against the gunwale. Gwenn took the hint, grabbed a wooden box full of porcelain, and stepped onto the jetty. She followed the other crewmen towards a warehouse and stepped through the wide open door.

Arvid showed her where to stack the box and said, "Come back to my place for breakfast, Faircrow? The Captain will be busy for a while with Per Drake's Son. My wife will make you welcome, I am sure."

Gwenn smiled and accepted his invitation with enthusiasm. Arvid had been a little suspicious of her at first, but once she defeated Keld, he had accepted her unquestioningly and became one of her staunchest allies on the boat. She thought this might be because Keld had been responsible for the jagged scar on Arvid's face, inflicted during a drunken brawl between the two men some years before.

She followed Arvid out of the warehouse and kept her face carefully averted when they passed the Magnus, who stood with Gunnar, admiring the boxes and chests full of valuables still to be unloaded.

Arvid said, "Come on, we can leave the thralls to get the rest. I am hungry and Gudrun will be expecting me to turn up soon. She always knows when the boat is coming in. Gunnar will come by later, when he is finished with our lord."

He stepped back on to the boat and shouldered his iron bound chest. Gwenn did the same, and followed him along the jetty and into the town. They walked side by side on the path following the sandy shores of the river and Arvid pointed out the tanneries and smelters hard by the dock area. Gwenn wrinkled her nose at the acrid odor of the chemicals used in leather processing. She peered with interest in the blacksmith's shop, and had a brief moment of homesickness when she saw a tall leather-aproned man bending over an anvil. But her attention was soon diverted as they passed over a bridge and into a precinct of craft workers. Gwenn eyed brooches and pins of all descriptions as well as glass bead necklaces, leather boots, and tunics with fancy braided edges. She decided she would come back and outfit herself properly as soon as she received her share of the spoils. The market also held an assortment of stalls selling foodstuffs, and other household goods.

Gwenn stopped before a wide table piled high with sweets. "What is this? Toffee? Can I have some? Please, it only costs a *fallin*..."

Arvid smiled tolerantly and obligingly dug in his leather wallet.

He led her down a wooden-plank walkway to a small but neatly kept house fronting directly on to the water. A woman sat outside in the morning sun, working intently at a loom holding an almost-completed piece of woolen cloth woven in a complicated pattern. She smiled and stood when she caught sight of Arvid, and called out a greeting. Nodding briefly in return, he pointed to Gwenn, who was hanging back by the path, suddenly shy.

He said, "Gudrun, this is Gwenn Faircrow. She joined the boat at Celeste and came back with us to Einar."

Gudrun seemed startled. She called over to Gwenn, "What in the name of Faysta were you doing in Celeste? Did your man accidentally leave you there?"

Gwenn laughed at this and replied breezily, "I have no man, Gudrun. I came to Celeste so I could join the Fynära as a raider."

Arvid's wife immediately looked suspicious. "What on Yrth? A raider? Per Drake's Son would never allow a woman on any of his crews. What is the meaning of this, Arvid?"

Arvid shrugged. "She killed Keld Thunder Blade in a fair fight, so we let her join the crew. Now I have invited her to breakfast, so stop asking stupid questions and go make us something to eat, wife."

Gudrun gave Gwenn a black look and went inside the low door-way. She returned, sullen and silent, a few moments later, with two bowls filled with cooked oats and fresh strawberries, and a pitcher of cream. After handing over the bowls, she went back inside.

Arvid called to her, "Don't forget the ale!" Gwenn politely declined when he offered her a beaker full, and asked him for water. He pointed to the well in the yard, saying, "Help yourself. But don't ever drink the river water, unless your stomach be as hard as your sword."

Gunnar joined them as they finished the porridge, and sat on the steps, contentedly smoking his pipe. He appeared very encouraged by his welcome at the jetty. "Per Drake's Son is might-ily pleased with our haul. He has invited the crew to a feast at his hall tonight." He glanced nervously over to Gwenn. "It is too bad you will not be able to attend, but I will make sure you receive your share of the spoils."

"What do you mean? Of course I am going. Why would I not be?"

"Women never go to feasts. It is our way, Gwenn Faircrow," Gunnar replied patiently,

"I don't give a damn about any of that. I am a member of the *Fire Drake*'s felag,* so I will be going to the feast. Have we not all sworn to be loyal to one another?"

"Gwenn, you have to understand. We Fynärans don't let our women do as they please. They have to be obedient, like thralls."

She roared with laughter at this.

"Let the girl go, Gunnar," Arvid urged. "She has earned it as much as the rest of us. Per Drake's Son will get used to the idea of a woman warrior. We all have."

Gunnar scratched his head, removed a flea, and crushed it thoughtfully between his fingernails. "You speak Dalvolk like a native, but you know nothing of our customs, do you? How did you learn our language, anyway?"

Gwenn looked a little uncomfortable at this. "I have... a friend who knows Dalvolk well, and she taught me when I was very small." Gunnar seemed disbelieving so she continued, "We were together almost all the time, this friend and I, so we had lots of time to practice."

His bright blue eyes narrowed and Gwenn got the impression that he did not entirely accept her story. But he said no more about it, and asked instead, "When are you going to tell Per Drake's Son your plan? Tonight?"

She nodded. "Of course. We haven't much time to get the camp established before winter. I need his cooperation right away."

A young woman, obviously upset, approached the group sitting on Arvid's step. She wore a ragged, filthy dress and worn leather shoes. Gunnar and Arvid recognized her as Stig's wife, Nanna Stormbringer. She said tearfully, "Is it true? Rebekka said Stig did not come back on the *Fire Drake*. What has happened? Where is he?"

Gunnar shifted uncomfortably. "Stig is dead, Nanna. He died in Celeste and we burned his body there. I sent Edvard to find you and tell you. He must have been held up somewhere. I am sorry."

---

* fellowship

She sank to the ground, covered her head with her hands, and started wailing. "What will I do now? I have twin babes, only three months old. Who will take care of us?" She looked up and noticed Gwenn for the first time. Her eyes widened. "Who is that woman? Why is she wearing Stig's clothes?" She rose and fingered the black tunic Gwenn wore. Her voice cracked miserably. "I made this for him with my own hands."

Ketha's voice rang in her head. "Don't tell her anything. She could make trouble for you."

Gwenn said carefully, "I needed some clothing and since Stig was dead, I took his. I will give them back to you as soon as I trade for some of my own."

This explanation did not seem to mollify Nanna, who said caustically, "Yes, thank you kindly. I don't need my husband. His clothes will be quite sufficient." She gave Gwenn a suspicious look. "Why will you not tell me what happened to him?"

Gunnar gave Gwenn a brief sideways glance and said, "He died when some villagers attacked us, Nanna. But you should be proud; he fought with blood and fire. He has joined the ranks of the mighty in Skyre."

"Will he be able to feed his little ones from there, Gunnar Strong Arm?" she asked bitterly. "When winter comes, will he be able to tend our stock so they do not freeze? What in Silent Brigga's Name am I going to do without him?"

She burst into a fresh round of tears and Gudrun hurried out of the house, wiping her floured hands on her apron. As the older woman helped the girl inside, she glared at Gwenn angrily. Apparently, Gunnar's transparent lie hadn't fooled her, either.

Gwenn sat quietly as Gunnar and Arvid discussed the coming feast. Remorse pricked at the back of her mind and Ketha spoke sharply. "A shield maiden never looks back. Stig was a threat to you and Gunnar, so he had to die. Forget that ninny of his, and get on with our plan." But as hard as she tried, Gwenn could not ignore the sound of Nanna's wails from inside the house, as she grieved for her dead husband.

Gunnar stood and stretched. "I am going to get some sleep before the feast tonight. Are you coming with me, Faircrow?" Arvid's eyebrows shot up, and Gunnar hastened to explain, "She doesn't have anywhere to live yet, Scar Brow. Do you think you and Gudrun...?"

Gudrun interrupted loudly from just inside the door. "She is not staying here! I will not have that murdering hussy in my house."

Arvid frowned. "I don't think so. Sorry, Faircrow."

"Don't worry about it. I will be fine. I can camp on the beach if I have to." Turning to Gunnar, she said, "Let's go, Strong Arm."

They walked along together, following the path by the river, and talked of the planned camp in Celeste and the men and weaponry needed. Gwenn passed many small houses, all set gable end towards the path. Each held an entire family — parents, children and often grandparents — in one or two small rooms. Smoke poured out of the roof holes as the women baked bread or roasted meats for the noon meal. Livestock wandered freely through the town, and she saw many small children leading pigs and cattle down to the muddy riverbank to drink. Though the water smelled noisome, other girls squatted by the river's edge, scrubbing clothes and bed linens. Gwenn noticed the houses looked progressively poorer as they made their way towards the high-palisaded wall. Finally, Gunnar drew up before a very run-down shack set in a rubbish-filled yard. The framing logs, set directly into the damp ground, had rotted, and the house leaned precariously to one side. The mud and wattle walls were cracked and had been carelessly repaired.

Gwenn stared at Gunnar in surprise and said, tactlessly, "This is where you live? I thought the Captain of a raiding ship would have a better house."

Gunnar raised his shoulders in an indifferent shrug. "I don't spend any more time in Einar than I have to, and I have no family to watch over my place when I am gone. One of these days I will have to rebuild it, but it hasn't fallen on my head yet."

"Where is your family?"

"My parents are dead, and I have no brothers. My sister married a man from Dagmar, on the mainland of Danica, and moved away. I haven't seen her in years."

Gwenn said distastefully, "Ugh. I wish I did not have any brothers."

Gunnar regarded her curiously. "Where are you from, Faircrow? Who is your family?"

"My mother is the Queen of Beaumarais, and my father died before I was born. I have an awful younger brother named

Tristan," Gwenn replied, ignoring Ketha's warning in her mind to keep silent. She trusted Gunnar, even if Ketha did not. But Gunnar merely roared with laughter.

"The Queen of Beaumarais, eh?" He chortled as he lifted the latch on the wooden door, which was badly in need of stain. "You certainly are full of good stories today."

"It is true. I lived in St. Valery, and I ran away from home a few months ago."

He answered sarcastically, "Yes, of course, and my father is Ods, King of Skyre."

Gunnar pushed at the door, which promptly stuck in the warped frame. He kicked at it in frustration and the door fell open, ripped off its rusty hinges by the force of the blow.

Gwenn laughed and said, "Have a care, Strong Arm, or your house will fall on your head this day."

Inside, the ash-filled hearth stood cold and empty. One chair, crudely hand-made, sat in a corner. An earthen bench, running along one wall, held Gunnar's bed. The house smelled of damp and rotten food. She wrinkled her nose as she saw the remains of a half-eaten supper on the table, now furred with blue-green mould and covered in rat droppings. As she wandered around the cramped interior, Gwenn caught sight of a shelf crowded with small objects. She crossed the room and carefully plucked one from its resting place. A small but exquisitely detailed bird, carved out of bone, rested lightly in her palm. Delicate jewel tones colored the wings and back. The shelf held a menagerie of other animal carvings and Gwenn recognized horses, seals, goats, bears, and elk, all executed with the same enchanting detail.

Turning to Gunnar, she asked, "Where did you get these little animals? They are so beautiful."

Gunnar was rummaging in a chest for some linen sheets. He replied from over his shoulder, "I carved them myself, from whalebone. In the winter, when I cannot go voyaging, there isn't much else to do around here. Do you honestly think they are beautiful?"

Gwenn nodded and felt a stab of pity for her Captain, whom she now knew must spend many cold and dreary hours alone in this hovel in the wintertime. No wonder he was so keen on leading raiding parties when the weather allowed. She watched as he pulled his tunic off over his head and idly scratched the thick red hair on his chest. His body odor assailed her once again in the closed confines of the room.

"Why don't you give me your clothes? I will take them down to the river and wash them while you sleep."

He looked at her in surprise. "You want to wash my clothes? Why?"

She stammered in return. "Because you have been, you know... kind to me. I want to do something nice for you. I don't need to sleep right now."

Gunnar could not keep the bemusement out of his voice. "You gave us the best haul we have ever brought back from raiding. I think that is payment enough. But, if you want to wash them, go ahead." He stripped off his woolen breeches and threw them in her direction, then climbed into bed, saying, "Wake me when it is time for dinner and we will go to the market and get some food. There isn't anything in the house fit to eat."

As she knelt by the riverbank, scrubbing Gunnar's filthy tunic with a bar of lye soap, Gwenn reflected that this town of the Fynära was very different than she had expected. When Ketha told her long ago of the warrior race she wanted her to join, Gwenn had imagined they would be incredibly fierce. But these townspeople acted almost just like those she had left behind in St. Valery — just a little more rustic, and certainly more self-sufficient. She smiled as a tiny blond girl passed her, carefully tending a flock of fat geese with a long willow wand.

When she had washed Gunnar's tunic and breeches, Gwenn hung them on the rickety fence to dry and sat down on the grass to wait for him to awaken. After a long while, she thoughtfully stood up again and headed back down the path towards the town.

Inside the house, Gunnar stirred in his bed, caught in a dream. The smoke and noise of battle surrounded him, and he gazed in horror at the blasted landscape in which he found himself. He wore no mail or helm, and his skin felt chilled and clammy in the biting wind. Somehow he had lost his sword and shield too, leaving his hands useless and empty. He tried to run away but his legs were strangely leaden, so that he could only stagger about, trying to avoid the blood-covered men fighting and dying all around him. Catching sight of a fallen figure in the distance, he made his way to a quiet dell, surrounded by tall evergreens. Gwenn lay on the sandy ground, pierced with many wounds. She clutched at him convulsively and a trickle of blood ran from her mouth as she whispered something to him in a strange language. He pulled her body close to his and felt her breathing slow to a ragged gasp.

As her head fell back, he cried brokenly, "Gwenn, my love, please. Don't leave me like this. Gwenn..."

He woke with a start and saw her framed in the open doorway. The late afternoon sun shone through her hair like a fiery nimbus. He blinked hard, trying to throw off the image of her in his dream. She asked, "Did you call me, Gunnar? Are you all right?"

His embarrassment made him cross and he spoke sharply to her. "I thought I told you to wake me! What in Od's name have you been doing? It must be long past midday. The market will be closed and I am hungry."

"I took Stig's brooch and traded it for some smoked fish and a loaf of bread, while you slept. It is there, on the table." He stood up and noted with some surprise she had scrubbed both the table and the wooden platters clean. A fire crackled in the open hearth. This sudden domesticity made him feel distinctly uncomfortable.

Gwenn handed him his clothes and turned away while he dressed. They ate, facing each other on opposite sides of the table, without speaking. Afterwards, Gunnar made an excuse and left the house. He walked beside the ocean and thought long on how he felt about his newest raider.

"Hurry up, Faircrow, or we will be late for the feast. The manor of Per Drake's Son is a good walk from here, at the top of Sandymount." Gunnar waited impatiently by the recently repaired door of his house, until Gwenn finally joined him. She had been trying to get the worst of the sea blown tangles out of her hair with a comb she bought from the market. Gunnar looked at her and shook his head. No doubt her appearance at the feast would cause a commotion.

He dug in the leather purse hanging from his belt and handed her a worn felted hat. "Put this on and try to look like a lad or you will be turned away at the door."

She nodded and pulled the hat down over her hair, then grinned at him wickedly. But inside, her stomach tied itself in knots at the thought of confronting the powerful Magnus, Per Drake's Son. She reached up and patted keth'fell, and thus reassured, followed Gunnar down the path.

Revelers had almost filled the high-roofed hall by the time Gunnar and Gwenn walked up the hill. The light from the wide-open doors lit up the summer dusk. The sounds of laughter and singing carried though the air towards them along with the pungent smoke from the cooking fires.

Gwenn paused at the door, as she took in the scene before her. Open fire pits filled the centre of the stone-flagged floor, and thralls tended to spits holding many cuts of roasting meat. Several long trestle tables held platters of food and jugs of ale. Men sat on benches on either side. Judging from the shouts and howls as Gunnar made his appearance with Gwenn, the men of the *Fire Drake* must have begun drinking quite some time ago. Per Drake's Son sat on an elaborately carved chair occupying a dais on the opposite end of the hall. The *skald** seated at his side seemed to have his full attention and the Magnus did not look up as they made their entrance.

Arvid called jovially, "Over here, Faircrow!" He waved a beaker of ale in her direction.

She took the empty seat next to him, and joined in the feasting. A serving wench came with the ale jug and Gwenn had to accept a horn full. As the men around her drank horn after horn, she delicately sipped the strong brew, knowing that alcohol-dulled reflexes would not help her later on if she had to fight. Gunnar sat at the head of the table and watched her in silence as she laughed and talked with the rest of the men. Perhaps it was not too much to hope the evening would end without trouble, especially since it looked as though Per hadn't even noticed her yet. Leaning back in his chair, he let the wench fill up his horn and drank it down with a contented sigh.

Ketha's voice cried out stridently in Gwenn's mind, "'Ware, behind you!"

---

* Storyteller or bard

Gwenn jumped up, and reached for her sword, as three of Per's men tried to lay their hands on her. Two managed to grab her arms as the men around her scattered. Arvid had already drawn a knife from the sheath attached to his belt, and was about to intervene, when Gunnar, belatedly aware his newest crewmember had been set up, rushed forward crying, "Let her alone! She is a member of the *Fire Drake's* crew."

Per's henchmen paid no attention to him as they struggled with Gwenn, three on to one. Per called to Gunnar, "Don't interfere, Strong Arm, or I'll have you gutted. The same goes for you, Scar Brow."

Arvid and Gunnar backed away and watched in disgust as the three men finally managed to overpower Gwenn and take keth'fell away from her. The other men looked on silently as the serving women, fearing a fight, cleared out of the hall as quickly as they could.

Per walked forward until he stood in front of Gwenn and ripped the hat from her head. "So, my dear. Did you think you could so easily hoodwink Per Drake's son? We don't allow little girls to come to the warrior's feasts, you know. What are you doing here?"

Gwenn gave him a withering look. "I am a member of Gunnar Strong Arm's crew. I came to celebrate the return of the *Fire Drake*, just like the rest of them. Why did you attack me?"

"I heard from Edvard Half Finger earlier today that you murdered five of the *Fire Drake's* men. Is this true? It hardly seems possible."

Edvard had made the mistake of trying to molest Gwenn while she slept on the boat, and suffered a broken nose as a result. Now he looked very smug as Gunnar shot him an angry glance.

Gwenn nodded proudly. "I killed four men who planned to mutiny and another after a fair contest of swordplay. I have done nothing wrong. Release me at once."

Per regarded her in astonishment. "You must be lying. No maiden could do such a thing. Even if she bears a sword as fine as this." He took keth'fell and studied it with interest. "From whence did you steal this sword? It is a well-worked blade."

"It is my own sword, keth'fell, made for me by my stepfather. I am the warrior known as the Faircrow."

Gunnar broke in, saying, "She is telling the truth, Per. I have seen her fight with my own eyes, many times."

The Magnus answered condescendingly. "So you hired her? After she slaughtered five of your crewmen? Even for you, Gunnar, that shows spectacularly poor judgment." Smiling, he moved closer to Gwenn and reached up under her tunic. Her eyes widened in disgust as she felt his sweaty fingers groping for her breasts. He leered at her. "Well, it does seem Edvard was right about one thing. You definitely are a woman." She spat in his face and he angrily slapped her in return. Arvid had to restrain Gunnar from going after Per.

He hissed, "Don't be a fool, Strong Arm. They will only kill you for your trouble. Gwenn has a plan — I see it in her eyes. They never would have taken her if she did not want to be caught. Wait and see what she does."

Per said to the men holding Gwenn, "Take her to my room and tie her up on the bed. I think I will very much enjoy getting to know this saucy young wench in private. When I have finished with her she will be executed."

Gwenn felt the men around her relax their hold slightly as they prepared to drag her forward. She cried out, "Now, Ketha!" and the crow burst out like a black thunderbolt from between her shoulder blades.

Per fell back in horror as the enraged crow pecked at the eyes of Gwenn's attackers. The men screamed in pain, clutching at the bloody sockets, as they dived for cover under the table. Ketha swooped overhead. Gwenn strode forward and snatched keth'fell from Per as he cowered before her. Then she leapt up on to the table, scattering plates and jugs onto the floor. Gunnar gave a fearsome war cry and jumped up on her right side while Arvid took the left. Ketha wheeled above them majestically, and came to rest on the girl's shoulder.

Dead silence filled the room as Per stood up and slowly smoothed his rumpled tunic. He said quietly, "What do you want with us mortals, maid of Skyre? You have merely to say and I will grant it." Per looked up at her, wondering fearfully if she would let any of them live to see the morning.

She laughed at him. "Well now, Per Drake's Son. It seems you have a polite tongue in your head after all, but I regret you will not be able to get to know me as well as you desired to." Then, all business, she barked, "I want you to give me control of five hundred men and enough ships to carry them to Celeste, in Secuny. We will build a permanent encampment there and use it as a base to raid the inland cities of Mardon and Beaumarais."

Per, forgetting his fear, said scathingly, "You must be mad. Even if I gave you what you desire, no man will follow the orders of a wench, even if she be one of the maids of Skyre."

"I will," said Gunnar, quietly.

"So will I," seconded Arvid. One by one, the other members of the *Fire Drake's* crew, with the exception of Edvard, climbed on the table and stood beside their Captain and the Faircrow.

Gunnar said, "Listen to me, Per. This maid is the reason our ship came back to Einar full of treasure. She has promised to lead us to coffers in the very heart of Yr. Further than we have ever been able to raid before. She could have us all bathing in blood and fire ere long."

But the other men in the hall murmured in dissension and Gwenn knew she would have to prove herself to them. She said, menacingly, "Who wants to be first? I will fight anyone in this room." Edvard, who was timidly backing away towards the door, tripped over a fallen bench and fell.

"How about you, little Edvard Half Pint? You were very keen to improve your standing in the eyes of your Magnus by betraying me. Why don't you come over and fight, and impress him even more?"

Per said sarcastically, "Yes, Edvard. Why don't you?"

Edvard licked his lips nervously and stepped forward, drawing his sword. Gwenn jumped lightly down from the table as Ketha took up a spot in the rafters. The fight finished in a matter of seconds and Edvard fell, split wide open, on the sawdust floor of the hall. Per looked on in wide-eyed disbelief.

"Anyone else want to fight?" Gwenn asked angrily.

"I will name the warrior for your next contest. If you defeat him, I will go along with your plan." Per narrowed his eyes shrewdly, thinking he might still find a way out of his predicament. "I choose... Gunnar Strong Arm." The rest of the *Fire Drake's* crew cried out in consternation and Gunnar swore in disgust. Per said imperiously, "May I remind you, Strong Arm, you are still a part of my *felag*, and must do as I command. I order you to fight the maid to the death."

Gunnar leapt down from the table to stand before Gwenn and slowly drew his sword. He raised his eyes to meet hers and nodded in resignation. "Strong Arm..." she began, softly.

"Go ahead, Gwenn," he said, before she had a chance to finish. "I know what needs to be done. I am happy to die here, in combat with you. The gates of Skyre will open wide for me now."

Gwenn stared back at him in confusion. "I can't do that... No, I *won't* kill you! You are my right arm, Gunnar. I need you." Gwenn had an idea. She turned to Per and said, "I cannot fight Gunnar, for he is my betrothed." Smiling at Gunnar, she cooed, "Isn't that right, dear?"

He stammered in return, "Yes... of course." She took his hand and squeezed it, and the men of the *Fire Drake* burst into delighted hoots of laughter as their Captain's face turned a spectacular shade of crimson. The atmosphere in the room lightened appreciably.

Gwenn smiled at Per and asked him sweetly, "You wouldn't ask a girl to kill her own fiancé would you?" Her expression hardened. "I would much rather fight *you* instead. Do you accept my challenge?"

The Magnus cursed softly, for he could see the maid had turned the tables on him. He said carefully, "I have seen your skill with a sword. You are young, and I am old. It would hardly be a fair fight, would it now?"

The men in the hall looked at their Magnus in surprise. It seemed to them he must be afraid of the girl's sword. She laughed and said, "Well, Drake's Son. How shall we even the odds? Shall I use my left hand?" After a calculated pause, she continued, "No! I have it. I shall fight you with my eyes covered." Per looked very dismayed. He could hardly refuse after she had given him such an advantage.

Gunnar hissed, through clenched teeth, "Gwenn! What in the hell are you up to?"

She smiled and said, "Don't worry, I can do this."

Jacq had given her many lessons in sword fighting over the years, and for quite a few he had insisted she cover her eyes. "That way you learn to use all your senses, Goldilocks, instead of relying on just your sight." Gwenn was sure she could best Per, who looked to be at least sixty years old, even if she could not see his sword.

The Magnus glanced around the room at the two hundred men who stood silently, waiting for his answer. He knew he had no choice, so he said, "I am ready. Let us begin."

She demanded they clear a wide space in the hall, so she could use her acrobatics if needed. Someone dragged Edvard's corpse away and kicked sawdust over the remaining puddle of blood. While the men occupied themselves in moving the tables and picking the broken crockery off the floor, Ketha floated silently down from the ceiling and entered Gwenn's body. No-one but Gunnar, who still stood next to the Faircrow, saw her do this. He looked at her fearfully and she shrugged.

"I told you I had a secret weapon," she said carelessly, and gave him such a dazzling smile he found himself wishing, for a brief moment, that she really did want to marry him.

One of Per's men came forward with a woolen scarf. He tied it securely around her eyes, making sure she could see nothing at all. Gunnar led her to the centre of the circle, whispering, "Are you sure about this?"

She nodded confidently as the Magnus joined her. They stood face to face, and Gwenn raised her hand. Before it fell, Per stabbed his sword forward, intent on taking any advantage he could. Ketha warned Gwenn, and she flipped neatly backwards, as Per's men booed his unsportsmanlike opening. He rushed her, and they traded ringing blows. Gwenn listened hard for the sound of his sword and with Ketha's occasional cues, she could accurately judge the direction of each thrust. She parried many attempts on his part before she decided the fight had gone on long enough. Grasping keth'fell with both hands, she began a whirling attack that left the crowd gasping. Her sword moved so quickly it became a metallic blur of light. Per turned from her and ran, but the men closed the circle tightly and would not let him through. Gwenn listened for the sound of his ragged breathing and homed in on him unerringly. The flashing sword came ever closer, and Per tried again to escape.

The ringing whine filled his ears, and he cried out, "Enough, Gwenn Faircrow, I surrender!" Then he fell to his knees.

Chapter Eight

Ice Dragon's Breath

The Numen turns and addresses Hieronymus, while ignoring Geya, who fumes silently at her side. I always liked young Dai. He has principles, that one. Doesn't believe in taking advantage of lesser creatures, eh, Hieronymus?

Geya makes an angry noise and the Numen smiles grimly.

Oh, are you still here? That's right; you asked me a question, didn't you? What was it again?

Jacq guided his dappled grey horse, Minerva, along a poplar-lined lane in the broad band of farmland to the west of the Mistmere. Katkin sat behind him on the horse's back, holding a covered wicker basket filled with food and a jug of wine on her lap. Her contingent of guards followed at a prudent distance behind them. The sun shone brilliantly, but a wall of clouds to the east threatened rain, and Jacq wondered about his wife's sudden urge to take him on a picnic lunch to the country. Especially this country, so close to their old cottage, Acorn — now nothing but a bramble-covered heap of blackened stones. The Guard had burned it down after they arrested him, during the War. Jacq shivered, remembering the tortures they had inflicted, trying to get him to divulge his contacts at the Citadel. He could never forget about that — the red-hot irons and the leering face of Tomas de Vigny still troubled his dreams.

After Katkin became Queen and they had gone to live in St. Valery he used to ride by the old place occasionally, but the sight of the crumbling stone walls depressed him, and he hadn't been back in several years. Now, as they climbed the last long hill, she reached up high and covered his eyes with her hand. He laughed and said, "What are you doing, Kat?"

She said, "No peeking. I have a surprise for you."

Minerva continued to trot up the lane and as they reached

the crest of a hill, she uncovered his eyes. Jacq first saw the grove of mature oaks that used to shelter their home from the bitter winter winds. As the yard came into view, he cried out in surprise, for he could see the ruined cottage had been completely rebuilt and the roof re-thatched with river rushes. Jacq reined Minerva to a sudden halt and leaped down. He held his hands up to Katkin and she jumped into his embrace.

"What is this? Did you have our house rebuilt?"

Without waiting for her answer, he ran down the hill to the dusty yard, still carrying Katkin easily in his arms. The guardsmen, already warned of the surprise, retired to a prudent distance away under the oaks and sat down to wait for the Queen to finish her picnic with the Dinrhydan.

They reached the porch, still smelling sweetly of newly sawn timber, and as he reluctantly put her down, Katkin produced a key from the leather purse hanging from her belt. She handed it to Jacq, saying happily, "Go ahead and unlock it."

They stepped through the open door. Although the interior held nothing other than a huge four-poster bed in one corner, covered in a pretty flowered quilt, Jacq's memories threatened to overwhelm him. He wandered around, running his fingers over the stone walls, and the rough timber mantelpiece. Many minutes passed before he could speak again.

Turning to Katkin, he said softly, "It is beautiful. Just like before. Why have you done this, my wife?"

She smiled and reached with her hand to wipe the tears from his cheeks. "It isn't exactly the same because now there is real glass in the windows." They had been too poor as newlyweds to afford anything so luxurious. She led him to the bed and they sat together, holding hands. Katkin sighed. "I meant to bring you here the day after Gwenn's sixteenth birthday. But when she ran away, well, it just did not seem like the right time to do it. I kept hoping she would return and we could come here as a family. But it seems that is not going to happen, and I decided I could not put my plans on hold forever."

He regarded his wife with confusion. "What plans?"

She gazed up at him and her green eyes were solemn. "I am going to abdicate. As soon as I can make arrangements for the transfer of power to a new ruler."

Jacq said in a shocked voice, "What on Yrth? Why? Are you tired of being Queen?"

She nodded sadly and said, "I no longer command the respect I once had. The deputies have made that clear. Now it is time for us to return to Acorn. As I promised we would sixteen years ago. You have been patient long enough, my husband."

He pulled her close and kissed her lovingly. "You have made me so happy this day. I never dreamed... How did you manage to keep it a surprise?"

Katkin laughed. "Come, let me show you something else. There are more surprises yet, my love." She pulled him towards two new doors in the far wall. Stepping through the first, she showed him the new washroom, complete with lavatory and a huge, claw-foot porcelain tub.

He smiled broadly. "Very elegant. I shall be spoiled, my wife." The second door led to a short hallway with two smaller rooms on either side.

She said quietly, pointing towards the room on the right, "This will be Tristan's, when he comes from school for the holidays." Jacq looked towards the other empty room, but said nothing. Katkin shut the door with a sigh, and they turned away together.

Now she took him back outside, to the yard. He walked to the side of the house, where stakes and twine marked the foundations of a structure yet to be built. "What is this going to be? Did you not have time to finish all your construction plans?" Jacq asked her.

Katkin came to stand beside him and gazed into the distance, where the lush green of the Ariane River valley spread vividly out below them. She said, very softly, "Do you recall the last morning we spent here, Jacq? Before Yannick came to tell us the Unity had taken Roseberry?"

He nodded uncertainly, lost again in painful memories.

"You were telling me about the barn you wanted us to have. To keep livestock in, remember? So, I asked the workers to lay out the foundations. I thought you might like to build it yourself, as you planned to do sixteen years ago." She wrapped her half-arm across his broad back. He hadn't spoken, so she asked him, "Does it not please you?" She saw to her distress he wept, and she pulled his head down so she could kiss him, begging, "Jacq, please, don't cry like that."

He smiled at her and said, "No, it's all right. I am just so happy, I can't help it." So she wiped his eyes and kissed him again, and then they set off to tour the grounds of their old house together. After a time, Jacq said thoughtfully, "There is one thing I will miss about living in the Citadel."

"What is that, my husband?"

"The food. Do you think we could persuade Chef René to come and live here with us?"

Katkin looked at him in surprise and asked, "What are you saying? You don't like my cooking?"

Jacq said laughingly, "I suppose my teeth are still strong enough to chew through leather. I might manage for another few years before I starve." Though, without a doubt, his wife had many other talents, Jacq knew she was a terrible cook, and he had struggled manfully through many indigestible dinners when they first married.

Jacq's comment caused Katkin to give a mock scream of rage, and he took off running across the yard to elude her furious pursuit. Once they reached an overgrown field, he slowed so she could catch him and fell to the ground with her in his arms among the wild daisies and buttercups. The sun warmed them as they spent a very pleasant hour hidden from view by the long grass. Afterwards, Jacq retrieved the picnic basket from the porch, and they ate the cold chicken terrine and baguettes provided by the Citadel mess hall. After they drank the last of the wine, Katkin lay back again in the grass, and gave a contented sigh. Jacq stretched out beside her and gazed down at her face. Her beauty always stirred him, even now, after sixteen years of marriage and two children.

He ran his fingers over her gentle curves, and kissed her mouth with such passionate intensity she asked with pretend severity, "Again? Do you think my men have nothing else to do today but sit around here while you make love to me?"

Jacq laughed and rolled over with her so she rested on top of him. "They can wait. I like having you all to myself for a change."

She smiled and said softly, "You will have me every day from now on, Jacq."

Huw Adaryi's broken ribs were on the mend by the time the Chandrathi finished their horse-trading in Beaumarais. As the men of his Kindred made ready to move south to Spanja, Huw stood by his caravan in the late evening and spoke quietly to Queen Katrione. She had come personally, without Jacq's knowledge and without her guards, to deliver a warning to the Firaithi, when she found out they intended to leave that day.

"Listen, Huw, you must take great care as you pass through Beaumarais. It may not be safe for you to travel in the open much longer. There is a dangerous drift towards incivility and disrespect amongst my people, especially in the rural areas. Even Jacq has been poisoned by it. You received a small taste when you tried to enter the City. I am so ashamed of the way my gatekeepers treated you."

Huw looked at her with concern. He said, "You have nothing to be ashamed of, your Majesty. I don't hold you responsible for what happened."

Katkin sighed exasperatedly. "You and I are friends, are we not? When are you going to stop calling me by my title? My name is Katkin. Anyway, I won't be Queen of anything for very much longer."

He said in a shocked voice, "Your M... I mean, Katkin. Why do you say that?" Just then, Padarn walked by, leading two black horses.

Padarn nodded a greeting to the Queen, and said to Huw in Firai, "The main column will be ready to depart in less than an hour. The forward scouts will leave in a few minutes. I am sending them far afield, Huw. There have been rumors of trouble at the border with Spanja."

Huw nodded and turned back to Katkin. "Please continue. Why do you say you will no longer be Queen? It seems to me, if what you say is true, the country needs your sweet reason more than ever."

She smiled and said, "Thank you for the compliment, Huw. I only wish my own subjects felt the same way." Her face grew somber as she continued, "Oh, I know I am still loved by the old folk, the ones who remember my healing work in Belladore, many years ago. But the younger generation don't care about any of that. Their minds have been infected by fear, Huw. Fear of anyone or anything different from themselves. The new Prime Minister, Philip Tremayne, has become their spokesman. He used to be one of my closest allies, but now he has betrayed the trust I placed in him. It was he who gave the guards the order to prevent any Firaithi from entering St. Valery. He has more than half of the house of Deputies in his pocket, and I can do nothing to hinder him — not any more."

"I am sorry to hear the foolish citizens of St. Valery do not appreciate their beautiful Queen any longer. I think it is something they will rue, sooner or later." Huw shook his head regretfully. "What do you plan to do?"

"I am going to abdicate. As soon as I can. I told Jacq I was doing it for him, and in a way, I am. Not for the reason he thinks, but because I can no longer rule the country effectively. My people have become cruel and unkind towards strangers, and I cannot change the hearts of so many. So I will retire with Jacq to the country and become a plain citizen again." She shrugged. "That way, at least he will be happy, even if I am not."

"Perhaps this will be the last year we Firaithi will come to Beaumarais. I doubt anyone will miss us much when we are gone."

Her eyes filled with tears as she said, "I would be sorry if you decided not to come back."

Huw's heart twisted a little bit inside him. He asked her softly, "Why, Katkin?" A chill wind stirred the fallen leaves at their feet as Katkin shivered and pulled her woolen wrap close about her.

She took his hand and squeezed it gently. "Because you are my friend. And because we have a secret connection. Something perhaps you don't realize..."

A cry from one of the Chandrathi interrupted her. A rider was approaching the camp, and from his size Katkin easily recognized her husband. He galloped across the damp field on Minerva and quickly dismounted. Katkin dropped Huw's hand as Jacq's voice rang out across the campground. "What in the hell are you doing here, Kat? You have no business leaving the Citadel without an escort. Especially to come here." He stared at Huw, and his eyes held nothing but contempt. All his earlier friendliness appeared to have melted away.

Huw stepped between the Queen and her husband. Jacq towered over him, but Huw spoke with quiet authority. "You need have no fear for your wife's safety, Mr. Benet. She will come to no harm while she is with the Chandrathi, I swear on the heart of the Un-Named One."

Jacq turned on him, snarling, "Look, darky, stay out of this."

Katkin said quietly, "Let's go, Jacq. Now." She took his arm and pulled him away from Huw, who could only stand by helplessly. Looking back over her shoulder, she mouthed the words, "I am sorry," to Huw just before Jacq began to shout at her once more. Huw sadly watched them go.

He called softly to her, though he knew she could not hear him. "Farewell, my Queen. May the moon light your path home. Someday, I hope you and I will meet again." Then he shook his head dejectedly, wondering what she had been about to say when her husband arrived.

"You were holding his hand! Don't deny it, I saw you with my own eyes."

Though they had left the Firaithi camp far behind, Jacq continued to berate Katkin as they rode together through the dusk. She did not bother to reply. Trying to reason with Jacq when he felt jealous was a waste of time, as she knew from long experience. She would have to wait until his anger cooled before she could explain. Meanwhile, he would probably sleep in the smithy.

Once they were safely back in the confines of the Citadel and Katkin's guards had taken their accustomed place behind her, Jacq gave Minerva a kick and rode towards the blacksmith shop without a word or backward glance. Katkin, on the Firaithi pony Alys, rode more slowly towards the tower doors. Night closed in around her, and the storm that had been threatening all day finally broke wide. Hurriedly she dismounted from the pony, and handed the reins to her waiting equerry.

Smiling tiredly, she urged, "Get inside, William, before you get drenched. Don't worry about me."

She dashed inside as the first huge drops of rain splattered the cobbles. A blaze of lightning split the sky, followed almost instantly by a terrific crash of thunder. Katkin stopped in the lower hall and turned back to make sure William and Alys had made it to shelter. What she saw brought her hand to her mouth. The bolt had hit the tower itself, and split the flagpole standing on the top. The proud flag of Beaumarais, three white swans on a field of red, fell, in flames, to the ground in front of the tower. Katkin, waiting just inside the double doors, watched it burn.

As the clock in the tower chimed eleven bells, she tapped lightly on Arkady's door, saying, "Kadya, do you sleep? I must talk with you."

He looked up from the T'Shanga text he was studying and bid her enter. She still wore her riding breeches and boots, and so he asked her what had called her out at so late an hour. A fire warmed the room, and Katkin wandered over and held her remaining hand out close to the flames. She explained, "I heard the Firaithi planned to leave tonight, and I wanted to warn Huw about something." Then, in a bitter voice, she said, "He says they may never come back to Beaumarais. Not that I blame him, the way things are going around here."

Arkady thought she seemed very upset and so he inquired, "Is there anything else that troubles you?"

She nodded sadly. "Tomorrow, you depart as well and you have no idea where you are going or if you will return. So I will lose two close friends in one day."

"I am sorry, but I have to go now, before the weather gets any worse. I have been here for far too long already." Arkady had actually wanted to leave some time ago, but family commitments kept him in St. Valery. He had visited his elder brothers, Nathan and Barlow and seen their wives and children. His sister Jessamine had come home from her boarding school especially to spend time with him. Jacq had pressed him to go hunting several times. The summer was slipping into autumn now. Arkady knew winter would be snapping at his heels as he made his way north to look for Gwenn.

Katkin's deep green eyes filled with tears. "There is a storm coming, I feel it in my bones. I am so afraid, my brother." Another brilliant bolt of white light flashed outside the window, and after a few seconds a faint rumble of thunder echoed in the distance. Arkady gave her a questioning glance and she shook her head. "Not like this storm. Something much worse." She walked over to the sofa and sat down beside him.

He looked at her with deep concern. Arkady knew she had been given foresight before, by Lalluna. He asked, "What signs have you seen, my sister?" and took her trembling hand in his own.

She told him of the burning flag she had just witnessed and then added, "I had a very clear dream two nights ago. I stood on a beach in the early morning. Somehow, I knew I was somewhere far away from Beaumarais. A thick mist rolled in off the ocean. A long, narrow ship, with a carved figurehead, appeared behind it. A tall, blond girl, dressed all in black, stood at the prow. The red sail bore the device of a white bird and so did her shield. There were many armed men with her, grave and fell. After I woke, the dream stayed in my mind, though I would have liked to forget it. I believe the girl was Gwenn." Katkin could not hide her deep dismay. "When we argued she used to tell me one day she would find a race of fierce warriors and become their queen. Then she and her new friends would make me sorry for the way I had treated her. She wanted everyone to be sorry, except Jacq, of course."

"Did she say where these warriors could be found?" Arkady asked her. Something gnawed at the back of his mind, some shred of memory that might be very important. Knowing it might reveal itself if he let his mind wander, he stared down at the aubergine silk coverlet protecting his knees against the autumn chill and studied the pattern intently.

"No. She would only say that Ketha knew."

Arkady's eyes widened in sudden understanding. "Gods. I know where she has gone. I know..." He closed his eyes, remembering her, as she boldly stood with her sword at his throat. What is it she had said?

I am not afraid of the Fynära. When we meet, it is they who will fear.

Her use of the word "when" had sounded, at the time, like nothing more than innocent bravado. Now it meant something altogether more deadly. Katkin waited impatiently for him to explain. "Where? Where do you think she is?"

"She has gone to find the Fynära."

Katkin vaguely knew of the Fynära. How could she not, when Secuny lay just to the other side of Mardon? But no-one in Beaumarais feared them, for they raided only the small coastal villages, never this far inland. "Are you sure, Kadya? Why would she ally herself with them? They would not present a threat to Beaumarais."

He nodded. "I am sure. It all makes sense now. She told me she was going to Danica. The settlement of the Fynära is off the coast, on a big island called Starruthe."

"I still don't know..."

Arkady interrupted her. "They dress all in black. Just like the girl in your dream."

Gwenn Faircrow stood on the pitching deck of the *Fire Drake*, with Gunnar Strong Arm at her side. A stiff wind filled the new red sail and the white crow design in the centre billowed prettily with each gust. Behind the *Fire Drake*, another longboat, the *Moon Drake*, rode as proudly through the waves. So far, the winds had favored their journey, and the oars remained stowed away. Gunnar looked at Gwenn, his eyes shining.

He said, with admiration, "I never thought you would get Per Drake's Son to agree to your plan. But he has given you everything you asked for and more."

She smiled at him. "I knew he would eventually come round, Gunnar. He'd be a fool not to. We are going to make him rich. All we have to do is get the encampment set up, and he will send all the rest of the men and boats we need."

Shading her eyes with her hand, Gwenn stared out at the coastline on the port side of the ship. They were passing by some high white chalk cliffs with a line of dark evergreen trees growing on top. She questioned her Captain about them.

Gunnar explained, "That is the Denbigh Scarp. Believe it or not, those cliffs are full of caves. They go on for miles underground. I heard smugglers sometimes used them for storage so we tried to raid them. It turned out to be a stupid thing to do. Six of my men were lost inside for a day and a night." He shook his head regretfully, and then smiled. "But when I went to look for them, I found a cave with pictures painted on the walls."

"What sort of pictures?"

"Many tiny stick men with spears. Also, lots of hand prints, and strange animals, like none I have ever seen. I drew some sketches and made carvings of them when I returned to Einar for the winter. Wait a minute and I will show you." Gunnar strode easily across the heaving deck to his chest and returned with a leather pouch. He reached inside and retrieved several small carvings. One looked something like a deer, but with huge spreading antlers. Gunnar had painted it cream and white. Another cat-like creature was colored with vibrant yellows and black. But Gwenn was most interested in the third carving — a shaggy dark brown beast, with huge ears, a curiously elongated nose and sharp white tusks on either side of its head.

"What is this funny looking animal? I have never seen anything like it."

"One of the Skryvinin* called it a mammut."

Gwenn studied the tiny creatures curiously, wondering what impulse made Gunnar carve them. He was undoubtedly the coarsest man she had ever known, and had probably never bathed in his life, yet his hands could create such delicate beauty. She asked, "Gunnar, do you truly like raiding? I mean, would you rather be doing something else, like... I don't know, maybe making these carvings to sell at the market?"

He stared at her, obviously bemused by her question. "I have never been anything besides a raider. I don't know what else I would do. Making carvings is just a foolish pastime for the winter. Anyway, that is a funny question for you to ask. You seem to enjoy raiding more than anyone I have ever met. Isn't that so?"

Because Ketha had left her some time ago to search the beach for some washed up dead creature to eat, Gwenn was able to think honestly about her answer. "It is Ketha that likes it, not me. She just wants more dead people to feast on. I like fighting and swordplay, but not kidnapping women and children to sell to the Haba. I feel ashamed of some of the things I have done — like killing Stig and leaving his children fatherless. Sometimes, I wish Ketha would fly away and never come back. She can be very cruel."

This unaccustomed honesty on her part frightened him a little. They had not talked of Ketha since the night of the feast at Per Drake's Son's hall. Gunnar asked, "What do you mean? Doesn't she give you a lot of power? I would like to have your sword fighting skills."

---

* Learned elders of the Fynära.

Gwenn said proudly, "That is not Ketha. My prowess with a sword comes from lots of practice and many lessons from my Papa. It is all my own."

"If you don't need her to fight, why don't you just tell her to go away?"

Gwenn bent down and began to unlace one of her leggings. Gunnar watched with increasing agitation. "What are you doing? This isn't a good time to get undressed."

She exposed one lean, muscular thigh. "Look, Gunnar. Do you see?" He did see, and he shook his head in confusion. Her thigh was criss-crossed with scars and deep puncture wounds. "That is what Ketha does when she is angry with me."

"How?" Gunnar whispered to her in horror. "How does she do that?"

Her blue eyes clouded briefly with sadness. "Like this." Gwenn took the knife from her boot and raised it. He watched in astonishment as the knife plunged downwards. With a cry, Gunnar caught her hand before she could complete the stroke.

He held her wrist in a grip of iron, but quickly released it when he saw the tears in her eyes. "Gwenn! Don't ever do that again. Are you mad?"

She frowned. "Maybe I am. I have to do what Ketha says. If she ordered me to kill you, I would do it. Do you understand? Even though I did not want to."

"I don't believe it. The Gwenn I know would let no creature, fair or foul, dominate her that way. She isn't afraid of anything."

Gwenn said wistfully, "I only wish you were right." She turned away and covered her leg again.

Gunnar stood next to Gwenn for a moment without speaking. Awkwardly, he took her hand and placed the little mammut in the palm. "You keep this one, Faircrow. To remind you..." His voice trailed away, and his discomfort showed plainly on his face.

"To remind me of what?"

He took a deep breath and continued, "To remind you that when you are ready to break free from Ketha I will be there to fight with you, to the death if need be. I mean it, Gwenn." His expression remained unchanged, for there were many men on the ship with them, but his blue eyes brimmed with emotion as they met hers. She looked down at the creature in her hand and smiled.

"Thank you, Strong Arm. I will remember," she said softly, and placed the bone carving in the leather pouch she wore around her neck.

Though she knew Gunnar could do nothing to help her, she still appreciated the fact he was willing to try. Leave Ketha? The Goddess had been part of her for so long she could not conceive of what her life would be like without her. Perhaps she would become weak and start wearing frilly dresses. That thought filled her with disgust. Even if Ketha did make her do unpleasant things, was it not better than being ordinary?

Gwenn walked back to the gunwale and watched absently as the coast slipped by. Sea birds followed the vessel, swooping and diving as they competed for the fish entrails the men tossed into the ocean. The sound of their shrieking cries reminded her of Secuny, and Kadya. Had he forgotten her, and their tryst in the dunes? She could not help wishing somehow she could see him again. At that moment, she saw a big black crow approaching the boat, and the gulls scattered in alarm as Ketha flew among them. Gwenn stiffened and waited for Ketha's entrance into her body.

Gunnar watched thoughtfully as Gwenn's face twisted in pain. The black bird disappeared as the Faircrow's face relaxed and her eyes gazed vacantly towards him. He stared down at the carvings still resting in his hand. Make such things for money, like the craftsmen at the River market? He closed his eyes and indulged in a happy daydream. He sat outside his newly rebuilt house and carved, while puffing peacefully on his pipe. The warm spring sun shone down on the laughing blond children scampering and playing in the yard. Gwenn was there too, inside by the fire, making dinner for them all. Later, when the little ones were asleep, he would hold her close in the wide bed he had crafted for the two of them to share.

She was so beautiful...

A jarring image of Ketha, perched on the end of the bed watching the two of them making love, ended the fantasy abruptly, and his eyes snapped open. Smiling grimly, Gunnar made a vow to himself — somehow, he would find a way to free Gwenn from her evil spirit so she might belong to him alone.

The *Fire Drake* and her sister-ship *Moon Drake* reached the coast of Secuny the next day. The men navigated far up a narrow waterway, and beached the boats close to a rickety jetty. The weather had turned quite cold, and Gwenn wrapped her fur-lined cloak around her closely as she tramped through the dunes toward the ruined village called Celeste, where she had first made the acquaintance of Gunnar and the other raiders.

"Come on!" she called back to the others. "Let's get the boats unloaded. I know a perfect place to build our camp."

They raced against the weather, felling trees to build simple gabled houses with stone fire pits, just like the ones in Einar. A hundred raiders needed shelter and food now, with many more to come in the early spring. Gwenn left most of the management of the new settlement to Arvid and Gunnar, for she knew little about building, and less about administrative matters. She led raiding parties to steal the winter stores of the surrounding farms and villages.

Ketha's voice whined and fretted inside her, wanting human flesh to eat. She forced Gwenn on several occasions to kill a hapless villager who had already surrendered, just to provide her with a fresh carcass. Soon the closest villages stood empty and silent as the few remaining residents, starving and cast adrift with their few possessions, headed towards the borders of Mardon or Spanja. Eventually, the Fynära had the whole corner of the coastal province to themselves.

Chapter Nine

The Call of the Budtime

Geya knows this mock forgetfulness is intended to provoke, so she tries mightily not to let her considerable annoyance show. I asked you if he had some new scheme to fight the Angellus.

Oh, yes! And I already told you if he did, it would be between him and me, and nothing to do with you.

She glances slyly at Geya, to see if her expression will give her feelings away.

The younger Amaranthine keeps her face carefully composed as she declares, I tell you it is, Numen! He has interfered once too often. Don't blame me if he gets hurt, this time.

The refugees began to trouble Beaumarais only a few days after Arkady's departure. A stream of homeless people approached the borders — their numbers increasing each day. Along with their meager remaining possessions, the exiles carried tales of cruel invaders from the North, and their leader, a ruthless man named Faircrow. Many asked for aid and shelter from the guards who manned the border crossings with both Mardon and Spanja. They were callously turned away, of course, on orders from Philip Tremayne.

Katkin stood on a wooden dais, and peered over the lectern at the members of the Chamber of Deputies. Lalluna had created this elected body so the people of Beaumarais could govern themselves after the end of the civil war. Now, though, reactionary politicians controlled most of the seats, and claimed to speak the will of the people. In fact, they spoke nothing but intolerant poison. The one hundred representatives waited impatiently for her speech to begin. Rumors abounded that she intended to resign, and this was cause for celebration among the allies of Prime Minister Tremayne.

"Fellow Citizens," she began.

"Get on with it, Queenie!" a young Deputy called from the back row, and several of his compatriots cheered his rudeness.

Katkin gave them a severe look and continued. "I come here today to address you on a matter of great importance. Dispossessed peoples have been arriving daily at our borders, seeking the aid of Beaumarais. They are victims of a wave of thuggery, perpetrated by a marauding group from the north, calling themselves the Fynära. In the past, these raiders have confined their activities to the coast of Yr, which was bad enough. Now they are ranging far inland, under a bold new leader, the Faircrow. It is our duty, as peoples of the free continent of Yr, to aid the victims of these attacks in any way we can."

Calls of dissent drowned out her next words and she had to hold up her hand for silence.

"Please Deputies! Hear me out. I would suggest there might come a day in the near future when we too may be in need of such assistance. Do not pretend to yourselves our location far inland makes us immune from their predation. The Fynära can attack Beaumarais, Deputies, by sailing up the Ariane River as far as the Mistmere. Their boats are shallow hulled and easily maneuverable. We must join in talks with Mardon and Secuny straight away, and develop a defensive strategy to cope with this menace. To isolate ourselves is suicidal madness."

Now the jeers grew louder and Katkin could no longer make herself heard. Cries of "Foreigners go home!" and "Philip for King," rang from the assembled crowd. Then, the same contingent of young Deputies began a chant. The other members of the Chamber, caught up in the fever of chauvinism gripping the country, took it up. Katkin listened to their cry with dismay.

"Ab-di-cate! Ab-di-cate!" She stood silently at the dais, shaking her head in disgust. Katkin knew she could do no more for the people of Beaumarais. Without speaking further, she removed her crown, laid it on the lectern, and walked away with her head held high.

Jacq Benet and his son, Tristan Dinrhydan, stood on the front row of the assembly. Though they did not join in the chant, neither appeared particularly concerned with Katkin's departure. Tristan looked up at his father, his eyes shining. "Now the new order will be able to rule the country, right, Father? We can make sure all of Beaumarais stays pure." Jacq nodded, and patted Tristan's shoulder.

Tristan smiled back at him. He had finally found the one thing he could do to earn his father's unconditional approval.

Katkin dashed angry tears from her eyes as she walked down the long corridor leading from the meeting hall to her private apartment in the Tower. The fact that Jacq and Tristan seemingly agreed with her enemies in the government only increased her present feelings of isolation. Katkin fervently wished Nicholas Reynard still lived. His steadying voice, added to hers, might have turned the tide for them this day. But Gwenn had killed him, probably so the isolationists would win the coming debate.

She called for her equerry. He brought Alys, and offered his hand to help Katkin mount. He asked respectfully, "Will your Majesty require any other assistance?"

Katkin gazed down on him from Alys. "I am Queen no longer, William. This is the last time I will ask you for anything. When I return from this ride, I will pack my things and leave the Tower forever."

He stared back at her sadly. "You will always be my Queen, ma'am. I hope I will be able to continue in your employ, somehow."

"Perhaps when I am settled at Acorn I will be able send for you. Jacq might need help with the farmland. You have been a true and considerate servant, William. I will be sorry to leave you and the other loyal Tower staff. But my position as Queen became untenable, and I could no longer continue in good conscience. I am sure you understand."

He nodded and watched unhappily as she headed for the Yoke and St. Valery's Acre all alone.

Katkin sat on the bench by Tomas' grave and finally allowed her tears to flow unchecked. She cried bitterly for many minutes before asking, "What must I do now, Tomas? I have no doubt that Gwenn leads the Fynära and she is bringing them to Beaumarais. She will have her revenge on me at last."

A small bird fluttered to the ground at her feet, and Katkin dug in the pocket of her cloak for a crust of bread. She crushed it into crumbs and scattered them about on the snowy ground. The bird pecked at them eagerly, and then settled for a moment on her boot.

Katkin lifted her foot gently, and the bird flew up into the oak tree. She sighed. "Kadya has gone to try and find her, but he may not be in time. Anyway, what can he do against an evil witch like Ketha?"

She pulled an embroidered handkerchief from within her kirtle, and wiped her nose. Katkin studied the three swans monogram for a long moment, and then threw the cloth away with a cry of disgust. "If only I could join with Lalluna and protect our City as I once did. But the voice of the Goddess has grown faint in my mind. She needs the belief of the people to continue. But they don't worship her anymore, only the Prime God. This new religion makes a mockery of her kindness and compassion to others. Now the people care only for purity, and the judgment of sin. They think by allowing the refugees across the border, the country will somehow be sullied. Their closed minds will be the ruin of Beaumarais. We are lost."

The dell, now forlornly bare in the chill winds of autumn, offered her no solace. She knelt and tidied the drift of soggy brown leaves that had almost buried Tomas' grave. After she had uncovered the grass mound, she ran her fingers over the worn gravestone. It bore the following inscription:

Captain Tomas Jean de Vigny
Aged 24 years
His life ended here but his love lives on

Katkin rested her forehead against the smooth, cold marble. A single leaf, dry and cool, wafted down from above and brushed against the nape of her neck. It felt almost exactly like a kiss.

On an icy night in Secuny, a freezing fog rolled in off the ocean, blanking out the stars. But inside the new longhouse, a fire blazed high in the pit, and the raiders sat around it, swapping stories and roasting chestnuts to eat. They were working their way through a huge barrel of a rich, dark brew, liberated some time ago from the cellar of a tavern in a neighboring village. Gwenn sat with the men, a little way from the fire, with a small beaker of ale at her side. The wind whistled outside the shuttered windows, making eerie sounds, and she shivered, thinking it sounded as bleak as the voices of the dead.

One of the younger raiders, Furga, called to his Captain.

"Give us a song, Gunnar! Something we haven't heard lately..."

"Yes," another raider agreed. "Do Lutyond's Lay."

Gunnar reddened and glanced over at Gwenn. "I don't know if I remember all of it," he began.

Arvid laughed. "Come on, Strong Arm, don't be bashful. You could sing it in your sleep. But I will help if you like."

"Please try, Gunnar. I have never heard you sing properly before," Gwenn begged.

He sighed, and stood with his hands behind his back, looking thoroughly uncomfortable. Gwenn smiled encouragingly, while wondering what she had just let herself in for. He probably couldn't carry a tune in a pail.

But Gunnar surprised her. She listened, enchanted, as he began the lay about Lutyond, the Mariner. He sang the words slowly, as one of the other raiders somberly tapped a drum. His voice, a deep, arresting baritone, seemed to fill her to the brim, as she felt herself lifted into the wild and lost lands of ancient Fynäran legend. Gwenn closed her eyes and let the words wash over her.

Came shrieking a beast, of foul design,
And harried the warriors of Fyn's wide land,
With curvèd fangs, and crooked spine,
Terror trod the glistening strand.
Was there a man who did not fight?
Who did not seek the warrior's true desire?
To pass singing before the shining height,
Of the great and golden gate of Skyre.
Nay, not so! All stood tall and bravely fought,
The beast in all its foul array.
Until cruel fate decreed their lot
The warriors failed and lost the day.
The unclean beast, triumphant,
Held fast before the archèd way,

He stood and laughed in scorn exultant,
And kept the fallen men at bay.
How would the gloomy dead join the feast?
Only silence stalked the hallowed halls of Skyre.
Would Atenfy's span be defiled by ravening beast?
O where was one possessed of blood and fire?

Arvid took up the story, in his gravelly bass:

In rays of light, before the dawn,
That lit the sky like pale ice night,
His sail was seen, rising up beyond
The furthest waves of horizon bright.
He came, aboard a dragon of gold,
Child of the North, grown to fullness,
Ancient strength, in twilight's hold,
Brought him to the warrior's witness.
The Mariner, seeker of the secret seas,
Bearer of the sword Ancarnen,
Anchored heart, spirit's ease,
Courage beyond the lore of men.
To Atenfy he came, and softly shed
Tears of sorrow for those denied their right,
And vow'd revenge on the beast of dread,
As he drew his sword, Ancarnen Bright.

The room was silent, the men sitting still as stones, as Gunnar finished the lay of Lutyond.

The beast didst roar, and growl in vain,
The Mariner would not quail,
He strode bravely forth to meet the bane,
Crying, "Either you or I must fail!"
The beast reared high its hornèd head,
And wide stretched its chilling maw,
With lolling tongue stained bloody red,
And dripping fangs to snap and gnaw.
Still he came, and the beast didst rise,
Its flashing teeth as pale as death,

The Mariner falls, in agony cries,
And prepares to draw his final breath.
But even as the beast crows, in victory taunting,
With the Mariner's leg caught fast in its jaws
His foe fights on, his courage unstinting,
Ancarnen shines, ice-locked light from the stars.
Its hideous body unhingèd, the beast's head falls,
On the bridge stained red, with blood and fire,
Forward and onward, the Mariner crawls,
And once more throws wide the gates of Skyre.
Each warrior finds his carven throne,
Round the groaning table, full and free,
But the one-legged Mariner sails on alone,
In the dreary dark of the cold, cleaving sea.

He held the last low, mournful note for a long while, and no-one in the room seemed to breathe until he had finished. Then the raiders roared their approval and raised their horns of ale to their Captain.

Gwenn let out a cheer at the end of the song, and clapped her hands in delight. Gunnar bowed modestly, and called for the ale jug.

"How about you, Faircrow?" he asked, a moment later, when he had quenched his thirst. "Sing us a tale of your Beaumaraisian Goddesses. Surely they must be a mighty race of warriors, to produce a daughter such as yourself."

But Gwenn only shook her head. The only story she knew was the story of her mother's triumph over Hythea, the sister of Lalluna, and she did not want to talk about that. Instead, she regaled them with tales about the exploits of the Dinrhydan, the legendary warrior of the Rising. They listened with shining eyes as she described his prowess with the sword, his incredible strength, and his indomitable spirit.

Arvid asked her, "Can this man, Dinrhydan, be real? Or is he just an oft-remembered hero from an old tale?"

She sighed and said, "Oh, he is real, all right. I knew him well." Her voice trailed away and she said nothing more. After a time, she wandered over to her bed and lay down, facing the wall.

Gunnar watched her go. Later, when the fire died down to red ash, and the others snored sonorously around him, he thought he heard a stifled sob. He rose silently and went to her. Gwenn lay wide-awake in the darkened longhouse and he could just see the tracks of tears on her face. He knelt beside her and whispered, "Is Ketha with you?" She shook her head. So he said, very softly, "Let me stay with you. Just tonight. You need make no promises."

Gwenn looked up at him and he could tell she was vacillating. He lifted his hand and touched her cheek, very gently, where a tear still lay, shining like a small white jewel in the moonlight. The memory of his voice, rising surely and tenderly through the Lay of Lutyond, somehow quashed her doubts. Gwenn raised her deerskins and he took shelter underneath them.

Chapter Ten

Dragon's Teeth

Now the Numen gets angry herself. He interferes! Your conceit would be laughable if it was not so dangerous, little Geya. You have interfered far more with the workings of this world. But come — let me reassure you, so that you will leave me alone, for now anyway. Dai became a human being for purely personal reasons. And yes, he asked me first and I gave him my blessing.

~~~~~~~~~~

Several days later, one of the scouts, a raider named Anders Fire Breath, gave his report as Gwenn sat eating a bowl of cold porridge for breakfast. "There is a Firaithi Kindred coming, maybe a dozen men among them. They have horses we can use, and women and children we can sell to the Haba." Gwenn, Arvid and Gunnar listened to this news with interest. Anders continued, "They ride on the coast road, and we can easily ambush them when they reach the dunes. Plenty of cover for us there. Shall we attack, Faircrow?"

Gwenn considered this proposal. The men were bored with their enforced lassitude and fighting with each other had become a favored pastime. It would do them all good to get some real raiding in.

She nodded firmly and ordered, "Tell the men to arm themselves speedily and well. We will need to move out quickly so that we can position ourselves in the dunes before the caravans reach there. And remember to keep an eye out for their forward scouts. If you come across any, kill them at once. We don't want the rest to have any warning as they approach our hiding place."

Obviously, the news of the Fynäran winter encampment had not reached the normally wary Firaithi, for they rode straight into the trap. As Gwenn and the others leapt up from behind the long grass, shouting and waving their weapons, several of the horses reared and threw their riders. The fallen men cursed and scrambled for their weapons as the Fynära moved in, slaughtering indiscriminately anyone who resisted them. Grigor Adaryi was among the first to die, as he stood before his daughter Eira and tried to keep Gunnar and Arvid away from her.

Eira screamed as he fell, and drew her own weapon. Leaping down from the caravan, she fearlessly attacked the men. She slashed her knife across Gunnar's cheek, laying his flesh open. He made a grab for her, and she stabbed his hand. He cursed, and thrust his sword at her midsection, but she whirled away. But Arvid stood ready with his knife.

Gunnar cried, "Take her alive!" But Eira, knowing that she would most likely be sold as a slave, was determined to go down fighting.

She shrieked, "Death to the Fynära!" and charged forward, her knife flashing in the sun.

Arvid slew her regretfully, for she was beautiful and would have fetched a good price with the Haba. Huw, unnerved by watching his sister die, was swiftly disarmed by his opponent, a tall, blond woman who fought like a demon from hell.

Now the remaining Firaithi stood huddled together, as the raiders decided their fate. Most of the men had been killed in the first moments of the attack. Huw and Padarn remained, and tried to comfort the survivors, but they had no illusions as to their fate. Mothers and children would be ruthlessly separated and sent far away. Huw glared at the blond woman, trying to burn her features into his memory. He swore on the heart of the Un-Named One he would kill her someday in payment for the deaths of his father and sister.

Leaving a few men to guard the captives, the Faircrow and her raiders walked to the other side of the road to talk. Squatting down in the white sand, Gwenn said, "Look, why don't we just let the women and children go? We don't know when the Haba traders will be coming this way, even if we had enough supplies left to feed all of the captives while we waited. Let us keep the two men to care for the horses until the boats come from Starruthe. Then we can send them up to Per as a present."

Gunnar, remembering what the Faircrow had told him on the deck of the *Fire Drake*, spoke up strongly in agreement. He knew she did not want to sell the women and children to the Haba. Arvid and the others seemed taken aback and he shrugged, offering no explanation.

Gwenn walked back over to the Firaithi captives and spoke to the guards. "Bind the two men. Let the others go free."

One raider opened his mouth to argue and she gave him a black look that sent him scurrying to obey. Padarn struggled as the raiders tied his hands, cursing in Firai and Maraison. His wife and daughters were among the group the raiders were leading towards the caravans. Neither he nor Huw spoke Dalvolk, so they did not know Gwenn meant to let the women and children go.

She spoke sharply to him in Maraison. "Do not resist us, fool, unless you *want* to die."

Padarn said angrily, "I would rather lose my life than watch you take my wife and children to the slavers, Fynära whore."

This insult earned him a vicious back-handed slap from Gunnar, who understood enough Maraison to get the gist of what he said. Padarn fell to his knees, half-stunned. Gwenn stood over him. "The others are free to go, Firaithi. We only want you men, and the horses."

Huw asked, warily, "Why are you doing this? We know you Fynära sell your prisoners to the Haba."

Gwenn glared at him fiercely. "I lead these men, and I decide what happens to the captives."

"You are a murderer and a bandit — still I give you my thanks for letting my family go free," Padarn muttered.

But Huw, remembering Eira's final gurgling screams as she lay on the ground with her throat slashed wide, said bitterly, "Do you thank the north wind when it blows down your house, if it leaves a single wall standing? These marauding animals deserve no gratitude from us."

He walked forward until he stood directly in front of Gwenn. A raider made to pull him away, but she said, "No. Let the Firaithi say what he wishes to me." Huw looked up at her with hatred in his eyes.

"These men you lead killed my father and my sister. For that crime alone you should die. I would cut out your heart right now if I could, Gruagá bitch. Someday, I will track you down, and

123

when I do you will suffer, do not doubt it." He clenched his fists threateningly. His guard pulled him backwards and bound his hands tightly together.

Gwenn gave a callous laugh, and said, "The Faircrow has shown you mercy, and that is how you would repay it? All I ask is that you serve me — by caring for these excellent horses you have so generously donated to our campaign."

Only the thought he might someday be able to revenge himself on the Gruagá known as the Faircrow kept Huw Adaryi sane in the wretched days that followed. He and Padarn were beaten and abused by their captors, and forced to sleep in the locked barn with the horses. They had little enough to eat, for the raiders had reached the last of the supplies brought from Starruthe. Gwenn and the others eagerly awaited the arrival of the ships and men Per Drake's Son had pledged to send them, so the inland raids could begin.

After the weather had been clear and unseasonably warm for almost two weeks, Gunnar said quietly to Gwenn, "I don't like this. There has been plenty of good weather for the long boats to make the trip from Starruthe. I wonder if Per has betrayed us somehow."

Gwenn had been wondering the same thing for quite some time. Even though Per had sworn on Lutyond's anchor to send the ships, she did not think he was above treachery, especially now they were far away. She asked him, "What do you think we should do, Strong Arm?"

Gunnar thought for a moment and offered, "I think I had better take the *Fire Drake* and pay him a visit with some of the men. Perhaps we can persuade him to keep his promises."

"I should come with you."

He shook his head. "The men here are restless. They have been cooped up too long already. If you leave they might revolt."

Gunnar set out the next day for Starruthe. Gwenn watched as her men dragged Huw and Padarn on board and chained them to the deck next to the oars. Gunnar hoped to convince Per to keep to their agreement by giving him the two Firaithi men as thralls, with the promise of much more spoil to come. He decided to leave half of the *Fire Drake* crew behind, including his first mate, Arvid, in case Gwenn had trouble with the men of the

Moon Drake. There was much grumbling, and several of the men said plainly they wished to go home to Starruthe. Gwenn knew they had better start successfully raiding soon or she would lose them altogether.

"Farewell, my Captain," she called to the retreating sail of the *Fire Drake.* "May Lutyond guide you safely over the waves."

All the villages within marching distance of Celeste were now ghost towns, but with the twenty horses provided by the Firaithi, they would be able to cover much more ground. Once Gunnar left with the *Fire Drake,* she held races to see who amongst the men could ride the most swiftly. The Firaithi horses were cruelly kicked and beaten until they learned to obey their new masters.

Gwenn chose the twenty best horsemen and created a new raiding party, with Sven Red Beard as its leader. Before their first outing, she instructed him, "Range as far and wide as you can within one or two day's riding of here. Bring back any foodstuffs you find, especially things we can store — like dried meat or oats. And remember; leave the women and children alone!"

Sven nodded his acceptance, but did not meet her eyes.

The others were employed felling trees and building houses for the expected influx of new raiders. Arvid was in charge of the construction. He spoke to Gwenn privately after a few days had passed. "My men are dissatisfied. Red Beard's crew have had women on several raids. It isn't fair, Gwenn."

"But I told them not to!" she said hotly.

"Well, obviously they aren't listening," he replied testily, and turned away to see to the work.

After Arvid's warning, Gwenn decided she would ride out with Red Beard to supervise his next raid. They headed southeast, towards a thickly populated band of farmland. After stealing several farm carts and draught horses, they began to load up with supplies. They met little resistance. The raiders took smoked meats, seed potatoes, bags of wheat and barley, and other foodstuffs as they found them. But because Gwenn dictated they leave the women and children alone, the men complained bitterly.

Ketha harangued her. "Why do you care what happens to some backward farm wives and their brats? Let the men have their fun."

But Gwenn would not rescind the order. Last year, in St.

125

Valery, the thought of leading a group of warriors had seemed dashing and romantic. Reality turned out to be far drearier. Killing and stealing for a living left her wracked with guilt and no encouraging words from Ketha could change that. Now, as she rode back towards Celeste ahead of the stolen carts, Gwenn could think freely, for Ketha had left her, intent on feeding on the fly-encrusted corpses of the farm owner and his wife they left behind at their last stop.

The long line of raiders trailed behind her, and they had several more hours of riding before they reached the camp. The country around Bruga consisted of mostly flat ground, with many wide expanses of marshland. Flocks of herons and egrets could be seen taking wing in the distance as the sounds of the raider's raucous laughter and singing reached them.

Hide the virgins in the bog,
Northmen coming!
Drown the gold and drink the grog,
Northmen coming!
Shift the kine and slaughter the hog,
Northmen coming! Northmen coming!

A solitary traveler also heard the ruckus, and paused on the road. He had been looking and listening for such singing for many days, criss-crossing the fens of Secuny, following the trail of destruction and murder left by his quarry. Though he wanted very much to hide, the ground was flat for miles around, and there was not a scrap of cover for him, never mind for his horse, Ylene. Arkady gave her a kick, and took off for the dark line of a pine forest several miles distant, hoping he could find shelter in the trees before they caught sight of him.

Gwenn, spying the fleeing stranger far down the road, decided to let him run. They still had a long way to ride, and the wagons were groaning with plunder. Anyway, she had seen her fill of death for one day, for the owner of the last farm had put up a good fight, and several of her own men rode home now with minor injuries. They had hacked and hacked the dead farmer's body in retribution, and hung the pieces up in a tree for the crows to eat. The farmer's wife had still been alive, and watched in horror as they did this. After they had finished with her husband, several men dragged her off behind the barn. Gwenn had screamed at them to leave her alone, but they had pretended not to hear. Later she found the woman also cruelly hacked to pieces.

A wave of nausea rose up to the back of her throat. She closed her eyes, trying not to think about the body, utterly appalled at the carnage these raiders inflicted in her name.

The lead rider, Red Beard, spotted the lone horseman. He took off in enthusiastic pursuit before she could call him back. Gwenn shrugged and waved a few more forward to join him. "Go on, get it over with," she said carelessly, thinking they might as well enjoy themselves while they had the chance.

When she caught up with the men a few moments later, they had the stranger face down on the ground and one of the raiders had his knee firmly on his back while another rooted through the saddle bags. He had obviously fought well, for an old man. His silver hair was braided with bits of yarn and turquoise.

Gwenn's heart hammered in her throat. She said, "Turn him over, so I can see his face."

Arkady stared up at her. Gwenn gave no sign of recognition, just licked her lips and swallowed audibly. Then she said brusquely, "Bind him and put him in the wagon with the other spoil. I want to question him later, back at the camp."

Two raiders started fighting over an object in the bag. They tore it to pieces before Gwenn could stop them. The ruined silk painting lay in the dust of the road, and as she knelt to retrieve the pieces, she caught Arkady looking at her. She shook her head angrily and turned away.

Gwenn's men bound Arkady so tightly with thongs of leather that he lost feeling in his hands and feet almost immediately. They threw him roughly in the back of a wagon filled with sacks of potatoes. It took him a long time to right himself and find a semi-comfortable position. His plan had been to follow the raiding party back to the main camp and try to talk to Gwenn privately. Now he had been captured, he did not know what would happen to him, but judging from her welcome he thought he might be in for a rough time indeed.

Chapter Eleven

Silent Brigga's Tears

Geya asserts, I don't interfere, I help. This turn of the Gyre I figured out a way to make the prophecy come true. Now the Dawnmaid can be born. Do you see, Numen? I did it for the good of all the worlds.

The Numen makes a dismissive noise. For your *own* good, you mean. You and your sisters want more power in the human sphere.

~~~~~~~

"What in the hell are you doing here?" Gwenn's voice cut through the darkness.

She entered the barn, where her men had earlier dumped Arkady, laughing crudely as he landed face down in a pile of fresh horse shit. In the hours since, he had managed to move himself to a sitting position and wipe his face with his sleeve. While the light lasted, he had hunted around the room for anything he could use to free himself, but could see nothing but some piles of straw and empty casks and chests scattered about. The hastily constructed barn had many gaps between the boards, and the freezing draught made his teeth chatter madly.

But still he replied calmly, "I came to find you, Gwenn."

She squatted beside him and lit a tin oil lantern. With her dagger, Gwenn cut his bonds and he groaned as the blood rushed back into his deadened hands and feet. Then she rose and rummaged around in a corner of the barn. She threw a woolen blanket in his direction and he wrapped it around himself thankfully, though it stank of horse urine.

She said, "So, you know who I am now. How did you find out, Kadya?"

"I saw your picture in the Citadel. Jacq told me who you were."

She smiled briefly. "I bet you were surprised, weren't you?"

"Surprised? I was horrified. I thought I had done something

very wrong when we spent the night together, because you were my blood relative. But now I know better."

"My mother told you the truth?" Arkady nodded and she appeared dumbfounded. "I did not think she would ever tell anyone about Tomas being my real father."

"I was so upset I think she felt she had to tell me the whole story. She sounded very unhappy. Katkin said you made her life miserable." Arkady stood up unsteadily and paced the barn, trying to warm himself and bring circulation back to his numbed limbs.

"Huh! She made *my* life miserable with her lies." She faced him and her eyes were full of worry. "Did you mean to get captured by the Fynära? How did you know I would be with them?"

"You said so yourself, that day in the dunes. It just took me awhile to figure it out. I left Beaumarais late last autumn. I have been traveling around and looking for you ever since."

She seemed to find this baffling. "Why?"

"Because I want to help you."

She barked in frustration, "I already told you that you cannot. Why do you not believe me?" She pointed to Ylene, who stood forlornly in a stall across the barn. "Now get on your horse and ride away. The men are inside, and if you hurry you should be able to get some distance before anyone figures out you have gone."

Arkady shook his head and said stubbornly, "I am not leaving unless you come with me."

She said angrily, "No! And you should not want me to. Did you know your father and mother are both dead because of me? You should hate me for that."

Arkady caught her arm and drew her close to him. She shoved him away ungracefully. He gave her a reproachful look and said, "You did not kill my father of your own volition, Gwenn. Ketha made you. But I don't think she can make you kill me. You and I belong together. I have known it ever since we met in the dunes. You must know it too. If not, why did you wait for me there?"

She shrugged. "I just wanted to see you again. You used to be my favorite uncle, you know."

"I don't believe it. If I was only your favorite uncle why did you let me make love to you?" Arkady looked more and more confused. This reunion was not at all going as he had thought it might.

Gwenn turned and walked away from him, so he could not see her face. "I wanted to find out what it was like."

His voice held an edge of frustration now. "I don't understand."

She said coldly, "You know. Sex."

"You had never been with a man before?" He walked over to stand in front of her. She could see the tears in his eyes and she knew her words had wounded him deeply. Still, he was not willing to give up on her. "So you hung around the dunes so you could lose your virginity with a man you hadn't seen in eight years? That doesn't make sense. Why don't you tell me the truth?"

"That is the truth, Kadya!" But she sounded unsure, even as she said it. Again, he tried to take her in his arms and she struggled briefly with him. He gently cupped her cheek with his hand and she found she could not keep fighting. Suddenly her mouth found his and they kissed passionately, until, with a cry, she pushed him away.

"No! Listen to me. I am going to invade Beaumarais with the Fynära. That is what Ketha says I have to do. You cannot stop her. So you must go, now, before it is too late. Back to St. Ekaterina or T'Shang. Anywhere but here." She started to cry, making Arkady even more determined to help her.

He shook her roughly. "No, you listen to me! Having chased you all over Secuny for the past two months, I am not going to give up and go away now I have found you. We will find a way to beat Ketha together. I swear it."

She stared at him for a long time without saying anything. When she finally spoke, her voice sounded bitter. "Stay then, if you like. You are my captive, and I will have to use you as a thrall. I will tell one of the men to put a collar on you."

His eyes widened. "What do you mean?"

"All slaves wear bands of iron around their necks. I can show you no favor, or the men would be suspicious. The life of a thrall is hard. You will have to sleep on the ground and eat whatever scraps I can scrounge for you. We hardly have enough to go around as it is."

He asked her why they had run out of food and she explained

the situation with the missing supply ships. Then she said, "Gunnar will be back soon with the rest of the men from Starruthe. When he returns we will make ready to invade the inland cities."

Her voice held a little catch, so he asked her suspiciously, "Who is Gunnar?"

"He is the Captain of the *Fire Drake*." She added defiantly, "And my lover. Do you see now why you should go?"

He stepped back and put his hand over his face. Gwenn forced herself to remain still. She would not offer him any comfort at all, though she desperately wanted to. If she could make him hate her then he might decide to leave after all.

After a moment, he said quietly, "I thought you might be happy to see me. All the time I searched for you, I told myself you cared about me, the same way I care about you. Even when we kissed just now, I felt it. But now you are deliberately trying to hurt me and I don't know why. You want to drive me away." He sighed and wiped the tears from his cheeks with the back of hand. "Look me in the eyes right now and say you want me to go. I won't stay here if you truly don't want me." He shook her roughly. "Do it. Tell me, if you can."

For a long time she stood before him, unable to say anything, though she knew she should send him away for his own protection. Gunnar would probably kill him when he returned, if Ketha did not make her do it beforehand. Why could she not speak?

He said, "I love you, Gwenn Faircrow. Would you have me go?"

Gwenn hissed angrily, "No! Damn you, I want you to stay." She continued, her voice soft and sad. "Kadya, I have just condemned you to death. You know that, don't you?"

He spread his hands in resignation. "Then I will die trying to save the woman I love. That is not so bad, is it?"

She smiled and shook her head. "I think you are mad. I am not worth it."

Before he kissed her again he said, "Yes, you are, my beautiful crow girl."

Arkady tried to tuck his shirt up under the iron collar he now wore around his neck. It had chafed the skin painfully raw on his collarbones. He glanced up from his position on the floor to where Gwenn sat with some of her men around a long table. The raider called Arne was arguing with another raider, Ulf, who insisted he wanted his share of the spoils now so he could go back to Starruthe. The two men's voices rose, and then Arne stood, drawing his sword. The other man issued an insulting challenge, and they began to fight, scattering chairs in their wake. Gwenn rebuked them sharply, but the men, intent on murdering each other, ignored her. Cursing loudly, she drew keth'fell and stepped between them. Arkady quickly rose to his feet, thinking she needed help, for she was fighting both men at the same time. One of the other raiders shoved him back against the wall, and he fell down, just as Gwenn slit Ulf's throat with her sword.

She turned away from his body and walked over to Arkady, then kicked him roughly. "Get back to work, thrall. Do not try to interfere in things that are none of your affair."

Arkady sighed and went back to scrubbing the floor. It was a noisome duty, for the raiders used it for both a spittoon and urinal when they were drunk. Gwenn had been right about the life of a thrall being miserable. At night, hunger kept him awake, as he lay chained to the wall not far from her bed. Backbreaking labor filled every day, and he was rarely allowed to see Gwenn for more than a few moments. He quickly found he could tell when Ketha was with her, for her eyes would stare through him blankly, as her lips moved in silent conversation with the goddess. She spoke to him with contempt, or not at all. Several times he watched in trepidation as she gazed thoughtfully in his direction and fingered the dagger in her boot.

But when Ketha left to feed, Gwenn would come to him, if she could get away from the men for a while. They spent the time talking quietly in Maraison, and she asked him many questions about her home and family. She seemed stunned to hear her mother had voluntarily left the throne of Beaumarais.

"Why would she do that? She had so much power and she threw it all away. Power means freedom."

Arkady said quietly, "You have a lot of power, but it does not make you free."

"What do you know about freedom?" she said dismissively as she touched the iron collar on his neck.

He pointed to his temple. "I am free up here. No man can put a collar on my thoughts, or my dreams. But as long as you have Ketha in your mind, you are not free, no matter how much power she gives you."

Gwenn stared at him and bit back the angry response she had been about to make. She asked softly, "Could you teach me how to be free like that?"

He nodded and said, "This is how Dawa taught me. You have to sit, like this." She crossed her legs as he did, and placed her hands, palm up, on her knees. "Now close your eyes and begin to think of your mind as a river, ceaselessly flowing. Each thought is like a leaf in the river. You just watch them slip by, without holding on to any of them."

"Humph... That doesn't sound very hard. Is that what you were doing when I first saw you in the dunes?"

"Yes. It is called meditation."

Obediently she shut her eyes, and tried to do as he suggested. In a moment, she opened them again with a frustrated cry. "I cannot! My thoughts keep running away from me."

He laughed. "Yes, it is not as simple as it sounds, is it? But if you practice every day, then in a little while it gets easier. Soon you will be able to quiet your thoughts and rest in the eternal silence of the universe. That will give you power beyond anything you have ever experienced." He looked at her and asked earnestly, "Will you try? I think this is the only way you will ever be able to break Ketha's hold on you."

She nodded obediently and closed her eyes once again.

"It is no good." Gwenn voiced her frustration and disappointment to Arkady as they sat on the sand in the warm spring sun. She had told Arvid she intended to take the thrall out to the beach for the morning to collect driftwood for the fire. Once they had passed beyond sight of the camp, she dropped Arkady's chain and walked along beside him. They worked together and amassed a decent pile of wood, and then took the rest of the morning off. After she finished her meditation, she complained, "I still cannot make my thoughts stand still, and I have tried and tried!"

"You have to be very patient. It takes more than two weeks of sitting before you can be successful. But I think it is time to give you something to help you. A tool."

133

"What is that?"

"A thing called a mantra. It is a phrase you repeat over and over in your mind. Mine is *Hana Hana sen mejum*."

"It is about Hana. The green lady from your special picture?" Arkady nodded and Gwenn looked sad, remembering the ruined painting.

He patted her hand and said, "Don't feel bad about what your men did. It was just a possession. I still have the real picture in here." He touched his chest. "Now I will give you a mantra, just as Dawa gave one to me. Closing his eyes he said, "*Ana Hana shawm tok duna*."

"What does it mean?"

"Hana lights my path to the heavens."

"I like that. It sounds very strong." Gwenn repeated the mantra until she was sure she had memorized it. "How do I use this tool?"

"Just repeat it when you are meditating, or whenever you need to. It will make you calm and give you strength. The more you use it, the more powerful it will become." He smiled at her but she could not help noticing the dark smudges under his eyes. The salt and pepper beard he had grown made him look much older than his twenty-seven years. Gwenn reached over and stroked his face, feeling a new gauntness under the cheekbones.

"Kadya..." she began softly, but then stopped speaking. What else could she say? He suffered because of his love for her, and she could do nothing to help him. They had been very careful, after their first meeting in the barn, not to touch each other at all, even when Ketha was gone. It would have caused too much controversy among the men. But now they were alone together, on the warm sand, Gwenn gave a little cry and threw herself on to Arkady, and he held her tightly. She whispered, "I am so sorry, my love. Why did you come here? Now you have become a slave for my sake."

He pulled away a little, to look at her, and she saw nothing but acceptance in his eyes. "It doesn't matter. I am glad to be here with you. Even with this collar on, I am as free as I have ever been. Do you understand?"

She nodded and said bitterly, "I am the slave, aren't I? Not you. I will never be free."

He shook her gently. "Don't say that. Somehow or other we will make Ketha leave. You must just keep practicing, and try to shut her out of your mind when she is with you. Can you do that?"

Gwenn sighed and said she would try. His arms tightened around her, and she brought her mouth to his for a long kiss. The new beard tickled her face and she laughed. Her hands found their way into his tattered shirt, and she unfastened it. Other pieces of clothing followed in short order, and he spread them out on the sand to make a blanket. Their lovemaking, this time, was a much more leisurely affair. Arkady wanted it to last even longer, but he could not hold himself back indefinitely, not when she lifted her body to meet his so hungrily, and cried out with such passion.

Afterwards he said, "Were you truly a virgin, that first time?"

"Yes," she agreed. "I was."

He said apologetically, "You should have told me. I hope I didn't hurt you. I probably wasn't very gentle."

She smiled and said it did not matter — she had enjoyed their lovemaking very much — the first time, and all the times after.

But there was something else worrying Arkady. "We really shouldn't be doing this at all. It would not be a very good time for you to get pregnant."

"Ketha would never let that happen. She told me so, last time. It would interfere too much with her plan to vanquish St. Valery." She stretched out beside him, intent on soaking up the sunshine, and he noticed for the first time the collection of scars on her thighs. He ran his fingers over them silently and saw her skin rise in goose flesh.

He sighed. "Don't you think we should be getting back?"

"Just a few more minutes. Please?" She rose, ran naked into the water, and called to him. "Come on, it is warm enough." He caught her in the waves as she splashed about. With a shout of laughter, she dunked his head under, and he came up roaring in mock anger. He picked her up, then staggered from the water, as she shrieked in protest and beat her fists on his back. With a cry of triumph, he dropped her back on the sand, and stood above her, panting. She lay as she fell, on her back, with her arms above her head, her hair tousled about her face. Her beauty was intoxicating, undeniable. As desire began building in him again, he tried to fight it.

He said, "Gwenn, we should go..."

But when she held out her hand to him, he fell to his knees before her, and buried his face between her breasts. He covered her neck and shoulders with kisses tasting like the sharp tang of the ocean. She gave a passionate cry and arched her back to receive him. He forgot the time, and his unhappy thralldom, as he immersed himself completely in the heat of her body. A few moments later, a black crow flew silently overhead. Ketha came to rest on a washed up tree trunk close by. Neither of the lovers saw her, and she watched them until they had finished once more.

Geya had been very clear in her instructions to her sister, and Raven, in her guise as Keth Dirane, knew she must do something to prevent Gwenn and Arkady from joining their bodies in this way again. While she resided in Gwenn, Ketha could prevent any pregnancy, but what if the girl found a way to break her hold altogether? But Ketha had all the cunning that years of fomenting evil had given her. She knew there was more than one way to send Arkady Svalbarad to his death — and bring together north and south.

Arkady staggered under the load of driftwood the two of them had collected as Gwenn dragged him back to camp by his chain. She shouted at him, "Hurry up, thrall! You spent far too long collecting the wood for the fire already."

This show of severity was meant to reassure the raiders, but Arvid listened with skepticism. He had heard the two of them whispering in Maraison many times.

Two days later, the *Fire Drake* landed on the shingle. Another ship slid in beside her. Sixty weary men jumped out and waded through the surf to the beach. Gunnar led them through the dunes to the camp and found the Faircrow in the main hut. She gave a shout of recognition when she saw him and rushed to his side. Arkady looked up from his work and his eyes narrowed as Gwenn and Gunnar embraced warmly.

"What took you so long, Strong Arm? We expected you weeks ago," she cried.

Gunnar removed his axe from his belt and threw it on the table with an exclamation of disgust. "It is as we feared. We have been betrayed. Per Drake's Son is dead."

"Dead?" repeated Gwenn. "How?"

"By the hand of Torsten Iron Fist. Now he commands the Fynära. He will send no more men and supplies until we send some spoil back to Einar. To this end, he let me take one extra ship and crew with me, but will allow us nothing else. What can we do now, Faircrow? We have failed."

Gwenn drew herself up tall and said proudly, "Indeed we have not! We will go ahead with our inland raids. Even if we have but a hundred men, our adversaries can still feel the sting of the Fynära. Instead of full-scale attacks, we will use stealth, moving in at night and hiding away by the dawn. As soon as we have filled the ship, we will send it back to Torsten. He will soon see what we are worth."

Gunnar's eyes lit up with pride. "It shall be as you say. I knew you would not be discouraged. Now, how about a meal?"

Arvid went to the corner and kicked Arkady. "Get up, lazy thrall. Make us some food." Gunnar looked over at him in surprise.

"Who in the Mariner's Name is that?" he asked, suspiciously.

Arvid said caustically, "Ask your friend the Faircrow. He belongs to her."

As Arkady shuffled tiredly from the room on his way to the cooking fire, Gwenn said, "We captured him on the coast road. We needed someone to do the cooking and cleaning around here after you took the two Firaithi thralls away."

Arkady's head snapped up and he barked out a question to Gwenn, in Maraison, "You had Firaithi thralls? Where did they come from?"

She spoke to him sharply in Dalvolk. "Go and make the food, thrall, and mind your own damned business or you will suffer a beating such as you have never encountered before."

Arkady shot her an angry look and left the room. Ketha watched all this with interest. When he returned, bearing a tray full of smoked fish and oat cakes, Gwenn and Gunnar sat at the table, their blond heads bent close together, discussing the upcoming raids. The bruised look of resentment in Arkady's eyes made Ketha very pleased indeed.

Later, Arvid found his Captain alone. He relayed his suspicions about the new thrall, saying, "I am telling you, she knew him from somewhere, before we captured him. They even speak the same tongue. I've been watching the two of them and something is definitely not right. He could be a Maraison spy, trying to find out when we plan to invade St. Valery."

Gunnar growled to Arvid, "Are you saying Gwenn is going to betray us?"

Arvid shook his head. "No, no, of course not. I don't think she would intentionally. But he is a good-looking man, and she is a woman, after all, no matter how well she wields a sword. Perhaps they were lovers in the past. All I am saying is we should not trust her thrall. Don't let your feelings about Gwenn blind you to the truth."

Arvid saw his Captain blush crimson. "What do you know about that, Scar Brow?" he asked gruffly.

"Come on, Gunnar. You and I have been shipmates a long time. I have seen the way you look at her."

"I will think on what you have said. If I find out the thrall is a spy I will kill him. It is as simple as that." Gunnar stalked off to find Gwenn, for he wanted to ask her when she thought they should leave for Mardon. The weather continued fine, and he wanted to get the boats underway as soon as they could. As he walked up the dune path to the main camp, an enormous crow fluttered down and lighted on a swaying piece of oat grass in front of him. The sun shone black-purple on its wings as the bird fixed him with a beady eye. Gunnar stopped abruptly and his heart began to hammer, for he was fairly sure who inhabited the body of this particular crow. A woman's voice, grating and nasal, spoke in his mind.

"Hail, Man of the North. Do not fear me. I come to you with advice and aid, if you will have it."

The crow looked at him intelligently. Gunnar licked his suddenly parched lips and said, "What advice would you have for me, Ketha? I am not your vessel, as Gwenn is."

"It is of Gwenn I would speak. I give you this warning, Gunnar Strong Arm. You must watch her carefully when she is with the thrall. There is a danger you will lose her. Have you not seen the way she acts when she is with him?"

He shook his head. "Why are you telling me this? I trust Gwenn and I have pledged to be loyal to her."

The sound of the crow's raucous laughter filled him with dread. "But you love and desire her as well, do you not?"

Gunnar nodded reluctantly.

"Why do you not go to her and make her your own? Before that groveling thrall usurps your rightful place in her bed. I know you have been with her before, in secret, when I am gone. Why do you not lie with her every night?"

"I... I would like to, but I don't think she..."

Ketha cut him off. "Don't be a fool! What does it matter, what *she* wants? You are the man I have chosen for Gwenn — a strong, proud warrior." Her voice grew softer yet in his mind and she whispered in honeyed tones, "Go to her tonight. While I am with her, she will welcome you. You may take her as often as you wish. I will give you sons with her, Gunnar."

He stridently declared, "I don't need your help with Gwenn. If I cannot win her on my own, what kind of a man am I? That stinking thrall is no competition."

"Well, it should be easy enough for you to get rid of him. Why don't you just kill him? If Gwenn is as trustworthy as you seem to think, then she should have no objection." Ketha made her challenge plain, and he felt determined to prove her wrong.

That night, Gunnar drank much more heavily than usual as he waited for Gwenn to excuse herself from the supper table. Once she had gone, he deliberately tipped his bowl of stew onto the filthy floor. The other raiders guffawed drunkenly as he said to Arkady, "Oops! Clumsy me. I seem to have spilled my food. You — thrall. Clean this slop up, right now." Arkady, who was eating his own meager meal of a bread crust and several raw worm-eaten turnips, slowly rose from his place in the corner.

He walked over to the upturned bowl, not bothering to hide his anger. Gunnar said, "Look men, our little drudge seems to be upset." He smirked at Arkady and asked mockingly, "What is wrong, slave? Are you hungry? Maybe you'd like to finish my supper for me." He stood and grabbed Arkady by the shoulder, then pushed him down roughly onto his knees. "Lick the floor, thrall." Another, harder shove sent him face down into the spilled food.

Arkady rose slowly, and wiped the stew from his beard. He frowned darkly, and for a moment it looked as though he might say something. But after taking a deep breath, he turned away.

Gunnar taunted him. "Come on, thrall. Why don't you fight me? Are you afraid?"

"No, I am not afraid," said Arkady quietly. "You just aren't worth the bother. Now leave me alone." He began to shuffle back to the corner. Gunnar followed, and shoved him in the back. Arkady whirled, and doubled Gunnar over with a knifing kick to his mid-section. Then he continued to walk towards the corner, as if nothing had happened.

Gunnar, with a cry of frustration, bowled into him and forced Arkady to the floor. The other raiders formed a circle and cheered their Captain on. It was not much of a contest, for Arkady was already weak from starvation and exhaustion. Gunnar thrashed him soundly and then said, "Get up, pig. On your knees." He grabbed Arkady's chain and yanked his head back hard, and made ready to slit his throat. "You will die for that unprovoked attack on your master."

Arkady's nose was bleeding profusely, as was a cut above his eye, but his spirit was undimmed. He said quietly, "You are not my master, dirtbag. I belong to no man."

Gunnar kicked him several times in the stomach, and Arkady fell face down and vomited weakly on the floor. Gunnar pulled his head up by the hair and lowered his knife for the kill. Just then, Gwenn wandered back into the room. She paused only for the amount of time it took her to understand what Gunnar meant to do. With a scream of rage, she threw herself headlong and tackled him, and the knife went flying. Gunnar landed heavily on the floor, with Gwenn on top of him. She gained her feet quickly and drew keth'fell before he could move away.

To the other raiders she shouted, "Move it, all of you. Now!" The men filed out quickly, for they knew from experience the Faircrow would blindly slay anyone who stood in her way when anger overtook her.

Gunnar stayed on the floor, knowing that to do anything else was to invite death. She stood over him, panting hard, and asked, in a voice choked with rage, "What in the hell are you doing, Gunnar? That thrall belongs to me."

He said, calculatingly, "He attacked me. I had to fight back."

She looked at him skeptically. "Did you provoke him?" Gwenn held his eyes, and he could not look away. He nodded slightly. She gave an exclamation of disgust and said, "Listen to me, Strong Arm. That thrall is in my *felag* and has my protection. Any attack on him is an attack on *me*. Do you understand? If you touch him again I will kill you."

She turned away and went back to Arkady, who lay on the floor, moaning. Carefully, she helped him to his feet, and led him back to the corner. Gunnar rose slowly and sat back down at the table. He watched in sullen silence as Gwenn took hot water and a clean cloth to tenderly minister to the thrall's cuts and bruises. Ketha's words to him in the dunes now had an uncomfortable sting of truth.

Later, while the other raiders snored around him in the darkened long house, Gunnar picked up his bedding and moved it next to Gwenn's. Arkady, who could not sleep because of the pain from his beating, saw him do it. He turned his face to the wall, but not before he had seen Gwenn casually raise her blanket to allow the Fynäran Captain underneath. Then a new torment began, far worse than anything else he had experienced since becoming a thrall. Though he tried everything to block out the sound, his position close to the bed made it impossible for him not to overhear Gunnar's groans of noisy satisfaction as he made love to her.

Chapter Twelve

Rindras Flow

Through narrowed eyes she stares at Geya, and says, Tell me of more of this cunning plan of yours, youngster.

Geya says proudly, I sent Raven to Yrth, in the form of Keth Dirane, to bring Lut and the girl together. North and South, do you see?

Really? *The Numen looks very interested at this.* Did you talk to Hana before you put this arrangement into effect?

~~~~~~~~~

"Do you, Tristan Dinrhydan Benet, solemnly swear fealty to the nation of Beaumarais?" Sixteen-year-old Tristan stood proudly by his father Jacq, as Philip Tremayne administered the oath of Kingship.

Tristan replied in his high, clear voice, "I will."

He already wore the purple, ermine-trimmed robe of office. It had been removed from storage just for this occasion, after lying unused for the past sixteen years. Queen Katrione had preferred a simple, white gown, feeling it brought her closer to her subjects. Philip wanted the boy to become a very different ruler than his mother had been, so he had decreed the ostentatious robe be placed on Tristan's slender shoulders.

"Do you promise to serve the citizens of this country with righteousness and honesty, so long as you hold the Kingship?" Philip looked at the boy, and smiled encouragingly.

Tristan said again, "I will."

Philip continued, "Do you swear to maintain the integrity of the borders and the purity of the populace?" This was a new part of the oath, added since Queen Katrione abdicated. She never would have agreed to those words.

Smiling broadly, Jacq patted his son's shoulder as he said, "I will."

The Chamber of Deputies broke into spontaneous applause. Tristan gazed around the high-ceilinged room with richly paneled walls at the men sitting at their polished wooden desks. They would soon be his subjects — all these powerful, wealthy men. He imagined he would have unlimited control over them, did young Tristan, but it was the man administering his oath who truly ruled the country.

"Do you promise to defend Beaumarais from all enemies, either without or within?"

Tristan again answered in the affirmative, and smiled at his father. Then he whispered, "I wish Mother had come. Why isn't she here?"

At Acorn, on the previous evening, Jacq and Katkin had argued. When he learned that Katkin planned to stay home from their son's coronation, he said angrily, "I always supported you even when I did not agree with your policies. I know you are not happy with the direction the country is taking, but it is the will of the people, and they want Tris as their King."

Katkin glared back at him, and said, "You mean Philip wants him. He rigged the whole process with the help of the Deputies. Now he has all the power, the country will just slip further and further into isolation. It is just wrong, why can you not understand? We should be reaching out to our neighbors, not closing the borders against them. Someday we may need their help. It is still not too late to form defensive alliances with Mardon and Secuny."

Jacq disagreed. "How can the country remain strong and pure if we let undesirables in? Take those darkies. You let them move in and pretty soon they will be marrying our own people. We don't need a bunch of half-caste brats running around. It would only cause trouble."

Katkin decided that telling Jacq that she was half-Firaithi herself would probably be a mistake, but she could not let his insulting reference pass without any comment at all. "They are not 'darkies.' The Firaithi peoples have traveled in Yr since before recorded history. Their society is just as advanced as ours. In fact, in some ways..."

Jacq cut her off, saying caustically, "You always defend them, and you think I don't know why? It is very personal with you, is it not? I saw you holding that darkies' hand."

She gave a long-suffering sigh. "Don't start that again. I have told you a hundred times, Huw Adaryi and I are simply friends. Let it rest. You know I love you more than anything."

He set his mouth in a hard line and said stubbornly, "I don't care. I know what I saw. If you truly loved me, you would stand with me as I am standing by Tristan. He is your son, damn it, and you should be there for his coronation."

"And let Philip think I agree with his policies? I don't care what you say, I won't do it."

She turned towards the fireplace, where a collection of mementos sat on the mantle. Picking up a white wood figurine of a swan, she turned it over in her hand thoughtfully. Huw had carved it for her when he found out that the graceful white bird was the symbol of her monarchy. Katkin wondered if she would ever see him again, now Philip and the other isolationists had control of the government. Seeing her blank expression and guessing her thoughts, Jacq walked over and snatched the swan from her hand. He dropped it on the floor and ground his heel down, crushing it into splinters. Katkin's eyes filled with tears and she turned away from her husband, saying, "How can you be so petty and mean!"

"You are my wife, and you should do as I say. Just because you used to be the Queen does not excuse you from your vows. Now, are you coming with me or not?"

Her voice was just as firm. "I will not give Philip the satisfaction. Nor will I appear in the Chamber of Deputies again after the disrespectful way they treated me last time. You obviously believe Philip is doing the right thing, so you go and cheer for our son's phony coronation. I am not going."

Jacq gave a cry of disgust and stalked out of the house, slamming the door. Katkin walked to the window and watched him cross the yard, heading for the barn. Most likely he would end up sleeping in there, in the workshop he made for himself when he built the barn. Jacq had spent many nights there already.

"Good riddance!" she muttered under her breath, and shook her head sadly.

The move from St. Valery had not worked out at all as she had planned. She had been happy enough at first, but after the first few weeks of her retirement, Katkin became restless and bored. Her life now was much different than it had been when she and Jacq first married and lived in Acorn together. Then she had maintained a thriving healing practice using her gift from Lalluna. Now she had nothing but the monotonous life of a farm wife, though Jacq seemed content with raising stock and winter wheat. Many arguments, over inconsequential things, marred their days together.

Katkin closed the shutters and walked back over to the fireplace. She knelt to pick up the pieces of the broken swan, and threw them into the flames. The blaze flared briefly, and then died down again.

As Tristan finished the last of his articles of Kingship, Philip walked forward carrying a slender gold crown.

He called out to the Deputies, "Do you, the representatives of the People of Beaumarais, promise to support the king in all his endeavors for the good of the country?"

To a man, they enthusiastically shouted, "Aye!"

As a young man, Philip had been one of the Guardsmen given the task of executing Katrione Benet for crimes against Beaumarais. Instead, her beauty and courage moved him to spare her life. In return, she had given him a great deal of responsibility in her fledgling government, including the rebuilding of the City of St. Valery after the earthquake. By the time he turned thirty-five, his political savoir-faire had made him prime minister, and he set his sights on the office held by his former heroine, Queen Katrione Arkafina. He engaged professionals to investigate her background. Once he found out her mother was a Firaithi it had been easy to convince the Chamber of Deputies to end their support for her. Only her popularity among the older residents prevented him from making his findings public. He still needed their votes, so he continued to speak highly of his Queen, while plotting her downfall.

Now, as he stood before her son, Philip reflected that while she was no longer a threat to the country, she could still create difficulties with Tristan's rule. He vowed privately he would marginalize her even further if he could. Smiling unctuously, he handed the crown to the Dinrhydan, saying, "It is only fitting the greatest savior of the realm should have the honor of enthroning the new King of Beaumarais." Though the former Queen had lost an arm in her battle to save the City, Philip conveniently forgot to mention her at all.

Jacq said to his son, "Kneel, Tristan Dinrhydan." The boy sank down and bent his head. His father's voice echoed proudly around the Chamber of Deputies. "I crown you King Tristan the First, ruler of all Beaumarais." As Jacq lowered the crown on to his head, Tristan could not help thinking gleefully he had at last surpassed his sister in their father's eyes.

Katkin waited until she was sure Jacq had left for the coronation. She mounted Alys and headed for St. Valery's Acre and the grave of Tomas de Vigny. Once she reached the walled compound, she dismounted and unlocked the gate. The branches of the oak tree whipped back and forth in the bitter wind, and a light dusting of snow covered the grass. Katkin wrapped her heavy cloak more tightly around her and sat down on the stone bench.

"Well, Tomas. Everything I feared has to come to pass." She spoke out loud to the gravestone bearing Tomas' name. "Philip persuaded the Deputies to nominate Tris as King. Jacq thinks it is because they respect the boy, but I know better. He will be a puppet in the hands of Prime Minister Tremayne. To think I once trusted that man with the rebuilding of the City."

Katkin sighed deeply and stroked her stump with her other hand, buried within her fur muff. "The country is in trouble. The pressure on the borders is increasing every day, as more and more refugees try to cross over. Gwenn's raiders are making deeper incursions into Mardon now. They have been attacking at night and killing everyone who crosses their path, then melting away in the dawn. Grenfell was sacked a few days ago with many houses burned. The raiders broke into the museum and took all the paintings they could carry. Then their trail of destruction took them to Arbith. They stole everything from the cathedral there, even the stained glass in the windows."

A freezing blast of icy air made her shiver and she huddled deeper into her cloak. She said in frustration, "No-one seems to be able to stop them. They are all fearsome fighters, just as Gwenn is. How long will it be before they come to St. Valery? I am so afraid for our daughter. Ketha continues to use her for her own wicked purposes and it is all my fault."

Katkin covered her face and wept. Never had she felt so lonely, and so absolutely powerless. A branch let go of a load of snow, and it sparkled in the spring sun as it feathered down to the ground. She looked up, sensing the presence of someone close at hand.

"Hello? Is anybody there?"

She shaded her eyes against the glare of the snow, and glanced about her in all directions. Then she could see him, like a wisp of mist, but one with true form, still wearing his ornate cuirassiers' uniform. He waited for her by the trunk of the oak. She stood, unafraid, and walked forward. He appeared unsubstantial, but when he raised his hand to touch her face, it felt as though a spider web had brushed against her. "Tomas," she whispered. "Why are you here? Can you not rest, my love?"

His voice sounded as though he spoke from the bottom of a deep well. "Cannot sleep, yet... Something to do, when the time comes."

"What must you do? Can I help you?"

He nodded. "Soon, Katrione. You will not always be so alone. Remember."

Already, he was fading away. She cried out, "Please, don't leave me. I need you now."

The whisper echoed through the empty dell. "Soon, love. Soon."

When Katkin returned to Acorn, she spied Minerva tied to the porch railing. Jacq was back from the coronation, then. She wondered why he had not unsaddled the horse and housed her in the barn. Once inside, she knew the answer. Jacq looked up from his packing, his expression cold and distant.

She met his eyes, and he looked away. "Where are you going? You are not leaving me, are you?"

He nodded at her briefly and continued to stuff clothes into an old valise.

"What!? Why are you doing this? I left the City so we could live here together. I gave up being Queen for you. Now you are leaving?" She walked to his side and pulled the suitcase off the bed by the handle, then hurled it across the room. It landed against the wall and fell on the floor, face down.

Jacq swore at her, and went to retrieve it.

Katkin was undeterred. "Talk to me. Will you not even tell me why you are going?"

"You never told me. All these years and I never knew the truth." His voice sounded bitter. Katkin wondered briefly if he had somehow found about Tomas, but his next words made his feelings clear.

"Your mother was one of them. No wonder you and that darky

were holding hands. How can I live with someone who represents everything I am fighting against?"

She stared at him in shock. "Jacq! I am the same person you married. The woman you promised you would love forever. Knowing who my mother was should not make any difference. What on Yrth has gotten into you?"

He scratched his head in confusion. "Philip said..."

Now she understood. "Philip said? You would allow that lying troublemaker to come between us?"

Outside the window, the snow drifted down softly through the chill spring air. The house was almost as cold inside, for Jacq had not bothered to light a fire. He glanced around the room slowly, thinking back on everything they had been through together. Should he be leaving? When Philip explained it, it had all been so simple. He said he needed Jacq to oversee the defense of Beaumarais against both the refugees and the Fynära. Tristan had begged him to come as well. But Philip had been quite clear on one condition. Katkin must stay away from the City. Her presence would be nothing but a distraction, and a political liability, given who her mother had been — the daughter of the Tane of the Firaithi kindred of Anandi.

She cried, "Why do you not speak? Has our whole marriage been a complete farce?"

"No!" he said hoarsely. "Kat, of course I still love you. But I am needed in St. Valery, and you cannot come with me. Do you see?" He walked across the room and took her in his arms. She buried her head on his chest and sobbed.

"You said you would never leave again. After the war, you promised me you would put away d'angwir forever." She looked up at him and her sorrowful eyes filled him with doubt.

"I know I promised. But things are different now. The country is being threatened by outsiders. I have to go, don't I?"

"Do you?" she asked sadly. "Let Philip get someone else. Have you not fought long enough for Beaumarais? Stay with me." He continued to hold her, but his eyes stared thoughtfully into the distance. Jacq could remember a time, long ago in the stables at the Foxhole, when his wife had left him, as he cried and begged her to stay. She went to pursue some important goal of her own. Now, it seemed, it was his turn to do the same. Abruptly, he dropped his arms from around her and went back to the suitcase, closing it with a decisive click.

He spoke briskly and would no longer meet her eyes. "I will be back as soon as I can. Meanwhile, I will send William to help you with the stock. I hope I can return here for a break occasionally, but it may be some time before I can get away. There is a lot to organize between the new border patrols and the increased defense for the City."

Katkin said nothing else. Jacq had obviously made up his mind and she would not humiliate herself by arguing further. She sat on the bed, debating inwardly about whether she should tell him who it was that led the fearsome Fynära. In the end, she decided to keep silent. Jacq would not have believed her anyway. The thought that he and Gwenn might meet on opposite sides of the battlefield filled her with misery and she began to weep once more.

Ketha wheeled in the sky above St. Valery, and came to rest on one of the flag poles adorning the Citadel tower. She watched the activity below with interest. The fools had obviously gotten word of the successful Fynära attacks and raids in Mardon. Companies of men scurried to and fro on the parade field, drilling or practicing small arms fire. Ketha recognized the tall man who crossed the grassy sward and entered the tower — Gwenn's stepfather, Jacq Benet. A moment later, he came back out, in the company of another man, and a teenage boy. That would be the Prime Minister, Tremayne, and the new king, Tristan. The three walked together to the Citadel rampart and climbed the steep stairs leading up to the parapet.

Jacq talked and gestured with animation. Ketha drifted lazily down and landed on the embankment, pretending to hunt for insects in the grass. She listened carefully to the men's conversation as they walked along the top of the wall.

Jacq was saying, in answer to a question from Philip, "The design of the Citadel will prevent any invaders from taking the City, should they be so foolish as to try. The pentagonal shape gives good views over every quadrant of St. Valery and the Mere. There are five revetments, each backed with earth, and five bastions. We have cannon strategically placed along the wall tops facing the Mere. A high parapet protects the artillerymen."

Jacq greeted one of the guards manning a small booth on top of the eastern bastion. "Hullo, Henri. Staying sharp?"

The young man nodded silently and saluted, but was too shy to address the mighty Dinrhydan.

"These bastions are like the points of a star." Jacq continued lecturing Philip and Tristan as they stood admiring the view of the City and Mount Hythea in the distance. "They allow the defenders to fire cross-ways at any attackers attempting to scale the walls with siege ladders."

They strolled along the wall-top until they stood high above a huge paved area called the Citadel Commons, home of many parades and public celebrations. A wide channel separated the revetments from this public square.

"Now here," Jacq said proudly, "we have another cunning defense." He pointed downwards. "This moat can be flooded by opening a series of deeply buried pipes fed from the Mere. Once the defenders cut the bridges leading to the main gate and the two minor gates, the Fynära will be forced to swim across a wide expanse of water in order to attack the Citadel." Jacq gave a satisfied smile. "Our people can pick them off one by one, like fish caught in a weir."

"What about the sides of the Citadel facing the Mere, Father?" Tristan looked up at Jacq with shining eyes, proud he had been included in this consultation between the mighty Dinrhydan and the Prime Minister of Beaumarais.

Jacq smiled. "It is even harder to attack the City from that angle, Tris. The sides dive straight down into the Mere with no banks at all. No enemy would be able to get a handhold on the sheer walls. We will concentrate our defense on the Yoke gate and the City gates."

Tristan was eager to show he could be of use in the defensive planning. "But the Rising managed to breach the walls when they saved you. How will we prevent that from happening again?" He had heard the story of the rescue mission, led by Nicholas Reynard, more than once. Thirty men approached in a boat, under cover of darkness, and blasted a hole in the Citadel wall below the level of the Mere. The water poured in the breach and flooded the lower floors, causing enough chaos to allow them to free the Dinrhydan.

His father shrugged. "I doubt the Fynära have any gun powder. They have not used it in any other attack I have heard of. Anyway, your mother ordered the construction of water snares all around the walls when she first became Queen. You cannot even pull a boat up to the side anymore, except for a small stretch next to the centre bastion."

The Prime Minister immediately protested. "Why is there a space at all?"

"There was once a door there, a long time ago, leading to a passage that used to be King Benedict's private escape route. But the tunnel collapsed when the lower levels were flooded by the Rising. No-one has been through it for years." As Jacq said this, they reached the area between the two westernmost bastions. The Yoke gate lay directly below them, and they could see the land bridge stretching off into the distance. Jacq said thoughtfully, "The Yoke may well be the weak spot. It must be well defended, in case they try to storm that gate directly. I will have the men concentrate the artillery pieces there."

Philip said, "Of course. I trust your judgment implicitly in these matters, Dinrhydan. But it seems from all reports that these raiders prefer stealth over an outright attack. What do we know of their leader, the one they call Faircrow?"

Jacq shook his head. He stopped and stared out across the Mere, towards the west. "No-one knows anything of him, except he fights like a spawn of the devil. The reports from Mardon are sketchy, of course, but it seems this man Faircrow is the greatest swordsman anyone has ever seen." He paused and put his hand on the grip of his own sword, d'angwir. "I would like to put that to the test someday soon."

Tristan laid a hand on his father's arm, saying, "I am ready to stand beside you when you fight him. Will you have need of my weapon, Father?"

Jacq smiled and patted his son's head affectionately. "Nay, Tristan. Your place will be here, safe in the Citadel. You are the King, and I have sworn to protect you."

Tristan swallowed his disappointment. He could not help thinking that if his sister had asked the same question, Jacq's answer would have been quite different.

Ketha listened to Jacq's defensive strategies with interest. As Jacq, Tristan and Philip walked down the stairs again, the battle crow rose, shrieking, from the wall, and flew off over the Mere, heading east towards the borders of Mardon.

Chapter Thirteen

Silent Brigga's Bewilderment

Geya looks confused. N... No. Should I have?

It might have been a good idea, since I happen to know she has chosen the Seed Bearer and he is *not* Lut.

~~~~~~~~~~

"The escape tunnel? Of course!" Gwenn spoke out loud to Ketha, who now resided once more in her body, after her three-day reconnaissance mission abroad. "I can remember playing down there as a child."

Ketha said, "Your stepfather seems to think the tunnel is impassable, so perhaps it would not be of much use to us."

"He is wrong. Fallen timbers block the tunnel in the middle, but there is a space large enough for one person to squeeze through and it could easily be made wider. We could move our men in by night, and assemble everyone in the tunnel for a sneak raid on the treasury."

"What news have you from Einar, Gwenn? We need those promised ships and men!"

"We have sent the extra ship laden with spoil to Starruthe three times now. Each time it returns with the same message... 'Not yet.' Torsten Iron Fist isn't convinced we can mount an attack on Beaumarais. I don't know what else I can do, Ketha, other than going back to Einar myself."

Ketha said angrily, "Foolish girl! You cannot leave the raiders alone for that long. We would lose control of them all together. I can make the journey in less than a week, if I wing my way straight across the ocean. When I have seen what the situation in Einar is, I will return." She lowered her voice and said tiredly, "I am already weary from my trip to St. Valery on your behalf, but I will leave right now for Starruthe. We must not allow much more time to pass before we attack Beaumarais. Already they make defensive preparations that could foil our plans." Of course, Ketha felt no such fatigue, but it never hurt to make the girl feel guilty.

Gwenn hid her relief effortlessly as she said, "I am sorry you have to leave again so soon. We will continue the raids until you return. I wish you a safe journey over the water. We would be lost if you did not return to us, Ketha." Actually, nothing would have pleased her more.

As soon as the battle crow left, Gwenn went to find her thrall. He sat listlessly, chained to his usual place on the wall by her bed. She looked at him with concern. Something had dimmed his spirit and Gwenn believed it began on the night Gunnar beat him up. Though she apologized for her Captain's behavior again and again, Arkady no longer spoke directly to her or met her eyes.

Now she squatted before him and said softly in Maraison, "I have good news, Kadya. Ketha has gone back to Starruthe, and will not return for a week. The *Moon Drake* has just arrived from Einar and all the men are busy unloading fresh supplies. Will you come with me now? We could lose ourselves in the dunes for a few hours. No-one will know."

He shook his head miserably and did not look up.

She stamped her foot in exasperation. "Will you not tell me what is wrong? I cannot read your mind, Kadya." Gwenn swallowed uncomfortably after she caught a whiff of the ox roasting on the cooking fire. Her stomach had been very upset for the last several weeks. Excusing herself, she turned away, rushed to the doorway, and vomited onto the ground.

Gwenn walked back to Arkady, wiping the sour taste from her lips with the back of her hand. He stared at her with burning eyes. "How long have you been sick like that, Gwenn?"

She answered carelessly. "A while. I guess I must have eaten something that disagreed with me."

His next question shocked her. "What of your moon cycle? Has it been timely?"

"I... No. I missed my bleeding last month and maybe the one before as well. I don't remember exactly. But that has happened before, lots of times. Mother told me it is because I don't have enough fat on my body. I hadn't thought..." Gwenn sat down abruptly and covered her face.

Arkady's voice was icy cold. "You said she would not let it happen. But she has. With him. She wanted it to be him. That bitch, she knew all the long."

"What are you talking about? Who is him?"

He snapped back, "Gunnar, that is who. As if you did not know. I have had it with listening to the two of you."

Gwenn seemed genuinely confused by this. "Listening to us? I don't know what you mean, Kadya. It is true Gunnar sleeps by my side, but he never..."

Arkady cut her off, spitting. "Why are you lying to me? I am telling you I have heard him making love to you, many times. It is killing me, Gwenn, do you not see?"

His gaunt face was twisted in sorrow and pain. Gwenn rose, and backed away from him. She ran to the other side of the camp, where her Captain worked, stripped to the waist, chopping wood for the cooking fires. Gunnar had sworn on Lutyond's anchor to be loyal, and Gwenn could not believe he would have taken advantage of her like that. She had no memory of the incidents Arkady seemed sure had taken place.

Gunnar stopped the swing of his axe when he saw her expression. "What is it, Gwenn? What has happened?"

"Kadya said you laid with me while I slept. Lots of times. Tell me you did not, Strong Arm. I trusted you."

Her eyes filled with tears, and Gunnar felt a tangled knot growing inside his stomach. He put the axe down carefully and stepped away from her, for she had keth'fell in her hand.

He assumed a carefully contrived look of confusion. "I don't know what you mean. What has the thrall been saying?" He hoped he might somehow distract her, but she could see right away from his hangdog look that he was guilty.

She took a step forward and pushed him hard. "How could you? You conniving jackass."

Gunnar hung his head, and whispered, "Ketha came to me. She told me I would lose you to the thrall if I did not do something. I... I did not want to, not like that, I swear it. Ketha insisted that I was the one she wanted for you. She said you would welcome me."

"Welcome you? I never even knew you were there. Ketha controls me completely when I sleep, for she has no need of rest." She pushed him again and he backed away from her anger. "Did you enjoy it, knowing you were with someone who had no knowledge of your presence? How many times did you take me?"

"I don't know. I stopped, once I knew, you must believe me. One night, when we had the shutters open, the full moon made it as bright as day inside. That is when I saw your eyes were blank. You looked right through me. She made you move, like a puppet. It was horrible."

Gwenn spat in disgust and touched the pouch on Gunnar's chest. "I gave you my hair. Remember? You swore you would be faithful, but you laid with me while I slept. Faugh! You sicken me. Do you not see how she used you?"

He nodded unhappily. "I see it now. I am sorry."

She spat back, "Sorry? Not as sorry as you are going to be. I should kill you right now." She raised keth'fell threateningly, but he did not move away.

Gunnar bowed his head. "Gwenn, listen to me. I love you. I should have told you a long time ago." He raised a hand to touch her face and she slapped it away angrily, disregarding the hurt look he gave her. Turning from him, she wiped her tears away with the back of her hand and ran back to the long house, ignoring Gunnar as he frantically called her name.

Arkady had shifted slightly, and now sat with his back to the door. He did not look up as she entered. Gwenn unlocked his chain from the eyelet on the wall and said roughly, "Get up. We are going for a walk."

"No."

She yanked hard on the chain, and he fell onto his side, but did not move further. "Kadya, do not make me drag you. Now please get up and come with me." Arkady rose stiffly to his feet. His clothing, now threadbare and filthy after months as a thrall, hung off his emaciated frame.

"Lead on, kind mistress," he said bitterly.

As she walked out the door, pulling Arkady by his chain, Arvid stopped her. "Gunnar has ordered the *Moon Drake* to make ready to leave again today, because of the spoils from the raids on Arbith and Grenfell. They brought some thralls from Einar with them to row and we have a fresh crew ready to join them. We wrapped the stained glass very carefully, and have stored it upright in the stern. Torsten should be very impressed."

Gwenn snorted. "I hope so, but we have sent many other fine treasures. Nothing seems to be good enough. See that the men guard the gold altarpiece from Arbith until the moment the boat casts off. We don't want anything to happen to it before it gets to Starruthe. I will come down to the beach in a few minutes." Arvid gave her a curious glance as she disappeared into the dunes with Arkady shuffling behind her.

Once they found themselves out of sight of the camp, Gwenn stopped and let go of the chain. Arkady immediately sat down in the shade of a dune, wrapping his arms around his drawn up knees. Again, he hid his face from her as she squatted in front of him.

"You were right, Kadya, but I swear to you I did not know what he was doing." Her voice grew plaintive. "You must believe me."

Arkady did not look up. "Must I? You told me when I first found you that he was your lover."

Gwenn said sharply, "That was different."

"It looks and sounds *exactly* the same to me."

"Do you not see? Ketha put him up to it. She is angry because she suspects I can block her out of my mind with the mantra you gave me, and she is using Gunnar as a wedge to drive us apart. Will you let her succeed?" She sat down close to his side and he moved away until several feet of sand separated them, then took up the same position as before.

Gwenn stared at him for a few moments and said bitterly, "I never asked you to come here. I begged you to ride away, remember?" The nodding stems of the oat grass clicked softly around them, and the ceaseless boom of the ocean sounded faintly in the distance. The sand was warm under her legs and she could not help thinking about the night they spent together in dunes just like these.

Arkady obviously had the same thought. He turned his head and gave her a burning glance. "Why did you let me make love to you that night, Gwenn? Do you know what torment you gave me? Do you even care?"

Her expression betrayed nothing of the hurt his words caused her. She said, "Of course I care. I have loved you ever since I was a little girl. When Ketha said I had to go away I wanted to see you once more. I waited for many months in St. Valery because Jessamine said you were coming home. Ketha said she could find you, so we left Beaumarais and made our way to Secuny, and you came. I did not plan... that is, the lovemaking just happened. But I was very pleased it did."

He was not at all appeased. "Yes, so pleased you abandoned me and stole the horse I worked so hard for. What happened to Ajax, by the way? Did you sell her to the slave traders or just kill her outright?"

"I let her go. Ketha would have run her to death. And I paid very dearly for that. Would you like to see the wound?" She rolled up her breeches and pointed to a particularly nasty-looking jagged scar. Arkady did not seem impressed. He gave her leg a cursory glance and put his head back down on his knees.

"So you let her go. Huzzah! Were you so merciful to the Firaithi your butchers ran down? Which Kindred was it, anyway?"

Gwenn shifted uncomfortably. She had no idea why the subject was of interest to Arkady. Her men had murdered hundreds of people since they began raiding the coast. "The Chandrathi, I think. The raiders killed most of the men. We let the surviving women and children go, and took the horses for our own use. Why do you care, anyway?"

"You would not understand. Words like family and loyalty don't mean anything to you, do they?" He spat angrily at her feet.

"Did you know them?" she asked softly. She crawled over to him, and tried to raise his head so she could see his face.

He slapped her hard, saying, "Don't touch me. Never again. Do you understand?"

She angrily drew her sword. "How dare you strike me! I would kill anyone else who did that."

He shrugged carelessly, saying, "Go ahead. What do I have to live for now? But before I die, I want to know one thing. What were the names of the two Firaithi men you captured and sent to Starruthe?"

Gwenn scratched her head, trying to remember.

Arkady stared at her, and she thought for the first time she could see hatred burning in his eyes. "You don't even know, do you? Two human beings, condemned to a life of miserable slavery by you, and you cannot even recall their names. That is truly despicable."

157

She snapped her fingers. "Now I remember! Huw Adaryi and Padarn... Somebody or other. We kept them alive to take care of the horses."

He cried hoarsely, "Huw? My Gods, Gwenn. How could you?" Arkady stood abruptly. The anger inside him suddenly flowered red and he drew his trembling hands together. Eira's voice echoed urgently in his mind. *No, Kadya! You must not kill her. She may be the mother of the Dawnmaid.*

Arkady shouted, "I don't give a damn! I have failed you, Eira. There will be no Dawnmaid."

Gwenn stared at him in confusion. "Who is Eira? Why are you talking to her?" Then her eyes widened as she saw the ball of glowing fire between his outstretched fingers.

He said, "Prepare to die, you murdering whore."

Gwenn did not move, though she could easily have felled him with her sword. She wondered briefly if he truly meant to kill her. The magic fire he held in his hands certainly appeared to be powerful enough, but the thought brought her no distress. As she looked up at him one last time, her blue eyes, as blue as the skies of T'Shang, held only sadness and love.

With a cry of horror, he threw the fireball into a patch of oat grass, which immediately erupted into a mass of fierce flames. The winds off the ocean dispersed the smoke and within seconds, nothing remained but a mass of blackened stems. Arkady fell to his knees and then on his face, sobbing into the sand. Gwenn did not dare touch him. She stayed on her knees a few feet away, and said nothing for a long while.

After a time, he raised his head. His face was a picture of misery. "I have to leave here before I try to kill you again. Next time, I might not be able to stop myself. I am sorry."

Her eyes filled with tears. She whispered, "Don't be sorry. I wanted you to. I know it is the only way I will ever truly be free of Ketha. But how did you make that fire?" Gwenn crawled forward until she sat close to him, and reached out her hand. Immediately, he stood up and moved away from her again, then gave her a poisonous glance.

"I told you not to touch me. The fire comes from Hana. She gave it to me, because I am the Seed Bearer."

Gwenn looked confused. "The Seed Bearer? What does that

mean?" A sudden gust of wind picked up the sand and whipped it across her face, stinging the skin there. She wiped the film of grit from her eyes. The sand stuck to her cheeks where her tears had fallen and left long white tracks.

"It doesn't matter," Arkady said wearily. "I have failed in the task she gave me, anyway. Failed you, failed Eira and, most of all, failed myself. All the things I learned in T'Shang have deserted me. I haven't sat in meditation for a long time. Not since... Well, you know, I am sure. I could cope with the hard work and the hunger and the abuse from the others, but not that. Now you understand why I have to get away from here."

"But where will you go? You are hardly fit to travel. What will you do?"

He fixed her with a burning glance. "There is only one thing I can do. Huw, my brother, is suffering. You sent him to Einar as a slave. I am going to try and rescue him, and as many of the others as I can."

She cried out, "No! You cannot go to Einar alone. They will kill you. I will remove your collar and give you a horse and some gold. Go back to T'Shang, and learn to be happy again."

"How can I?" he snarled. "Would it be right for me to ignore Huw's agony? I cannot undo all the wrong you have done, Mistress Faircrow, but I can try to save one or two. If I perish, I will have failed for the last time."

She begged him, "Kadya, please, don't do this foolish thing. I never wanted..."

He interrupted her sharply. "Why should I care what you want anymore, Gwenn? You don't have the right to ask me for anything. You lost it the moment you raised your blankets and let that murderer underneath them. Now get out of my way. It is a long walk to Danica."

She drew herself up proudly, so he would not see the pain his words caused her. After taking a deep breath, she said, "If you are truly determined to go, then let me help you. It is the least I can do, since you blame me for everything that has happened."

"Why should I not blame you?"

Gwenn refrained from pointing out that she had not chosen to become a vessel for Keth Dirane. Pride kept her eyes free of tears and her lower lip from trembling. She said quietly, "I will tell Gunnar I wish you to be sent to Einar on the *Moon Drake* as a present for Torsten Iron Fist. Once you get there, you will be on your own. I don't expect I will ever see you again."

Arkady nodded curtly. "Very well, Mistress Faircrow. I accept your offer." He added venomously, "You can run off to your boyfriend now and tell him I am going. I am sure he will be pleased."

She whispered sadly, "You did not have to say that. I am hurting enough already. Soon Ketha will return and force me to start the invasion of St. Valery. You don't know how very tired I am of killing and stealing, but I am not allowed to stop. If I had my wish I would be as dead and burned as that bush over there."

Arkady's angry expression softened. "Gwenn, I..." he whispered, as he reached out to brush the sand from her cheek. Just then, Arvid crested the top of the dune. Arkady dropped his hand abruptly.

The first mate, uncomfortably aware he had walked into some scene between the two of them, cleared his throat. "I am sorry to interrupt, Faircrow, but the *Moon Drake* is ready to leave with the tide. Gunnar is waiting by the shore and he wants you there too, to wish them a safe voyage."

Gwenn said listlessly, "Of course, Arvid. I was just coming."

She glanced over at Arkady, whose face had hardened again at the mention of Gunnar's name. He gave her an imperceptible nod. "Take this thrall, clean him up and put him aboard. I am sending him to Torsten." She grabbed Arkady's chain and handed it to Arvid, whose eyebrows shot up in surprise. He took the chain from her and walked away. Arkady gazed back over his shoulder and saw her crying, and the tears washed the rest of the sand from her cheeks. He closed his eyes, trying hard to forget the image of her face, and allowed Arvid to drag him along by his collar.

A few minutes later, Gwenn stood by Gunnar on the beach as the men of the *Moon Drake* prepared to cast off. There were thralls on board to do the rowing and Gwenn knew Arkady would soon be brought down to take his place among them. Her insides churned painfully, and she left Gunnar's side and ran into the dunes. Falling on her hands and knees, she waited for her stomach to empty itself. Then she felt gentle fingers gather up her hair and hold it away from her face. Once she had vomited, she straightened up and found her captain standing beside her.

His voice was full of concern. "What is wrong with you, Gwenn? How long have you been sick like that?"

"This is all your fault, you idiot. I have been sick for weeks. I am pregnant, Gunnar," she said in exasperation.

He stepped back, stunned by her news. "Are you sure?"

She replied, "I have missed two or three moon cycles already, so yes, I am quite sure. Ketha used you and you fell right into her trap. I don't know why she wants me to be with child, but I believe it is for some evil purpose." Gwenn sighed deeply as she peered across the dunes. "We had better get back, the boat must be about to leave."

Gunnar caught her arm as he said softly, "Wait, Faircrow. Let the ship go. I don't give a damn about raiding any more. You say you have my child growing inside you? I know it is my fault and you probably hate me for it, but still I am filled with joy." Pulling her back, so she stood close to him, he whispered urgently. "We can leave here now, and be far away before Ketha returns. I will take care of you, I swear it. Can you not be happy with me?"

She raised her eyes to meet his. He could see the bitterness there. "I can never get away from Ketha. There is an invisible thread connecting us. Only death can break it."

"No! There must be another way. We can find it together. You have to let me help you now. I promised I would, remember? When I gave you the *mammut*." His resolve made her fury evaporate. He had been tricked and lied to by Ketha, just as she had. It seemed the goddess would stop at nothing to keep control of her vessel. What would happen to the child after it came into the world? Gwenn started to weep, and Gunnar put his arms around her.

She buried her head on his shoulder and whispered, "How? How can you help me?"

"There is an old woman I know, who lives far up the coast from Einar, in the wilds of Starruthe. She is a witch and communes with the spirit world. Perhaps she knows a spell to break the bond between you and Keth Dirane. She is very powerful." His voice grew strong with hope. "If we leave right now on the *Fire Drake*, and sail straight across the ocean, we can get to her before Ketha returns here."

Gwenn sounded doubtful. "Sail the *Fire Drake* across open water with a crew of two? What if we hit rough weather?"

Gunnar replied proudly, "There is no man in Einar who handles a longboat better than Gunnar Strong Arm. I have sailed from here to Starruthe many times with only the stars and winds as my guide. We will not founder as long as I am at the helm; I swear it, on the Mariner's anchor. You must trust me."

A small seed of hope began growing in her heart, but still she hesitated. "Who is this witch of whom you speak? How do you know of her powers?"

"I know her well. She is my grandmother. I lived with her after my parents died in a fire. She had a house in Einar, the same house I live in now. When the Magnus found out she practiced spell-casting he exiled her, though she never harmed a soul." He added sadly, "She went away when I was twelve. I have been on my own ever since." She met his eyes and saw they were filled with tears. "Will you come with me or no?"

Gwenn stood by quietly, torn by indecision. All her life she had told herself no other man could ever take Kadya's place. Now he had rejected her so unfairly she did not know what to do. Should she give her heart to Gunnar? He said he loved her and had promised to care for her and the baby. The sudden cry of a sea bird passing above reminded her of Ketha. Did she have any other choice? She must do anything she could to protect her unborn child from the battle crow.

Gwenn made her decision. She would try to forget Arkady Svalbarad, though the thought of him still filled her with longing. But rubbing her eyes made his gaunt features disappear in her mind, and there was Gunnar standing before her, waiting patiently for her reply. She put her hand on his chest, over his heart. "Are you sure she still lives? That was a long time ago."

He took her hand and kissed the palm softly. "I have had messages from her every year. I believe she still lives, and I know where to find her. Don't be afraid."

She nodded and said, "Then let us go together. I am not afraid. But there is one thing I must tell you before we set out." To Gwenn, it seemed a fountain of happiness and hope bubbled up inside her now that she had made up her mind. Suddenly it spilled over into a peal of laughter.

Gunnar scratched his head, and removed the obligatory flea from under his black-rimmed nail. Her amused expression confused him. "What is that?"

She grinned at him wickedly. "You smell awful. I am afraid you are going to have to learn how to bathe." He gave her a shy smile in return and nodded obligingly.

As Arvid led him along the path from the camp running down to the beach, Arkady watched at a distance as Gwenn ran headlong towards the dunes. When he arrived at the *Moon Drake*, he saw Gunnar turn to follow her and his anger multiplied until he could feel the burning in his solar plexus presaging the formation of a fireball. He knew he could easily hit the Fynäran captain from where he stood on the beach. The thought he could burn Gwenn's lover alive in front of her cheered him momentarily, and he slowly moved his hands forward until they rested in front of his stomach. Arvid was busy giving instructions to one of the departing crewmembers and did not notice Arkady's intent expression. He was calculating how many of the other raiders he might be able to kill before they took his life away from him.

Eira's voice echoed in his mind. *What have you become, my brother? You would not kill Huw for his terrible crime against you, the night the men from Mardon attacked. Why are you so quick to condemn this man to death? Save your fire, for our brother has need of it. He is very close, Kadya.*

Her calm words poured ice water on his anger and the burning pain slowly lessened and disappeared. He allowed Arvid to pull him into the water, to where the *Moon Drake* lay beached with her shallow hull on the shingle. His chain was given over to Sven Red Beard, who tugged at it mercilessly while Arkady tried to scramble aboard the vessel. Twice, his weakened condition made him fall back into the freezing ocean before he at last managed to pitch forward onto the deck. He lay motionless, soaked and shivering, for a few seconds. A wicked slash with a leather strap made him cry out in pain.

Sven said callously, "Get up, lazy thrall. You will row for me, now!"

A second blow with the whip followed before Arkady could gain his feet. Sven dragged him along by his chain until he reached a vacant spot on one of the benches. He was shoved down into a sitting position and his chain attached to a cleat on the deck, making it impossible for him to rise. Another thrall sat close beside him, his head turned away, resting on the oar.

Arkady gave his rowing partner a cursory glance. He found his gaze locked on the man's back. It festered with many suppurating wounds, and flies hovered about the livid flesh, laying eggs. The putrid, sweetish smell of gangrene assailed his nostrils and he wanted to retch. Just then, a flurry of activity announced the raiders had finished loading the spoil and made ready to get under way.

Sven strode forward along the deck and stopped next to Arkady. Without a word of warning, he slashed his whip across the injured thrall's back, scoring a new wound across his shoulder blades. He shouted, "Get rowing, dirtbag!" as the thrall threw his head back, his face frozen in a rictus of pain, an anguished scream escaping his lips.

Arkady forgot at that moment to put his own hands on the oar and was rewarded with a vicious blow across the face, laying open his cheekbone. He hardly felt the pain, or the blood dripping down onto his shirt as he stared in horrified recognition at his rowing partner. The emaciated, tormented figure now pitifully sobbing beside him was all that remained of his blood brother, Huw Adaryi. In that sudden realization, something very quietly snapped inside Arkady. Then he swore to himself two unbreakable resolutions — he would somehow rescue Huw from his terrible torture and he would watch Sven Red Beard die in the most painful way he could contrive. As Arkady pulled on the oars, an expression very akin to madness settled in his hazel eyes and stayed there. Huw did not speak or even look at Arkady, just kept rowing. Each time he pulled back on the oar, he gave a little cry of pain.

Hand in hand, Gwenn and Gunnar walked back down to the beach. The crowd that had gathered to bid farewell to the *Moon Drake* had already dispersed. The boat was far out to sea, and the rhythm of the oars carried it further and further away as Gwenn watched, shading her eyes with her hand. It carried Arkady Svalbarad towards his death, and as she turned away to follow Gunnar back up the path to the long house, one small sob escaped from her throat before she could stifle it. He did not hear her cry, for he was telling her of his plans for their voyage.

"We will have to wait until darkness falls. Then we can catch the next tide, and get out to sea without rowing."

Gwenn quickly wiped her eyes and caught up with him. "What about supplies? We need at least a week's worth of food and water."

"The *Fire Drake* has been stocked and ready for some time, in case we had to go out to sea to avoid pursuit, but I will go down and check the water casks just to make sure. There is enough ship's biscuit on board for forty men, and we can catch fish on the way." He grinned at her. "We will not starve even if you are eating for two."

They walked back towards the camp and passed though to the outskirts of the old village of Celeste. She led him into the yard of a house that was hardly more than a ruin, a casualty of a long-ago raid. One wall and part of the roof remained, half-buried in drifting sand. A graveled path led around the side to a tin-shingled lean to shed that stood miraculously intact. Someone had planted a row of pansies by the door.

"What is this place?" he asked her.

Gwenn smiled as she opened the door. "You will see."

A wide horse trough stood close against the inner wall. A threadbare rag rug covered the floor, except where Gwenn had carefully excavated a channel in the dirt to drain the tub. The stub of a candle sat on a shelf over a wooden airing rack draped with a towel. A pretty pastoral watercolor hung on the opposite wall.

Gunnar stepped inside and wandered around, bending his head to avoid the low ceiling. He gave her a questioning glance. "Where on Yrth did all this stuff come from?"

"I found most of it in Celeste. I guess it was left behind when the villagers cleared out."

"You brought it here yourself?"

"Yes. I wanted a private place to bathe and do my washing."

Gunnar appeared nonplussed by this. "What for? All the rest of us use the common washbowl. You southerners sure have some funny ideas."

Gwenn had seen what passed for ablutions among the men of the Fynära when she first allied herself with them. Sometimes, before a meal, they passed around a single basin of hot water and rinsed their beards and hands. Once she saw what the water looked like when they finished she decided to forego the practice all together.

She laughed, shaking her head at his ignorance, and handed him the bucket. "Come on, I'll show you where the water butt is."

After many trips back and forth with the bucket, the trough brimmed with cold water. Gwenn wrinkled her nose. "It isn't as nice as my bathroom at the Citadel, of course, because we had hot water piped in there from a big boiler down in the basement. Cold baths are not so pleasant, but they are better than nothing." Pointing to the tub, she ordered, "Now, in you go, Gunnar."

He replied dubiously, "In there? Should I take my clothes off first?"

She nodded encouragingly, so he pulled his black tunic over his head and dropped it in the corner. Gwenn watched him undress without embarrassment. A winter spent indoors with the men had made them all very familiar with one another. His heavily muscled chest was deeply tanned from many shirtless days at sea, but his legs, when he removed his breeches, were lily-white. Still unsure what he was meant to do, he hesitated by the trough, scratching his flea bites distractedly.

Gwenn could not hide her laughter. "Look, I will show you. It is perfectly harmless." Quickly, she stripped off her clothes, and stepped into the bath, trying not to shiver. He finally joined her, loudly cursing as he sank down into the cold water, and sent a wave splashing over the sides. But when Gwenn took a soapy rag and scrubbed the crusted dirt off his skin, he relaxed and finally sighed with pleasure.

"This isn't half bad. How often do you southerners do this sort of thing? A few times a year?"

"At least once or twice a *week*, Gunnar. Now let me wash your hair." Obligingly, he bent his head and she rubbed the soap bar over his greasy locks. When she had created enough lather, she used a fine-toothed ivory comb to remove as many of the fleas and nits from his hair as she could. He sat patiently through this procedure and did not complain.

"Did you truly live in the Citadel at St. Valery?" he asked her after she dumped a bucket full of water over his head to rinse off the bubbles.

"Yes, I told you my mother used to be the Queen of Beaumarais, did I not? Turn around so I can wash your other side." He did so, managing to slop a good deal more water onto the earthen floor in the process.

"You did, but I did not believe you." He squirmed happily as her hands massaged the soap onto his shoulders. Once she sluiced water over his back, the muddied colors of a sizeable dragon tattoo became bright on his newly clean skin. Gwenn ran her fingers over the design, which extended all the way across his broad back and over both powerfully built shoulders.

She whispered, "How beautiful! Your back is a work of art. The colors are like the stained glass windows we took from Grenfell." He shivered with pleasure, both at her touch and the admiration in her voice. Her next words did not please him as much. She asked enthusiastically, "Where did you get that tattoo? I want one just like it!" as she continued to scrub his lower back with the rag.

Gunnar rapidly changed the subject. "Why do you want to invade St. Valery if it used to be your home? Do you not have people you care for there?"

The scrubbing stopped. Gwenn said, "Ketha told me I should and I believed her. She made me think my mother was a terrible person who deserved punishment." Then the rag moved again as she sighed deeply.

"Do you still believe that, Faircrow?" he asked her softly.

"No, I don't, not any more. Ketha lied about so many things. I thought she was my best friend, but all this time she has been using me to get what she wants." She finished with the soap and pulled him backwards so he could lay against her chest with his head resting on her shoulder. Gunnar said nothing else for a few moments, lost in the thought he had never known happiness before, not like this, even though he could not get used to the powerful smell of the soap now clinging to his skin. But soon the water's chill drove them out of the trough, and they shared the towel equably. As Gwenn reached for her clothes, he caught her hand.

"Don't get dressed for a minute. I want to..." Gunnar stopped talking, and colored up in embarrassment. He put his hand on her slightly rounded stomach and stroked it softly. A second later, he felt an almost imperceptible fluttering under his fingers and his eyes went wide.

She smiled tenderly. "Can you feel that? It is our child, moving."

He nodded, unable to speak for the wonder and joy threatening to overflow from his heart. With a cry, he fell to his knees and buried his face in her belly, with his arms tightly around her waist.

She stroked his hair and murmured, "Mmm... You smell very nice now, my Captain." A second later, Gwenn joined him on the floor of the bathhouse. They had little space to maneuver in, so Gunnar stretched out with his back on the rug. She straddled his chest and kissed him, and then traced the dragon pattern inked on his shoulders with her tongue. He found this attention intensely pleasurable and his little shivers of delight pleased her as well. She slipped further down until she rested on his hips just above his groin.

He tried to sit up, wanting to swap positions with her. She pushed him back down. "Not this time, Gunnar. There isn't enough room in here. Anyway, it is nice like this. I like it."

Gunnar stiffened. "You want to be on top of me? The woman isn't supposed to..." He looked up at her nervously and started again. "A Fynäran man..."

"Never takes baths," she finished for him, laughingly. "But you took one today, and you liked it, did you not?"

He nodded distractedly, then involuntarily arched his back and groaned as she lowered herself down on to him. She rocked slowly, as she whispered, "See? It is not so bad, is it, letting a woman control things for a change?"

Gunnar did not say anything in reply but when she saw the mottled red stain spreading wide on his neck and chest, she knew the answer to her question. Forcefully, he grasped her hips, wanting more of her, completely absorbed in the novel sensation of having to lie still while she moved. She leaned forward, and let her hair fall around his face, while her hands stroked his ribcage and belly. He cupped her cheek and pulled her down to kiss her mouth roughly, and then let his lips play on her breasts for a long while. Gwenn quickened her pace, as her passion increased, until Gunnar gasped her name, and thrust his hips up high again and again, finally carrying her over the edge with him.

"Are you happy, Strong Arm?" she asked him a bit later, when they had finally managed to get dressed.

Gunnar busily tried to tame his unexpectedly fluffy hair into braids. "I am more than happy, Faircrow. But I will be even happier when we are far away from this place and from Ketha."

"What will the others do when we are gone? I don't feel right just abandoning them like this. We have been through a lot together, after all. The men of the *Fire Drake* are part of my *felag*."

He gave up on his hair, and allowed her to plait it for him in a single braid hanging down between his shoulder blades. "I am going to tell Arvid we are leaving. He has been my first mate for many years and he deserves to know the truth. He can take the men and go back to Einar on the *Sea Drake*." Gunnar smiled ruefully and said, "He understands how I feel about you. I could not keep it a secret, for he knows me too well."

She opened the door and peered outside. "It will be getting dark soon. Why don't you go down and check the *Fire Drake* while I empty the trough?"

He nodded but did not leave right away. Gunnar turned back and took her in his arms again. "Faircrow, I..." He swallowed and started again, finding it difficult to put into words everything he held in his heart. "I just wanted you to know no matter what happens, I will never forget today. I love you so much. Do you believe me? You must."

"Yes, of course, Gunnar. Why would I not?"

"Because of the terrible thing I did to you." He sighed. "Can you ever forgive it?"

"I already have." Her feelings for Arkady had been carefully tucked away in her heart and she found she could truthfully say she cared almost equally for the man who stood before her now. She took a deep breath and said, "I love you too, you know."

He hugged her again and disappeared into the grey evening light. Gwenn stood at the door a long time and listened to the distant sound of the ocean. The baby fluttered inside her, and she stroked her stomach softly, wondering whether she carried a boy or a girl. *Gunnar will want a boy*, she thought, *but a little girl to dress up and play with would be nice too.* Gwenn remembered the wardrobe full of beautiful gowns she had been given over the years. Had her mother been sad that she did not want to wear them? The idea that she would not, after all, have to invade St. Valery gladdened her, and she hummed a jaunty Dalvolk sea shanty as she bent and pulled the stopper from the drain hole on the trough. The dirty water emptied into the channel and under the wall, disappearing into the sand outside.

A sharp cry from outside made her lift her head sharply. Gunnar drew up, out of breath and shaking. "Hurry, we have to go now. She is coming."

"Who? Ketha?" A dark dread spreading outwards from her solar plexus utterly swallowed the feeling of hope and happiness filling her a moment earlier. "Why? She is supposed to be gone all week."

He tugged at her arm urgently, but she remained rooted in the doorway, staring wildly into the twilight. "Come on!" he begged. "Torsten has sent ships, twenty at least. One of the men saw them with the spyglass. They are sailing down the coast, and a big black crow flies before them. We can still get away if we leave now."

She shook her head despairingly and pointed off into the distance. A black form glided low across the dunes, obviously searching for something. Gunnar uttered a stream of profanity and drew his sword. Gwenn stared at him in dismay. "What do you think you are doing? You cannot fight her, Strong Arm. She will peck your eyes out, just as she did those men at the feast, remember?"

He stepped between her and the approaching battle crow. His voice was grim. "I don't have a choice. I will not let her take you again."

She curled her right hand into a fist and tapped him lightly on the shoulder. When he turned back, she landed a blow that spun him around and left him lying face down on the sand, out cold. Just then, Ketha slammed into her chest with vicious abandon. The excruciating pain made her faint, and she slumped down on top of Gunnar's prone form, just as Arvid came running up with the news that Torsten had relented at last.

Chapter Fourteen

Sailor's Graveyard

Not Lut? *Geya pales and squirms in her chair.* Are you sure?

The Numen nods firmly.

Oh dear. I told Raven not to let anyone else... *Geya rubs her hands together worriedly.* Is there anything I can do?

~~~~~~~~~~

After Sven took his place at the stern by the steering oar, and Huw still had given no sign of recognition, Arkady touched his hand and whispered in Firai, "I am here, my brother. It is Arkady and I have come to help you."

Huw moaned, "Kadya, is it truly you? Eira told me you were coming but I did not believe her."

Arkady looked around wildly. "Eira? Where is she?"

Huw shook his head but carefully kept his face turned away. "Our sister has passed through *Tsmar'enth*.* She speaks to me from Death's kingdom and offers comfort as best she can." This unexpected news devastated Arkady and he could not hide his grief.

He cried, "Eira is no more?" Sven's head snapped up, seeking the source of the disturbance. Arkady quickly dropped his tear-filled eyes and concentrated on rowing until another raider walked back to begin a conversation with the helmsman. Then he asked quietly, "How did she die?"

His brother said, "She was very lucky. Eira died defending our caravan from those Gruagán scum, the Fynära. They captured me and made me their slave, along with Padarn. I have wished many times since that I had shared her fate instead. Are you sure you are truly here?"

He squeezed the Firaithi's hand reassuringly. "Just look. I am right here beside you."

Huw slowly turned his head so that Arkady could see his face.

---

* The Moon-Gate—death.

171

His once-sparkling brown eyes had become milky white, and rough red scar tissue covered the lashless lids. He said softly, "I cannot see you, Kadya. The raiders poured lye in my eyes after I tried to escape. I am only kept alive so I may row for them."

The mounting horror of Huw's situation threatened to overwhelm Arkady, and it was many moments before he could speak again. He said hoarsely, "I am going to get you away from here. I swear it."

Huw patted his hand. "Don't endanger yourself on my behalf, my brother. I am leaving soon anyway. Death will come for me before long, and I will be very glad when He does. But tell me, how did you come to be made a slave too?"

Before Arkady could answer, Sven barked an order and his shipmates scurried forward to raise the square sail. They had rowed straight out to sea for an hour, but now Sven turned the ship to the north, so it ran parallel to the coast, which lay just on the horizon. Wind filled the sail and carried them along at a good clip, so he gave the order for the oars to be stowed. All the thralls were herded up into the bows.

Arkady and Huw sat together, on the wet deck, as the salt spray quickly drenched their clothes. Huw trembled uncontrollably and Arkady took off his own shirt and wrapped it around his brother's wounded shoulders. He pulled him close and sheltered him as much as he could from the wind. The other thralls sat silently with their heads down, some twenty in all.

Arkady watched them for a moment and then he whispered to Huw, "Why do they not speak?"

"The thralls come from many different lands. The Fynära deliberately place as many different nationalities together on a boat as they can, so the thralls cannot communicate with one another. That way we cannot plan any sort of mutiny. But most of them can speak a little Dalvolk — otherwise, they would not be able to follow their master's instructions. I can speak more because I worked as a record keeper for the Magnus, Per Drake's Son, until I tried to escape. If Sven sees us talking together now he will punish us and we will be separated. When we are forced to row again he will probably put you on a different bench anyway, just to make sure."

Huw did not speak again, and presently Arkady found his

brother had passed into a fitful slumber. His head rested heavily on Arkady's shoulder. He studied Huw's ravaged face for a long while before closing his own eyes.

When Gunnar regained consciousness, he found himself lying on his bed in the long house. He stared up at the ceiling, trying to piece together what happened after he and the Faircrow made love on the floor of her bath shed. He sat up and looked around, her name on his lips. Arvid crossed the room and squatted beside him.

He spoke reassuringly. "Easy, Gunnar. Gwenn is well enough, I reckon. She is out with Torsten, inspecting the ships by torchlight. How do you feel?"

Gunnar rubbed his jaw and winced. "She hit me, Arvid. Right in the mouth."

His first mate seemed quite shocked. "Why in the name of Ods did she do that?"

"I wanted to fight Ketha."

"It is a good thing she did, Strong Arm. What were you thinking? You saw what happened at the banquet."

Gunnar dropped his voice, so the others could not hear. "Gwenn is pregnant. My child. We were going to take the *Fire Drake* and go back to Starruthe. I thought my grandmother could help her." He said despairingly, "Now Ketha is back, I don't know what will happen."

Arvid looked at him in dismay. Gunnar whispered something he never expected to hear from his normally unshakeable Captain. "How can I stop that demon from making her fight now? Everything is lost."

"Come on. Let's talk outside." Arvid stood and Gunnar rose with him. They walked outside together into the warm spring night. The full moon lit the sky, and the dunes cast flat, black shadows on the sand. Gunnar took the path to the beach, intent on finding Gwenn. Arvid tried to reassure him. "I know the Faircrow. She will find a way out." He stopped and offered his hand to Gunnar. "But if it comes down to fighting, well, you know I stand with the two of you. We will all go to Skyre together, Strong Arm."

Gunnar clasped his hand in gratitude but said sadly, "I don't care about the blood and fire anymore. I only want to be with her and our child, somewhere in peace. Do you understand?"

He nodded. "Of course. You love her. But have a care, Gunnar. Ketha already knows the two of you were up to something. She jumped back into Gwenn so ferociously it made her pass out from the pain. I doubt she will be so careless as to leave her again."

Gunnar growled, "She will pay for that."

They walked together in silence, each man caught up with his own worries, until the dunes parted to reveal the brightly moonlit ocean, and twenty ships. Each lay on the shore, harmless for the moment, though the carved dragon figureheads testified mutely to the death and destruction that surely lay ahead for the City of Isle St. Valery. A pair of torches bobbed around the biggest ship, the *Drake Storm*. This was Torsten Iron Fist's own flagship. Not content with allowing Gwenn to lead the invasion, he had come himself with eight hundred of his warriors.

Gunnar crossed the shingle and waded into the water until he stood by the gunwale of the *Drake Storm*. He watched as Torsten showed Gwenn the stockpile of weapons aboard the ship. After a time, she looked up and saw him there, and gestured for him to come aboard. He lifted himself over the side with practiced grace, and crossed the deck.

Torsten hailed him jovially. "Welcome aboard, Gunnar! How was your nap?"

Iron Fist's head came up to just below Gunnar's chin, and his girth spoke of too many rich meals. But the width of his shoulders and neck showed he would be a formidable opponent in battle, and his prowess with an axe was legendary. Gunnar nodded a greeting to the Magnus and studied Gwenn's face closely. She stared back at him blankly, as if all the loving warmth he had seen in her eyes earlier in the day had simply been drained away.

Torsten had brought many arms and men with him from Einar. He wanted to mount a full-scale assault on St. Valery, and sack the city completely. Gwenn argued fruitlessly for a more stealthy approach, using the secret lakeside doorway, and limiting the raid to the treasury. Now she understood the extent to which she had been used by Ketha, she no longer desired to avenge herself on her mother. But Torsten was unmoved.

"I was there when you described the riches of Beaumarais to Per Drake's Son. You said our hands would run with gold! Why do you now wish to skulk in the darkness? We must take everything we can from Beaumarais, and deal death to whomever stands in our way."

Ketha's voice rang raucously in her mind. "Listen to him, little fool. When St. Valery falls, you will be Queen. Would that not be the sweetest revenge against your lying mother?" Gwenn was indifferent to this, but she could not change Torsten's mind.

In the end, they compromised. The Faircrow could lead a small group and infiltrate the Citadel, using the secret door. Once inside they would spread confusion while Torsten and the main force attacked the walls outside the wharf.

Gunnar, standing silently by during this discussion, immediately volunteered to go with Gwenn. Torsten said, "I want you with me, Strong Arm, and all the crew of the *Fire Drake*. The Faircrow can take some of the others on her mission. I need your strength and experience to get the boats into the wharf and the men onshore as quickly as we can."

Gunnar sullenly agreed. They left the *Drake Storm* and walked back to the camp, as Torsten and Gwenn discussed her stepfather, the Dinrhydan, and his defensive plans for the City.

Gwenn passed through the door of the crowded long house and accepted a bowl of thin stew from one of the men. With the addition of Torsten's eight hundred raiders, the accommodations had now become very inadequate and food scarce. The men made no secret of their displeasure.

Torsten looked around and said under his breath, "The sooner we get this lot moving, the better. We leave for Beaumarais first thing tomorrow morning. Once the men get a taste of the booty and women to be had they will soon forget their troubles."

Gwenn hardly heard him. In the locked-off portion of her mind, that Ketha could no longer reach, she was considering a last desperate plan to free herself of the battle crow.

As Huw predicted, Sven made sure the two brothers were seated separately when they were pressed into rowing once more.

Arkady's muscles screamed with the exertion of rowing non-stop for four hours, and the sweat poured off his brow, stinging his eyes and the welt on his cheek. The wind had died down to a whisper, and Sven pushed them cruelly, intent on getting as far up the coast as he could before it became totally dark.

As Arkady removed a hand from the oar to wipe his streaming face, a strap came whistling down on to his other arm. The overseer grumbled, "No slacking, thrall! Both hands on the oar at all times."

Arkady gritted his teeth, not wanting to give Sven the satisfaction of hearing him cry out in pain. Hana's fire ignited inside him, but he could not risk damaging the ship with a fireball now they were so far away from the coastline. Huw would undoubtedly drown before he could make it to shore. Arkady damped the fire down resolutely, promising to himself the time would come, very soon, when he would be able to use it. The man beside him, a Secunian, fell forward, insensate from the heat and exertion. Sven used the strap mercilessly, but the man did not move.

Finally, he came to life, with a moan of pain, and croaked, "Water, please, I beg you, just one drink..."

Sven laughed cruelly. "Come on fellows. This one needs a draught of cold water. Let's give him more drink than he can stomach." Rough hands grabbed the Secunian and dragged him to the bow. They tied his legs together and attached long lengths of rope to each of his arms. He struggled frantically and the raiders subdued him with many fierce blows, until Sven warned, "Don't kill him — we want him awake for his bath. Now, over the side, boys!"

The Secunian begged for mercy as they threw him over the prow and lowered him down to well below the dragon figurehead, so that their prisoner became a grisly second decoration for the front of the boat. Each time the prow dipped down into a wave trough the man's head went underwater, and surfaced again briefly as it lifted.

Sven turned and loudly addressed the other thralls. "Let that be a lesson to you. Any whiners get the same treatment as our lovely new figurehead." The Secunian's screams continued for several hours, gradually growing weaker, until finally they stopped all together. A raider strolled forward and casually chopped at the ropes holding the hapless Secunian. He disappeared without a trace into the ocean.

When night fell and Sven allowed them to stop rowing at last, Arkady staggered forward on the deck and fell down beside Huw and the others. The raiders passed among them, offering each of them a ladle full of water and a stale ship's biscuit. Arkady hungrily ate the offering and between bites he spoke quietly, trying to remind Huw of happier times. But his gentle words were no comfort to his brother, who could only recall all that he had lost in the deadly morning attack.

After they had finished their meager meal, Huw said sadly, "I wonder what has happened to Padarn? I have not heard news of him for several weeks."

"What sort of labor was Padarn forced into? Did he work for the same master as you?" Arkady asked softly.

Huw shook his head. "He works on the docks, unloading the ships as they come in full of spoil. Torsten Iron Fist is his master. He is a hard man and beats his slaves unmercifully."

Sven gave the order to drop the anchor, and the boat came to rest for the night on the quiescent waves. Huw fell asleep almost instantly, but Arkady, though desperately tired, could not. He passed the time mentally designing more and more elaborate tortures for Sven, as the raiders on watch paced back and forth along the deck. At the end of each grisly fantasy, Arkady was forced back to the present. Sven still lived and seemed intent on making Huw's life as close to a living hell as possible. There would be no end to his brother's suffering except death, unless Arkady could find some way to free him.

After four endless hours, another pair replaced the watch, and Arkady considered a desperate plan. His hands were loosely chained, and he could easily conjure a fireball. But he knew such a weapon would give him away far too quickly. He wondered if he could change the fire's colour so the light did not draw attention to him.

He prayed, "Hana, I need your help. Give me fire from the depths of hell. Not firelight, but fire-dark I need now, my goddess."

He felt her answer as the burning inside him increased, and then he could no longer see the fireball forming between his fingers. He shaped it carefully, ignoring the pain of the deadly cold flame piercing his own flesh. When the watchman stopped by the gunwale to urinate over the side, Arkady launched the fire unerringly, hitting the man square in the middle of his back. The raider did not cry out, just pitched forward over the side, making a small splash as he hit the water and sank out of sight. The other watchman drifted over to the side to investigate the noise, and joined his partner in the deep. Suddenly spent, Arkady drifted to sleep, content in the knowledge he would get at least four hours uninterrupted rest before the watchers were missed.

In the grey dawn, Arkady woke, feeling cold and stiff. He lay curled up close to Huw, who had stretched Arkady's shirt over the two of them in a vain effort to keep off the chill morning dew. The raiders huddled down at the stern, holding a whispered conversation.

Huw, feeling him stir, said quietly, "Kadya, two raiders went missing off the boat last night. No-one knows what happened to them. They don't want to admit it, but the rest are afraid. I hear it in the sound of their voices. I don't know what misfortune caused the two men to disappear, but I am gladdened by it. Now there are nineteen of us and only eighteen Fynäran. If only we could communicate with one another, we might plan some sort of uprising."

Arkady answered him in a whisper, "Just wait until tonight, my brother. The odds will tip even more in our favor. Tomorrow, I will begin to organize the rebellion."

"How can you do that? Do you know what happened to the missing men?"

Arkady nodded, and then belatedly remembered Huw could not see him. He murmured, "Yes, I know, but I am not going to tell you, not yet. And remember, I can speak the language of every man on this ship, except for the man from Shadion. But he speaks a little Mard, so I think I will be able to make him understand."

Huw said worriedly, "Kadya, you must not risk yourself for me. These raiders will stop at nothing to prevent a mutiny. I have heard of such tortures that make what they did yesterday to the Secunian seem kind."

Sven strode forward and spoke to the thralls, cowering on the deck before him. "Now, listen, you lot. Two of my men went missing last night, and I think one of you had something to do with it. I don't know who, so every one of you is going to get ten lashes with my whip. You, dead eyes. You are going to be first."

Two raiders grabbed Huw, who struggled weakly, and held him upright with his arms stretched wide. Arkady forced himself to look on as the sadistic Sven brought the lash down again and again on Huw's already shredded flesh, until the screaming Firaithi sagged between his captors in a faint. Sven continued his punishment until Huw had borne the full ten lashes, then he was dragged back to the bow and thrown down next to Arkady. He did not move, but his ragged breathing showed he still lived.

Arkady watched as five other thralls were given the same penalty, and then they came for him. The first stroke made his bladder release, and he felt the humiliating warmth flow down his legs and on to the deck as Sven and the other raiders taunted him unmercifully. The second, laid close to the first, caused him to curse incoherently in Maraison, and as blow followed blow, he could no longer think of anything but the pain as he screamed in anguish. He sank to his knees, and the raiders holding him twisted his arms viciously to get him on his feet again.

In his mind, from somewhere deep inside, he heard Eira and Dawa urging him, "Call on the Eastern Star. She will help you."

He did so, by an effort of superhuman will, and began to repeat his mantra steadily in his mind. The pain lessened slightly, as Hana's touch brushed against his wounded shoulders. Sven finished the last stroke and the raiders half-carried, half-dragged Arkady back to the others. He lay on the deck, fighting for his breath, as his choking sobs continued. Huw took his hand and squeezed it feebly.

The screams of the succeeding victims almost drowned out Arkady's mutterings, but Huw just made them out. "Those bastard sons of scum. I am going to make them pay, all of them. When I am finished, not one Fynära will be left alive to stain Yr. They will all feed the secret flame, every one in his turn. I swear it on the name of Hana." Huw's chest contracted in fear, for in Arkady's furious words he heard nothing but the baying hounds of madness.

Gwenn stood on the deck of the *Fire Drake*, blindly staring ahead. Gunnar watched her silently, his heart filled with fear. She had hardly spoken a word to him since Ketha returned, and when he tried to look at her face, she turned away. But in those brief glimpses, he saw something new in her eyes, a fell expression speaking only of death and despair.

The proud ships sailed up the Ariane River, on their way to the Mistmere and the City of Isle St. Valery. If the favorable winds held, they would reach it by the evening. Presently they passed through a land of cultivated hills and lush wooded valleys, and Gunnar let his mind wander freely, seeking an escape from his unhappiness. He worked the soil with his sons, and on the hot summer days she would come, in a pretty dress, barefoot and laughing, with a bucket of cool water for them to drink from. He would take her hand and lead her through the fields of golden ripe grain, and then tumble down with her amongst the rippling stalks, under a cloudless blue sky. Now as he lay back, she lowered herself down on him, and he felt himself slowly, so slowly, slipping inside her warmth as her hair fell down around his face. He felt a surge of passion, and shifted so she could take more of him inside. She continued to move, quickly now, with her mouth fastened to his, and he shivered as the first wave of ecstasy took him. It took her as well, and she called his name again and again, while the thundering rush of blood filled his ears with music.

"Gunnar... Gunnar..."

His eyes snapped open, for he realized the voice was not his mind. Gwenn called to him from the prow, and he started, guiltily aware he sported an obvious physical reaction to his previous train of thought. He walked forward and leaned casually against the gunwale, trying to hide his embarrassment.

"What were you thinking about? I have been calling you for ages, but you would not answer and you had the strangest expression on your face." She looked at him with amusement as he blushed hotly.

He said nothing in return, thinking the battle crow spoke through her and would cruelly mock any explanation he might give for his happy daydream. After a moment, she surprised him by saying softly, "Ketha has gone ahead to see what the men of St. Valery are doing to prepare the city for our invasion. She doesn't think they will have word of our movements, because they have sealed the borders with Mardon and Spanja, and the warnings will not get through. I just wanted to talk to you for a little while, before she returns." Gwenn sighed. "She will not leave me again, not once the fighting starts."

Reassured by her words, he moved behind her and put his arms around her waist, and felt the thickening bulge that was his child. She said, in surprise, "What are you doing? The men will not like it."

He shrugged. "I don't care anymore. Everyone knows how I feel about you." They stood together silently, and studied the brown foam-flecked water that parted on each side of the prow. A line of wild ducks, disturbed by the boats' passage, left the water and flew away to the north, calling to each other raucously. Gunnar watched them until they passed from sight.

Presently, Gwenn whispered, "Once we get to the Isle, I will have to leave you. I just wanted you to know, no matter what happens to me, I did love you, Gunnar. You must remember that."

Gunnar choked back a cry, understanding exactly what she meant to convey with her words. He said hoarsely, "I will find you after the battle, I swear it. Once Ketha has her victory she may leave you alone. We can still go away together, and raise our child in peace, somewhere far from here."

Shaking her head sadly, she leaned back against his body, and he tightened his arms about her. The deck pitched and rolled beneath them. She said, "You must not keep holding on to empty hope. There is none, not now."

He moaned sorrowfully, burying his face in her hair as he felt the child move under his hands. Gunnar understood he hovered just above an abyss of despair. One false step and he might fall forever. Only his hopes kept him from catastrophe. So, softly, he disagreed with her. "I don't care — I will not give up, no matter what you say. As long as we both live, there is still hope."

She covered his hands with her own and said bitterly, "I did not think it would end like this, Gunnar. Just like you, I used to be full of hope, believing all the lies Ketha told me about my destiny. I would be the warrior queen and take over the world, with you at my right hand. What a fool I was! Now I have nothing left."

"You still have me. I will always be there, at your right side. After the battle, if I find your..." Gunnar could not bring himself to finish his sentence, so he continued, "I will lie down beside you, and open my veins and let my life flow away. We will be

181

together in death, if we cannot be in life."

She turned to face him and he saw the tears on her cheeks. "Will you not die fighting, my love? Go to Skyre and drink with the heroes of your people. Then I will be happy, knowing you are where you belong."

He shook his head. "No. My place is beside you. I pledged as much on the beach, that day." His mouth found hers and held it, the two no longer even aware of their crowded surroundings. Afterwards Gunnar thought unhappily that her lips tasted of salt, like blood.

The men of the *Fire Drake* watched in silence as their Captain held the Faircrow close, and stroked her hair. No-one thought to speak or interfere, understanding the unbreakable *felag* between the two of them.

Arvid studied the edge of his sword, and ran the whetstone over it again. He knew, as every old campaigner does, that this battle might be his last. He wondered what Gudrun was doing, and whether she missed him. Their four children had grown up and gone, and he thought how long the hours must be for her when he was away, with only her weaving for company. Once they had been full of love and fire for one another, just like Gunnar and the Faircrow, but now they had only the easy familiarity of long experience. He felt a sudden ache in his chest for Gudrun, and if she had been with him, he would have taken her in his arms, and told her he loved her. She would have been very surprised.

Chapter Fifteen

Silent Brigga's Dream

The Numen says somberly, it is too late to do anything now. Moera has already woven the design for this Gyretime. We will have to live with it, whether 'tis pleasing or no.

~~~~~~~~~~~~~

Tristan looked up from his book, unable for the moment to concentrate on the mathematics exercises his tutor had assigned, and sighed profoundly. When he had been made king, he naturally assumed his life would be a great deal more exciting than it had been in the past. He had imagined addressing the Deputies in the opulent Chamber with stirring words, attending high-level cabinet meetings where important matters of state were discussed, and traveling through the countryside in luxury, while visiting his grateful subjects. None of these things had come to pass. Instead, he toiled at his schoolwork with the very same teachers, while the business of the country continued to be managed exclusively by his Prime Minister, Philip Tremayne. He now suspected just how much of a figurehead he actually was, despite his father's reassuring words to the contrary.

To make matters worse, he missed his mother in a humiliatingly childish way. At least she had always made time to listen to his complaints and worries. He had not seen her since the day before his coronation, for she was no longer welcome in St. Valery. No-one bothered to explain the reason for this to Tristan, and he wondered if she had done something terribly wrong. His father always seemed busy with the defense of the City, and had only time for hurried greetings and patronizing pats on the head when they passed in the hall. Gwenn had been missing for most of a year, and no-one knew where she had gone to. At that moment, Tristan felt so isolated, he would have been glad to talk to anyone, even his sister.

As he stared off into the distance, pondering his lonely position at the top, the door to the study room flew open and Philip stepped through, followed by his father. The two were almost always together these days. Tristan greeted them eagerly, pleased to have some company at last. But they had not come to exchange small talk with a dejected boy.

Philip said curtly, "I need to talk to you about your sister, Tristan. I understand you were the last person to see her before she left St. Valery?"

Tristan nodded uncertainly; amazed his sister would be on anyone's mind at the moment, with the Fynäran invasion imminent.

Jacq asked urgently, "Did she say where she was going when she left here, Tris?"

He tried to think back and could not remember her saying anything as specific as that. "No, I don't think so; she just made a lot of vague threats. Why are you asking me about Gwenn now? She has been gone a long time, already."

Neither man answered his question. The Prime Minister's face grew somber. "What sort of threats, Tristan? You must tell us exactly what she said."

"I... Uh, I don't..."

Philip strode forward, grabbed him by the shirt front and shook him angrily, crying, "Think! It is very important."

Jacq stepped in and extricated his son from the Prime Minister's grasp, saying quietly, "Leave the boy alone, Philip. It is obvious he doesn't remember anything. Can you not let this ridiculous theory go?"

Philip turned to Jacq and said angrily, "Listen, Dinrhydan. I know you don't believe it, but the last reports filtering in from Secuny before we closed the borders said they were led by a tall, blond woman who fights like a demon."

Tristan's eyes went wide. "You think Gwenn leads the Fynäran raiders?" He smiled broadly. This unpromising day had just become much more interesting.

Jacq said resolutely, "There is not a scrap of proof it is Gwenn. Only some vague rumors, several weeks old, I don't believe we should be paying attention to. She is only sixteen, for the Gods' sake. How could anyone so young mobilize and lead a force of hundreds of men?"

Tristan added helpfully, "She *is* almost seventeen, Father," and Jacq gave him a black look.

Philip said placatingly, "Please, King Tristan, you must tell us what you know. Did your sister hold any grudge against the City?"

Tristan answered him sullenly. "She had no grudges I know of. Except..." He paused, unsure if he should reveal Gwenn's last words about their mother.

Philip, in his eagerness to extract the necessary information, forgot to be polite to his puppet ruler. "Go on, boy, tell us what she said."

The King replied truculently. "First let me hear you address me properly, Prime Minister. I am no-one's boy."

Philip snarled and made to shake Tristan again, and Jacq stepped hastily in between the two. "Come on, Tris. This is important. If you know something you must tell us right away." He looked worriedly at his son, afraid the boy held some piece of information that might implicate Gwenn further in the attacks by the Fynära. Jacq still did not believe she could be responsible. He had taught her honor and fealty as well as swordsmanship. But Tristan's next words did not reassure him.

Tristan stared at his father and said uncertainly, "She said she was angry at the Queen. That she would bring her to her knees. That she would make us pay — all of us, Father."

Philip gave a cry of dismay. "Why did you not mention this before now? Can you not see how important it is?" He paced back and forth across the study room, gesturing wildly. "She has the skills, thanks to you, Dinrhydan, and now she has the motive! It all fits, can you not see that? If only we had known sooner." He turned to Jacq angrily. "Your brainless son might have just cost us the battle for the City. I never should have made him king. His inferior breeding has obviously ruined him."

Jacq turned to the Prime Minister, and his eyes narrowed. "Have a care what you say of my son, Philip."

Philip said breezily, "Don't take it personally, Dinrhydan. I meant on his mother's side, only. Your bloodline is pure, beyond repute. I just wish the boy had more of your qualities."

Tristan stammered, "I did not think... That is, it did not seem important at the time. Gwenn always seemed angry about something. It was eerie, the way she used to go around talking to herself all the time. I thought they were just empty threats." Jacq gave Tristan a warning look, but the boy continued to speak. "She said our mother had lied to her about something, but she would never say what it was. What difference does it make anyway? If Gwenn leads the Fynära, I mean."

Philip gave an exclamation of disgust, leaving Jacq to explain. "If Gwenn is their leader, we have to change the whole defensive plan. She knows the Citadel inside and out, and that would give the Fynära a huge advantage in any sort of invasion. Do you see why it is so important now?"

The boy nodded, and the men turned to leave him. He said, "Wait! Can I not come with you? I want to help in the defense of Beaumarais." He added proudly, "I am the King, after all."

Neither man gave him a backward glance as they passed out through the door and left him with his books. He spent the rest of the day forlornly alone, as men scurried back and forth outside, obviously on important errands for the Prime Minister. Tristan, profoundly depressed, went to his room in the middle of the afternoon, crawled into bed, and pulled the covers and the pillow over his head, so that his personal contingent of guardsmen could not hear their King weeping.

As the day wore on, Arkady teetered on the edge of complete exhaustion. The sun beat down on him and the other oarsmen, and not a breath of wind stirred. The sea, broad and almost flat, stretched around them like a vast wasteland. Wearily, he pulled back on the oars again and again, praying the wind would pick up before he collapsed. Sven pushed them even harder than before, now that the two men had gone missing in the night. Arkady stole a glance at Huw, sitting across from him on the other side of the boat. Somehow, the Firaithi managed to keep going, though his excoriated back dripped blood onto the deck with every agonizing pull of the oars. The raiders muttered as they went about their business, and he could almost smell the apprehension infecting the ship's crew. Sven continued to bluff breezily, but Arkady reckoned even the big overseer felt fear. He smiled grimly, thinking after the coming night they would all feel much more afraid.

A welcome gust of wind puffed up the slack sail at last, and the ship picked up speed. The thralls were released from their benches, and herded up to the bow. A raider was left to stand guard over them. Arkady knew he would not be able to talk to any of the others until night fell and the darkness made a close watch impossible. He settled down to rest while he could, and soon he slept deeply.

A dream overtook him, in which he became a sea bird, skimming over the waves. In a burst of exuberant freedom, he flew high into the sky, looking down on the wide oceanscape below. He saw a tiny speck moving on the waters and swooped down to investigate. The speck became a recognizable shape — a ship, square rigged, and dragon-prowed, like those of the Fynära. Arkady flew closer and landed on the mast. The ship appeared to be empty, with the steering oar tied in a fixed position. No, there were two people on board after all. A blond woman lay on her back on the deck and moaned with pain, while a man squatted beside her.

Arkady woke abruptly, disturbed by the dream, and unable to piece together any meaning from it. He lay in the darkness, aware the motion of the ship was rapidly increasing. The wind shrieked a sinister song through the ropes, as waves slapped at the side of the boat like angry hands. The raiders were having a hurried discussion at the other end of the deck and Arkady strained to listen.

Sven said, "This storm is going to be the death of us. We need to make landfall as quickly as we can. Let's raise the sail and head for shore."

Another raider, evidently a more experienced sailor, stridently disagreed. "If you raise the sail now, we will surely founder. The coastline here is rocky and inhospitable. We need to lie ahull* and ride out the storm in deep water." Most of the other raiders appeared to agree with this second plan, but Sven was not convinced.

He said, "We cannot afford to lose any more men. With Dag and Furga gone, the thralls already outnumber us. I still say we should try to get back to land, while we still have control of the craft."

---

* Take down all sails and let the unanchored vessel drift where it will

The other raiders shouted down his objections, and one went forward to furl the sail. As he leaned forward, Arkady hit him in the back with a deadly black fireball, and he disappeared without a trace. The noise of the waves covered the sound of his lifeless body hitting the water.

Smiling grimly, Arkady waited for another raider to come within range. Soon a second man came to check on the first. The fire hit him in the side of the head, and he managed to scream before he fell over the side. Several others rushed forward, swords and axes in hand, as the heavens opened and rain fell in great sheets, drenching thrall and Fynära alike. After a quick headcount, the raiders knew their number had once again been reduced by two. Terrified, the men huddled together in a circle, swords pointing outwards, as the ship yawed wildly from side to side. Arkady clung to the deck as best he could, and sought Huw's arm, to prevent his brother from being swept away by the waves now breaking over the prow.

Occasional bursts of lightning illuminated the night. Arkady continued to pick off the raiders one by one. He did not bother now with stealth, for the panic-stricken raiders ran madly whenever one of their number fell to the deck.

Sven watched from the stern, and as a jagged bolt of lightning lit the sky, he saw Arkady call upon the fire and toss it towards one of his men. The man stiffened and fell, clutching at his chest. But Sven did not tell anyone amongst the crew what he had seen. Instead, his voice boomed out of the darkness, "Stop running, you idiots! Get down and cover yourselves with skins. Don't give whatever it is a target." He did not want to risk an insurrection if his men knew the truth — the white haired thrall was a wizard with the power to kill them all.

Huw shouted to him, "What is happening, Kadya? The raiders cry out in fear, as though some evil demon walked among them."

Arkady leaned forward and put his lips to Huw's ear. He said, "I am the demon."

The men hurriedly obeyed, and soon the deck stood empty save for the waterlogged bodies sloshing back and forth with the rocking motion of the boat. The wind speed increased, and Arkady hung on to the bales of cargo occupying the bow. An enormous wave almost sent the boat on its beam ends, and Huw lost his grip on Arkady's arm and slid down the deck. With a frantic cry, Arkady dived after him, as a jagged bolt split the towering clouds. Somehow, he was able to grasp Huw's breeches and hold on, as wave after wave pounded the ship.

Several other thralls rolled past them and were washed away, screaming, "Help us! By the gods, please..."

The next few hours were more hellish than any other Arkady had ever known. He became lost in a nightmare of darkness, with rolling seas, punishing waves and howling winds bearing ever more tumult and terror. Speech and even thought became impossible — life was reduced to clinging to whatever solid handholds could be found. Finally, Arkady managed to gather up Huw and get him back amongst the cargo. Then he untied one of the bales, and used the rope to tie them both to the deck. They held on to each other, until finally the wind spent itself, just as the sun rose through the bloody storm-wracked clouds.

Now the raiders warily uncovered themselves from their skins and looked around. Sven grunted forlornly. Only nine of his men remained alive, and several of those had lost their weapons in the general panic during the storm. He eyed the thralls uncertainly, trying to ascertain their number. He counted sixteen bedraggled slaves at the bow. Sven saw to his disappointment that Arkady stood among the survivors.

One of the other raiders whispered, "I don't trust that one, Captain. We never had any trouble before he joined the boat in Celeste."

Sven nodded silently in agreement. He watched while Arkady carefully untied the little blind thrall from his position among the cargo. His eyes narrowed. He knew he needed to act decisively, right now, to stop the thralls from taking over the ship. Nevertheless, Red Beard was well aware that a direct attack on the white haired thrall might mean death for them all. Within seconds, he had come up with a cruel, cunning plan. He whispered a few terse words to his men. They busied themselves carrying out his orders while Sven made a great show of removing his sword and laying it on the deck.

Arkady watched curiously as Sven walked forward, with his hands held open before him. The Fynära captain spoke with false humility, saying, "Who amongst you will speak for the thralls?"

Arkady immediately said, "I will. What do you want, filth?"

Sven, forgetting all pretence in the wake of this insult, raised his hand, saying, "Filth? Is that how you address your master?"

Huw said quietly from behind, "Be careful, Kadya, that man is still very dangerous."

But Arkady's escalating madness continued to eat away at his discernment, and he did not wish to listen to his brother's warning. He stepped forward until his face was just inches away from Sven's. "You are not our master. Not any longer. But you still need us to row, do you not?" He smiled cheerlessly and continued. "All the water casks have been washed overboard, and most of the food. The ship now lies becalmed, and her sail is in tatters. You are in trouble, Red Beard, and you know it. Tell your men to throw all their weapons overboard and then we will talk, not before."

During this speech, Sven kept his hands behind his back, and gestured to the raiders at the stern. He said loudly, "Do as this thrall says. We are all going to have to work together to get out of this alive." Several of the raiders walked casually to the gunwale and removed their weapons, as if they were about to follow the Captain's order. Arkady did not notice as others approached closer to the bow.

Urgently, Huw cried out, "Don't listen to him. He is lying — I hear it in his voice."

Huw's warning came too late. Several raiders rushed past him as Arkady spun round. He saw a raider now held his brother's head back by his ponytail, with a knife across his throat. Sven growled, "If you move so much as a muscle then this one dies. Do I make myself perfectly clear?" Arkady nodded slowly and dropped his hands to his sides.

Sven barked further orders as his men dragged Huw over to the mast. They threw him down on his knees and tied his hands behind his back with a rope that had been tossed over the yard — the high crosspiece holding the sail. Arkady watched in horror as Sven sauntered over to the other end of the rope, which dangled invitingly before him.

"Now let me show you something, filth. If I were to, say... pull down on this rope, your friend's arms would go up. Like this, see?"

He pulled down on the rope and Huw's arms were yanked up from behind, causing him to cry out in agony as his shoulder joints were cruelly twisted backwards. Sven smiled sadistically and slowly lowered the rope.

Then he said, "Now I would not want to have to pull that rope again, and haul this slave up by his arms to hang from the yard. It would not kill him, not right away, anyway, but it would be very, very painful. He might hang there for several days before he actually died. Isn't that right boys?"

The other raiders murmured in agreement as Arkady paled. Sven faced him and said, "Now get rowing, you lot, or I make a new pennant out of your friend here."

The other thralls looked at each other fearfully and shuffled forward to take their place at the oars. The raiders quickly moved among them, fastening their chains to the cleats. Arkady stood indecisively, his fists clenched in rage, and Sven pulled up Huw's arms again, this time a little bit higher. Huw sobbed raggedly, and Arkady could not bear to witness his brother's torment any longer. He sat down on the nearest bench, furiously cursing under his breath, and began to row.

Gwenn paused to listen as she crept along the dank passage that passed through the Citadel wall, leading to King Benedict's escape tunnel. She and her party of ten raiders had left the main invasion force at midnight, and made their way up the Ariane alone, after stealing a fishing dory from one of the docks on the river. Their progress across the Mere had been undetected, and it had taken her only a few moments to locate the secret lakeside door and open it. They had scuttled the dory so it would not be seen in the morning, and piled into the narrow passage, only lighting torches once the door had been shut again. The walls dripped with moisture, and cobwebs festooned every surface. The chittering of panicked rats could be heard further down the tunnel, but no other sound, other than the persistent dripping of water, met their ears.

She said softly, "The tunnel is relatively straight for the first hundred yards or so, and then we will come to a cave-in. We will have to squeeze through a narrow opening before we get to a ladder leading up to the main levels of the Citadel. Everyone must stay close together, for there will be other tunnels branching off right and left. Do you understand?"

The men, all from Torsten's *felag* and therefore unfamiliar to her, nodded one by one.

"Let's go, then."

As they traversed the tunnel, she heard them muttering behind her. "What are we doing down here, skulking around like sewer rats, I'd like to know?"

"Aye. There'll be no blood and fire for us here, I'll wager. How're we to earn our ticket to Skyre in this stinking hole?"

Another raider spat in contempt. "And to be led by a maid! If my sons get word of this I will never live it down. If Torsten hadn't ordered..."

Gwenn turned and glared at them, and they abruptly fell silent. She hissed, "Now listen carefully as I tell you what we must do. There is a group of pipes running from the Mere to the dry moat around the Citadel. In times of attack, the valves are opened to allow water to fill the channel, making it much more difficult to gain access to the three Citadel gates. Our first task is to disable the valves so the pipes cannot be opened. Do you understand?"

She looked back and saw the men nod in unison. "I know where the intake room is located, but it will most likely be heavily guarded. We will have to fight our way in, and hold off any further attempts to win it back. Meanwhile Torsten will attack the wharf area, and storm the front gate of the Citadel."

Gwenn paused as they reached the caved-in section of the tunnel. The raider carrying the torch stepped forward so she could see the extent of the blockage. A section of the roof had come down, scattering rocks and heavy beams across the tunnel. Subsequent flooding had made the floor a quagmire. Gwenn picked her way gingerly through the mud until she reached the last fallen beam. It ran diagonally across the tunnel from floor to ceiling, and behind it lay a solid mass of earth and stone.

The raider who carried the torch, Birger Lost Tooth, spoke up, saying flatly, "It is completely blocked, Miss. We will have to go back."

He did not sound upset.

Gwenn looked back and said impatiently, "I know it looks

blocked, but I managed to get through when I was a child. It can't have changed that much in ten years. Hold the torch up higher. The opening is close to the ceiling, if memory serves me aright."

She climbed up the diagonal beam, until she reached the top. Then she shifted sideways, scrambled up a few feet and disappeared through an almost invisible hole in the fallen earth. A few seconds later she poked her head through again and said brightly, "Come on, there is a wide space up here. We can pass through easily."

The men muttered disappointed curses, but followed her obediently through the hole before dropping down eight feet to the floor on the far side. Once assembled there, they moved forward again.

The tunnel on the near side to the blockage had been much more carefully maintained. Gwenn led them along the corridor swiftly and silently until she reached a long iron ladder, stretching up into the darkness above her head. This was the first part of King Benedict's escape route, and it once led directly to his private dressing room. More recently, the room formed part of Queen Katrione's private suite in the Citadel Tower, so Gwenn was quite familiar with its location. She started up the ladder and one by one the others followed. The light-bearer, Birger, had to grasp the torch in his teeth, and nearly singed his bushy beard.

Gwenn scampered up easily enough, but the others were soon sweating and breathing heavily.

She called back to them softly, "Quiet, you lot. We are in the inhabited part of the Citadel now."

The ladder went on and on, up four or five levels before it came to an abrupt end under a trap door. Gwenn gave the order to douse the light. She pushed up on the trap door, praying it would not be locked or covered by some heavy piece of furniture. To her surprise, it opened easily and she was able to hoist herself into the almost empty dressing room. A clerestory window let in plenty of moonlight, and she waited to let her eyes adjust before moving further. Several bits of clothing were scattered about on the floor. A tailor's dummy in the corner held an opulent looking purple robe. She crept over to examine it as the rest of the raiders made their way into the room. The dummy's featureless head had a slender gold crown resting on it.

Ketha said, "That is right, the new king sleeps just on the other side of the door over there."

Gwenn asked, "Who is it, Ketha? Who is the new king?"

Ketha chortled. "Why don't you go and see for yourself?"

Holding her breath, Gwenn opened the door into the bedroom and crept across the floor, with a line of raiders trailing behind her. A blanket-shrouded figure snored on the bed against the far wall. Moving with utmost caution, she made her way to the outer door of the room. She had just groped for the handle when the last raider to leave the dressing room tripped over a book carelessly left lying on the floor, and banged into the wall.

The occupant of the bed sat up, saying, "Father, is that you?" in a cracked voice.

Gwenn crossed the floor, and covered his mouth before he could call for help. The new king struggled but he was no match for her strength. He never had been. With sudden recognition, Gwenn stared into the panic filled eyes of her half-brother, Tristan Dinrhydan.

Ketha screamed in her mind, "Kill him! Now, before he can raise the alarm." Gwenn considered her options desperately, trying to find a way around the battle crow's order. She did not want her brother to die now, even though there had been many times in the past when she might cheerfully have murdered him.

Then she said quietly, "He will be more use to us alive, as a hostage, if he truly is the new king."

Reaching down, she removed the pearl-handled dagger from her boot and held it before Tristan's face. His eyes widened in fright and he made a whimpering noise under her other hand. Gwenn leaned forward so that she could whisper close to his ear. "I am going to move my hand now. If you cry out I will cut your throat, understood?" The boy nodded, staring in uncomprehending terror at the line of black-clothed men ringing his bed.

He whispered, "Gwenn, is that you? Have you come to take over the City with the Fynära?"

She nodded.

He said, "Father did not believe it was you they were talking about. He's going to be very angry when he finds out."

Gwenn made no answer to this. She could not allow herself

to think what terrible effect her betrayal would have on her Papa when he met her on the battlefield, so she whispered brusquely to one of the raiders, "Bind his hands and feet and gag him. He is coming with us." Then to a second man, "Check and see how many guards are outside the door."

After he had tied Tristan securely, one of the raiders slung him over his shoulder. Gwenn stepped silently into the anteroom, where three guards sat with their backs to the door, playing cards. Keth'fell flashed in the candlelight. None managed as much as a cry before she slaughtered them. Tristan closed his eyes in horror and began to cry, unable to watch such efficient brutality from his sister. The raider holding him shook him roughly in an effort to make him stop.

Gwenn listened as the tower clock chimed five times. They now had only one hour to secure the intake room before Torsten began the main invasion.

"Come on," she hissed. "We must hurry."

She led them out the door and across the narrow hallway into the room that used to be her own. Now it stood forlornly empty and as she crossed it, heading for the window, she briefly wondered where all her things had gone. Then her mind snapped back to the task at hand — climbing down the ivy covered Tower. She went first, so the others could watch her route. Once she reached the ground, the raider carrying Tristan began his descent. The boy clung to his captor in terror as the ivy creaked and swayed under their combined weight, but they made it safely down.

Seven other raiders followed one after the other, as Gwenn waited impatiently in the shadows. The last two, who inexplicably decided to climb down together, were not so lucky. Abruptly, the ivy sheared off the wall and they fell, screaming, thirty feet onto the parade field. One howled in pain, clutching at a compound fracture in his leg. Tristan could see the ends of the bone gleaming whitely in the moonlight and it made him want to vomit. Dogs started barking all over the Citadel, as Gwenn stepped out of the shadows. She dispatched the injured man with a casual thrust of her sword, and kicked at the lifeless body of his partner in frustration. The fools had cost her the element of surprise. Doors were thrown open in the barracks across the parade field, spilling light out on to the grass.

"Come on, we'll have to run for it now!" she cried, and set off for the low-roofed building next to the rampart facing the Mere.

The storm had driven the *Moon Drake* hopelessly off course in the night. Once the brightening sky heralded the dawn, Sven turned the boat back towards the east. He spoke to Olaf, his second in command. "The ship will never make it to Starruthe now. We'll have to take our chances on the mainland."

"It doesn't much matter where we wash up," Olaf agreed. "There are fishing villages all up and down this coast. We can find a sea-worthy boat to get us back to Einar. But what about victuals? There is hardly a mouthful of fresh water left, and no food to speak of."

Sven sniggered. "We are raiders, remember? All we have to do is drop in on some isolated farmstead. We can steal everything we need for the journey home, and maybe some women too. We can use them for rowing *and* entertainment."

"What are you going to do about the thralls?" Olaf asked nervously.

"Kill them all," said Sven. "Once we are in sight of land. The incoming tide will bring the *Moon Drake* the rest of the way to shore." Olaf sauntered off to inform the other remaining crewmembers of the Captain's plan.

Sven studied the white haired thrall, and fingered his knife. He would enjoy making that one suffer as much as he could before taking his life.

Arkady also watched the Fynäran Captain, when he could find the strength to raise his head. He knew the punishing pace Sven set for the rowers had a dual purpose. Certainly, he wanted to make land before nightfall, but he also wanted to incapacitate the remaining thralls so they could not fight. As hour followed hour of rowing, the pain unraveled his already fragile grip on reality. He watched in frustration as Huw, still on his knees by the mast, was subjected to a constant barrage of abuse by the raiders.

Arkady wondered if he would have to set the ship alight and perish along with the Fynära, in order to alleviate Huw's suffering. Just then, he saw a raider, who had been keeping watch at the bow, hurry back and whisper something to Sven. No doubt, he had just sighted land.

Arkady smiled grimly to himself. *Very well, it was high time for them all to die.*

He felt the fire burning in his belly and he let it rage until it felt as though his body must explode into flame.

Abruptly the air around him seemed to thicken and grow dark, and he no longer felt the smooth wood of the oar under his blistered fingers. A resonant pulsing rang in his ears, frightening him, but it was only the beating of his heart. Arkady stood up, forgetting the chain that attached him to the deck. His collar no longer restrained him. The images around him were faint and insubstantial, and he wondered if he had passed into some waking dream.

Then she came. She looked like Eira, except Eira never had skin as green as chrysoprase, or as luminous a drop of dew in the morning sun. He waited, holding his breath, as she walked towards him, and then she spoke. Her voice sounded like the whisper of wind through new spring grass. "My Seed Bearer, what is your purpose in this? I chose you to father the Dawnmaid. Will you now lose your life in the pursuit of some pointless retribution? My people need you."

He stammered, "He has to pay for the things he did to my brother, Hana. He has to..."

Hana smiled gently. "Can you feel no compassion for him?"

Arkady's reverent expression hardened. "No, I cannot. I have seen too much and experienced too much. Hatred burns in me. Why did you give me your fire if not to use it to cleanse the Yrth of scum? Shall I waste it?"

"My Fire will not be wasted, Seed Bearer. I gave it freely, for you to employ as you see fit. You have chosen to use it for destruction rather than healing. But do you not see? Hatred and revenge will not ease the pain you feel, nor the pain of our brother Huw. Think on what I have said. Farewell."

The darkness lifted and Arkady found himself back on the deck of the *Moon Drake*, with Hana's strange words still echoing in his mind. He could not shake the feeling there was something missing in his understanding — something that, in his rage and hurt, he had been unable to see before now.

Arkady watched as Sven casually rose from his seat by the steering oar and walked towards the mast. He did not doubt that the raider Captain meant to kill Huw now they had sighted land. The fire raged again, deep inside Arkady, and for the first time he questioned its purpose.

What did Hana mean when she said her fire could heal as well as destroy?

He knew he should send the fire straight for Sven, to save his brother's life, but for the first time since coming aboard the *Moon Drake*, indecision plagued him. He took his hands off the oar and formed the glowing ball between his fingers, but did not release it. What had she said?

Hatred and revenge will not ease the pain you feel...

Sven had reached Huw now, and the knife flashed as he raised it. The other thralls cried out in alarm. Time slowed to a crawl.

Something missing...

Suddenly, it came to him, an insight so paralyzing he hesitated until it was almost too late to act. He felt the fire change in his hand — change from blistering heat to comfortable warmth, from blood red to pure white. As the others watched in horror, he threw the fireball directly towards his brother, Huw Adaryi. He screamed when it came in contact with him, and Arkady had a blinding moment of self-doubt.

He saw Huw's body stiffen as the rippling flames took him — white fire to cleanse utterly. Sven dropped the knife and backed away in terror, crying "Holy Father of Ods!"

Huw floated up before him, no longer bound by the rope, or even the bonds of Yrth. He hovered above the deck, now only a vague halo of fire, rotating gently as a sudden fresh breeze fanned the white flame and carried with it the scent of frangipani. The pulsing of the flames increased and subtle colors appeared, like a rainbow in a spray of water.

As abruptly as it began, it finished, and Huw's form appeared again as he sank gently down to the deck. He was naked, but no more did his brown skin bear the mark of whip or chain. The putrid flesh on his back was smooth and whole. The scars on his eyelids were gone. The others muttered fearfully at this astounding transmutation, but Arkady did not hear them. He rose slowly, as far as his chain would allow, and softly called his brother's name.

Huw's eyes were tightly closed, and as he opened them for the first time, he cried out, then covered his face with his hands. "The light! Ach, it burns. I can see the light, Kadya."

Huw staggered forward, using his hand to shade his face, and unhooked Arkady's chain from the cleat. They stood close together without speaking, while Huw tried to wipe the moisture streaming from his eyes. He said, in a voice filled with wonder, "I am healed. You made me whole again. I thought that madness had taken you, my brother, and I felt very sad. But you have conquered the demon, have you not?" Then he stepped forward into his embrace.

The raiders, huddled at the stern, did not move or speak. Even Sven, who would never have admitted to fear, kept his eyes downcast as Arkady walked towards him. A long moment passed as their former thrall made his way to the back of the boat, unhooking the chains of the other thralls as he went. Each man stood and stretched, and silently followed behind.

Chapter Sixteen

Berbiroc

Geya looks stricken and the Numen laughs heartily. Never mind little Geya, we all make mistakes. I am sure this one will be rectified sooner or later. But the next time you decide to help, ask one of us elders first.

The younger Amaranthine has the grace to look abashed.

~~~~~~~~~

Once inside the shed housing the water intakes, Gwenn ordered her men to lock the door. The man carrying Tristan unceremoniously dumped him in the corner and he landed hard on the packed earth floor. He gazed around the bleak, whitewashed room in dismay. It held little, except for a fireplace along one wall, and a table and chairs, recently vacated by the guards. A game of cards lay half-played on the table, and the scattered remains of someone's breakfast. The bodies of six Guardsmen lay just outside, where they had fallen. Though they had fought well, they were no match for keth'fell and the swords of the Fynära.

The furious sounds of pursuit echoed across the Citadel walls — many men had poured out of the barracks once it became clear who the fleeing figures were. Gwenn peered through the barred window and shivered as she saw the man who rode before all the others, on Minerva, hurriedly pulling a shirt over his head. It was her stepfather, Jacq Benet. Soon he would be at the door, and then...

She barked an order, "Break off those handles somehow. We must disable the system. Lars, get to work with the sledgehammer."

The eight pipes came through the ramparts at a ninety-degree angle, and disappeared under the floor. Each had a metal, wheel-shaped stopcock. They were massive, and made of brass. Gwenn remembered watching Jacq forge them in the smithy, when she was just a little girl, to replace the older, narrower ones. How proud and grown up she had felt as he explained in detail about the defensive potential of water.

Tristan whimpered and Gwenn kicked him roughly. She snarled, "Don't make me have to kill you, little brother. Our situation here is desperate, and I will not hesitate to take your life if it suits me."

He fell silent, though his shoulders continued to tremble as he cried soundlessly. At that moment, Gwenn felt the crushing weight of every one of her unhappy choices over the years, though Ketha's voice, as always, disagreed stridently. Gwenn said to the battle crow, "Go out and check on the men outside. I need to know how many there are, and what kind of weapons they bear."

Ketha reluctantly agreed. As her head appeared from Gwenn's chest, Tristan tried to crawl further into the corner, squeezing his eyes shut in absolute terror. Once Ketha left, Gwenn knelt and touched his arm awkwardly. His eyes flew open and he shook his head in a silent plea for mercy. Gently, she removed his gag, forgetting for a moment her vital mission and the men massing outside the doors.

She whispered, "Shhh... Don't cry, Tris. I will not let anything happen to you, I swear it."

He gulped audibly. "What... What was that thing? It came out of you."

She sighed. "It doesn't matter. Soon she will be gone from me forever. Look, I know you are afraid and I don't blame you, but you must trust me. Just do as I say, and don't try to escape. My men might kill you, before I could stop them. Can you do that?"

He nodded uncertainly and gave her a half smile. Tristan could not help bragging just a little, now he was not quite so scared. "I bet you were surprised to find out I am the new king of Beaumarais, eh Longshanks?"

She grinned at him in return. "Just goes to show how bad things must have gotten since I left, little Shrimp." One of the raiders called for her, so she gave him a reassuring pat on the leg and stood up.

As she turned to go, he asked nervously, "Gwenn, are you going to fight Father?"

She shrugged. "I don't know. Probably." She had to shout over the incredible racket her men made as they pounded at the stop-cocks with their axes and the sledgehammer.

He pleaded with her. "Please don't kill him. Promise me you will not."

"There is no chance of that, I swear it. In fact..."

She paused and turned away. He called after her, "What were you going to say?"

"Nothing. Just forget it. I have to go now."

Ketha fluttered back down the chimney, and lit on the mantle. She spoke silently to Gwenn. "There are two hundred men just outside the door. Your stepfather and the Prime Minister lead them. They know you hold the king hostage and that is the only reason they have not yet attacked. But we have only to hold them off a few more minutes. Even now, Torsten is crossing the Mere with his twenty ships and he will soon set upon the wharves with fire and steel."

She entered Gwenn, as Torsten's men watched fearfully. They had succeeded in disabling the water system and now they clustered about the window, staring out into the grey dawn. They muttered amongst themselves, sure they would be unable to fight their way past the many grim men waiting, with swords in hand, outside the locked door.

One asked uneasily, "What would you have us do now, Faircrow? Fight to the death?"

"No. We will move out, with the king as our hostage. They will not dare touch us if they think it will endanger his life. I will guard the boy, while you make your escape up the ramparts. Once there, try to destroy as many of the cannon as you are able. Then jump into the Mere and swim for it. You should be able to meet up again with your Magnus at the main gate of the Citadel. Do you understand?"

Most of Torsten's men felt no *felag* to this strange, possessed girl. They nodded, their relief plain, except Lars, who said thoughtfully, "How will you escape, Faircrow? Once we are gone, you will be left to face them with no-one at your back. I would stay and stand with you, if I may." He did not think such a beautiful maid should have to die alone.

She smiled and refused his gallantry. "I have another task yet to complete. But I thank you for the offer, Lars. Now make yourselves ready. Once we get outside, run to the left and straight up the stairs. There may be some guards on the top of the rampart. You will have to kill them if they get in the way. Od's fortune to all of you."

Ignoring the questions Ketha screamed in her mind, she cut the bonds holding her brother's legs with the pearl handled dagger. "Get up," she hissed to him, and he rose uncertainly. She held the knife to his throat, and only her reassuring words of a moment before kept him from crying out in fear. After dragging him over to the door, she said to Lars, "Open it wide, so they may see their king."

The door swung open and she looked straight into the eyes of her stepfather. Horrified recognition spread across his face. He took in her black clothing, and the desperate looking men that crowded around her back. Keth'fell dangled from the baldric he had lovingly made with his own hands. Jacq looked physically ill. He said hoarsely, "Goldilocks, my Gods. I cannot believe it. How could you betray me like this? Let your brother go."

"I am sorry. That I cannot do. Hear me, Jacq; the king dies if you attack. Now tell your men to back off."

The men behind her stepfather murmured in consternation as Philip ordered, "Let the bitch kill the boy. What does it matter? His blood is tainted anyway, just as hers is, by her Firaithi grand-mother. Is it any wonder she is a traitor? We must free those intakes or risk the whole City. Give the order to attack. I can eas-ily find a new king once the battle is over."

Jacq shook his head violently. "No! Those are my children you speak of."

He turned and addressed the waiting Guardsmen, "Stand back, all of you. No-one is to move without my order."

Philip gave him a poisonous look, but did not object further. As the Guardsmen stepped back, Torsten's men broke away and up the rampart stairs. Several men started to follow, so Gwenn tightened her grip on her brother and raised the knife higher. Jacq cursed and called them back, as the raiders disappeared over the edge of the wall.

He studied his daughter for a long moment and spoke qui-etly, as though she was the only person on the parade ground with him. "What do you want, Goldilocks? Why have you come back here?"

The tears in his eyes almost broke her heart, but she had come too far to lose her resolve now. Gwenn said harshly, "I came back to fight you. To prove once and for all I am greater than the mighty Dinrhydan. Do you accept my challenge?"

He stared at her uncomprehendingly. "I cannot fight you — not like that. This is not some practice contest between the two of us. You are my daughter. I will not have your blood on my hands."

Gwenn sighed deeply as she regarded her stepfather, and noticed for the first time the grey stubble on his cheeks and the silver hair at his temples. Somehow, he looked so much older now than she remembered, though it had been only a year since she had last seen him. His broad shoulders, that had provided so much comfort to her as a little girl, sagged with sorrow. But she knew she would have to intensify his pain and humiliation, in order to make him fight. She took a deep breath and forced herself to continue — though it was the hardest thing she had ever done — to destroy the man she loved more than any other.

She screamed, "You are *not* my father. Do you hear me? You are nothing to me." Her voice echoed harshly around the parade field. Tristan gasped aloud, unable to believe his sister's cruelty. Jacq fell back as though she had struck him, and put a hand to his face. His eyes, when they met hers again, held a look of unmitigated wretchedness, like a dog that has been beaten after proudly bringing his master a bone.

Still he kept his voice low, and ignored the consternation of the men around him. "Don't say that, Goldilocks. Have you lost your wits? Of course I am your father." Jacq felt sure now his daughter had somehow been unhinged by her experiences with the Fynära. He took two slow steps towards her with his hand outstretched, saying, "Just give me the knife, sweetheart. Then I can fetch your mother. She will know what to do for you."

Gwenn backed away from him while keeping the knife close to her brother's Adam's apple. How could she say what needed to be said next? It would truly break him. But Gwenn, in her desperate desire to be free of Ketha's torment, could see no other way. She said, through her tears, "My mother is a lying whore. All these years you thought I was yours, did you not? But she betrayed you, with Tomas de Vigny. He is my real father. Do you understand me? While you rotted in prison she gave herself to him."

Tristan screamed, "Stop it, Gwenn. How could you?" She nicked his cheek with her knife, and he abruptly fell silent again. The guardsmen around them shook their heads in horror. Would the Dinrhydan do nothing to stop this girl's mouth from dripping further poison?

These words from his beloved Goldilocks pierced Jacq to the core. It was as though she had cut his heart out with a flaming knife and handed it to him on a platter. He said, brokenly, "No, it cannot be true. Your mother would not... Not with him."

Gwenn fumbled in the pouch she wore on her belt and retrieved the braid of hair she had stolen from her mother. She held it up for him to see, and threw it down at his feet. "I took this from her. She kept it hidden from you, Jacq, in a locked chest. It is his hair, and hers, entwined together, just as their bodies were, when they made me..."

He picked up the hair and studied it, and Gwenn thought she might die from seeing his anguish exposed, so raw and naked in front of her. His lips trembled uncontrollably and he bit down hard. He would not cry now, not in front of this hideous monster he had once loved as his own child.

Instead, he screamed at her, and drew his sword, d'angwir. "No! You are lying. You must be. Kat would never do that. Take it back, or I swear I will kill you."

Jacq's eyes brimmed with his utterly broken-hearted sorrow, and Gwenn found she could no longer look on him. She dropped her eyes and said softly, "You know it is true. Look at me. Do you not see the face of your enemy?"

A mounted Guardsman, pressing his steed to the limit, could be seen flying across the parade field. He reined hard and dismounted, then whispered a message to the Prime Minister. Philip blanched and tugged urgently at Jacq's sleeve. "Dinrhydan, listen to me. The rest of her men are attacking the wharves. You must go and direct the defenses."

Jacq ignored him completely, wrapped up as he was in the study of his daughter's face. Now that he knew, he could plainly see Tomas' features, still sharp in his mind from so many years of nightmares, in hers.

He put a hand on his mouth and stifled a broken cry, then turned to the Prime Minister, saying woodenly, "Take the men and go, if you will. I have something to finish here first, with this cursed spawn of that devil, de Vigny."

Jacq paid no more attention to Philip's protestations, and soon the Prime Minister gave the order for the guardsmen with them to hurry to the wharves for the defense of St. Valery.

There were only four people left on the parade field as Gwenn stepped away from the deep shadow of the rampart wall. Jacq, who had not taken his eyes off her since she told him who her true father was, waited silently while she let go of Tristan and pushed him away from her. He fell to the ground, and crawled back inside the door of the intake house, crying openly at his mother's terrible betrayal and his father's pain. Philip followed him inside, and simply stepped over his prostrate form. He only wanted to see if anything could be done to salvage the water system.

Gwenn stared back at her stepfather, and saw the hatred writ plain on his face. There was no doubt in her mind he meant to kill her now and she smiled grimly. She knew he was the only person on Yrth with enough skill to defeat her in a sword battle. It was what she wanted, was it not — to die at his hand? To be free of Ketha forever? No more killing or stealing, no more running and hiding, only an endless sleep without dreams. She only hoped she might have a moment before she died to tell her Papa Bear that she truly loved him.

Drawing keth'fell with a flourish, she stepped into the wan sunlight, and they began.

It did not take Gwenn very long to see that her carefully thought out plan had somehow gone grievously wrong. Perhaps it was because she now had a whole year's experience with fighting and killing many men, or maybe her unhappy revelation had completely unmanned her stepfather, but it soon became blindingly obvious he was in no way capable of besting her in their present contest. His reactions were glacial, his sword thrusts feeble. She parried him with ease, and soon had to take care not to injure him, as he stumbled before her, weak and sweating.

"Come now, Jacq!" she taunted unmercifully. "Where is the Dinrhydan hiding? If I did not know better I might believe I was fighting one of the lead-footed farm boys I trounced in Secuny."

But even with this provocation, he did not improve. He was the Dinrhydan no longer, only a pathetic fool who had just lost everything he cared for. Gwenn cursed her own ill-conceived hope and easily disarmed him, just as Philip and Tristan stepped back on to the field.

Jacq fell to his hands and knees, utterly broken, as Tristan cried, "Gwenn, no! You promised me."

Ketha's voice, silent during the brief battle, sprang to life. "That is right. Now finish him off so we can go down into the City and help Torsten. What are you waiting for, girl?"

Gwenn did not strike. She stared wildly around for a few seconds, delirious with grief, and then started running, following the route her men had taken earlier, up the rampart steps.

Just as she reached the top of the stairs, Philip Tremayne produced a flintlock pistol from inside his frock coat. He shot the fleeing girl in the back. She screamed, and fell over and over, back down the stairs, before landing in a crumpled heap at the bottom. With a cry of absolute horror, Jacq rushed to her side, and knelt there, as she gasped for breath. Mechanically, he straightened her twisted limbs, while she cried out in her terrible pain. He cradled her broken body close to his chest and sobbed, his grief now unfathomable.

She raised her hand and touched his face, leaving a bloody smudge on his cheek. "Papa Bear..." Her voice was so weak he had to lean right over to make out her next words. "I am very sorry I hurt you. I wanted you to kill me, you see. Ketha would not let me go. I did not mean any of it. You truly are my father and I love you more than anything, even if..."

She stopped to gather breath, and a moan escaped her lips before she could bite it back.

Jacq wept softly. What difference did it make now who had planted the seed to give this child life? He had raised her, taught her everything, loved her fiercely and protected her from all harm, up until the moment she left him, on her sixteenth birthday. Was she not his true daughter in all the ways that mattered?

He said in a choked voice, "Don't talk, Goldilocks. I understand what you are trying to say. Save your strength, sweetheart."

She smiled at him, and the blood welling from her mouth stained her teeth and her lips bright red. Her tongue had been half bitten off in her fall down the stairs. "Am I still your Goldilocks, Papa Bear? I only wanted you to be proud of me..." Her voice trailed off, and her blue eyes, once so vibrant and alive, slowly closed, until the lashes lay dark and luxuriant on her pale skin. At that moment, she looked just like her mother.

He lowered her gently back down to the ground and stood, as Philip joined him by the rampart stairs. Jacq said angrily, "You shot her. You shot my little girl. How could you do that, Philip?"

Philip had never been a tactful man. He shrugged as he handed Jacq d'angwir, saying brusquely, "She was getting away. Good riddance to bad rubbish, eh Dinrhydan? I knew she was no child of your loins, not after the way she behaved. It just goes to show you, everything we believe about purity is absolutely true. Now let's go and see if we can exterminate the rest of the scum that washed up with her."

Jacq turned on him, in such a blind and unreasoning rage that the Prime Minister cowered in fear. He hissed, "She *is* my child, and always will be. I am proud of her, and of Tristan. I don't give a damn about purity and bloodlines anymore. Now shut your mouth or I will kill you, I swear it."

Philip unwisely snapped back, "You disappoint me greatly. I thought I could always count on you to protect the sanctity of Beaumarais. I can understand that finding out that your wife is a lying trollop might upset you, but I still take your threat very seriously."

With an inarticulate cry of rage, Jacq swung d'angwir. The Prime Minister fell and his blood stained the grass a bright, pure red. Philip's head rolled until it lay at Tristan's feet, separating itself from its periwig along the way.

He looked down at the grisly trophy and then at his father, crying in dismay, "You murdered the Prime Minister, Father! Who will lead the country now?"

From behind them, Gwenn called out, "Papa, are you there? Don't leave me."

Jacq quickly turned from his son, saying coldly, "You lead them. You wanted to be King. Now go and do your job."

Tris stared helplessly at his broad back as he walked away. He pleaded, "But Father, you have to stay and help. You gave your oath to defend me, remember? The City will be lost without the mighty Dinrhydan."

Jacq shot back over his shoulder, "The Dinrhydan is dead, son. I have nothing left to give St. Valery. I don't even care about this cursed city anymore. Let her fall to the Fynära, it is no more than we deserve. I was a fool to listen to Philip's lies. Your mother was right all the long."

"But where will you go?"

"Home to Acorn. I am taking Gwenn home to die. Farewell, Tristan."

Tristan watched as he bent and gathered Gwenn up as carefully as he could, but still she cried out in agony. A short whistle brought Minerva to his side, and he mounted the horse awkwardly, with Gwenn slung over one shoulder. Once in the saddle, he cradled the girl gently on his lap, and guided the horse into a gallop, heading for the Yoke and Acorn. He prayed Katkin would be there, and could somehow heal their daughter as she had once healed him as he lay under an oak tree, gravely injured. De Vigny had shot himself under the very same tree.

Jacq had never believed his wife's version of the events on that day — that Tomas had killed himself so Death might take his soul instead of Jacq's. Now as he passed quietly through the Acre, with his dying daughter in his arms, he wondered again why de Vigny had given up his life, especially if he knew the child Kat bore was his own. Was it possible Tomas had actually done it out of unselfish concern?

And why in the gods' names had his wife given herself to de Vigny in the first place? Jacq steadfastly refused any further conjecture. That path led only to additional torment, and he could cope with nothing more, not now.

Tristan stood for a long time in the empty parade field, with Philip Tremayne's beheaded corpse as his only companion. The twisted braid of hair Gwenn had thrown at his father's feet still lay on the ground, trampled and muddy. Bending down, he extricated it from the grass, and thoughtfully put it in his pocket.

He found himself thinking gleefully, "*At least she will soon be dead. Serves her right, after all the terrible things she said about Father.*"

But then he dashed angry tears from his eyes as the bitter truth sank deep. His father, the True Heart, had chosen the illegitimate daughter of his worst enemy over Tristan — his own flesh and blood.

Chapter Seventeen

Lut's Hammer

Hieronymus gives a cry of alarm and sits up. The Numen narrows her eyes, and listens with grave attention. Then she turns to Geya and says abruptly, What have you done, wicked one? This is no foolish attempt to help!

Geya rises to her feet and quickly backs away. What do you mean, Grandmother? I have done nothing. Nothing at all.

The expression on the old woman's face frightens her.

The Numen stands as well, much more slowly, and gropes for her staff. She limps toward Geya, crying, "Murderer!"

She throws up her hands in mock horror. "It was not *me*, Numen. Raven..."

~~~~~~~~~~

When Jacq arrived back at Acorn, the house stood cold and dark. He carried Gwenn into her bedroom, calling frantically for Katkin as he passed through the house. When she did not answer, Jacq knew he would have to care for his daughter himself, as best he could. After he had laid her carefully on her side, he steeled himself to look at her injuries. He saw immediately that her left leg was broken. After checking to make sure that she was unconscious, he set it, and the bones made a sickening grinding noise as they came together again. Next, he methodically set her broken right arm, and removed the pistol ball from the flesh in her back with his knife, before tightly bandaging the bleeding hole. Though Jacq had never had any medical training, he had been performing such rough first aid on battlefield casualties for many years and his work was efficient, if not terribly pretty.

He knew his daughter had lost a lot of blood already, so he covered her warmly with a quilt, and sat by the bed morosely, waiting for her to breathe her last. But she did not. After a time she stirred, as though she felt great pain, and he stroked her forehead.

Inside her, Ketha seethed at Gwenn's betrayal, and wondered what she could do now her vessel was incapacitated, paralyzed from the waist down, where the pistol ball had shattered her spine. Ketha did not have the power to mend such a grievous wound. She could keep the girl alive, forever if need be, but that would gain her nothing if she was locked in a broken body.

Ketha turned her attention to the human sitting by Gwenn's side. She had an errand to complete with this man. Something her sister Geya seemed to think was very important.

Gwenn's body stiffened as a curious mound formed in the covers. Jacq leaned towards her, intending to hold her close to him before she died. He stared in horror as the black head of a crow poked its way out from under the quilt. The crow sat on her chest for a second or two and then flew over to the footboard of the canopy bed.

Jacq asked, "What manner of foul being are you? Answer me, or I will slay you, here and now."

He drew d'angwir and stood ready to stab at the crow. With a rustle of iridescent feathers, it rose from the bed and then, in a motion seemingly both sharp and blurred at once, an opaque stain spread from mid-air to the ground. Jacq found himself staring into the dark eyes of a petite, raven-haired woman. He colored and quickly averted his eyes, for she wore no clothing, although he was not so foolish as to turn his back on her. Ketha laughed at him.

She said, "Do you honestly not know who I am, Jacq?"

He remembered then what Katkin had told him about their daughter and the fell creature who lived inside of her. So this was the battle crow, Keth Dirane. Jacq stared at the woman she had become and said angrily, "Yes, I know who you are and what you have done. Gwenn lies dying now because of it." He raised d'angwir, but hesitated as she spoke again.

She said softly, "Kill me and you lose all chance of seeing your daughter whole once more. I can cure her of all her wounds."

Jacq replied harshly, "She desired death at my hand rather than endure another hour of your presence, carrion-eater. Begone and trouble her not. Let her die in peace."

Ketha smiled cunningly. "I will do as you ask, in return for one small boon from you. Otherwise, I will have to keep your daughter alive and in agony, until I can find another to grant it."

Jacq scratched his head in confusion. "What is it you want from me, Ketha?"

She stepped forward until she stood very close to him. Her body smelled fetid, like some rotting thing. Ketha raised her hand and ran it down his chest. Her hideous black nails made him, who feared nothing, want to run from her, and cower in some dark place like a terrified beast. But he found his trembling legs would no longer obey him.

She whispered, in a voice full of menace, "I want your seed, human. You must couple with me, now, and in return I will leave Gwenn alone." Looking down, he saw her filthy, matted hair was crawling with vermin.

Jacq regarded her with pure loathing. "No... I will not. I am married and my wife..."

She did not allow him to finish. "Did not your wife dally once with another? She would tell you it was for a good cause." Her hands searched lower, and Jacq's eyes went wide as he felt the inevitable physical reactions to her touch. How could someone who filled him with utter revulsion elicit such a crushing need?

He tried again to escape her. "I said I cannot. I feel no desire for you, whore crow, only disgust. I would never be able to do what you ask of me, because of it."

She smiled at this, and he could see her teeth were yellow and pointed, like a rats. Once more, her carrion stench assailed his nostrils, making bile rise to the back of his throat. Nevertheless, when she pulled him by his shirt front, he followed along behind her, as though he had lost the will to control his own body. When they reached the big double bed in the main room, she shoved him backwards and he fell across it. His hands, without conscious effort on his part, unlaced his trousers.

She watched in amusement as he struggled against himself. "It will not help, you know. I will have your seed. I can make it pleasant for you, human, or painful. It is your choice."

She climbed on the bed beside him, and Jacq shivered uncontrollably as the need to have her took him completely. Yet in all the time they coupled, as he pressed into her again and again, he was aware of a degrading horror sickening him to his very core. He knew he would never again be completely free of it. The end was painfully intense, almost making him pass out, and completely without pleasure.

Once he had finished he felt her control of him slacken and he rolled away as quickly as he could. The black edges that had feathered his vision during his climax remained, leaving him drained and dizzy. He fumbled with his trousers and staggered back towards Gwenn's room. In a matter of seconds, a pounding headache developed in his temples, and he clutched at his brow in agony. Black spots danced in front of his eyes, and his vision retracted into a narrow tunnel.

Her voice came merrily from behind him. "What is wrong, lover? Do you miss my touch already?" She laughed harshly as he fell to his knees.

Jacq's heart began to beat wildly, as though it wanted to bang a hole through his chest and leap forth. His breath came in great, shuddering gasps. "What have you done to me, you filthy whore?"

She walked over to where he had fallen, and stood before him, still naked, openly gloating. He tried with all his might to crawl away from her, but he could no longer make his muscles obey.

"I took your seed from you, human, as I said I would. But I might have forgotten to mention I needed your *anafireon** as well. A lesser man would be dead already, but you... Well, even a most extraordinary specimen like you will die without it, very soon. A pity, for I had hoped to feast on that magnificent body of yours before I left. No matter."

Her voice became brisk and businesslike. "Now, you must excuse me, for this female form tires me greatly and I must hurry back to your poor, injured little girl. But don't fret, Jacq, I will make sure she lives a long, long time. So long, that life itself becomes unremitting torture as the muscles putrefy on her crumbling bones. Then perhaps, when there is nothing left of your darling daughter but an agonized, quivering lump of flesh, I will release her. Rest in peace, lover boy."

A limitless blackness filled Jacq's soul. She had tricked him, and stolen the very marrow from his bones. Now he lay dying and could do nothing to stop her as she went to prey on his daughter

---

* The eternal element, latent in all living things. The soul.

again. He cried out in frustration as she sauntered past him, "No! Don't do this, please..." and vainly clutched at her thighs.

She turned and raked her black fingernails across his cheek, and he screamed as the flesh was ripped to the bone. Jacq fell onto his face, writhing as the last drops of life were squeezed from his veins. Pain wracked every nerve in his torso, such pain as he had never imagined he could feel, as his body failed. He tried to retreat into the comfort of memory, to the unfettered creature he had once been. But it seemed Ketha had stolen even his deepest sense of himself, for Dai could no longer remember the feeling of his strong grey wings carrying him across the heavens, to the silence between the stars.

With a final gasp, he rolled over onto his back, and gazed up at the ceiling of the house Katkin had rebuilt for the two of them to live in together. Everything he had given up had been for her. Why had he ever left her alone? Slowly, the darkened beams faded to blackness.

Katkin sat by the lonely grave of Tomas de Vigny. She had been talking to him most of the last hour, as the spring sun warmed the stone bench. Blue forget-me-nots covered the grass around his burial mound, and a clinging vine grew up around the headstone, framing the inscription in white flowers. The morning was filled with extraordinary peace in the tranquil and silent grove.

She reflected on the latest word William had brought from St. Valery, when he came yesterday to help her move the cows from one paddock to an adjoining one. "There is no news of the Fynära, ma'am. Some people are saying that the whole thing is just a joke."

She asked him seriously, "What of the Dinrhydan? Does he say so?"

William shook his head firmly, "No ma'am. Your husband says if it is a joke, then he is not laughing."

Katkin lingered long by the grave, unwilling to return to her empty house now William had returned to the City. A breeze picked up and sent the forget-me-nots flailing wildly. The sun passed behind a cloud, making the temperature under the tree drop sharply. She shivered and anxiously looked around her.

In the deep shadow under the oak, she found him at last. As

Tomas approached her, she noticed his form now looked more substantial and the colors on his tattered uniform were bright. Tomas stopped in front of her, his expression somber.

He whispered, "Go home at once. Your husband and child have need of you."

He touched her face briefly, and this time it felt as though a feather brushed her cheek. Then he passed her, swiftly and silently gliding down the path leading into the Acre.

She wondered at his increasing presence in the material world, and what it might foretell. Katkin cried out, "Tomas, what has happened? Where are you going?" He did not answer her. After watching him disappear into the forest, she mounted Alys and kicked her hard, sending the pony galloping back to Acorn.

As she drew up into the yard, nothing appeared out of the ordinary and she gave a relieved sigh. She saw Minerva straying free on the grass and smiled, thinking Jacq had come back to her. Katkin dismounted and hurried towards the house. Her brief flicker of happiness died once she saw the trail of fresh blood leading across the porch and up to the front door. The splashes of blood led to the new wing, and she almost tripped over her husband's inert form in her haste to follow it.

She uttered a choked cry as she knelt before him. Shaking him gently, she said, "Jacq! Jacq! Please wake up." But he did not respond to her touch.

Automatically, her medical training took over as she tried to fight down her panic. With a trembling hand she checked him for signs of life, and injuries. Other than a nasty laceration on his cheek, he had no visible wounds — nevertheless his condition was obviously grave. His pulse and respiration were almost too faint to detect.

She stood and pulled the quilt off the bed, and covered him. His eyes fluttered open. Katkin knelt again as he said, very faintly, "My wife, are you here with me? I prayed you would come, before the end." She nodded, and then stared at him fearfully when he did not respond. His wide-open eyes were blank and almost lifeless. Katkin picked up his hand and held it up to her cheek.

"I am here, my love. What happened? Can you tell me?" She tried hard to make her voice sound strong, so he would not know how much his haggard countenance frightened her.

He whispered, "She came. Out of Gwenn. She made me..."

Katkin did not know, at first, what he meant, so she asked, "Gwenn? You have seen our daughter? Where is she?" She took the edge of the blanket and gently wiped away the trail of spittle that leaked from her husband's mouth and dripped down the grey stubble on his cheek.

Jacq's remaining strength was almost gone, but he tried to make his wife understand. "She lies in yonder bedroom. Philip shot her in the back. I killed him — for that, and for what he said about you. You were right about him all along. I never should have listened to his poison." He paused for a long moment, breathing raggedly, and Katkin wondered if he would ever speak again. Then he said, slowly, "I know about you and de Vigny. Gwenn told me."

She put her hand over her mouth to stifle a moan. How could she now explain to her husband the difficult choice she had made on that summer day long ago? Sighing deeply, she said, "Jacq, I thought you were going to be executed, so I made a bargain with Tomas. It was the only way he would let me see you. I know I should have told you afterwards, but he made me swear I would not. He thought you might not love Gwenn if you knew. I am so sorry..."

Jacq shook his head, almost imperceptibly, and put his hand over her lips. "No need... to say anything more. I just wanted you to know it doesn't matter. I should have forgiven him long ago. He gave me a daughter, and seventeen extra years with you." He blindly ran his fingers over her face. "My beautiful girl... You stole my heart from me, on the day we first met." Now he trembled uncontrollably, and cried through his chattering teeth, "Cold... I am so cold, my love. Everything is dark now. Will you hold me, just for a little while?"

Katkin could not dam up her tears any longer. She stretched out full length beside him on the floor, wrapped her arm across his chest, and cried bitterly. He twined his almost numb fingers in her hair, and comforted her as best he could.

After a time, he said urgently, "She has gone back into Gwenn. You must..." He stopped and coughed, then shuddered as a fresh wave of pain hit him.

Katkin raised her head from his chest and stared at his face. Now his skin had turned a sickly color, the color of ashes, cold and long dead. She knew the end was very near. "Who are you talking about? Ketha? You saw her?" The realization sank in. "Gwenn's demon did this to you?"

He nodded painfully. "Ketha made me lay with her. I did not want to. You must believe me. The putrid stench of her fills me, even now. She says she will keep Gwenn alive, keep her in pain forever. You must stop her... Ach, where is Death, my love? It is so dark, and I cannot see him. I am afraid... so afraid of this blackness."

Jacq's voice sank into a mumble, and she had to strain hard to catch his words.

Katkin grasped his hand and squeezed it hard. "What is it, Jacq? Tell me, if you can."

Though she did not see how he could possibly go on, his voice grew strong again. "I gave up my wings for you, Katkin. I loved flight — the freedom of it was my greatest joy, but I loved you more. Always, I loved you more..."

Her eyes went wide with sudden understanding. "Dai?"

His breathing took on a rasping, hollow timbre, and he said nothing else intelligible. Katkin was not sure he could still hear her, but she wanted him to go on his last journey free from anxiety and pain. She whispered into his ear, "I will spend the rest of my life finding a way to free Gwenn from Ketha, I swear it. Sleep in peace, my dearest, and never forget I love you."

His hand, which covered hers, twitched convulsively, and she prayed it meant he had heard her and understood. Afterwards, his massive chest stopped its ragged motion under her head, and his arm fell down, slack, by his side. Katkin buried her head on his shoulder and sobbed. How could he be dead? She still needed his strength. Katkin pounded Jacq's lifeless chest with her fists, crying, "Don't leave me again. How can I face everything without you? Please... I need you."

An hour passed as Jacq's body cooled next to her, and still Katkin could not force herself to leave his side. She knew she should go and see to her daughter, who must still be unconscious in the back room where Jacq had left her. There was nothing, now, she could do for her husband except weep and curse Keth Dirane to hell forever for what she had done.

Slowly, she rose and wandered around the front room, touching things he had made, lost in the memories of her life with

Jacq. She remembered their first passionate kiss, upstairs at an inn called the Compass Rose. How she had begged him to stay the night with her, and how he had steadfastly refused. The next day he surprised her by taking her to the church in Belladore and making her his wife. Katkin smiled through her tears, as she recalled the wedding ceremony, and how nervous Jacq had been when they found themselves alone at last, upstairs in Yannick's mill. Their happiness had been tempered with many sorrows since then, but through it all they had stayed together. What would she do now?

In the next room, Gwenn cried out weakly, "Papa Bear, where are you?" Katkin thought of her last promise to her husband, that she would somehow free their daughter from Keth Dirane's clutches. That at least was something to live for. Katkin went to the cupboard where she kept her medical supplies. Passing back across the main room, she paused only to pull the quilt over Jacq's pale grey face, to cover him completely, before she went to find her daughter.

Gwenn lay on her side, and a dark red stain marked the place where the covers draped over her back. Katkin drew her breath in sharply and tried to let her medical training guide her hand. Her daughter's eyes opened and she whispered. "Mother? Oh, Mother, I am so sorry. I told him about Tomas..."

Katkin said, "Ssh... Don't worry, he understands. He told me so before he..." She stopped abruptly and focused on changing the sodden bandage around her daughter's ribs.

Gwenn moaned as her mother cut away the pad of cloth Jacq had bound over the gaping hole in her back. "Before he what? Has Papa gone somewhere?"

Katkin bit her lip hard before she answered, so her voice might sound calm and untroubled. "Yes, he had to go away for a little while. He said I should take care of you while he is gone. All right?"

She nodded and said softly, "I need to tell you so many things."

Katkin replied, "Not now. You must rest. I am going to make some tea for you to drink. It will help with the pain."

Gwenn said thickly, "Everything above my waist hurts, but I cannot feel my legs at all. What is wrong with me?"

Katkin turned away so Gwenn could not see the concern on her face. She said, as brightly as she could, "Don't worry about it now. I am here, and I will take care of you. Now, I had better make the tea." She went out, closing the door softly behind her. A few minutes later she returned, bearing a steaming mug. Gwenn could not sit up, and could hardly swallow because of the injury to her tongue, so Katkin fed the drink to her a spoonful at a time. After a time, she said quietly, "Arkady came back to St. Valery last summer. He told me he'd been with you. Then he left again in the fall. He said he was going back to find you again."

Gwenn said dully, "He met up with me. In Secuny. But things were very difficult, because I was with the Fynära. When he found out about the Firaithi thralls, he became very angry and left. I don't know where he is now."

Katkin could tell the subject was an unhappy one for her daughter, so she said nothing else about it. As the opium poppy tea eased her pain, Gwenn said, drowsily, "Ketha sleeps now, deep inside me. I don't hear her words in my mind anymore, but I know she is still there. Gunnar and I were going to go away, back to Starruthe. His grandmother is a witch. He thought she could help somehow, with Ketha."

Her mother regarded her with interest and asked, "Who is Gunnar?" then saw her daughter's eyes had closed, and she slept, her expression relaxed and peaceful. Katkin kissed the girl's damp forehead and pulled the quilt up over her, and then went back into the front room. She could not bring herself to do anything with Jacq's body, so she sat down in a chair across the room, wondering what she could do to help Gwenn. The grandfather clock in the hallway chimed the passing quarter hours. Katkin stood up and paced in frustration and worry.

The door flew open and William entered the room, wildly disheveled and obviously in a great hurry. When he saw her, he cried, "Quickly, Your Majesty. We must leave here at once. Your son is on his way here with a detachment of Guard. Does the Princess Gwenn still live? Where is the Dinrhydan?"

She stared at her former equerry, nonplussed by his panicked questions, and remembered he did not yet know about her husband's death. She choked back a sob and said, "William, Jacq is..." Katkin could not bring herself to say the rest, so she dragged him over to the quilt-shrouded body on the floor and pulled the corner away to uncover the face. William's eyes went wide with dismay.

219

"My Gods, what happened? How did he die?"

Katkin, unwilling to go into the difficult story of Gwenn's involvement with Ketha, said dully, "I am not sure, but I think his heart stopped. I found him when I came back from the Acre." She could not look on his face without breaking down further, so she turned away and forced herself to make more tea.

William came up close behind her. "Your Majesty, please..." She let him gather her into an embrace, and cried on his shoulder as he hesitantly patted her back. Her distress almost made him forget the pressing reason for his trip from St. Valery. Suddenly he cried, "Your son, the King. He is coming here with some Guardsmen to arrest you and the Princess. You have to get her away from here..."

She interrupted him, saying, "What? William, you must slow down and explain yourself." Katkin had not thought to ask why Gwenn had come back to St. Valery, but now a horrible certainty dawned on her.

He said tersely, "The Fynära attacked the City early this morning. The battle still rages. Your son hopes to take the Princess Gwenn prisoner, and torture her publicly in order to make them surrender. Do you see why you must go? He has gone mad, and will stop at nothing."

They both looked up at the sound of running feet crossing the yard towards the house. The tall blond man that burst through the door made both Katkin and William step back in fear. His black clothing hung in tatters from his body, and streaks of blood and grime covered his face and arms. He looked around wildly, panting hard, obviously close to collapse.

William stepped in front of Katkin and drew his sword. He hissed, "He is one of them. The Fynära. Stand back, your Majesty. He looks desperate." But Katkin had seen another figure beyond the Northman, watching silently from the door. Tomas gave her a pleading look, and vanished.

She said, "Wait, William. I don't believe he means to hurt us." She stepped forward, and extended her hand to the stranger, saying, "Gunnar? Are you looking for Gwenn? She is here."

Gunnar spoke very little Maraison, but he did understand one word she said. Ever since the specter appeared to him on the battlefield, he had followed it blindly. Somehow, he knew the quaintly uniformed man who glided before him would lead him to his love. Now he nodded, and said softly, "*Ja*, Gwenn." Katkin took his hand and led him back to the bedroom. As they passed Jacq's body, he gave her a questioning glance, but she avoided his eyes and gave no explanation.

Gwenn turned her head as they entered the room. Gunnar gave a sharp cry and rushed to the side of her bed. He leaned over and kissed her mouth warmly, then stroked her hair as he spoke soft words in a language Katkin did not understand. She did not want to intrude in what was obviously a tender reunion between the two, but she knew they could safely linger no longer at Acorn. "Gwenn, is this the man you spoke of earlier?" she asked. "Can he help you get away from here now?"

Gwenn looked up at her mother and tried to focus on her face. "This is Gunnar Strong Arm. He is my Captain. Why do I have to go? I am so tired."

Katkin spoke urgently. "William says Tris is on his way here to arrest you."

Gunnar, hearing the concern in her voice, fired a rapid question in Dalvolk. Gwenn quickly translated. He said to her, "We'll have to get back down to the Ariane. The *Fire Drake* is there, hidden in a grove of willows. Ask your mother if we can take that horse outside and a cart."

Once she understood Gunnar's request, Katkin said to William, "Get Minerva and hitch her to the hay wagon, hurry! You will have to ride with them and show Gunnar the back way to the riverbank. Once they are gone, make your way to wherever you will be safe, William."

William shook his head. "Your Majesty, I cannot leave you to face the Guard alone. What do you think they will do when they find you have helped the Princess to escape? Let me stay behind."

Katkin sighed wearily. "No. Tris is my son and I do not fear him. As long as Gwenn gets safely away from here, I will be all right. I can stall the Guardsmen longer than you would be able to. Now go, quickly." Gunnar touched Gwenn's face softly and then went out with William. Katkin sat by her daughter's bed, and took her hand, deeply unhappy that she had to leave again so soon.

Gwenn whispered tiredly, "Will my legs start working again? I need to know the truth."

"I don't know. The pistol ball hit your spine and damaged it. Maybe not."

Her eyes filled with tears. "What about the baby? Do you think it will be all right?"

Katkin looked horrified. "Baby? What baby? You mean to say you are pregnant?"

Gwenn nodded miserably. "Gunnar is the father. I think I am about four months along. Am I going to lose it?"

"I cannot say for sure, but your abdomen appears to be uninjured. I can only pray you will be well taken care of when you leave here. You must tell Gunnar to keep you warm and keep your wounds clean until they can heal. I will give you some supplies to take with you."

William came back through the doorway, and said urgently, "I saw them coming from the top of the hill. We have less than fifteen minutes to get away." Katkin stood as Gunnar came back through the door. He put his arms under Gwenn and picked her up with the utmost gentleness, blankets and all, then carried her from the room. By the time he stepped over Jacq's body, Gwenn had closed her eyes, and so did not see him lying on the floor.

Once Gunnar had arranged Gwenn carefully upon a bed of hay, William climbed on to the driver's seat. Gunnar sat beside Gwenn and held her head in his lap. Katkin handed him a bag containing bandages and soap, and a glass bottle with a stopper, containing dried and chopped *papaver somniferum* heads. Using hand signals she managed to show him how to make the tea for Gwenn. Now, as they made ready to depart, Katkin's eyes filled with tears. How could she keep her last promise to Jacq when she did not know if she would ever see her daughter again?

She asked anxiously as William snapped the reins on Minerva's back, "Where are you going to take her, Gunnar?" Gwenn quickly translated.

Gunnar replied in fractured, heavily accented Maraison, "We to Celeste now. Starruthe later time." Then he smiled shyly at her and added, "Thank you, Katkin. Good woman you — like my Gwenn. Gunnar save daughter, promise. *Adjö*."

Chapter Eighteen

The Ice Demon's Paint Brush

The Numen does not let her finish. Faugh! *You* told your sister what to do. Now *you* will pay the price. *She takes a step forward and Geya turns to flee. The old woman raises her hand and the younger Amaranthine stops abruptly, then shuffles slowly back towards her, obviously fighting every step.*

Geya Banthet! You will be banished to the fifteenth azimuth of the outermost pellicle until the end of this Gyreturn for the murder of Dai Irrakai. Go there at once!

On the heaving deck of the *Moon Drake*, Arkady approached the remaining raiders fearlessly, knowing the demonstration of his power in healing Huw had frightened all the remaining fight out of them.

He ordered quietly, "Throw down your weapons."

They obeyed instantly, and the other thralls picked up the swords and axes as they clattered down to the deck. Arkady took Sven's leather strap away from him, and fingered it thoughtfully. He herded the raiders forward and made them take to the oars. Arkady studied the approaching coastline. High cliffs, formed of some dark stone, towered over the rocky shore, on what looked to be a narrow headland. The coastline did not look at all familiar to him, and a quick survey determined none of the other thralls knew where they were either. Now, as they passed a series of barrier islands, shallow crescents of rock and dunes anchored by sea grass, Arkady gave the order for the rowers to ship the oars and the boat glided to a halt. The headland was still a mile or more distant.

He faced Sven and the other raiders. "This is where you get off the boat," he said firmly. "I don't trust you not to try something when we reach the mainland. Once the tide goes out you should be able to swim for the shore. By then, we will be long gone. Now get moving."

He used the whip to point towards the gunwale, and waited impatiently as the first of the raiders shuffled forward. The man hesitated, and Arkady glared at him. With a frightened cry, he launched himself over the side and into the freezing water. A second later, his head broke the surface and he swam frantically for the nearest island. The rest of his shipmates quickly followed, until only Sven stood on the deck before Arkady. He walked forward, with his head down, ready to join the others.

Arkady said coldly, "Not so fast. You and I have something to settle first, Red Beard." Sven paled, and a sweat broke out on his brow.

Huw said unhappily, "Do not revenge yourself on him for my sake. Now that I am healed, I hold no anger in my heart. Let him go with the rest."

But Arkady could not forget Huw's anguish so easily, nor the agony and humiliation of his own lashes at Sven's hand. At Arkady's command, the gleeful thralls tied their former master to the mast. He took one of the swords and cut Sven's black tunic away. The raider looked on fearfully, but he was too proud to beg for mercy.

Arkady gave the whip to the man from Shadion, saying, "Give him ten lashes, as hard as you like."

He seemed confused until Arkady mimed his instruction, and the man chortled jubilantly. He brought the whip down across Sven's naked shoulders with a sizzling blow, and the raider gave an involuntary whimper through his clenched teeth. The rest of the thralls lined up behind the Shaddite, eager to take their own turns with the whip. Each tried to make his stroke more firm than the last, and to flagellate a different portion of skin.

Soon Sven was howling in agony as the blood ran down his back and pooled onto the deck at his feet. Forgetting his pride, he begged tearfully, "Please, no more! I cannot bear it."

Arkady stood unmoved. He said, "So did my brother cry to you for mercy, but you gave him none, Northman. Now you feel but a small portion of the hurt he endured. I hope you never forget this agony." The other thralls cheered approvingly.

Only Huw, unable to bear the sound of the torture, turned his head away, and cried.

Sven sank down, and only the rope around his wrists kept him upright. He sobbed wildly. One hundred and fourteen lashes had been applied to his back by the other thralls and now Arkady handed the whip to Huw, saying, "Go ahead, my brother. You give him as many as you like."

Huw stared down at Sven's back, which now looked like a piece of poorly carved meat. He backed away from the proffered whip, shaking his head madly. "No, Kadya, please let him go. He has suffered enough. This revenge is wrong, can you not see? To punish him further makes us just as culpable. Please, my brother, I feel only pity for him. If you continue, he will die." Arkady gave an exclamation of disgust and turned back to Sven, intending to lay into him with the whip again.

Sven's voice, hoarse from his screams, was barely audible as he said, "You swore your own revenge on the Faircrow, Firaithi. Remember, on the coast road? If she were tied to this mast, would you open her flesh with the whip?"

Arkady said under his breath, "I would."

Sven continued, loyally, "I don't want your pity. Save it for her."

Huw looked horrified at this reminder of his own threat, and Arkady's response. The other thralls murmured in surprise as he picked up a fallen axe and chopped through Sven's bonds before Arkady could prevent him. The raider staggered to his feet and dashed for the gunwale. As he hit the water, he gave a scream of agony as the salt water soaked his flayed back. Huw rushed to the side, in time to see his red hair disappear below the surface. He came up again, floundering uselessly, his body quickly going into shock.

Within seconds, Huw followed him to the water, and cast around wildly before he managed to grab Sven's arm. Sven weighed almost twice as much as the Firaithi and Huw struggled to keep the drowning man's head above water. He cried out to Arkady, "You must use your healing fire or else he will die. And I will die with him, because I will not let him go. Do you want his blood and mine on your hands?"

With a sigh, Arkady formed a ball of white fire and threw it towards the struggling pair. The water hissed and steamed as the raider's body rose up into the air. Within seconds, the flame engulfed Sven's body, as Huw, helped by many willing hands, scrambled back aboard the *Moon Drake*. The other raiders, now ashore on one of the barrier islands, watched fearfully as their leader's body was bathed in fire. Abruptly, he fell back into the water, and the fire was quenched.

He surfaced, treading water while he looked up at the row of faces above the gunwale. Finding Huw's, he said, "You, Firaithi. You saved my life, after all the terrible punishment I gave you. Why?"

Huw shook his head. "I don't know. Perhaps because you asked for mercy for your leader."

Sven said, "So be it. I am in your debt, and I will not forget." He turned and swam strongly for the island, and joined his shipmates. Then he stared at the departing *Moon Drake*, shaking his head in confusion.

Once the ship landed on the shingle, and they disembarked, the other thralls gathered around Arkady and Huw. A dreary, cold rain fell, and the thralls, dressed in little better than rags, shivered and clutched their arms. Arkady spoke to each man in turn, in his own language. Several argued vociferously. Huw could follow little of what was said, but from the looks of disgust on the thrall's faces, he could tell Arkady's replies did not please them. One by one, they turned away. Within a few moments Huw and Arkady stood alone on the beach, the rest of the thralls having melted into the gathering dusk, after dividing up what little food there was on board the *Moon Drake*. The brothers stood side by side, both more than a little miffed with the other.

"What did you say to them, Kadya?" asked Huw, after a few moments had passed in uncomfortable silence.

Arkady shrugged. "I told them I planned to repair the sail on the *Moon Drake* and take her back to Einar."

"Why would we do that? We need to find out what country we are in, and how to get back to Beaumarais from here. If the Fynäran fleet we passed the day before yesterday is on its way to attack St. Valery, Katkin may need our help. I fear for her safety."

Arkady answered him sharply, "She has my brother to protect her. Or have you forgotten she is married? What about Padarn and the other thralls in Starruthe — don't you think they need our help even more?"

He stared belligerently at Huw, who dropped his eyes, and

kicked at a broken cockle shell with his foot. Huw ignored the caustic comment about Katkin and tried again to convince Arkady. "What will we be able to do in Einar, except get ourselves killed? There are but two of us. Do you think we will be able to defeat all the remaining Fynäran forces? You are being a stubborn ass." Arkady said nothing in reply, merely turned his back and walked towards the cliff. Huw hurried to catch him, cursing himself for failing to keep his temper in check.

They strode along together in silence, until finally Arkady said adamantly, "I am going to Einar, alone if needs be. If I lose my life trying to free the others, so be it. It is the only thing I have left to live for anyway."

As they rounded a low hill, a forlorn-looking shack came into view, close against the rock wall, the windows blank and uninviting. The surrounding vegetation grew thick and wild, and they had to pull through many brambles to reach the entrance. Arkady found a rounded stone and hammered the rusted lock. The door opened with the sound of protesting hinges, and a puddle of drifted sand spilled across the earthen floor.

The shack's cramped interior was no more inviting than the outside, but it did provide some shelter from the cold winds off the ocean, and the persistent rain. Two wooden beds with rotted rope webbing stood against one wall. A table and two chairs occupied the centre of the room. Piles of rusty and tangled fishing tackle filled the corners. A thick layer of dust and cobwebs covered everything. Water dripped down one wall from a hole in the roof and pooled on the floor, making the room thoroughly cheerless and damp.

Huw looked around him in dismay. "Whoever lives here has not been home for a long while. I suppose they will not mind if we stay here for a few days."

But he brightened when he found several woolen blankets and even some cooking vessels.

"Look, my brother," he said, "The Un-Named One has provided us with all we need for the moment. I will see if I can warm this place up while you walk back down to the *Moon Drake* and get the rest of the food and water." He busied himself making a fire in the partially collapsed hearth, while Arkady shrugged cheerlessly and headed out the door.

Once he reached the shore, Arkady ran the last few yards and stared out to sea, cursing wildly at the retreating sail of the *Moon Drake*. He screamed and waved his arms, crying, "No! Wait for us! Come back, do you hear me? Come back!" But, as he watched in despair, the sail passed irretrievably over the horizon.

Arkady turned away. He found kegs of salt beef and ship's biscuit on the shore, close to where they had beached the longboat. He placed one keg under each arm and headed back for the shelter, wondering if it had been the thralls who stranded them, or if the raiders had managed to swim from the island and make off with the boat. Either way they were in trouble. Parts of Yr were very thinly populated, and if they had fetched up in such a spot it might be thirty miles or more to the nearest village.

When he returned, Huw had a good blaze going in the hearth, and had blocked up the holes in the chimney to stop smoke from entering the room. He had hung up the mildewed, moth-eaten blankets on a makeshift clothesline to dry out. Huw had discovered a rain barrel outside the back of the shack, fed from a pipe from the roof, and was busy making some rose hip tea. Arkady accepted a cup gratefully and sank down by the fire after telling his brother about the stolen vessel.

Huw said, "I think it must have been the other thralls who took the ship. The raiders would not have left any food behind for us. I am very glad they did! But it will not last us long. Tomorrow we will have to explore this coastline and see if we can find out where we are."

He turned back to the fire and poured himself another cup of tea, trying to hide his relief. The loss of the *Moon Drake* prevented Arkady from going ahead with his suicidal plan much more effectively than any argument could. Arkady made two plates of food and handed one to his brother. They ate in silence, neither willing to break the temporary truce that had sprung up between them. It had been several days since either had had a proper meal, but still they ate sparingly. Both worried silently about the raiders they had left on the sand bar. They would be making their way to shore before long, if they hadn't already.

As the light faded outside the windows, Huw asked softly, "Did you ever find the woman you were looking for? The one who gave you the talisman?"

Arkady stared into the flames without speaking for so long, Huw felt sure he did not mean to answer at all. Finally, he said wistfully, "I did find her, but she was not the person I was looking for, after all."

Huw looked puzzled. "I don't understand. Did the prophecy not mention a woman who would be the mother of the Dawnmaid?"

"Yes, but the woman I told you about — the one I met in the dunes, was the same woman who captured you and Padarn. She is evil."

He stood and poked the fire, and Huw studied his back, before saying thoughtfully, "I see now why she made such an impression on you — for she is perilously fair and cold." He scratched his chin thoughtfully before continuing. "So, the girl known as Krikka is also called the Faircrow. Did you know that when you told me you cared for her?"

"No, I only found out after I went back to Beaumaris. And I found out something else as well. She is Katkin's daughter, Huw."

Huw's eyes went wide at the mention of Katkin's name. "Her daughter? But how can that be? That would make her your..."

Arkady grimaced and said, "It is a long story, and I cannot tell you all the details. But she is *not* my kin."

Huw asked softly, "Do you love her still?"

"I thought I did, before I knew she was the one who led the men who killed Eira. Now I think she is wicked — beyond redemption." He turned to face Huw with an expression of utter hopelessness. "I believed I could help her, but in the end I was so angry I almost killed her instead. I failed completely. That is why I had to leave on the *Moon Drake*."

Huw rose and stood by his brother. He reached up and put his arm around his shoulder. "I am very glad you did, Kadya. You saved my life. It is as Eira said — *the wind does not change direction by chance.* Do you see? You did not fail, my brother."

All at once, Arkady did see, and the remaining jealous rage inside him crumbled and blew away, like the drifting sand outside the door of the shack. Why had he blamed Gwenn for everything, when she had been just as much a pawn in Ketha's game as the rest of them?

Now, belatedly, he wondered if he might have been able to

free her from Ketha if he had only known the correct use of Hana's fire before he left Celeste. This thought filled him with such desperate sadness he broke into anguished sobs, as Huw pulled him into a comforting embrace.

The next day dawned misty and cold. Arkady staggered outside, flapping his arms in an effort to get warm while Huw lit the fire. There was no sign of either the raiders or the thralls, and again he wondered who had taken the *Moon Drake*. After another meager meal, Huw and Arkady set off to reconnoiter the land around the shack. They set out in a southerly direction, following the line of the basalt cliff, hoping it might prove possible to climb up the face further along. It rose steeply from the ocean side, and in some places they were forced to scramble over slick tide-swept rocks to reach the next sandy bay. Many caves pockmarked the cliffs, and shaggy bushes clung to the sides in little grassy indentations. Sure enough, after an hour, they found a faint trail up the side, obviously made by some agile creature. They followed it carefully, and after thirty minutes of almost vertical climbing, they stood, sweating and breathless, on the top.

Huw turned around in a circle, shading his eyes with his hand, peering hopefully in all directions. "If there are people anywhere around, we should be able to see their houses or stock from up here."

Arkady studied the horizon thoughtfully and observed, "Well I certainly don't see anything that looks like a settlement or even a farmstead. Maybe they are further along to the west, away from the prevailing winds." After a drink of water, they continued walking again.

A few bent trees, twisted into tortured shapes by the wind off the ocean, were scattered here and there. The day remained chilly, and shreds of fog blew across the cliff top. They wandered silently for another half an hour before stopping to rest near a weathered tor. Arkady remarked, "Brrr... I am cold! Let's get moving again. It doesn't feel like late spring. I wonder how far north we are?"

Huw smiled and shrugged. "Let's find some people and ask them, Kadya."

As they climbed together, heading for the crest of a rocky prominence, bemoaning the fact they might have to travel many miles to find a village, the view opened up to show the far side of the cliff top they traversed. A similar view stretched both east and west. Arkady and Huw both stopped and looked at each other in alarm. There could be no doubt. They had landed on an island, in the middle of an expanse of wind swept waves. Dark forms in the far distance spoke of other, perhaps larger islands to the south, but there was no possibility that they could reach them.

Arkady could not remember later how he and Huw made it back to the beach. He stumbled along in shock and profound dismay at the circumstances in which they found themselves. Without a boat, or the materials to make one, they might be stranded on this blighted island until they died. Only the presence of the fishing cabin was a slender thread of hope. Perhaps whoever owned it might come back again, and find them there.

As Arkady slumped by the fire, utterly demoralized, Huw said cheerfully, "We must not lose heart. We will get off this island someday. I know it. Ketha may think she has beaten us, but the Un-Named One will yet prevail. Her aims are mysterious and her strengths are hidden, yet she is all the more powerful for it. This island is her Gift, and we will make use of it while we wait patiently for her to make the next move. Now we had better sort out some of this fishing gear, and see about catching some dinner, and may the Un-Named One forgive me for eating the flesh of a fellow creature." He grinned and patted his brother's shoulder. "Don't worry. I have lived off the land my whole life and you can be sure I will find things for us to eat. Now is your chance to experience asparitus first hand, my brother!"

Arkady stood up, ready to help him. Though he did not share Huw's optimism about their eventual rescue, he wanted to make the best of their days together, at least until they starved.

Chapter Nineteen

Tamis

Geya pleads with the Numen. No... Please, grandmother, don't send me back. I have so many wonderful plans to catch the Angellus this time. They will all be ruined! *Her mouth forms a pout.* Anyway, it is *so* dull there.

The Numen is unmoved. *You wanted the death of one human too many, this gyretime, Geya. I should have done this long ago. Leave my sight, Fexella!**

With a dismissive wave of the Numen's gnarled hand, Geya disappears, though her angry scream lingers long in the air. The Numen limps back to the fireplace, talking to Hieronymus as she goes. *There, that's better. Good riddance to bad rubbish, eh?*

She slumps back into her rocking chair. *My heart... I shouldn't get so angry. It isn't good for a frail old thing like me.*

~~~~~~~~~~

As soon as the wagon carrying Gwenn passed out of sight, Katkin turned and ran back into the house. She hurriedly gathered up the remaining sheets off her daughter's bed, and used the pillowcase to wipe up every drop of blood on the floor between the bedroom and the front door. As she did, she talked to her husband. "I have to hurry, love. Tristan is coming, and he wants Gwenn. I must try to convince him you never brought her here. What can I say, Jacq? Wait, I have an idea... Surely he will not expect his own mother to lie to him?"

Katkin scurried outside and kicked dust over the blood spots on the ground, then took the stained sheets out into the barn. She buried them deeply under a pile of hay in the loft. As she crossed the yard on her way back to the house, she could see the first rank of mounted guardsmen cresting the hill. Katkin wiped her hand nervously on her apron and carefully composed her expression.

---

* One-celled organism. An insult.

She could see Tristan now, riding in the middle of the guards-men, sitting tall and proud on his black horse, Castor. The four men who rode in his immediate company used to be her own personal guard. The horses clattered to a halt in the yard, raising a cloud of dust, and scattering the chickens. The geese retired to the pond behind the barn, hissing madly.

Tristan dismounted and walked stiffly towards his mother. She rushed towards him, and threw her arms about his neck, wailing, "Thank the goddess you have come, Tristan. How did you find out so quickly?" Katkin hoped to confuse the boy with this strategy. She succeeded.

He held her at arm's length and said, "What are you on about, Mother? Calm down and tell me slowly."

Katkin could easily produce very real tears as she told him about his father's death. "When I came in, he was on the floor. He only said a few words, and then he just... died." She continued to weep copiously as she dragged him inside the house to where Jacq lay on the floor. Tristan knelt at his father's side, his face con-torted with the effort he had to make not to cry in front of his men. The other guardsmen crowded around, and looked down upon the body of the Dinrhydan in dismay.

For a long moment, no-one spoke, and Katkin wondered hopefully if she might get away with her ruse. Then Tristan stood, wiped the moisture from his eyes with his sleeve, and snapped, "Where is she, Mother? Where is my sister? Father told me he was going to bring her here to die."

Katkin pretended to be confused by his questions. She grabbed his hand and dragged him towards the door, saying, "I don't know what you mean, Tris. Gwenn hasn't been here as far as I know. What are we going to do about your father? He needs a proper burial. Come and help me find a spot for him outside. I was thinking under the oak..."

Tristan barked an order to his men to spread out and search the house. He snatched his hand away and said to Katkin, "Shut up, you whore. I cannot think with your prattling."

Katkin thought, irrelevantly, how much deeper his voice had gotten in the weeks since she had last heard him speak. Then the meaning of his words registered.

She stared at him, profoundly shocked. "What did you call me?"

"Don't act so innocent, mother. I know all about you and that torturer, de Vigny. You traitorous bitch! How could you betray my father like that?"

Katkin hadn't expected this from Tristan. She stepped forward and slapped her son across the face. "How dare you! You have no idea what I went through to help rescue your father from prison. I am no traitor. Just because you are King doesn't mean you can speak to me like that."

He caught her hand, and pushed her across the room, so that she fell backwards over Jacq's body. She lay on the floor, breathing heavily, trying to think of some other distraction she could use to keep him from expanding the search for Gwenn. Jacq's sword still lay at his side, and she wondered briefly if she might have need of it. D'angwir was both long and heavy, so she carefully pulled it half way out of the scabbard so it could be quickly retrieved, all the while praying she would not have to draw a weapon against her only son.

Tristan wandered around, obviously hunting for some sign his sister had been present at Acorn. Katkin's heart sank as one of the guardsmen hurried back into the room, bearing the bloody bed sheets she had concealed in the barn. Tristan snatched them away, and hurled them on the floor next to where she lay. He screamed at her, "Now, Mother. Tell me. Where is my sister? If you lie to me again I will have you executed. I have the power to do whatever I like — now the Prime Minister is dead."

His rage frightened her a little, and she belatedly wondered if William had been right about her son's insanity. She stood up slowly, and carefully folded the sheets over her arm, all the while thinking up a new story. "I am sorry. I know I shouldn't have lied, but I was scared. Jacq did bring Gwenn here, but she died soon after from massive blood loss. He buried her somewhere in the Acre. I... don't know where. The effort of digging the grave must have affected his heart. That is why he collapsed. You must believe me." Tristan glared at her coldly and she could see the skepticism in his eyes. Another guardsman entered the room and saluted smartly.

"The dogs are here, Your Majesty. What object do we have that bears the girl's scent?"

Tristan pulled the muddy piece of braided hair from his

pocket and handed it to the guard. He spoke crisply. "This was in her pocket. It should carry enough of her traitorous stench on it. Have the dogs search the grounds to see if they can pick up her trail. The handlers must hurry — I think she has at least a half an hour lead on us already. Tell some of the other men to join me in here." He turned back to his mother and continued coldly, "I need someone to watch over this lying... trollop, in case she tries to escape."

At the sight of the braid — that damning piece of ancient history — Katkin's heart sank utterly. "Where did you get that, Tristan?"

His mouth formed a thin, hard line. He spat, "Gwenn threw it at father's face, in front of *everyone*! She broke him, right there and then. What a callous bitch she turned out to be — just like her mother..." He stepped forward, and Katkin felt sure he meant to strike her. Bending down, she drew d'angwir the rest of the way out of the scabbard. She pointed the weapon at Tristan, resting the heavy sword on her stump. He swallowed in surprise, and dropped his hands to his side.

The guardsman looked at her with alarm and made to draw his own weapon. She hissed, "Drop your sword, or the King dies!" He did as she instructed, shaking his head in disgust at the former Queen's treason. She said, "Now, move slowly over to the door, and bar it. Don't try anything funny, or I will use this to cut his throat, I swear it."

Tristan, already reeling from his father's desertion on the parade field, could hardly hold back his tears. He snarled, "You both loved her more. I was never good enough! I hate you, Mother. You will not get away with this, you know. There are forty men outside, and you cannot hold them off indefinitely."

Katkin smiled grimly and raised d'angwir a little higher. She knew she did not have much time before the men outside rushed the house, but she hoped she could delay them long enough for Gwenn to make her escape. Someone hammered persistently on the door outside and she heard the sound of many excited voices filtering through the stone walls of Acorn. She asked Tristan, "How does the City fare? Are the defenses holding against the Fynära?"

He looked at her with loathing. "Your precious daughter's

forces are no match for the magnificent Citadel of St. Valery. We have beaten back their advances twice this day, already." Given what William had told her, Katkin wondered how much of what Tristan said was just bravado. He seemed very afraid, despite his efforts to put on a calm face. She cursed Ketha for making her choose between her two children, and wondered if her son would ever forgive her.

She said softly, "I know how bad this looks, and I am sorry. You are my son and I love you, but I have to protect your sister's life. Someday, perhaps you will understand."

Tristan said angrily, "I will never understand nor will I ever forgive you. I no longer think of you as my mother at all. Now you are just another traitor to my realm and you will be punished accordingly." As he spoke these harsh words, the room shook. The door exploded, smashed to pieces by a heavy log, and many guardsmen piled through with swords drawn. Katkin backed away from them until she could feel the wall behind her. Tristan's men charged forward as he shouted frantically, "Take her alive! I want her for questioning."

As rough hands seized her, and a matchlock butt smashed down on her head, Katkin's last conscious thought was that her own son meant to torture her.

Gunnar cradled Gwenn closely, trying to spare her as many jarring bumps as he could. The hay wagon banged over a pothole in the road bed, and Gwenn moaned in pain. Gunnar swore in frustration as he saw her back was bleeding again. He scanned the road ahead anxiously. Once they reached the *Fire Drake*, he knew they would be safe, for no man could catch Gunnar on water, but for now he had to rely on this stranger to keep ahead of their pursuers. He pressed down hard on the bandage and tried to stanch the blood seeping from her wound.

Gwenn's eyes flickered open when she felt his hand on her back. She said, weakly, "You should just leave me, Gunnar. I am going to die anyway." He did not even dignify this with a response, just shook his head mournfully and held on to her as the wagon swayed from side to side.

William drove Minerva as fast as he dared on the rutted track that wound around the long hill leading down to the Ariane plain. He knew they had little time to make the river. Despite the Queen's brave words, William held no illusions about her son's intentions. He would not allow himself to be delayed overlong, not while the leader of the Fynära remained at large. So far, though, their luck held. No sound of following hooves disturbed the sultry afternoon silence.

Once they reached the plain, he slapped the reins hard across Minerva's back, and she picked up speed. They traveled quickly through well-ordered fields, each protected by a windbreak of poplars or hedged pine trees. The river snaked along in the near distance, and the afternoon sun glinted on the water's surface, glimpsed between the rushes growing on the banks. Gunnar pointed excitedly towards a clump of willows to the left of the track, and William guided Minerva on to the grassy verge of the riverbank. He peered back along the road and cried out in alarm.

William, forgetting Gunnar did not speak Maraison, said, "You must hurry! Save the Princess."

A detachment of mounted guardsman, their horses at a dead run, made their way quickly down the last stretch of the hill road.

But Gunnar had seen their pursuers and was already scrambling out of the wagon. He ran to the *Fire Drake* and checked to make sure she had a clear path out into the open water. There were five other longboats tied up by the willows, left behind by Torsten. He had taken only the largest ships in his fleet, and loaded each to capacity with men and arms. Fortunately, the *Fire Drake* stood at the far end of the line. As Gunnar made ready to cast off, William carried Gwenn on board and laid her carefully down by the mast. As he turned to go, Gunnar grabbed his arm and said something in Dalvolk.

Gwenn, her voice a ragged whisper, translated. "He says you should come with us, William. If you remain here, they will kill you."

William steadfastly refused. "I will stay and hold them off as long as I can. Then I must make my way back to Acorn and see if I can help your mother somehow."

Gunnar listened as Gwenn translated. He offered his hand to William and said in Maraison, "Thank you."

William clasped it briefly and then turned and ran for the wagon. Gunnar strained mightily to raise the heavy, square sail. He knew the strength and direction of the wind was all that lay between them and disaster. Fortunately, the sail filled immediately, and the *Fire Drake* moved smartly to the centre of the river. Gunnar moved back to the steering oar and kept her steady, all the while watching the progress of the mounted guardsmen. They had reached the riverbank now, and William stepped out to meet them, his sword drawn. Gunnar sighed and closed his eyes briefly as the former Queen's equerry fell, screaming, pierced with an arrow through his eye socket. Now the horses turned downstream, and began a furious pursuit along the road that followed the bank. Arrows whistled over his head as Gunnar doggedly kept the *Fire Drake* on course down the Ariane.

"Mariner, heed my prayer," Gunnar pleaded. "Send your living breath, enough to carry us safely into Mardon." He knew the men from Beaumarais would not dare follow them over the border. Just then, the wind picked up, and the ship shot ahead. He smiled grimly at the cries of dismay coming from the riverbank.

Now the road veered away, passing behind a narrow copse of willows, and he lost sight of the pursuers. The trees had many drooping branches that partially blocked the watercourse, forcing him to steer the *Fire Drake* towards the left bank. On his right, the willows thinned out and Gunnar watched intently, expecting to see the mounted Guardsmen emerge from behind the trees at any second. He gave a cry of alarm as he saw them — well ahead of the *Fire Drake*, busily launching several small fishing vessels from a jetty, just before the place where the river divided to flow around a small island. About fifteen men piled into the biggest boat, while those remaining on the shore had bows at the ready. Gunnar jumped up from the steering oar and lashed it with a loop of rope to keep the boat on course. He moved forward, holding his round wooden shield high, and stepped in front of the mast, to where Gwenn lay helpless on the deck. Arrows flew through the air, peppering the boards, as the archers let off volley after volley. One found its mark, lodging deep in his thigh, but he hardly felt it.

The guardsmen had managed to get their vessel into the centre of the river, though she was askew and drifting rapidly downstream. Gunnar watched calmly, confident that the larger and heavier-built *Fire Drake* would have the advantage in any collision.

As the distance between the two boats closed, he called over to Gwenn, "Hold as fast as you can, Faircrow!"

Though the impact was jarring, he easily kept his feet, and he gave a whoop of victory as he saw the shattered pieces of the fishing boat in the *Fire Drake*'s wake. But his relief was short-lived. He watched in dismay as five guardsmen who had managed to cling to the sides of his vessel hurled themselves over the gunwale and stood up, dripping pools of river water onto the deck. They drew their swords and moved unsteadily forward as the ship pitched and rolled in the rough currents of the Ariane.

Their leader, Captain Egmont, said in slow and precise Dalvolk, "Drop your weapons, and we will do you no harm. We only want the girl."

Gunnar swore colorfully at Egmont and said through gritted teeth, "Get off my boat, southern swine."

Egmont gave him a patronizing smile and gestured to where Gwenn lay on the deck. "Come now, my good Fynäran. Why waste your life on the defense of this traitorous bitch? I give you my word you will be allowed to go free if you surrender her to us. You are already wounded and hopelessly outnumbered; surely you see that you don't stand a chance?"

Gunnar spat derisively. "Is that what you cowards do, here in the South? Trade your worthless hides for the lives of your comrades? We Fynärans are men of honor and pride."

The Captain said angrily, "Don't lecture me about honor. You Northern scum are the lowest form of life on Yrth." Egmont glanced at the four well-armed guardsmen who stood at his side, swords at the ready. He cried, "Come on! We can take him easily. Attack!"

In his long career as a raider, as he rose from the lowest oarsman to Captain of a longboat, Gunnar had faced many other dire situations, but none so desperate as this. This time he did not fight for blood or fire, or a glorious rebirth as a hero in Skyre. Those contests of the past — those things he had once battled for and thought important — meant nothing to him now. The five men who approached from the prow of the *Fire Drake* meant to take from him his woman and his unborn child. He was going to stop them — it was that simple.

With a furious roar, he ran forward, blond braids flying, and hurtled into their midst. Nung the Demon himself could not have fought more ferociously. As he reached the first man, he drove his sword straight through him, as he raised his shield arm to fend off the attack of another. With a backhanded swipe, he felled a second man, then smashed in the face of the third with the iron boss on his shield. The fourth man's sword came ringing down onto his iron helmet, and Gunnar's vision temporarily faded into a panorama of stars. He staggered forward and dropped his shield, but managed to unhook his axe from his belt as the guardsman unwisely pursued him across the deck. A vicious arc of the axe separated the man's head from the rest of him.

Gunnar whirled and almost fell over a coiled rope as he heard Gwenn cry out weakly. The remaining guardsman, Captain Egmont, stood over her, his sword poised to strike straight down into her heart. He said, menacingly, "Don't move or she dies. Drop your weapons, now!"

Instinctively, Gunnar launched himself through the air, slamming into the Captain with his entire body weight and sweeping him over to the side of the boat. The two men rolled on the deck, wrestling furiously, both trying to lay a hand on any weapon they could find. Gunnar screamed in agony as Egmont caught hold of the broken arrow in his thigh and brutally twisted the shaft. Blood poured from the wound. He tried to push the guardsman off him, and succeeded only in rolling closer to where Gwenn lay, helpless, next to the mast.

From the sounds of the frantic conflict beside her, Gwenn knew Gunnar must be in trouble. Raising herself up weakly, she groped for the dagger still concealed in her boot, the same dagger that had once belonged to Tomas de Vigny.

She cried out, "Father, help me..."

Her eyes could hardly focus on the struggling pair beside her, but when Gunnar managed to throw off his attacker, Gwenn saw her chance. With every ounce of her remaining strength, she plunged the knife downwards, into the throat of Captain Egmont. With a gurgling scream, he twitched violently for a few seconds, and died.

240

Gunnar crawled over to Gwenn, who had fallen back, utterly exhausted. He prised the dagger from her clenched fingers and tried to make her comfortable. She whispered to him, "Are they gone? Did you get the rest of them?" He nodded, and squeezed her hand, so she smiled, saying, "We always made a pretty good team, you and I, eh, Strong Arm?"

Her eyes closed, and Gunnar felt her hand go slack in his. He watched her chest rise and fall, fearfully, before he remembered the boat had no-one at the helm. After brushing his lips across hers, he rose uncertainly and lurched across the deck towards the steering oar. Now that the battle had finished, the wound in his thigh burned like fire, and he felt exhausted and light-headed.

After making sure the *Fire Drake* still occupied the centre of the river, Gunnar rummaged through the medical supplies Katkin had given him. He bandaged up the arrow wound as best he could. After he had thrown the bodies of the five Guardsmen overboard, watching with a satisfied smile as their bodies hit the water and sank out of sight, he dragged a chest over to the oar and sat down. It would be many hours before he could rest properly, but Gunnar felt content. They were deep into Mardon territory now, and there would be no more pursuit. By tomorrow, the *Fire Drake* would carry them back to the coast of Secuny, and the abandoned village of Celeste. After that... Well, the morrow could look after itself, as his grandmother used to say.

But the journey to Celeste soon became a waking nightmare for Gunnar. He found that after a few hours he could hardly keep his eyes open. A combination of shock, blood loss and battle fatigue threatened to undo him and this enemy would be a far more difficult one to subdue. After checking the way down river was clear, he stood up and walked unsteadily to the gunwale, then reached over to splash a handful of water onto his face. A wave of nausea hit him, and he groaned.

Gwenn called over to him in alarm. "Are you all right, Strong Arm? Who is steering the boat?"

He made his voice obey him. "I am fine, Gwenn. Do not worry."

But Gunnar knew that everything rested on his shoulders. The Ariane's currents were treacherous, and even for a shallow-hulled vessel like the *Fire Drake*, dangerous shoals lurked where she could easily run aground. Yet he knew they must reach Celeste as soon as possible. Unless he could find a safe place for Gwenn to rest, where he could properly tend to her wounds, she would doubtless die. He stumbled over to her with a cup of water, and held her head so she could take a few sips.

"How much longer, Gunnar? Everything hurts so much..."

"Not long," he lied. "We'll be there very soon. Then I will make some of the tea your mother gave us."

Though he had originally planned to sail all night, if the wind held, so that they might reach Celeste by daybreak, he could see now it would be impossible. They would have to hole up in some narrow inlet so he could rest until it grew light enough to sail again. Gunnar lifted his head wearily, and stared into the westering sun. Gwenn's eyes had closed again, and her ragged breathing filled him with dread. He stood, slowly and painfully, clutching the mast to take the weight off his injured thigh, and hobbled back towards the stern. The hours of the afternoon passed with agonizing slowness. Several times, he only managed to prevent the *Fire Drake* from running aground at the last second, after his eyes closed involuntarily.

He stood and shook his head in an effort to stay awake, and then shook it again, more violently, as a figure appeared in the twilight, kneeling over Gwenn's sleeping form — a man with long blond hair, tied back in a queue, and wearing a ragged blue uniform with red epaulettes. At first Gunnar thought exhaustion was playing tricks with his mind, but as he continued to stare at the apparition, he recognized it as the specter who had led him from the battlefield to Acorn.

Gunnar approached him carefully, and said, "Hail, Man of the spirit world. What has called you from your rest?" Though Gunnar did not fear any ghost, it was only prudent to be respectful of the dead.

Tomas brushed the hair from Gwenn's face, and stroked her cheek briefly before rising to his feet. She did not stir, but she smiled in her sleep, as though his touch had soothed her pain somehow.

Gunnar asked again, "What do you want with us?"

Tomas did not reply. His presence in the physical world was marginal at best and he had no strength to waste with talk. He floated slowly back to the stern, and took up a position next to the steering oar, then stood silently, grim-faced, studying the river ahead for obstacles. The wind picked up, and the boat glided gracefully through the water with Tomas at the helm. Gunnar watched him for a long moment, and sighed, thinking he had little choice but to trust the apparition yet again. He laid down next to Gwenn, curling his body up close to hers, and pulled a reindeer skin up to cover them both. In less than a minute, after he pillowed his head on his arm, he slept.

The red sun of early morning woke him, and he jumped up in alarm. The specter no longer stood at the helm, and Gunnar swore, sure they had run aground sometime in the night, for the *Fire Drake*'s sail lay slack against the mast. He looked around wildly, and saw they lay beached on a shingled inlet, by a rotted quay. Sea grass nodded in the breeze, and the ceaseless booming of the ocean filled the dawn with sound.

"Celeste," he said out loud to himself. "We are in Celeste."

He bent, jubilantly, and shook Gwenn. Her eyes fluttered open. "What is it, Gunnar? Are we there?"

He nodded happily and gathered her up into his arms. Carefully he stepped on to the gunwale and leapt lightly down on to the sand, biting back a cry as he landed on his injured leg. Gunnar bypassed all the new long houses the raiders had built and headed for the ruined village. Several of the cottages in the village seemed habitable, and he chose the one closest to Gwenn's bathing place. After laying her down carefully, he busied himself making a bed for her to sleep on, with a pile of hay and many deerskins. Then he made the tea, and sat with her while she sipped it carefully.

Once the tea had lessened her pain, Gwenn could talk more freely. "What are we going to do now, Gunnar? We cannot stay here forever."

Gunnar scratched his beard thoughtfully. "The journey to Starruthe would be too hard on you right now, so we will wait awhile. Once your wounds are healing well, we can sail the *Fire Drake* up to visit my Grandmother. In the meantime, you must not worry. I promise I will take care of everything."

The following days and weeks passed swiftly for Gunnar. He spent most of the time finding food for Gwenn to keep up her strength. By day, he wandered on foot, searching through the remains of the village for overgrown vegetable plots and fruit trees. He caught fish and shellfish in the estuaries surrounding the village. Though he had never bothered to cook much of anything for himself, he tried to prepare meals for her to tempt her poor appetite. After ranging far and wide, he found a wandering goat and brought her back to the house.

"Look here, love," he told Gwenn, as he brought her a cup of the foamy milk. "You must try to drink this every day. It will make you strong again." Gwenn smiled and thanked him, but he could see the pain and unhappiness writ plain in her eyes.

At night, he held her in the bed he made, and sang songs of his homeland to keep her loneliness at bay. Each morning he carefully cleaned the bedding, and carried her into the washhouse for a shared bath. He focused his entire being on taking care of Gwenn, but still she did not recover the use of her legs.

The bandages and medical supplies Katkin had given him were running out, and he worried about how to replace them. The nearest village was thirty miles or more away, and he could not leave Gwenn alone all the time it would take to walk there and back. If her condition worsened only a little, Gunnar feared she would die. During the busy daytime hours, it was easy to keep such dismal thoughts at bay, but at night he tormented himself with the possibility she would leave him alone forever, and take the child with her.

One evening while she slept, fitfully, he walked down to the beach. Gunnar had never been a particularly devout person in the past, but now he faced north, across the dark water from his homeland, and prayed fervently to every God and Goddess he could think of for help.

The answer to his prayers appeared rather unexpectedly the next day. A rail-thin, shaggy horse wandered over the dune top and into the yard of the house, then began nibbling on the flowers Gwenn had planted in front of her bathing shed. Gunnar approached her warily, holding out a carrot he had found in one of the abandoned gardens. The horse nickered softly, and took the offering. She wore no halter or saddle. When Gunnar turned away, and walked back to the house for some rope, she followed on her own.

He had left Gwenn outside in the morning sunshine, propped up against the wall, her useless legs wrapped in a blanket. She gave a cry of recognition when the horse appeared. "It is Ajax! I let her go last year, and now she has returned."

When she explained about the stolen horse, he asked, in consternation, "So you did know that thrall, Kadya, before he came to Celeste? Arvid suspected as much."

She nodded.

Gunnar knew he should ask no more questions. Gwenn's use of the painkilling tea dulled her mind, and she often said thoughtless things to him, without restraint. Whatever answer she gave now, it would probably hurt. But it was like a scab — tight, itching, and he could not leave it alone, so he asked, "Did you love him?"

She stared at him, her blue eyes cloudy and far away. Then she said, "Yes."

Just that one word. He could still stop, and pretend it never happened. But Gunnar did not, even though the scab had cracked and a trickle of blood seeped from underneath it. "Do you love him still?" he asked, and waited silently, his heart hammering in his chest.

Ajax wandered between them, and put her head down to sniff at Gwenn delicately. Her answer came out from behind the horse. That word again. It did hurt, a lot. Now the scab was gone, and the wound was bleeding freely.

Gwenn said softly, "Sit beside me. Please, Gunnar. I cannot get up and come to you."

He did, and she took his hand. She told him the whole story, leaving nothing out, even the final harrowing scene in the dunes. At the end of it, she said, "I love you, too. I swear it." Her eyes filled with tears as she looked at him, and saw the hurt on his face. Above their heads, the sun passed behind a cloud, and threw the yard into shadow. Ajax poked around, looking for more flowers. Neither of them said anything for a long while.

At last, she asked, "Can you take me inside, please? I am tired and I want to lie down."

So he carefully picked her up, carried her into the house, and made her comfortable. After she had drifted off to sleep, he walked back down to the beach and stared at the white-tipped breakers rolling onto the sand. He picked up a small, grey spiral shell, studying its intricate whorls as he went over the story in his mind. Though he wanted very much to hate Arkady, he could not help admiring his courage in seeking to free the other thralls. No wonder Gwenn thought so highly of him — no, she loved him. She loved him — and had done so since she was a little girl. The pain made him choke back a cry. How could he compete against such a man?

He remembered his conversation with Gwenn, long ago, on the deck of the *Fire Drake*. She had told him then that raiding made her unhappy and ashamed. Why had he not taken her seriously? With a look of grim determination, he hurried back to the bathing shed. A few minutes later, he emerged, beardless for the first time in his adult life, and with his long flaxen hair roughly chopped at shoulder length. After scrounging through several houses, he found some rough linen breeches and a torn, dirty shirt that must have once belonged to a farmer. Then he built a fire of driftwood, down on the beach, and burned the black clothing of the Fynära he had once worn so proudly. After a time, the ocean came up, with the tide, and washed away the ashes.

With his new, less menacing appearance, and the help of Ajax, Gunnar visited the nearest village, St. Martin, and traded some of his carvings for medical supplies and food. As he wandered through the shop on the main street, a tiny pair of blue leather shoes caught his eye. He picked them up, and studied them with wonder. With the aid of sign language, he managed to trade another carving for them.

Even with the horse it took him most of a day to make the trip, and he worried about Gwenn every minute he was away. When he returned, he quickly unsaddled Ajax, and hobbled her on a patch of grass. As he passed across the courtyard of the cottage, he heard Gwenn's voice, speaking softly. Startled, he drew his knife and crept closer, hoping she might just be talking to herself, or lost in a dream. He dropped low and peered over the windowsill. A clean-shaven man, with greying, shoulder length hair and tattered clothing, bent over Gwenn with his hands outstretched. With a cry of alarm, Gunnar rushed through the door, his knife raised high. The stranger whirled, and only Gwenn's weak cry of warning prevented Gunnar from murdering his first mate, Arvid Scar Brow.

Later, as they sat together outside in the long sunshine of a summer's evening, and Arvid sipped a cup of tea, Gunnar asked him, "How did you get here, Scar Brow? What happened in the battle for St. Valery?"

"In the beginning the attack went well. We took the wharf area, with few casualties, and then marched for the main gate into the City as the guardsmen retreated before us. Torsten led the men carrying the battering ram, and they soon had the gate swinging wide. The defenders fought fiercely, but again we prevailed, and made our way into the City itself. I was sure we were going to be victorious."

Gunnar handed another cup of tea to Gwenn, after allowing it to cool. She asked, "Did they manage to flood the Citadel moat? Lars and the others tried to disable the water system."

He replied, "Not at first. We were able to storm the inner ramparts without difficulty with siege ladders. They had a few men with matchlocks, but our men inside managed to kill most of them. Once on the top of the walls the fighting began again in earnest, and we lost a few warriors. They had archers posted on the bastions. I led a group of our people to take them out. We threw many down off the walls to their deaths. I though we had turned the tide in our favor, but then he came, and rallied the guardsmen."

Gwenn interrupted. "Who do you mean? Some General from St. Valery?"

Arvid shook his head, "No General. Just a lad. But he wore a crown. Valiant, too. He strode to the front of the lines and just started issuing orders."

Gwenn's eyes went wide with shock. "Are you talking about my younger brother? King Tristan?" She could not believe the boy she had once called "Little Shrimp" could be capable of such feats of bravery.

He then imparted a far more upsetting piece of news. "I don't know what his name was but the guardsmen called him 'the new Dinrhydan.' He fought like a demon."

She bit back a cry. "They called him that? Was my Papa there too?"

Arvid stared at her in confusion. "Is your father the one they call Dinrhydan? The one you told us about?"

"My stepfather, yes." Gwenn's expression changed radically. She asked, her voice urgent, "Did you see him in the battle? Does he still live?"

Scar Brow was focusing on Gwenn rather than Gunnar and so did not see his frantic gesturing. He answered, unhappily, "I did not see him. I am sorry. Perhaps he fought somewhere else."

Gunnar looked at Gwenn with concern. He had decided long ago the dead man on the floor of Acorn must be her stepfather, but he had not told her anything. But now her face, already thin and haggard, bore a new stain of fear and worry.

She said, "I hope he is all right. Maybe they locked him up for killing the Prime Minister." Gwenn started to cry, brokenheartedly. "I can do nothing to help him. I am useless like this!" Gunnar eased her forward, and sat behind her, with his back against the wall. He put his arms around her and stroked her hair.

He said gently, "Don't worry about him. If he is the man of your tales, what prison could hold him?" Gunnar wiped her eyes, then tried again to reassure her. "When you are well we will go and look for him, if you like. All right?" She nodded distraughtly as Gunnar, still with his arms about her, said, "Finish the tale, Arvid. What happened after the lad arrived?"

Arvid sighed and stroked his bare chin pensively. "The defenders fought like madmen, and soon they forced us back through the main tunnel of the Citadel. The gate detail had closed the portcullis, trapping us, like rats in a sewer. Our men fought to the death and many joined the heroes in Skyre trying to defend Torsten. Then, the portcullis started to rise, and Torsten thought we might yet be able to escape and regroup for another attack. We raced through the tunnel. The bridge had been demolished so we had to jump for it — down into the dry channel." Arvid grimaced in disgust, remembering. "It was a stinking trap. As soon as we landed in the moat, they somehow released a huge wave of water, ten feet high. It washed everyone away."

Gunnar gazed dolefully at his first mate. "Did anyone else survive?" As he spoke, six or seven grey doves fluttered down on to the roof. They still nested in the rafters of the old cottage, even after their owner had abandoned it, and them, to ruin. Their mournful cooing filled the evening air as they settled down for the night.

"I don't think so, Strong Arm. Only you and I remain." The two men locked eyes, both feeling keenly the loss of the rest of the *Fire Drake's felag*. Arvid hung his head sorrowfully. "The wave washed us back down into the Mere, through a new hole they had blasted in the wall. A few soldiers, stationed on the banks, shot our men with matchlocks as they came to the surface. They picked them off one by one. I managed to swim underwater to a reed bank, and used a hollow stem to breathe through. All the rest of the day, I stayed there, under water, until the cold almost killed me. Then I managed to creep away in the twilight. Luckily for me, some local folk took me in, and I stayed with them for quite awhile. Once I was recovered, they gave me some different clothes and I made my way here."

Gwenn asked in surprise, "Did you not wish to die in battle with the rest of the men — to earn your place in Skyre?"

Arvid shook his head. "I knew Gunnar had gone to find you, and I started thinking about Gudrun. Suddenly, I just wanted to see her again. Maybe it was wrong to leave the rest of our *felag* to go to Skyre, but I don't care. I am tired of fighting, Faircrow."

The sun disappeared behind the dunes and the evening grew chill. The cooing of the doves faded away. Gwenn shivered, and Gunnar immediately took her inside, and made her comfortable on the bed of fresh straw. After brewing an extra-strong cup of the poppy tea, he sat with her while she sipped it and showed her the tiny shoes. She smiled with delight and kissed him, forgetting all her worries for a brief moment. Arvid watched from the doorway, his heart troubled by Gunnar's tender devotion to Gwenn.

After a few minutes, Gwenn dropped into an uneasy sleep, and the two men walked back outside together. They sat on a fallen tree not far from the door and conversed in low tones, so Gunnar could keep within earshot of Gwenn. Both men pulled out their pipes and lit up, puffing restfully in the twilight.

Gunnar drew out his knife and began carving a piece of soft wood. Arvid, watching curiously, asked, "What is that you are making, Strong Arm?"

He smiled and shrugged. "It is a rattle, for the baby. He will need some play things when he arrives." Under his skilled and careful attention, the wood soon took on the rounded shape of a ball.

Arvid put an arm around his shoulder. He said, quietly, "Listen, Gunnar, old friend, you have to know, chances are..."

Gunnar interrupted him forcefully, hissing, "Of course I know! Just don't say anything more. I have to go on believing she and our baby will be all right. Do you see, Arvid?" His blue eyes filled with tears and he put a hand to his face.

Arvid patted his arm before saying, sympathetically, "All right, Strong Arm. But what are we going to do now? If she is to have any chance at all, we need to get back to Starruthe right away. Do you have a boat?"

Gunnar nodded enthusiastically. "I took the *Fire Drake*. She is hidden in one of the estuaries. We can leave as soon as I gather enough supplies together. I will sail up the coast to Feringhall, where my grandmother lives, then you can take the boat back to Einar."

"It will be a difficult run, even with the two of us," Arvid mused thoughtfully.

"We will make it, Arvid. We have to."

A sudden piercing scream from Gwenn brought both men to their feet. Gunnar tore back across the sand and through the open door, Arvid at his heels. She had curled herself up into a ball and now clutched at her middle. A large stain of pinkish fluid soaked her breeches and spread across the floor.

He fell to his knees by her side and cried out in alarm, "Gwenn, what is it? Are you in pain?"

She moaned. "I feel like something is pushing on my chest. What is wrong with me? Everything hurts again." She thrashed about on the hay, as Gunnar held her down. Though she had been incontinent since her injury, he had a horrible feeling the wetness spreading across the floor now was not urine.

Arvid alone seemed unruffled. He said, "The baby is coming. We will have to deliver it."

Gunnar stood and ran his fingers through his hair in agitation. "What?! Holy blood and fire! No, it can't be. We have to get to Starruthe first. Gwenn, you must stop, do you hear me? You can't have the baby now." His voice rose, and Arvid could hear the underlying panic, only just contained. He grabbed Gunnar by the shoulders and shook him roughly.

"Go and find something to wrap the baby in, and boil some

clean water in a pan. I will stay here with her. And don't hurry — it will be ages yet before it comes." Gunnar dashed from the room, and Arvid shut and barred the door from the inside. He knelt down by Gwenn, saying reassuringly, "Now, Faircrow, don't worry about anything. I helped Gudrun do this four times." He moved her so she rested on her back, and removed her breeches. Her breath came in short painful gasps.

"Where's Gunnar?" she cried.

"I sent him out. He'd be no use in the state he's in."

She moaned as another contraction came, very close to the last. "Arvid, help me. It feels like someone squeezing me in two," she cried breathlessly. Arvid could see the baby's head quite clearly now, a tiny red ball with a fringe of dark hair.

"You need to push, Gwenn."

"I... I can't. I can't do it."

"Yes, you can, Faircrow. Now come on. Fight! Fight for this child," he urged.

She tried, feebly, and then the baby was there, in his hands. He cradled it to his chest, and cast about for his knife to cut the cord with. Gwenn continued to writhe and moan on the floor. Arvid said, "You can stop pushing now. You have a boy, and he seems to be healthy and strong." Then he looked back down at her in alarm.

Thirty minutes later, Gunnar walked back to the cottage, bearing a more or less clean linen bed sheet, and a steaming bucket of water. As he passed the shuttered window, he heard the sound of an infant, crying weakly. He pounded on the door and Arvid opened it, looking very bemused.

Gunnar asked anxiously, "Is Gwenn all right? Is the baby?" He added reproachfully, "You said it would be ages, Arvid."

Arvid smiled and held out his hand for the bucket. "Gwenn is all right, Strong Arm. But you had better get to work on another rattle right away."

"What?"

Arvid laughed. "She just bore you twins — two sons, and they both look fine."

The sand made a soft crunching noise as Gunnar fell backwards, in a dead faint.

Chapter Twenty

The Ice Demon's Roof

Hieronymus blinks at her. You are right, my friend. We must do something for young Dai. Perhaps our brother can help us, eh?
She begins to whistle a haunting tune.

~~~~~~~~~

Katkin marked the endless days of her captivity by scratching marks on the mildewed wall of her dank cell, deep within the bowels of the Citadel, although it was not always easy to tell when one day ended and the next began. She had no window to watch the movement of the sun, only a shaft of light filtering in from a crack in the ceiling, high above her head. Once a day, perhaps in the morning, a hatch opened in the bottom of her door, just large enough for her gaoler to shove a tray through. The tray held a plate of food, a stoppered bottle of water and an empty chamber pot, nothing else. She took the food and the water, and then placed her full chamber pot and yesterday's dishes on the tray, which he promptly removed.

At first, she had begged and pleaded with the gaoler on the other side. "Speak to me! How fares the City? How is King Tristan? You are his gaoler; can you not carry a message to my son?"

He never replied, nor did she ever see his face. His cracked leather boots were her only contact with the outside world. She took to studying them with a passion for the minute or so they filled the slot in the doorway each day. Were they muddy? Dusty? Had a new nail worked loose on the hobbed soles?

Forty-five days passed, by the scratches on the wall, and in all that time Katkin never saw another person, nor heard a voice. At first, she had been afraid her son would question her, as he had promised, or even resort to more crude methods to get information. But it seemed Tristan had another, more subtle, form of torture in mind. Now that the City had been successfully defended against the Fynära he no longer needed his sister, so he decided to lock up his traitorous mother in solitary confinement, and throw away the key.

After finishing the first part of her allotted food, Katkin sat on her bed with her back against the damp wall of her cell. In a little while, she would begin the series of exercises she did each day to keep herself fit — running in place, sit-ups and one-armed push ups all helped make her strong, and kept her incipient madness at bay. She passed the time until she could exercise by balling up little crumbs of bread for her friends, when they chose to join her. After a few moments, a rustling sound from the straw covered floor revealed the presence of four brown rats, which crept over to sit by her feet. The first time she had seen them, Katkin had screamed and screamed, sending them chittering away in panic. But now they were her faithful and trusted companions, and each one had a name.

"Well, Arlo, your whiskers look fine today," she murmured, as she held a ball of bread delicately between her fingers and thumb. The rat sniffed it and clutched at the offering with his tiny paws. His "wife", Desdemona, scuttled up for her share. Katkin stroked her soft fur, and said, "And how are your young ones, Desa?"

The two other rats, both juveniles, hung back nervously. She tossed a shower of breadcrumbs over to them and they scurried about, collecting them. Arlo and Desdemona, both completely unafraid, climbed into her lap and washed themselves. Without the companionship of these rats, Katkin knew, she would already have lost all hope. She often wondered if Lalluna had somehow sent them to her, for though the Goddess had little power in the sphere of men, she could enter the minds of animals and ask them to do her bidding.

After their meal and ablutions, the rats squeezed back through a tiny crack in the wall, leaving her alone.

She called softly, "Good-bye my friends. Come and visit me again, soon."

Once a week, in addition to her rations, the tray held a basin of warm water and a sliver of soap for her own ablutions. She looked forward all week to this occasion, and washed both herself and her clothes thoroughly, hoping in this way to prevent any of the scabrous skin conditions she knew plagued prisoners. Katkin recognized that her health would eventually fail, from lack of sunlight, and decent food, but she intended to last as long as she could, if for no other reason than to spite her son. While her clothes dried, she huddled in her scratchy woolen blanket and talked endlessly to Jacq, or Tomas, or her sister Willow. The fact they never answered her had ceased to be a problem many lonely days ago.

One evening, on the fiftieth day of her imprisonment, Katkin readied herself for bed. She combed out her hair with her fingers, and removed her prison issue dress, hung it carefully from a hook on the wall, then ate the last of her ration of food for the day. This late meal, she had found, kept her hunger pangs at bay, so she could sleep. Katkin shook out her thin mattress and fluffed it up as much as she could. Still, before morning, the uneven boards of the bench on which it rested would be digging holes in her back. She stretched out, and placed her hand behind her head. Judging by the glimmer of light filling her cell, there must be a full moon outside.

Katkin waited for sleep to take her. In the first days of her imprisonment, missing Jacq, and fearing for Gwenn's safety, she had cried herself to sleep every night. Now she just lay still, and thought about the next day, and what she might do to make it different from the last. In this way, she usually dropped off, sooner or later. Tonight was no exception, and soon she was dreaming of Tomas de Vigny.

He stood before her, glowing with eerie phosphorescence. She saw that the light came from some object he held carefully in his cupped hand. He still wore his cuirassier's uniform, of faded blue with red epaulets. Bending down, he shook her shoulder softly, and said, "Wake up, Katrione. I have come to free you."

The dream appeared uncannily clear and realistic, but still it took her quite a long time to come to the realization she slept no longer, and Tomas truly stood before her. With a cry, she jumped up from her bed and threw herself into his arms. His uniform smelled musty, as if it had been in the back of a wardrobe for many years, but his form felt solid, warm and alive.

She whispered, "Is this a dream? Please tell me it is not or I shall truly go insane."

He raised her chin with his hand, and gazed long at her face before answering. "It is no dream, my dear. I am sorry it took me so long to come to you, but I have traveled far in the Vastness, and time does not seem to pass there as it does in the land of the living. To me, it has been less than a week since the last time I saw you, when I led Gwenn's young man to Acorn, but I can see now you must have been here many days."

Katkin nodded. "It has been fifty days. But how on Yrth did you get in?"

"I came through the Vastness, and you and I must leave the same way, if you choose to come with me."

She looked at him in dismay. "Am I to die? Has Death sent you to collect my soul?"

He smiled at this and shook his head. "I am no errand boy for old man Death. With my help, you will be able to enter the Vastness alive."

"Then what are we waiting for?" she cried.

"Hold for a moment," Tomas urged softly. "There is something I must show you before we go." He opened his hand, and revealed a shard of light, like a small diamond, glowing in his palm.

"What do you have there, Tomas?"

"This is all that remains of Lalluna. I searched long in the Temple, before I found her, swept into a corner and surrounded by dust."

Katkin looked down at his cupped palm in shock. What had happened to the beautiful winged Goddess she had once served? "My poor Lalluna," she said sorrowfully. "Is there anything I can do to help her?"

Tomas nodded slowly. "But I have no right to ask it of you."

"Why ever not?"

He stared at the glowing shard in his hand before answering, as if he were trying to make up his mind over something. "It would place you in grave danger," he answered finally.

"I don't care, Tomas," she said resolutely. "I want to help Lalluna, if I can."

"Will you join with her, and let her shelter within you, until she regains her strength?" She nodded uncertainly, wondering why Tomas would be so concerned about a Goddess he had never worshipped in life.

255

"You must be sure, Katrione. In all the turns of the Gyre, no human has ever joined with an Amaranthine three times. Lalluna does not know what will happen to your earthly body the next time the two of you must separate. You may die."

"If I do this now, can I still go to Gwenn, and help her escape from Ketha?"

"That is what I hope we will do together."

She did not hesitate. "Let Lalluna come to me. I am not afraid." Katkin looked around her cell and shrugged. "There are some kinds of living that are far worse than death."

Tomas raised his hand, and said, "Open your mouth."

She did as he instructed, and he carefully tipped the glowing spark between her parted lips. Katkin was aware of faint tingling warmth on her tongue that quickly spread to her throat. In her other experiences as Lalluna's vessel, she had been given senses like those of the Goddess. She could see, hear, smell, taste and touch with incredible clarity. But this time, with the exception of that reassuring warmth and a disconcerting fluttering sensation in her chest, Katkin felt no different than she had before.

She looked up at Tomas and said, "Now what?"

He smiled. "Now we go." He took her hand, and stepped sideways.

Katkin was aware of a fractured moment of unreality, like a wavering distortion just on the edge of her vision. When she looked around, it seemed as though they were still in her cell in the Citadel — the same uncomfortable bed, the same smelly chamber pot in the corner, and the same scratches on the wall. Yet everything felt profoundly different.

When Tomas walked over to the door and pulled it open, she asked, "How did you manage to unlock it?"

"There are no locked doors in the Vastness," he replied.

They walked down the corridor together, into an unfathomable stillness. It felt as if nothing had ever moved in that stillness, and that once they passed through, nothing else would ever move again. The flat, grey light cast no shadows. Katkin held Tomas' hand tightly, and did not speak. She felt to break that silence would have been ungodly, and wicked. Such solemn immensity reminded her of a cathedral, or rather a world of cathedrals, one after the other. As they traversed the corridor, she turned her head from side to side, searching for any sign of life. There was nothing. Then her heart quailed, for up ahead she could vaguely see someone or some*thing* sitting on the floor and blocking their way.

Katkin breathed in slightly, and whispered, "Tomas? Do you see..."

Tomas continued to walk forward, seemingly unconcerned. He stepped around the seated figure as if it was not there, and nothing happened. Katkin turned her head and stared behind her as they walked away, remembering her first glimpse of such a creature. Then she had been eight years old, in the company of her future husband, Jacq Benet. She had never known, until now, the name of the place he had taken her — the Vastness. She still did not know how he had done it.

Tomas said nothing until they had made their way up through the many levels of the Citadel, and out of the Yoke gate. By then, Katkin had seen many other silent, seated figures. In some places, they appeared to be layered three or four deep, yet when she stared directly at them, her vision resolved the picture into a coherent whole, as if space itself bent to encompass all the sitters. Now, on the Yoke, she paused and gazed across at the Mistmere. The water looked like a black mirror, not a ripple or breath of wind disturbed the surface. Here and there, dotted about the Mere, more of the sitting figures floated on the surface. The sky above their heads was as dull and black as the water — the stars shone only faintly and seemed as insubstantial as motes of dust.

Once they crossed the Yoke and passed through the mouth gate, into the Acre, Katkin looked around her, struck by something odd. She said to Tomas, "There are trees here, in the Vastness! How can they be here if they are alive?"

He nodded. "The trees exist in all the spheres at the same time. No-one knows how or why, for they are silent, and give up their secrets to no-one."

Tomas stepped sideways again and Katkin could tell right away they had left the Vastness. The night rang with sound — of birdsong, and rustling leaves, and the waves slapping against the shore. She took a deep lungful of air, drinking in the keenness of the chill night breeze.

"We can walk through the Acre in the living world," said

Tomas. "No-one will be looking for you yet. Tomorrow they will wonder in vain where you have gone, for your cell door will still be locked."

Shaking her head in awe, Katkin said, "I have so many questions to ask you, I don't know where to begin. But the main one is — where are we going now? I need some different clothes and a decent meal before we set off for Starruthe." She glanced down distastefully at her prison-issue dress of drab grey linen.

"I think we should go to Acorn for the rest of tonight," Tomas said thoughtfully. "Your clothes and things are still there. We can set out tomorrow, early, for the coast of Secuny."

They stepped in and out of the Vastness on their way to Acorn and Katkin could soon make the transition without Tomas' help. When they passed through a village or crossroads — anywhere there might be people about — a sideways step would carry them back into the profound silence of the Vastness. In this way, they reached Acorn quickly, without being seen.

Once inside, Katkin lit a candle, and rummaged around for a change of clothing and a pack. She made some tea, and offered some to Tomas, but he shook his head. The moon had set and it was very late.

"Go to bed, Katrione. You should probably try to get some sleep. I will wait here for you until you awaken."

She asked, uncertainly, "Do you... sleep, Tomas? I mean, can you?"

He smiled at her confused expression and shook his head. "Not really. I just close my eyes sometimes and rest, and it is like a waking dream."

As he finished speaking, Katkin gazed blankly into space for a moment, as if trying to make up her mind about something. Then she walked over to stand before him, and took his hand in hers.

"Come with me?" she asked. She tugged at his hand, to lead him towards the bed, but he did not move.

"Katrione, I don't understand. Why would you... I mean, after everything I did, when I was alive?"

She shrugged. "Why not? I am alone. So are you. Why should we not find comfort in each other this night?"

His vehemence shocked her. "Because I don't deserve it! I

tried to rape you, remember? I tortured your husband for five days. Do these things mean nothing to you now? Why don't you hate me?"

Katkin replied sharply. "You also gave me seventeen extra years with him. Years I would not have had otherwise." She continued, pensively, "I would have married you, if he had died. I wouldn't have had any other choice, with your child on the way. You knew that, did you not?"

He slowly nodded.

"But you sacrificed yourself anyway. For me. And for Gwenn. So how could I hate you? For whatever sins you committed, in your former life, you paid long ago. I forgave you, and so did Jacq, before he died." She looked up at him, in the candlelight, and smiled ruefully. "You look just the same as before. I am much older than you are, now. Maybe you just don't want me any more..."

He cut her off. "No! Of course, I still desire you. You are just as beautiful to me now as you were sixteen years ago. But how can I possibly make you happy? I don't know anything about giving. I never learned how. All my life, I just took the things I wanted."

"Then you shall learn now, my gallant Captain," Katkin said softly, and kissed his mouth with such passionate longing he found he could argue no further. When she tugged at his hand again, he followed her.

Later, as she lay next to him in bed, and stroked the damp curls in his hair, she asked inquisitively, "What is it like? Being dead, I mean."

He stared up at the dark beams on the ceiling for a long while before answering. Then he admitted, "I don't think I know, properly. Nothing happened as it should have."

"What do you mean?"

"After I shot myself, and Death came, we went to the Vastness together. We were still under the oak tree, but everything felt different."

Katkin nodded, remembering.

"Then he rode with me through the Acre and to the shores of the Mistmere. He never said a word, although I tried to talk to him and ask him what would happen to me. I did not feel fearful,

I just wanted to know. We rode out on to the Yoke, about half way across, and that is when I saw the Uri'el."

She interrupted to ask, "Is that what those things are called? I saw one too. They have wings, like Lalluna. What do they do?"

"They are the guardians of the *anafireon*." Katkin appeared baffled, so he explained. "That is the life force of our kind, Katrione. When someone dies, their spirit travels to the Vastness, to rest until the end of the world. The Uri'el cradles them and keeps them safe in the exact same place they passed away."

Katkin remembered the Uri'el she had seen in the corridor. It possessed a long worm-like body, covered in pearlescent scales. Even more striking were its double set of wings — fine-veined and transparent, like those of a dragonfly. The creature also had arms, and long silvery strands of pellucid hair surrounding its face. But the face itself had been blank — completely featureless. She asked Tomas why.

"They say the spirits of the dead can see a face, of the one person whom they loved more than any other on Yrth. That way they feel at peace, sleeping in the arms of their beloved."

She sighed at this, remembering, for a moment, her husband's death. Then she propped up her head on her hand, and said, "Go on with your story. What happened when you reached the Uri'el by the Yoke?"

He said, very quietly, "I saw myself. Sleeping in the arms of a guardian who bore your face."

She sat up in bed, profoundly shocked, and wrapped her arms around her drawn up knees. "I don't understand. Lalluna came to us in the Mere. She healed your leg. She saved us."

He shook his head in the darkness. "She saved *you*, Katrione. I died. But my body stayed in the living world anyway."

Katkin said dreamily, "I saw you... As I slept in the wards at the Infirmarie. You were resting in the arms of your Uri'el." She sighed. "That was such a long time ago. But do you have any idea why you were made to stay?"

He said, "For the longest time, I did not know. Death would say nothing, though I begged him to speak. He just left me standing there on the Yoke, and rode away on his black horse."

"Oh, Tomas, that is horrible — beyond horrible. What did you do?" Katkin wept softly, in sympathy for his plight.

Tomas stroked her hair, trying to comfort her sorrow. "At first I stayed on the Yoke, waiting to see what would happen. I hoped, you know... that my body would somehow merge with the sleeping one. But the Uri'el just stared at me mournfully, and after a time I could not bear it, so I left and started to wander around. I did not know what else to do, and I was very lonely. Eventually, I went to find the rest of my family. My father slept at Havenwood, on his bed, and his face in death bore the same angry expression it had all the time I knew him. Then, I visited my mother's spirit, still in her room at the Infirmarie, and her arms held the form of my stillborn brother, just as the Uri'el held her. I stayed there for a very long time, and told her everything that had happened to me since she died. But it was no comfort, being in that silence. Well, you have felt it, I expect you understand what I mean." Katkin nodded and shivered. "As I rose to leave her, I thought I heard her voice, telling me to go home."

"But you had already been to Havenwood..."

"Not there," Tomas interrupted. "That moldering crypt was never home."

Katkin looked very surprised at this. "Where then?"

"When I was nine years old, my mother took me to see my grandparents. They lived on an island, far from Beaumarais. I visited with them for several years, and would have gladly stayed longer if the old man had not forced me to return to St. Valery and attend military school. Anyway, I decided to go back to their house, and spend eternity there, if I had to spend it anywhere, in the company of my happiest memories. So I traveled through the Vastness to the island. It took me a very long time, because I did not know the way, and there was no-one to ask."

Katkin sighed, thinking of this lonely passage. In the seventeen years since Tomas de Vigny's suicide, she had often prayed that his soul had found peace. It seemed her prayers had not been answered. "Did you find their house? Was it still there?" she asked hopefully.

He nodded enthusiastically. "It was more than just there. When I walked up from the beach, I saw warm light filtering through the shutters, and I could hear the sound of music playing softly from within. After so many days of silence and darkness, I wondered if I had gone insane. Then the door opened and my Grandmother appeared on the threshold, welcoming me."

261

She stared at him in confusion. "Your Grandmother was *alive*, in the Vastness? How could that be?"

"I do not know, exactly. It seems my Grandmother has powers beyond that of ordinary mortals, but she would tell me very little. We mostly just talked about my lives and all the awful things I had done this time around. I begged her for another chance to make things right with you. Finally, she said I should come back here and wait under the oak tree where I shot myself. So I returned to the Acre, and after a time I saw you there, sitting on a stone bench, talking to me. It was autumn then. After that, I hardly ever left the dell, because I did not want to miss your visits. Nothing else mattered to me."

"You could see and hear me, even though you were in the Vastness?" She felt him nod and she said softly, "I could tell, when you came, that autumn. It gave me great comfort. I would have gone mad without you." Katkin rolled sideways, and rested her head on his chest. His heartbeat sounded curiously slow and hollow. After a time, she asked, "What keeps you alive, now? If you don't eat and you don't sleep, why does your heart go on beating?"

Tomas did not speak for a long time. He seemed to be weighing his answer carefully. "Because I was chosen by the immortals, Katrione. I have become one of the Amaranthine."

Katkin found this idea quite unlikely at first, but within a few seconds, she accepted it. It was the only logical explanation. "How did you find out?"

"Here is the story, as I understand it. When we were in the Mere, I drowned, though I was not meant to die so soon. That is why my body now lies on the surface of the Mistmere, with the Uri'el. Geya sent Lalluna to bring me life again because I had more things I needed to do. I had to make a child with you..." Katkin stirred in his arms and he kissed her softly. "Lalluna gave me the *anafireon* of an Amaranthine who had perished in the war against the Angellus. So after my human body died a second time, and I was left in the Vastness, I started to remember other lives, and other battles." He sighed. "Far too many battles. Each time things happen differently, but in the end..." His voice trailed off and he gazed up at the ceiling.

Katkin shivered at the bleakness in his voice. She asked, though she did not want to know, "How *does* it end?"

"We lose the war. The Angellus consume everything and make their way down to the next level."

That name filled her with fear. She remembered the vision of the pulsating Void she had seen long ago, in the Temple of Lalluna. In her breast, the Goddess fluttered desperately, like a trapped and dying sparrow. "Who are the Angellus? Why do they attack the Vastness?"

"They came from the unknown future, and make their way back through the rising Gyre. Every age they touch is destroyed. So far they have not been able to enter the living sphere, but we greatly fear that they will soon find a way."

"What on Yrth is the rising Gyre?"

"Time. Time is the rising Gyre. When the worlds were made the Gyre began, and it winds around the infinite passage of time. Within the Gyre, everything that is or ever has been or ever will be exists. Now the Angellus have infected it, and they want only our destruction."

Katkin shivered at this. "How can the immortals fight them?"

"With such weaponry as we have at our disposal. So far, we have found nothing that stops them for long. But there is a prophecy — something to do with the Firaithi, and our daughter is a part of it."

Katkin said nothing for a long time. Her journey as the vessel of Lalluna now took on a clear and unassailable meaning. She whispered, "I am a part of it too, am I not? When I joined Lalluna, in the Temple, the day we healed Hythea, I saw all my past lives stretching out like an endless ribbon."

"Yes," he agreed softly. "You and Lalluna are also connected, both as Amaranthine, and as Avatar. No-one else, in all the turns of the Gyre, has been both."

"And Jacq? I saw his face in all my past lives too. Which Amaranthine is he? ...Dai?"

He stared at her and Katkin thought she saw a flash of anger in his eyes. "Dai is a traitor. Your husband has always been the son of Shiqaba."

She said beseechingly, "Please tell me more."

"I know little else to tell you. Only that our lives are like a play, with the same cast of characters, but a different story each time. And you and I have been together in many other pasts, but never like this." His fingers lightly stroked the bare skin on her back, and raised a shiver.

"Have we never been lovers before?"

"No, Katrione. Always you have to make a choice, and always you choose the son of Shiqaba instead of me." He sighed and Katkin suddenly realized the true identity of the man who lay beside her.

"You are Fyn, are you not? The Amaranthine that Lalluna told me she loves. No wonder you went back to the Temple for her!" Katkin's eyes filled with tears. "My choice has kept you apart from her in every lifetime. Lalluna must hate me." She wept, and Tomas wrapped his arms about her tightly.

"Don't be sorry, love. Lalluna and I have always known our fate, since the beginning of time. She has ever chosen to protect you. She loves you, as she loves herself. How could she not? You are one and the same."

Katkin sought his mouth in the darkness. She knew they had little time together, and she wanted to give him all the love she held in her heart — to somehow make up for all her unhappy choices. Lalluna's love and her own, joined as one.

Tomas had only a moment to wonder what this new choice might mean for this turn of the Gyre. Then her passion engulfed him like an undulating flame, and he was carried with it — beyond ruin, battle and death — beyond the Gyre — to the very heart of heaven itself.

Early in the morning, Tomas left Acorn to scout the road ahead for Guardsmen, telling Katkin to be ready in fifteen minutes. She dressed in a plain, muslin gown and sturdy boots, and stuffed a few extra articles in a worn bag. When she had finished her packing, had a cup of tea and a hasty breakfast, Katkin stood quietly in the main room of Acorn, thinking back to the last time she had been there — the day Jacq died. Following an irresistible impulse, she stepped sideways into the silence of the Vastness. A white-winged Uri'el sat on the floor, close to the door leading to the bedrooms. Katkin saw, to her dismay, that its arms were empty. Suddenly, the Uri'el raised its head and gazed right at her. She saw herself, as in a mirror, but with an expression of infinite sadness.

Katkin asked of it, "Where is my husband? Why is his *anafir-eon* not here in the Vastness? Tell me, Uri'el."

The Uri'el's voice echoed through the silence of the Vastness, though it whispered only one word — "Raven."

After a moment, it raised one alabaster hand and opened its fingers. Jacq's crystal feather talisman rested in its palm. Reaching downwards with a trembling hand, Katkin took the talisman, slipped the thong over her head and placed it next to her heart. The Uri'el withdrew its hand and dropped its eyes to study its empty lap. Katkin got the impression that it was no longer aware of her presence. An unexpected flash of movement at the edge of her peripheral vision, black and menacing, filled her with terror. She fled back to the living world. When Tomas questioned her later about where she had found the talisman, she unashamedly lied.

Huw whistled cheerfully as he scrambled over a rocky outcrop and down into a dark, damp gully, hunting for wild mushrooms. When he came upon a cluster, he carefully picked the largest caps, and put them in a bag hanging at his side. Though mushrooms were not terribly nutritious, Arkady liked them, and Huw wanted very much to please his brother. The wind from the ocean penetrated easily through his tattered shirt, and Huw paused to tie the piece of blanket he wore around his waist up over his shoulders, like a cape. Though in the southern parts of Yr summer would still be in full flower, here, on the northern island that had become their home, autumn had been sovereign for many days. Already the tubers, roots and gull's eggs they depended on for food were growing scarce, and Huw did not want to think about what would happen once winter arrived.

As he made his way down the rocky cliff face with his full bag of mushrooms, he was closely followed by a one-legged tern, who hopped along, giving the occasional hopeful shriek. Huw spoke to the bird affectionately. "All right, Bran. I suppose I can spare one for you." He tossed a small mushroom to the bird, who gobbled it down eagerly. Huw sighed as Bran shrieked again. "You are just like Kadya, always hungry. Go and catch yourself a fish!" The bird spread its wings and took off easily from the cliff side. Huw watched it fly away. "I wish I could grow some wings like

265

yours, my friend. If I could fly, then I could go to the mainland and bring back a boat for us to sail away on." Sighing again, he packed up his mushrooms and headed back to the cabin.

He found Arkady sitting cross-legged on the floor with his eyes tightly closed. A blanket was wrapped over his thin shoulders. Within the first week of their arrival on the island, he began his meditation exercises again. Now, after many weeks of practice, Arkady spent four or five hours a day sitting — his lean, ascetic face composed and calm. Huw entered the fishing cabin, and put the mushrooms in a pot of water on the hearth to stew. Later he would go fishing, and perhaps collect some dandelion leaves for a salad. Without complaint, Huw had quietly taken over most of the food-gathering duties, leaving his brother free to meditate.

After a few moments, Arkady's eyes opened. "That smells good. I am hungry. Did you find many mushrooms?"

Huw peered down into the pot thoughtfully. "Enough for our supper, but not enough to dry for winter stores."

Arkady looked at him blankly. "Winter stores? What is the point, Huw? We will not make it through a winter on this gods-forsaken rock."

This pessimism bothered Huw, and he said, with forced cheer, "I intend to make sure we do. I just have to collect a little extra food each day. We should not give up hope. Rescue could come at any time, you know."

His brother did not seem convinced. "I appreciate what you are trying to do, but I just cannot feel hopeful any more. How long have we been here? Seventy-three days, is it not? The weather is only going to get worse. Face it, this island used to be inhabited, but the people who lived here abandoned it because of the climate and lack of trees. They aren't coming back."

In their exploration of the island, those first few weeks after they landed, Huw and Arkady had found the remnants of a settlement on the south side, now just a ruin of tumbled stones and holly bushes. A few hardy sheep and goats, probably the descendants of animals left behind by the former occupants, still roamed the grassy cliff top. Occasionally they managed to catch an unwary one by chasing it off the precipice.

Huw said patiently, "I am not ready to give up, just yet. I still believe the Un-Named One will come to our aid. Now, I am going fishing." He grabbed a hook and line, a pot of fish heads from the table, and stalked out the door, calling back over his shoulder, "Keep an eye on those mushrooms, and don't let them dry out." A blast of freezing air entered the room as he went out, and Arkady huddled further under his blanket.

Arkady marveled at his brother's capacity for cheerfulness and hope in the face of their dire situation. It seemed likely he would go on fighting to the bitter end. Arkady, meanwhile, contented himself with meditation, to prepare his soul for the turning of the wheel. He moved closer to the fireplace, and held his hands out to the small blaze. Huw insisted they must conserve peat for winter, so the draughty cabin always felt cold. He peeped at the mushrooms, and decided they were in no danger of drying out. Then he lay down by the fireplace for a catnap, before beginning a new round of contemplation.

Almost at once he dreamed — of an isolated cottage, on a wild and rocky coast, with shadowy green pines growing tall, all around, like sentinels. The fresh scent of the needles filled the air, mingled with the salt tang of the ocean. He walked towards the house — a curiously built structure, with deeply overhanging eaves, and tiny, shuttered windows — and opened the low door. To his right lay the main room, a jumble of odd chairs, small tables and piles of dusty books. Many shelves hung on the walls, haphazardly filled with jars, boxes and pouches. He opened a glass-stoppered bottle of some poisonous-looking yellow fluid and wrinkled his nose at the sharp smell.

A very old woman, sitting in a chair by the fireplace, greeted him. "Welcome, Seed Bearer. I am glad you have come to me, at last." She wore a long, shapeless robe of bright blue and boots of red leather. Her white hair was very thin, and the pinkness of her scalp showed through on the top of her head.

Arkady asked, "Who are you? Why have you brought me here?"

The old woman smiled. "I am Eydis. I did not bring you. You came because your heart is here. It calls to you."

He gazed at her in confusion. "My heart? I don't understand."

She rose slowly, and groped for her walking stick. "Do you not? Come then, I will show you."

Eydis took his hand in hers. Her skin — translucent, blue

veined — looked just like white marble. She led him to a hidden alcove in the back of the room. Behind the curtain, a deathly pale, thin-faced girl lay on a bed, with a snow-white coverlet tucked up around her shoulders. Her blond hair clung damply to her skin, and her cheeks burned with fever. She stirred restlessly, and moaned, as though she felt great pain. Her eyes, when she opened them, were as blue as the skies of T'Shang. She stared fixedly, without seeing, and then her dark lashes rested on her cheeks again.

Arkady watched the girl silently for many moments, the old woman at his side forgotten. Then he asked, hoarsely, "Is she going to die?"

Eydis nodded. "Very soon, unless you can heal her."

He never took his eyes off Gwenn as he said, "How can I? Did you bring me here just to torment my soul? If there is hope, tell me, old woman."

"Remember what Dawa taught you, long ago. There is another way to leave your island, without a boat. Use it. Quickly, Seed Bearer, she does not have much time left." The old woman's voice faded away, as the alcove and the girl dissolved into a sparkling mist.

When Huw returned a moment later, carrying his meager catch of fish in a wicker creel, Arkady was curled up by the fireplace, weeping bitterly. With a cry, Huw dropped the basket and hurried to his side.

He shook his brother's shoulder. "What is it? What has happened?"

Arkady took a deep, shaky breath, then another. "I had a dream. I saw her. I saw Gwenn. She is ill, somewhere. The old woman with her said she would die soon. I don't know how to help her. I don't know what to do..."

He was crying again and Huw looked on him with pity and concern, unable to find any words of comfort. But he knew such a vision should not be discounted, so he asked, earnestly, "Did the old woman say anything else? Anything that might help us find a way off the island?"

"She said..." He paused to catch his breath, and Huw patted his back. "She said there was a way to leave the island without a boat. Something Dawa taught me."

Huw shrugged, thinking of his words to Bran. "How can that help us? The only way to leave this island without a boat would be to grow some wings."

Arkady stared at Huw, realization dawning in his red-rimmed eyes. He said, breathlessly, "I think I know now what she meant. I need to go out and get something. I will be right back." He jumped up, grabbed his blanket and ran out the door, slamming it behind him, leaving his astonished brother still kneeling by the fireplace.

He returned an hour later, just as Huw was ladling out mushrooms and fish onto tin plates. Ignoring the food, Arkady dumped a crumpled handful of odd-looking vegetation on the table. The large, pale green leaves had deeply toothed edges, and fine light hairs growing all over them. Huw recognized them at once. He said, in alarm, "This is black henbane, Kadya. It is very poisonous. I have seen goats and hens grow sick and stagger about after they ate it, and then die."

Arkady said nothing in reply, just began tearing up the leaves with his fingers and placing them in the cooking pot. Huw wondered if his brother had lost his mind. He said again, "What are you going to do with this? We cannot eat it."

After adding water to the pot, Arkady pushed it close to the fire. He turned to Huw and said, matter-of-factly, "I am going to make a decoction of the henbane leaves and drink it."

"What? Have you gone mad? It will kill you."

Arkady shook his head. "Dawa told me once of a method the ancients used to travel long distances from place to place. By ingesting the leaves of certain potent plants, the *anafireon* may leave the body and fly free in the air like a bird. I can go to her. Help her." He gripped Huw's shoulders. "Don't you see? I have to try this. It is her only hope."

Huw threw off his hands and turned away. He said angrily, "How is killing yourself going to help her, or us? You don't know what you are doing."

After a few minutes, the boiling liquid in the pot smelled revolting, and had taken on a green, slimy appearance. Arkady took it from the fire with the edge of his blanket and placed it on the table to cool. Then he said, "Let's eat. I should probably have something in my stomach before I drink it."

269

Huw sat down at the table and picked at his fish and mushrooms listlessly. His eyes filled with tears. "Please don't do this. What will I do if you die? I will be all alone here."

"I won't die. I just have to be careful about the dose. You must stay and watch over my body while I am gone. Will you do that for me?"

Huw nodded unhappily.

After making sure the decoction had cooled sufficiently, Arkady dipped a cup into it. Without saying anything more, he drank the foul liquid straight down, and then lay on the floor again, by the fireplace. His brother squatted beside him and watched him anxiously for signs of distress. Within a few moments, his eyes closed and he appeared to be sleeping. Huw took his hand, and the skin was cold and clammy under his fingers.

It was many hours before he stirred, and Huw never left him alone, even for a few minutes. Arkady, his face pale, weakly rolled onto his side and vomited up a sickly green liquid. Huw crossed the room in alarm and helped him into a sitting position.

Arkady whispered, "Huw?"

"Yes, my brother. I am here."

Arkady groaned and clutched his abdomen as another wave of nausea hit him. A flood of the green fluid shot from his mouth, soaking his shirt and breeches. Huw tried to mop up the mess with a rag as Arkady ran his sleeve over his face and said weakly, "He will be coming soon, Huw. You must keep me alive until we get to Starruthe." His voice grew fainter. "I tried to heal her, but I failed. Hana's fire could not work like that. But then I went to him." Arkady screamed in pain as his gut cramped into a fiery knot, and his bowels released. He scrabbled with his hand on Huw's arm, saying, again and again, "Promise me." Then his eyes rolled back in his head, and with a final, gurgling moan, he passed out.

Chapter Twenty-One

Lut's White Horses

Welcome, Shiqaba. Raven has stolen Dai's *anafireon* and his seed. That meddling Geya put her up to it. I have punished her, but now I need your help to right this wrong.

The tall, grey-haired man before her nods.

He says, I can create a receptacle for the life force, and place it back in the Gyre so that we can make use of it. But the seed, Eydis... I fear the child of such an evil union can be nothing other than a demon.

~~~~~~~~~~

Gunnar sat by the ancient cradle, rocking it gently back and forth. The wood felt worn under his fingers, smoothed by a century of use. The cradle had been his, as an infant, and his father's and grandfather's before that. Now it held the most miraculous of all treasures — his two sons — each so like the other he could not tell them apart. He watched, transfixed, as one of the tiny mouths opened in a yawn, and a pink fist, no bigger than a rosebud, waved briefly in the air, before settling back on the lamb's wool blanket.

Gunnar laughed softly and offered, "Come, little boxer, do you want to fight me?"

He very carefully picked up the hand to tuck it back under the cover, and the fingers briefly curled around one of his and held on, with only a whisper of pressure. Each perfect finger, rendered in shell pink, ended in an impossibly diminutive nail. He caught his breath, unable, for a moment, to fathom the depth of feeling these two tiny beings evoked in him. His sons — Jakob and Arvid. Already he loved them more than he had thought it possible to love anything, and in his fierce devotion he divined the seeds of utter heartbreak.

His grandmother had already told him, "They are very tiny, Gunnar. Born much too soon, probably. We will do our best to save them, but they may not have much of a chance, especially after a long sea voyage."

But Gunnar would not be dissuaded. He said firmly, "No Grandmother. My boys are strong, like me. They want to live." He could tell by the way they rooted for their mother's nipples and suckled with such determination. They drew life from her, and each day, as they grew stronger, Gwenn seemed to fail a little bit more.

They were only three weeks old, his sons, but already they had braved the long voyage from the coast of Secuny to Feringhall. The crossing had been rough, and the days at sea endless. Arvid had stayed at the steering oar for four nights and days straight, going without sleep, so Gunnar could care for Gwenn and the babies. Gunnar knew that without his first mate none of them would have survived. Still, it had been touch and go, as Gwenn lay on the deck, feverish and sick, too weak to hold a child to her breast. He had turned her on her side, and given the boys to her one at a time, and covered them up with a reindeer skin to keep off the rain and the freezing winds. The other baby he kept tucked in his leather tunic, next to the warmth of his skin and the beating of his heart. Once they arrived in Feringhall, his grandmother had taken over Gwenn's care, leaving Gunnar to tend to his sons, which he did, all day and every day, with complete dedication.

The tapping of his grandmother's stick could be heard now in the passage, and as she entered the room he asked her quietly, "How is she?"

"The same, Gunnar. She clings to life by a thread. I fear only the demon inside her is keeping her alive now. I am doing all I can, with poultices and herbs, but we must pray more help arrives soon."

Gunnar re-tucked the blanket around Jakob and Arvid. He said bitterly, "No-one is coming here to help us."

Eydis came to stand beside him, and put a comforting hand on his shoulder. She said, "Help *is* on the way, I promise you. The stones told me a few minutes ago." Just then, a large, very fluffy orange cat bounded into the room, meowing and trilling conversationally. She said in reply, "Is that right, Hieronymus? Tonight, you say?" She glanced over at Gunnar and smiled. "Did you hear? Hieronymus says they are coming this very evening."

Gunnar smiled in return and shook his head, bemused by her strange habit of holding conversations with the cat. It was curious though, how Hieronymus had been with her ever since Gunnar could remember. The cat still looked just the same, though he must be close to twenty-five years old. His grandmother was full of little mysteries like that. How had she known to make everything ready? When they arrived, the cradle had been set up by the fireplace, and a bed made up in the sick room with fresh sheets, though Gunnar had sent no word. And how had Grandmother understood everything about Keth Dirane and Gwenn, without being told a thing?

One of the boys began to cry lustily, and woke the other.

"Must be supper time," Gunnar said.

He carefully scooped up both babies with practiced ease, and carried them through to Gwenn. She lay in bed, in the alcove, pale and unmoving. Only the rise and fall of the white coverlet showed she still lived. He touched her shoulder gently, and her eyes opened. As he propped her up with pillows, she smiled bravely at him, but she could not hide the pain in her eyes. Gunnar lay beside her as she nursed Jakob and Arvid, but did not try to engage her in conversation. Talking made her tired, and she needed all her strength.

After both boys had been fed, he kissed her forehead softly, and carried them back into the main room. He changed their sodden wrappings and cleaned them up, all the while singing a hearty sea shanty to keep them entertained.

Gunnar stopped singing when he heard Gwenn's panicked cry from the alcove. "Don't go!"

He hurriedly tucked the babies back down in the cradle, and ran to her side. She was struggling to sit up, talking incoherently. He caught her shoulders and gently pushed her back down on the bed.

"Easy, love. What is it? Tell me what you need and I will bring it."

She caught his wrist and held it, and her voice sounded desperate. "Where is he? Tell him to come back, Gunnar."

He did not want to know who she meant, but he asked anyway.

She started to cry. "Kadya. He was here, just a minute ago. I think he was trying to help me, but something went wrong. I could not hear what he was saying. Then he vanished. You must find him. I need him."

Gunnar inhaled sharply, and sat beside her, trying not to show his hurt. He took her hand and said softy, "I think you must have been dreaming. He has not been here."

But Gwenn would not be consoled. Ripping her hand away from his, she cried, "Don't lie to me, Gunnar! What have you done to him?" She struggled violently as he tried to soothe her with soft words. As she called Arkady's name again and again, asking for his help, he felt his composure slipping.

"Gwenn, please. I swear to you, I have done nothing to him. Don't fight me, girl, you are only going to hurt yourself."

"Why should I listen to you? You tried to kill him once before. You murderer! Murderer!" Her voice had risen to a scream now, and every word was like an ice pick through the heart to Gunnar. She snarled, "I hate you and I hate your brats! They will grow up to be filthy, stinking Northmen, just like their father." Even though he knew she was not in her right mind, still he could not suppress a cry of anguish at her words.

"Please don't say that. Please, Gwenn..." His grandmother swept through the curtain, carrying a bottle made of black glass, with a heavy rubber stopper.

Eydis ordered, "Hold her head, Gunnar." He gripped Gwenn's jaw as she gnashed wildly, trying to bite his fingers. Blood dribbled from her mouth and ran down her chin.

Once she had doused a cloth with the sweetish-smelling liquid from the bottle, Eydis clapped it over Gwenn's nose and mouth and held it there. As the ether took effect, she went completely limp. Gunnar withdrew his bloodied hand, and thoughtlessly wiped it across the front of his shirt. As he stared down at her face, he did not believe he could ever again be free of the misery her words had given him.

His grandmother murmured, "I will stay with her now. Don't take on so, boy. She did not mean any of it. The battle crow's poison has infected her mind, that is all. We must persuade Raven to leave her soon, before the madness becomes permanent." Then she said, casually, "Gwenn's mother and father are walking up from the landing now. Go and talk with them, while I sit with her."

Gunnar gaped at her, wondering if his grandmother had been struck with the same madness. Hadn't Gwenn told him her father was dead? He asked incredulously, "How in the name of the Mariner did her parents get here?"

His grandmother smiled at him, and offered sweetly, "Why don't you go and ask them? Now out!"

He wiped his eyes hastily and opened the curtain. Hieronymus meowed and wrapped himself around his legs, purring loudly. Gunnar found the cat a piece of fish for his supper, and checked on Jakob and Arvid, who were both sleeping, snoring sweetly, with one tiny fist next to each face. When he heard the faint sound of voices outside, he crossed the room towards the door. He flung it open and peered into the darkness. Two figures, shrouded in fog, were crunching their way up the shingle from the beach. Gunnar scratched his head in confusion when he recognized the mysterious specter from the battlefield, which had steered the *Fire Drake* down the Ariane River for him. Then he had seemed as insubstantial as a ghost, but now he appeared to be thoroughly alive as he strode along beside Gwenn's mother.

As the pair approached the door, Gunnar stepped through and said, "Welcome to Feringhall," in halting Maraison.

Katkin smiled at him and said, "Thank you, Gunnar." She pointed to Tomas and said, in Dalvolk, "I believe you have met Gwenn's father, Tomas de Vigny." Gunnar gaped at her in amazement. When had she learned to speak his tongue like a native?

He opened the door wide, and stepped aside to let them in. Katkin paused on the threshold just long enough to remove her cloak, and then she spied the cradle and its precious contents. With a cry of utter delight, she flew across the room and stood quite still over it, admiring her first grandchildren. She looked up at Gunnar with shining eyes. "Twins! They are so beautiful. What did you name them?"

Gunnar blushed, feeling shy about his boys. He said softly, "Your daughter and I picked the names together. Arvid Tomas and Jakob Leif. Arvid is my first mate, and Leif was my father's name. The other names are for Gwenn's two fathers."

Tomas glanced up at the mention of his name, and smiled as Katkin told him about his namesake. He asked which child was which. After Katkin translated the question, Gunnar's face went even redder as he admitted he could not tell them apart. Then she asked him quietly, "How is Gwenn faring?"

Gunnar's proud expression immediately turned melancholy. "She is as well as can be expected. My grandmother is with her now. You can see her when she wakes up."

Katkin sat down on a threadbare upholstered settle, close to the fire. Gunnar offered her some tea, and she accepted gratefully. As he busied himself filling the kettle, out of the corner of his eye he watched Tomas sit down by the cradle and begin to rock it, his expression one of rapt wonder. Gunnar could not figure out how he could possibly be Gwenn's true father. He seemed to be no older than Gunnar, himself. As he carried a steaming mug of tea to Katkin, he asked her about it. She translated the question to Tomas, who smiled again, shook his head and returned his full attention to his sleeping grandsons. She said, "It is a very long story and Tomas thinks it would be easier if I told you about it, now that Lalluna has given me your language."

He thought any tale would be a welcome relief from his worries, so he said, "I would dearly like to know how you both came to be here, even if it takes all night to tell." Gunnar poured a mug of tea for himself, and settled down next to Katkin on the sofa.

Katkin sipped her tea, looking fondly over at Tomas, and then, more sharply, at Gunnar. There was something uncanny about the two of them. They were enough alike to be brothers, and it was not just because of their blond hair. Katkin shrugged, thinking it just some bizarre coincidence. She began her story with the bargain she had made resulting in Gwenn's conception. Gunnar raised an eyebrow at this, but did not question it. When she spoke of Tomas' suicide, he said softly, "So in the end, he became a good man, did he not?"

She nodded. "Yes, Tomas is a very good man now. I think, underneath, he always was. But he was angry and confused and in terrible pain for a long while. The Amaranthine saw the truth though. Otherwise, why would he still be here?"

Gunnar cast his eyes back towards the alcove, thinking on Gwenn, and her pain. Katkin had obviously forgiven Tomas for all the hurtful things he had done. Could he ever forgive Gwenn? He honestly did not know the answer to that. Turning back to Katkin, he asked her, "What happened after we left with William?"

She told him of her imprisonment, and Tomas' unforeseen appearance in her cell. "After we left Acorn in the morning, we made our way here, sometimes in the Vastness and sometimes in the living world. Tomas said we should not spend too much time in Death's kingdom, because time is so unpredictable there. We only crossed over to avoid seeing other people. It took us two weeks of walking to reach the coast of Secuny. Once we arrived, we had to figure out how to cross the water. I wanted to steal a fishing boat, but Tomas thought the passage would be too difficult in the living world, because of the winds and currents."

"So what did you do?"

Katkin smiled. "This became the strangest part of the whole adventure. We went back to the Vastness. An old boat lay on the shore, with one of the Uri'el sitting on the deck, cradling some unfortunate fisherman who had perhaps died while hauling in his nets. I followed Tomas as he stepped on board, and I asked him how we would make the boat sail, since the air in the Vastness never moves. Nothing ever moves there, Gunnar — the ocean is as smooth as a sheet of green glass. Tomas told me we had only to set the boat in motion and it would not stop until we reached the island. I did not believe him, but when he took the oars and gave them a pull, the boat started moving very quickly and steadily through the water. It was amazing."

Gunnar could not bring himself to accept this. "But how did you navigate? You have not sailed to Starruthe before, have you?"

"No, I have not. But I am not so sure about Tomas. I asked him about it, but he rarely speaks now, and he would not answer me. He just stayed at the rudder and brought us here, without any charts for guidance. I think he must have had help from the Goddess."

The curtain to the alcove opened, and Eydis stepped into the room. Gunnar rose quickly to his feet. "How is she?" he asked his grandmother, and Katkin saw the terrible fear in his eyes.

"Still sleeping, Gunnar. Leave her be, for now."

Eydis crossed the room, and went straight to Tomas, who rose to meet her. As Gunnar and Katkin looked on in confusion, they embraced warmly, and Tomas said haltingly, in Dalvolk, "I brought her here, as you said I should."

She regarded him seriously, and said, "Thank you, Tomas.

You have had the most difficult journey of all, and seen things that none of the living have seen. I am very glad you are here now, for I have need of both of you."

He answered simply, "I know, Grandmother. I came as soon as I could."

Gunnar spluttered, "Grandmother? Lutyond's anchor! Why do you call her that, Southerner?"

Eydis answered for him. "Tomas Jean de Vigny is the son of my daughter Lara. He is your cousin, Gunnar."

Gunnar stared in disbelief. Another of his grandmother's little mysteries stood before him, in the form of his cousin Tomas, and this one was the most amazing of all. He wondered, not for the first time, about her and her magicks, and whether Gwenn's distressing problem might form part of some larger pattern she controlled. Certainly a spiraling web of connections appeared to be drawing them all closer to some unknown fate.

Eydis said, "Sit down, all of you, and I will explain. But first I must welcome our other guest." She turned to Katkin and said, "I am thankful you have come, Katrione." Eydis raised her hand and touched Katkin's chest with her fingers. A feeling like the fluttering of butterfly wings awoke there, inside Katkin. "I know of the One you bear with you, and to her also I give greeting." Katkin, feeling more than a little abashed, smiled shyly. Obviously, the old woman who stood before her was a mage of great power and insight.

"Don't just stand their with your mouth open, boy. Make me some tea!" This was delivered sharply to Gunnar, who started guiltily and went to fill the iron kettle again.

Eydis pulled a chair close to the cradle and sat next to Tomas, who smiled at her warmly. She said, "My eldest daughter, Lara, married Charles de Vigny and moved to the south many years ago. I rejoiced when I heard she bore a son, and had named him Tomas, after her father. When the boy was old enough to travel, she brought him to visit, and he spent several years with us in Feringhall. He was happy here, I think, but his father wanted him to go to military school and so Tomas left us and went back to Beaumarais when he was twelve."

She patted Tomas' hand, which still rocked the cradle, steadily. "His mother died that same year, in childbirth. After my husband passed away, I left Feringhall and moved to the town. Later, after his parents died, Gunnar came to live with me. I don't suppose he ever knew his cousin Tomas even existed."

Gunnar, still making the tea, growled, "You are right, he did not." He took the steaming mug to his grandmother, who smiled and thanked him. He asked, "Now Katkin and Tomas are here to help, is it time to try and separate Gwenn and Ketha?"

"We must wait just a little bit longer. There is yet one more piece of the puzzle to fit. In one week's time, on the night of the full moon, we will call on Sister Raven to come out and play. In the meantime, all of you must stay here and rest from your journeys. Is that all right?" Eydis smiled over at Tomas, thinking she would be pleased to spend time with him in the living world before he performed the final task she had set for him. There would be no time, afterwards, except perhaps for goodbyes.

The week passed in peace. Katkin spent a great deal of time conversing with Gunnar as they kept Gwenn company in the alcove, and heard the story of their sojourn in Celeste and the unexpected arrival of Arvid. Although she had heard rumors of the Fynära's defeat at the hands of her son, King Tristan Dinrhydan, she wanted to know all the details. When told of William's courageous death, she wept, for he had been with her almost since the day she had been crowned Queen Arkafina. Her reign had truly come to the most bitter of endings.

Tomas talked with Eydis as they took long walks together through the high firs. She asked him, one day, "Do you feel you have redeemed yourself now, Tomas? You begged me for this chance, so you could atone for the wrongs of your past life."

Tomas stared up at the high green canopy over his head. He said, thoughtfully, "I did not think so at first, but Katrione taught me otherwise. When I knew she had forgiven me, I was finally able to forgive myself. I have learned much from her about giving and forgiving, these last weeks we have been together, and I have found happiness I never thought I deserved." He turned to his grandmother and said with intensity, "Something has changed. She gave herself to me, willingly. That has never happened before, in all our lives before now. Perhaps this time things will end differently..."

Eydis shrugged. "It is beyond my power to know such things,

but we can always hope, can we not? But for now we must finish what that wicked Geya began. Are you ready?"

"Now I have seen my grandsons, I am ready to depart, Grandmother. Only you and I know what lies ahead. Are you afraid?"

His grandmother regarded him seriously, and said, "Indeed I am, for though we have faced this battle before, only Moera knows whether we will win or lose this time. Raven may try a new trick."

Tomas smiled. "You have plenty of tricks of your own, and you know it." His expression turned solemn as he asked, "What will happen to Katrione?"

"I know not, this time. But do not fear for her, Tomas. Moonlight would never allow her vessel to suffer, if she could prevent it."

"But what if she cannot? She is very weak now," he said quietly.

His grandmother sighed. "Yes, I know. She lost a great deal of power when I sent Geya to the outer pellicle. But I had to punish them for what they did to Dai."

"That traitor! Surely whatever they did to him was just?" Tomas frowned as Eydis shook her head.

"Traitor? Nay, not he."

"But..." Tomas began.

"I have sight," Eydis softly insisted. "Only to the turn of the Gyre. Beyond it, I know not what will transpire. But heed me. For this I do accept as true. Though you have been enemies in every life, that enmity will be cast aside — there will come to pass a time when you and Dai Irrakai will stand together in the last battle against the Angellus."

He shook his head in disbelief.

Chapter Twenty-Two

Silvinna

The Numen shakes her head sadly.

Geya, what seed have you sown? What wickedness will the worlds harvest?

I weep for all my children.

~~~~~~~~~~~~

On the seventh day, as the sky darkened and the full moon swept up across the horizon, Eydis asked Gunnar and Tomas to pull Gwenn's bed away from the wall of the alcove. Gwenn lay on top of the coverlet, naked from the waist up. Eydis enclosed the bed in a triangle, drawn on the floorboards with chalk, and placed a tall brass candleholder at each of the vertices. Then she sprinkled protective herbs — angelica, deersbane, rue and motherwort — on Gwenn's chest.

Gunnar stood beside the bed and held Gwenn's hand. It felt icy cold in his, as though death had already claimed her. Eydis looked over at him in concern. Anxiety had etched deep lines to either side of his mouth, and his blue eyes were pale with fear. His grandmother said softly, "Go back out to the main room. Wait with your sons, Gunnar. There will be no place for you here once we start."

He opened his mouth to argue, as Gwenn's eyes flickered, half-open. "Go on, love" she whispered. "Take care of the boys. Don't worry about me." He kissed her mouth and then backed out of the room, never taking his eyes off her face.

Eydis called Tomas and Katkin to the alcove. She closed the heavy velvet drapes and lit the beeswax tapers. The utter silence in the room disconcerted Katkin, and she licked her lips nervously. She did not know what Eydis expected of her, other than to anchor one side of the triangle. Tomas stood across the bed, beside the other leg of the triangle. His eyes met hers and he gave her a reassuring smile. His lips moved silently, forming the words, "I love you," as Eydis, standing at the base, began chanting in a strange tongue.

The chanting went on for some time, and Katkin became aware of a subtle shift in the energy of the room. The candle flames flickered wildly back and forth as the shadows chased each other over Gwenn's pallid skin. Eydis raised her voice to a shriek and clapped her hands, three times. Katkin and Tomas watched as a darkly feathered head pushed forth from between Gwenn's breasts, parting the skin and bones. Gwenn screamed in pain.

Gunnar, over by the fireplace, rocked the cradle with intense concentration, and tried not to think about what might be happening to her.

Once Keth Dirane had emerged completely, she stood still, blinking in the candle light. Then she hopped to the end of the bed, and transformed into her female form. Katkin stared at her grossly distended belly. She shivered, remembering Jacq's words to her, about his unwilling congress with the Goddess.

Ketha remained squatting, hunched over her knees, in a parody of her bird shape. Giving Eydis a venomous glance, she hissed, "What do you want this time, Numen?"

"You must leave her now, Raven."

"No."

Katkin felt again the curious fluttering sensation in her chest. It seemed Lalluna had also awoken, and wanted to obey this command from Eydis. The old woman turned to her and said, "It is not yet your turn, Moonlight." The fluttering abruptly ceased. Katkin noticed, for the first time, a narrow golden thread, sinuous and glowing, connecting her daughter to Keth Dirane. It stretched from Gwenn's solar plexus to a place between the shoulder blades of the naked woman who sat hunched over on the bed.

She stared at Ketha with loathing, and the battle crow turned her head to face her. She croaked, "What are you looking at?"

Katkin cried, "You killed my husband. What did you do with his spirit? It is not in the Vastness where it belongs. Answer me!" Tomas gave Katkin a look of alarm and put a finger to his lips, trying to silence her.

Eydis said, more firmly, "Leave the girl now, and come back with me. You have done your work."

Again, the battle crow said, "No."

Eydis nodded patiently. "So be it. Cut the thread, Tomas."

Ketha jeered, "No living man can cut the thread binding us."

Tomas said, softly, "I am already dead this time, Sister Raven."

He drew his sword, and swung it high. Keth Dirane screamed, "Think, Fyn! If you do this, she will die. Only my power keeps her alive. You would murder your own daughter?"

Gunnar's head snapped up in alarm as he listened to this exchange through the curtain. He had trusted his grandmother's intentions implicitly, thinking she meant no harm to his beloved. Now doubt filled him. Hadn't Gwenn told him, long ago, that only death could break the connection with Ketha? Is that what his grandmother meant to do — kill her? All the tensions of the day concentrated themselves into a single point that lodged like a sharp pain in his chest. He drew his own long white knife, and stepped over to the alcove.

As the sword flashed downwards in the candlelight, Gunnar dived through the curtains. He tackled Tomas, driving him to the ground. Katkin screamed as two of the tall candle holders tipped back and forth, before falling against the curtains. As the velvet drapes caught fire, Tomas threw off Gunnar, and stood up, with the knife protruding grotesquely from his chest.

Eydis, who had been grappling with Keth Dirane, shouted, "Hurry Tomas! You must cut the thread now." The skin on her arms and cheeks already hung in ribbons. Ketha's wicked claws slashed across her neck and she screamed in pain. Her blood covered the white coverlet and spattered Gwenn's pale skin. Tomas swung wide as Gunnar tried to tackle his legs, and missed the mark, cleaving the foot post of the bed neatly in half.

The heat from the fire became unendurable, and as Tomas fell again, Katkin groped for his sword by the bed. Smoke filled her eyes and her lungs, and she bent double in a spasm of coughing. Ketha laughed maniacally and slashed with her deadly black fingernails.

Lalluna's voice, almost too faint to hear, echoed in her mind. "Close your eyes. I will guide the sword." With a cry, she cut the glowing thread, and Ketha seemed to waver, or was that just the shimmering heat from the fire? A glowing spark leapt from the battle crow and struck Katkin's throat, and she cried out in pain.

Eydis screamed to Gunnar, "Get your children out before the whole house is aflame." She collapsed across the foot of the bed, as Tomas gained his feet again.

He cried to Katkin, "Hurry, Katrione. Help him. I will see to them."

Gunnar remained rooted in place, staring wildly at Gwenn's deathly still form on the blood-soaked bed. But over the roar and crackle of the flaming curtains he could hear his sons' pitiful wails of terror.

Katkin shook him, saying, "Come on, we have to save the babies, before it is too late. I cannot carry both of them."

With a cry of utter desolation, he turned from Gwenn and ran back out through the burning curtains to the main room. Already the walls and ceiling were alight. He snatched up Jakob, and cradled him closely, trying to shelter him from the rain of ash and sparks falling thickly from the burning ceiling. Katkin did the same with Arvid, and they fled through the door into the night.

After running a safe distance from the burning house, Gunnar carefully laid Jakob on the sand. Katkin placed Arvid beside his brother. Gunnar gazed down at the two of them for a few seconds and said grimly, "Stay with them. I am going back in. I have to save her."

"No!" she cried. "Look, Gunnar, the roof." Flames licked at the eaves, and it looked as though the house would soon collapse. She pointed to the infants, lying in the sand. "They need you now. You cannot leave them."

Gunnar stared at the flames uncomprehendingly. How could she die like this? He had done everything, worked so hard, and now it had all been in vain.

He gave a cry as Tomas emerged from the door, carrying Gwenn in his arms. His uniform and skin was somehow untouched by the fire as he walked over to Katkin and laid the girl at her feet. Gunnar immediately knelt by her side and took her hand, to see if she still lived. Tomas, with a grimace of pain, silently drew out the knife protruding from his chest and dropped it onto the sand. He turned away and stalked back towards the inferno.

Katkin ran to his side and tried to restrain him. "Don't go

back in there. She must be dead by now, anyway. Did you not see what Ketha's claws did to her?"

He did not answer her, and as she could see her words had no effect on him, she dropped her hand from his arm. Once he had disappeared back inside the house, Katkin, sure he would never emerge again, walked back to Gunnar, who sat disconsolately by Gwenn's side.

The fire's heat had given her thin face a rosy glow, in a horrible mockery of health. But it was clear she would not live much longer. Her eyes opened and she smiled as she saw Gunnar's face hovering over hers.

He could hardly bear to look at her. "By the heart of Silent Brigga, Gwenn. I never meant... Some cursed madness overtook me. I have killed you, and my own grandmother."

She smiled gently. "What does it matter? Ketha has gone from me, at last. I can feel it, inside. Now I can die in peace. Don't grieve love. Not too much. You have our sons. Teach them..." She coughed, and a red ribbon of blood dribbled down her chin. Gunnar remembered his long-ago dream in Einar, and as he had in the dream, he gathered her up into his arms, and cried.

Gwenn spoke again. "Teach them to be mariners, bold and strong. Like their father. Remember to tell them the story of Sif, of the golden hair..."

The house collapsed into a pile of burning rubble, and the flames leapt high into the twilight. Katkin stared, almost disbelieving, as Tomas, still unscathed, somehow managed to push through the blackened timbers and escape. She watched him approach, carrying a limp bundle in his hands, something far too small to be the remains of the old woman. When he joined the little group on the shingle, she saw he held the body of the cat, Hieronymus. He placed it gently on the sand and stroked the orange fur, now badly singed.

She said, "Could you not find her? Eydis, I mean?"

"I found her. This is all that is left of my grandmother. Her familiar. The rest of her *anafireon* returned safely across the heavenly plane, with Sister Raven. Later, when you have time, you must bury Hieronymus, so he will be waiting for her next time she has need of him."

Gunnar stared up at him, perplexed by his cryptic remarks.

He shook his head, thinking it was only the last of his grand-mother's little mysteries. This one she would carry to the grave. He could not accept her death — could not make any sense of the events that led to it, or his own part in them.

Gwenn weakly called his name and he turned his attention back to her. She whispered, "Would you bring our sons to me? I want to hold them once more." He bit back his tears, and gathered the two boys up, then knelt beside her. She could not raise her arms, so he held each child to her bare chest in turn. Both boys searched hungrily for their mother's nipple, and wailed when it was denied them. Gunnar looked down on them, his grief limitless, sure they would die without her.

Tomas went to stand beside Katkin. He said softly, "Now I must leave you, my dear. My time in the living world has come to an end. Together you and I have accomplished our task."

She turned to him, her eyes full of tears. The thought of losing both him and Gwenn together was almost too much to bear. "Do you have to go right now?" she begged. "I still need you."

He smiled and said, "You don't need me, Katrione. You are the strongest woman I have ever known. I think that is why I loved you so much in this life, from the moment you threw the water at me. You reminded me so much of my grandmother." Tomas suddenly looked very old. "Forgive me, love. But I am tired. I have wandered alone for so long."

Katkin nodded guiltily, a little ashamed of her selfish desire to keep him close. "I understand. I will never forget you, my gallant Captain. But will you now be able to go to your rest? Does another Uri'el wait for you under the oak tree?"

He heard the worry in her voice. Staring thoughtfully at the burning house, he said, "Of course. I am going there, as soon as I may. You need have no concerns for me, Katrione."

Katkin seemed reassured by his words, so he met her eyes again and gave her a cheerful smile. The curious fluttering sensation in her chest returned, as though Lalluna had once again awoken, and wanted to leave her body. She shivered, and he took her into his arms.

He whispered, "I am very glad we had this time together, my dear. Farewell."

She clung to him and he kissed her. Then he pushed her arms

gently away, and stepped backwards and a little to the side. The fluttering increased sharply and suddenly went quiet.

Katkin stared for many minutes, with tear-filled eyes, into the void he created, before a shout from the direction of the beach made her turn sharply. She could vaguely see three figures approaching. The darkness yielded few clues to their identity until they were very close. A man with sandy grey hair and a small dark-haired man supported another man. The third man appeared to be ill or injured, for he could only stumble along between them. Katkin thought he must be very old, because he had long silver hair.

She stared hard and then ran forward with a cry. "Huw! Huw! Over here."

Gunnar looked up from Gwenn's side, and saw his first mate, Arvid. He also recognized the Firaithi thrall, and the other man — his rival, Arkady Svalbarad. Cursing, he bent down and retrieved his knife from the sand. He moved forward, holding the hilt loosely between his fingers, without any real idea of what he might do when he reached them. The flickering light from the burning house lit his way. He heard Gwenn cry out weakly behind him.

Arvid eyed the bloodstained knife. He said quietly, "We have not come to fight, Strong Arm. Huw says Gwenn's thrall can heal her. You must let him try."

Gunnar looked askance at him. "He tried to kill her last time they were together, Arvid. Why should I let him near now?"

Arkady raised his head. His lips, dark blue against his parchment colored skin, might have belonged to some long-dead creature. He coughed up a mouthful of blood, and spat it out on the ground at Gunnar's feet. It was like a red flower, growing there in the sand. He said, with great effort. "Because she is already going to die, Northman. Even now, I see Death standing over her. You have nothing to lose and everything to gain. I have so very little time left. Now get out of my way or I will kill you, I swear it."

Gunnar locked eyes with him, and the two men stood frozen in place, bitter enemies who shared only one thing — the love of Gwenn Faircrow. Katkin pleaded, "Please let him try, Gunnar. Perhaps he can help her."

Gunnar cursed and stepped aside.

Arkady placed his hands together, steeling his will for this last and most important attempt to bring forth Hana's fire. As his remaining strength drained away to form the fireball blossoming between his fingers, his legs collapsed. Arvid and Huw dragged him forward until he stood directly over Gwenn. With a convulsive shudder, he dropped the white fire. It struck low on her belly and consumed her utterly.

With a cry of horror, Gunnar rushed forward. As he saw Gwenn rise into the air, he fell to his knees, crying "Holy Father of Ods! What have you done to her?"

He buried his face in his hands as Katkin came to stand beside him and placed a comforting hand on his shoulder. Arvid and Huw lowered Arkady's limp form carefully to the ground. He curled into a fetal position, and began trembling violently. Huw squatted next to his brother, and held his hand. Arvid walked over to the squalling infants and picked them up, then stood by in awe. The burning house lit the scene garishly, but its light did not overpower the white fire still surrounding Gwenn's form.

Gwenn found herself inside a white orb, but she was not alone. A beautiful green-skinned woman came to stand before her, and smiled. "Welcome, daughter."

"Who... Who are you? You look like the lady in Kadya's painting."

Hana nodded. "I am she. My name is Hana, and I need your help."

"How can I help you? I am dead, right?" Gwenn could see nothing but white all around her. Hana's laughter sounded joyous, like rushing water. Jasmine scented the night air.

"No, foolish one. My Seed Bearer has healed you. Now you can be the mother of the Dawnmaid. You must join with him, my daughter."

"With Kadya? But he hates me, and anyway, Gunnar..."

Hana's form faded. "Go to Khalama. The answers you seek will find you there."

The whiteness began to fade too, and Gwenn felt herself settle back down to Yrth. The unaccustomed sensation of standing upright almost made her lose her balance, and as she staggered, Gunnar caught her up in his arms.

"Gwenn! What miracle is this? Are you all right?" His smoke-blackened face was streaked with tears.

Katkin hurried over to offer her a blanket, and Gwenn wrapped it around herself thankfully. Gunnar never took his eyes off her.

She smiled and touched his face. "Why are you crying?"

"This feels like a dream. I prayed so many times for you to get well, but I never believed..." Gunnar turned to where Arkady lay on the ground and said in a voice filled with despair, "He made it happen. I think... I think he is dying. You had better go and give him your thanks now, before it is too late."

Gwenn put a hand over her mouth, and walked away from him. He watched her for a long moment, then turned and headed into the dunes. Arvid followed him, still carrying the twins. As Gwenn approached Arkady, Huw rose and blocked her path. Her eyes widened as she recognized her former thrall. She stopped, and in a moment of forgetfulness, groped for keth'fell, before dropping her hands uselessly to her sides. Huw stared at her, recalling Eira's death and his own torture at the hands of the Fynära. Though he reminded himself she was Katkin's child, and the victim of Keth Dirane, still he could not damp the hatred boiling up inside him.

Then Gwenn said something that struck him as extraordinary. "I am sorry, Mr. Adaryi. My men killed your sister and father, and many more of your people. I don't expect forgiveness. If you wish to slay me, so be it, but I would like to say goodbye to Kadya first."

Huw opened his mouth to speak, but no sound came forth. He seemed to be engrossed by something behind her left shoulder, so she turned her head. A brilliant green curtain of light filled the sky from horizon to horizon. Shimmering waves of radiation washed out the stars with their brilliance. Huw brushed past her, unseeing, walked a few more steps and fell to his knees.

Gwenn knelt at Arkady's side and took his hand. "Kadya," she softly said, and his eyes opened. His face, previously twisted in a grimace of pain, softened, and his lips curved upwards in the dim shadow of a smile. He lifted a trembling hand and brushed her cheek. She grasped it in her own and held it to her lips. "Kadya," she murmured again and then could think of nothing else to say

289

because she knew he was dying. He had given his life for hers, the moment he drank the henbane decoction.

"Gwenn," he whispered, and she had to lean close to hear his words. "I came to you, do you remember?"

She nodded, and stifled a cry as he threw his head back in a spasm of pain. After a moment, it passed, and he continued. "I wanted... to say I was sorry. But you could not hear me, could you?" He squeezed her hand weakly. "I should not have blamed you for... everything."

Gwenn wept. What did Hana's words mean now? She said, through her tears, "I saw her. Your green lady. She is very beautiful."

"She came to me, too. To tell me I hadn't failed her. I don't understand why. You and I... we were supposed to have a child. Did you know?'

"Yes, she told me so, just now. I think that is why Ketha feared you so much. She tried to make Gunnar kill you, and when he did not, she tricked him into making me pregnant instead." But at that moment, Gunnar and the twins seemed a part of another lifetime, as distant as a misty star.

"Does he... take good care of you?" Arkady's eyes closed, and he sighed.

"Yes," she said. "He loves me very much, and the babies."

His chimerical smile appeared again. "That is good, otherwise I would have to come back and haunt him."

Gwenn sobbed, "How can you make jokes? You are dying because of me. I never should have asked Ketha to find you."

He stroked her hair. "I am glad you did, even though we did not manage to fulfill the prophecy. You gave me so much, my crow girl. My beautiful crow girl..." He said nothing else for a long while, and to Gwenn it felt as though the whole world stood still, watching with her as he drew one last breath. Suddenly his eyes snapped open again and his grip grew firm in her hand. "I have to go back to T'Shang. Hana says... Don't let them bury me here. Please, love, don't let them..." His eyelids slowly sank downwards, and his face went slack. She put her head down on his chest and listened to his heart falter and stop.

Huw watched in awe as the green light continued to light up the heavens. Somehow, he knew it was a sign from the Un-Named

One, to show he must forgive the blond maiden known as the Faircrow. Eira's voice spoke in his mind, "Yes, my brother, for we know now she will be the mother of the Dawnmaid, the deliverer of our Kindreds."

"But how? Our brother Kadya is dying."

"That I do not know." Her voice faded, as the lights dimmed to nothingness. The fire at Feringhall finally burned itself out, and the beach went very dark. Huw turned back to Arkady. Gwenn's head still rested on his chest.

She said dully, "I think he is dead."

Huw gave a cry of distress and walked away to find Katkin, who had been as spellbound as he by the green light. When he reached her side, she wrapped her arms around him for comfort. Only the wailing of the twins, who hungrily cried for their mother, broke the mournful silence.

Gwenn stood, like a sleepwalker, and went in search of Gunnar and Arvid. When she stumbled into the dunes, following the sound, Gunnar handed her Jakob without a word. She sank down onto the sandy ground and fed him, and Arvid handed over his namesake to join his brother. Gunnar walked away again, to the water's edge, and watched as the full moon appeared from behind a cloud. The red dragon prow of the *Fire Drake* looked pitch black in the flat white light. Arvid walked up beside him, and put an arm around his shoulder.

Gunnar stared desolately out to sea. "Now that she lives again, I am going to lose her to a ghost. She told me in Celeste she still loved him, and now he has given his life for her, how can I ever be equal in her eyes? I should just climb aboard the *Fire Drake* and sail away. There is nothing left in Starruthe for me."

Arvid said wisely, "Don't go yet, Strong Arm. I believe Gwenn loves you more than you know." Gunnar was shaking his head, so Arvid continued, "At least talk with her before you leave. She still needs you, and so do your sons."

Gunnar felt very tired, and his body ached from his fight with Tomas. He said, "I am going aboard the *Fire Drake* to lie down. Tomorrow, I will decide what to do. I don't want to think about anything else right now." He sloshed through the shallows to the boat, and hoisted himself aboard. Arvid watched him until he disappeared into the shadowed stern and then went back into the dunes. Gwenn still sat, disconsolately, holding the babies, both sleeping quietly after their feed. He squatted before her and she looked up. Even in the dark of night, her eyes were a startling shade of blue.

"How is he, Arvid?"

Arvid frowned. "Unhappy. He thinks you don't care for him. That your heart is given only to the thrall. Is he right, Faircrow?"

She sighed. "No. He isn't." Vehemently she continued, "Why can I not love them both? I do... love them both. As I love my two sons. It is not fair, Arvid. I should not have to choose between them."

"Go and talk to him. Let me stay with the boys." Shrugging off the blanket, she stood and laid the babies down on it, wrapping them up well against the chill breeze from the ocean. They slept on peacefully. Arvid stretched out on the sand beside them, and pillowed his head in his arm. Gwenn thanked him and headed for the boat.

Once she climbed aboard, she stood still, trying to pick out Gunnar's form on the shadowy deck. The moonlight caught his blond hair, making it shine white, and for an instant she was reminded of Arkady, lying still and silent on the sand. She walked down the sloping deck to where he lay, wrapped in a deerskin coverlet, facing the side. Silently, she squeezed underneath and curled her body into his. Gunnar said gruffly, "I am trying to get some sleep. What do you want?"

Gwenn whispered, "Do you remember the last time we made love? In my bath house?" She felt him nod in the darkness. "I told you then I loved you. Nothing has changed."

He rolled over on to his back and stared up at the stars, blinking on and off as the clouds scurried overhead. "Everything changed when *he* came back. You called me a stinking Northman. You said you hated me and our children."

"Did I? I don't remember doing that."

"You did. I want to forgive you, but I don't know if I can. It hurt."

She found his hand and squeezed it. "I am sorry. The last few weeks seem like a horrible dream to me. But now I am well again..."

He interrupted her, saying bitterly, "Yes. Thanks to him."

Gwenn rested her head on his broad chest. "Yes, thanks to him. But *more* thanks to you, Gunnar." she declared. "You were the one who rescued me from my brother's men in Beaumarais, cared for me in Secuny, and brought me here to Feringhall so your Grandmother could help me. I would not be here now, if not for you."

He growled, "So you want to stay with me, out of gratitude?"

She raised her head. "No! Damn you, Gunnar! Why can't you get it through your thick, northern skull? I am here because I love you. Why will you not believe me?" Staring down at him, her eyes full of tears, she wondered what else she could say to convince him.

Finally, somehow, he did believe. He gave a cry and wrapped his arms around her. A second later, her lips found his. A powerful need drove them onwards very quickly, and within a minute, Gwenn was straddling his belly as she had in the bathing hut. She said, "There is plenty of room here. Do you want me to move?"

He guided her firmly downwards to meet his rising hips, and took several deep breaths, trying to control himself. The heat inside her was almost overpowering. He inhaled sharply and replied, "No, you were right. This is very good... just like this." Then he said nothing else but her name, again and again, as many months of unfulfilled desire overtook them both.

Chapter Twenty-Three

Fyn's Gift

Fyn makes his way through Death's Kingdom, but not back to the oak tree in the dell. He knows there is no gentle Uri'el waiting for him, anywhere or anywhen in the Vastness. Geya's thoughtless soul transference has seen to that.

He carries his grandmother's stones in his pocket. After a time he draws a single rune and studies it, then smiles to himself, for it is Fyn's Gift.

As long as Katrione and Lalluna are safe and happy, Fyn is content to set off on his long journey, utterly alone. He is determined to go now to the very heart of the Vastness, and fight the Angellus, as he has done so many times before.

~~~~~~~~~~

Katkin and Huw, standing side by side on the gently rolling deck of the *Fire Drake*, watched the coast of Starruthe slipping by. They spoke softly to one another, exchanging stories. After telling Huw of her sojourn in prison, she listened as he described his life with Arkady on the lonely island. Katkin wanted to know how Arkady had managed to get a message to Einar.

"I knew the henbane decoction would be very dangerous, but Kadya's mind was made up. Once he took it, I watched over him for many hours as he lay unconscious. When he woke, the illness struck him right away, but he managed to tell me what he had done. After drinking the poison, he said his spirit felt light, like a bird, and he knew he could fly across the waves. When he came to Feringhall, he found Gwenn, but he could not use the Un-Named One's fire to heal her. It would not work without his physical body there to manifest the flame. The old woman, the sorceress, was her name... Eydis?" Katkin nodded and he continued. "Eydis... She appeared to him, as she had in his dream, and said he must fly instead to Einar. So he did, and found the house of Sven Red Beard. At first, Sven did not want to help him. Then he explained that I, too, waited on the island, and Red Beard agreed to bring a boat."

"Why did he want to help you and not Kadya?" Katkin asked.

"Because I saved his life," Huw said self-consciously, and changed the subject. "I had to spend every waking minute caring for Kadya in the days that followed and I felt very unhappy. I thought he would likely die from the poison he had ingested and I did not believe his rambling tale of finding Sven and asking for his help. How could Red Beard be back in Einar? We left him stranded on a sand bar. You can imagine how astonished I was after five days, when the raiders arrived in a long boat, captained by none other than Sven Red Beard. He helped me carry Kadya on board and we headed straight back to Starruthe."

"How *did* Sven get from the sand bar to Starruthe?"

"From the beginning, we were never sure who took the *Moon Drake*. I thought it must have been the other thralls, because they left us some food. Kadya and I lived in fear that the raiders would turn up again and try to murder us in our sleep. It turned out Sven knew all the long that the coast we headed for belonged to an uninhabited island, because the Dalvolk had once had a settlement there, called Asaruthe, that had been abandoned long ago. Once the tide went out, he and the others swam to shore and spent the night on the beach. In the morning, they found a somewhat seaworthy vessel that the settlers had left behind and set out for Starruthe. We never even knew they had been there on the island with us."

"Weren't you afraid to go with them, knowing they might make you a thrall again?"

"Yes, I did feel afraid, at first. But Sven explained about the defeat of the Fynäran force in St. Valery and he told me of Arvid's return to Einar. He was the sole survivor of that battle, besides Gunnar, of course. After Arvid made himself Magnus, he decreed there would be no more raiding. He said the Fynära must become traders, like their Dalvolk cousins, and live in peace. Then he freed all the thralls, and sent them back to the mainland."

"He must be a good man."

Huw's expression darkened. "He murdered my Patre and my sister Eira."

"But he was following Gwenn's orders. I am so sorry you lost your family because of it."

Huw turned to watch Gwenn, as she stood talking and laughing with Gunnar by the steering oar. He said thoughtfully, "I know now she was not responsible for what happened. I had to forgive her when the Un-Named One came to us in the sky last night. How could I not? She must somehow be a part of the Prophecy. But I don't understand how it will be fulfilled through her, now that Kadya is gone."

Huw pictured his last moments with his brother, as Arkady lay on the beach, writhing in agony as his liver failed completely. He sighed deeply. "I will miss him so much. Why did he have to die?" He stared out to sea. Katkin laid a sympathetic hand on his arm when she saw the tears spilling down his cheeks.

She said softly, "I will miss him too. He was a brother to both of us. But he loved Gwenn, and wanted her to be whole again, so he sacrificed himself for her. She told me he was at peace in the end, even telling jokes." Katkin studied the greenish waves, remembering how the brilliant aurora had lit up the night sky with a sheet of viridian flame. "Your Goddess must be very beautiful to be able to create such a display in the sky."

Huw blushed and hung his head in embarrassment. "I think she looks just like my sister Eira." He turned to Katkin and asked her curiously, "Why do you think Gwenn stopped Gunnar and Arvid from burning Kadya's body? She seemed very determined."

"She told them Kadya had begged to be taken back to T'Shang before he died. Still, I felt very surprised when Gunnar agreed to take his remains on the *Fire Drake*. You would think he would want to be rid of him. It is a very long way to Khalama, the village where Kadya's old teacher, Dawa Tinley, lives. But Gunnar said his people have sailed the rivers of Ruboralis for hundreds of years and he can find a way there."

"I don't think the Northman wants to go to T'Shang — he just agreed because he loves your daughter," Huw replied. "That is the one thing he and Kadya had in common." Then, he said with concern, "I wonder if Gwenn believes Kadya will somehow be brought back to life by his teacher? I think she should not be so unrealistic. It only leads to heartache."

Katkin wondered briefly what Huw knew about heartache that made his voice sound so despairing. She realized that she knew very little about the Firaithi man who stood beside her. Did he have a woman of his own somewhere? She pushed that question to the back of her mind. As soon as the *Fire Drake* reached the mainland, they would most likely be going their separate ways.

She saw her daughter bend down and pick up a wriggling blanket-wrapped bundle from a wooden box securely lashed to the deck. Gunnar reached out and took Jakob from her. He cradled the infant loosely in his arm, and kept his other hand on the steering oar. His weathered face held nothing but joy and contentment as he puffed on his pipe. Arvid stood by and held out his arms for his namesake. From where Katkin stood, at the prow, the happy picture before her seemed flat, and somehow impossibly remote.

Huw must have guessed her thoughts, for he asked, "What will you do now, Katkin?"

Katkin shrugged and said tiredly, "I don't know. Gunnar and Gwenn are traveling on to T'Shang after they take Arvid back to Einar. They told me I could go with them, but I think I would just be in the way. Gwenn doesn't need me anymore, Huw. No-one does. My son despises me and I am wanted for treason in my homeland. I can never return there."

Huw said nothing for half a minute or more. He appeared to be occupying himself with an intense study of the decking at their feet. Then he took a deep breath and said, very softly, "I know of a place where you will always be Queen." He raised his dark brown eyes to meet her astonished gaze, and gently took her hand and placed it over his heart. "I would be greatly honored if you would come with me. I am going to cross Yr on the greater Ambit, and search for the rest of my people."

Her eyes went wide. "I... I don't know what to say, Huw."

He quickly dropped her hand and said bitterly, "Let me say it for you then. While you hold me in the highest regard, you could not possibly live with a darky. We come from different worlds, you and I."

To his everlasting surprise, she laughed merrily at this and found his hand again, then laced her fingers through his. "You could not be more wrong, Huw. Don't you remember what I tried to tell you once before — that we have a secret bond? We come from exactly the same world. I also was born to one of the Kindreds."

He stared at her, unwilling to believe this. "But I know of your childhood. Your parents were wealthy landowners. How can this miracle be true?" When she had explained about her mother's defection from the Kindred of Anandi, he shook his head in amazement. "No-one ever suspected?"

"Only my treacherous Prime Minister, Philip Tremayne. He used the information to turn the House of Deputies against me." Katkin paused and sighed deeply, then said, "And my husband." Her green eyes clouded with sorrow. "You were right about one thing — I *do* hold you in the highest regard, Huw. But I lost Jacq and I lost Tomas. I just don't know if I am ready to try again, at least for a little while."

He took her hand and placed it to his lips. "You don't have to say anything else. I will wait until your heart mends."

Katkin smiled. "Then I would be pleased to travel at your side and find the rest of our people."

Together they stood at the prow of the *Fire Drake* and gazed to the eastern horizon, as the sun swung high in the cloudless blue sky.

Appendix I

The Linnun

The Linnun, or water runes, are the oldest known form of divination among the settled peoples of Yr, and are used by both the Fynära and the Dalvolk. They consist of twenty-five round stones, kept in a pouch of reindeer skin. Each is incised or painted with a symbol, representing one of the many physical forms of water. The sea-faring peoples use them to predict the outcome of a journey, or any other situation calling for guidance. Stones are drawn from the pouch one at a time. No more than three stones make a reading, or Linn.

Sailor's Graveyard (Whirlpool) – Confusion and fear will reign.

Dead Men's Lick (Waterspout) – All plans will be upset.

Ice Dragon's Breath (Freezing Fog) – The mist hides the cold heart of darkness, where nothing comes and goes.

Tamis (Spring Tide) – Passion, birth.

Silvinna (Neap Tide) – Harvest, day of reckoning.

Nung the Demon's Snare (Thin or Rotten Ice) – Do not proceed. The situation is not as it seems.

Silent Brigga's Dream (Steam) – The rising spirit. Heaven is near.

The Mariner's Abode (Ocean) – Search the mysterious depths for meaning.

Faysta's Gate (Estuary) – A new way will be found.

Lut's Hammer (Tidal Wave) – Death and destruction are imminent.

The Ice Demon's Roof (Thick or Iron Ice) – You can depend on this person or situation.

Lut's Leviathan (Iceberg) – Travel is likely.

Silent Brigga's Tear (Snowflake) – There is beauty, but it causes only sadness.

Dragon's Teeth (Hail) – A violent confrontation.

The Ice Demon's Paint Brush (Hoarfrost) – Now it is time to wait.

Fyn's Gift (Gentle Rain) – Happiness, warmth and companionship.

Silent Brigga's Bewilderment (Sleet) – Confusion over which way to turn.

The Call of the Budtime (Open Ice) – Adventure is at hand. Seize it!

Feathers of Fyn (Storm Clouds) – A time of darkness approaches, but will pass away.

The Grasping Hands of Old Mother Cinnus (Undertow) – Beware. This situation could prove overwhelming.

The Wild Horses of Grandfather Ods (Aegir) – A powerful man or woman is on their way.

Berbiroc (Waterfall on the edge of the Yrth) – Judgment, the end of adventuring.

Orlinir Flow (Warm current running against cold) – Love triumphs over all.

Rindras Flow (Cold current running against warm) – Love will fail.

Lutyond's White Horses (Whitecaps) – Unlooked for help is on the way.

Appendix II

Glossary

Acorn – Jacq and Katkin's stone cottage on the grounds of her late father's former estate, Tintaren. Burned down by the King's Guard after Jacq's arrest for spying.

Anafireon – The spirit of the living.

Beaumarais – A small country in the continent of Yr. Bounded to the east by the Mistmere and Mardon to the west. The northern border is shared with Secuny and the southern with Spanja. The capital is Isle St. Valery, an important trading hub on the inland sea.

Citadel, The – The five-sided fortress that overlooks the City of Isle St. Valery. The abode of the ruling monarch and the Guard.

Chamber of Deputies – The ruling body of Beaumarais, consisting of one hundred representatives elected biannually.

Cottar – Peasant or serf.

Dinrhydan, The – Jacq Benet's code name. Translates as "true heart" in the old tongue.

d'angwir – Jacq Benet's sword. Means "justice for all" in the old tongue.

Firaithi – A wandering people, comprised of twenty Kindreds, who traverse Yr trading in horses and handcrafts. Their earliest history is unknown to outsiders, but it is surmised that they may have come east a thousand or more years ago from the mountainous region now known as T'Shang. They speak an obscure language unrelated to the other tongues of Yr. The Firaithi peoples are dark-skinned with brown or hazel eyes. They tend to be small in stature with a wiry build. Their hair is thick and lavish, and both men and women prefer long tresses, done up in braids. Their Goddess, whom they refer to as "The Un-Named One" is Hana, the Eastern Star.

Felag – The unbreakable fellowship between Fynäran raiders.

Fyn – A god of the Fynära, beloved of Lalluna.

Fynära – A marauding, seafaring race. For more details on the history and customs of the Fynära see Appendix III.

Geya – A Triple Goddess of the Amaranthine. Her sisters are Raven and Moonlight.

Gruagá – Firaithi name for the settled peoples of Yr. Means "white devil." Pl. Gruagán.

Gyre – Everything that is or ever will be winds around the infinity of time in the Gyre.

keth'fell – Gwenn Faircrow's sword. Means "death crow" in the old tongue.

Keth Dirane – The name that the Amaranthine Raven was given by the Firaithi when she came to Yrth. Lit. "Death's Shade."

Kindreds, The – Divisions of the Firaithi people. Normally a group of around thirty to forty adults and children.

Knar – Dalvolk tradeship.

Linnun – The divination method of the Dalvolk. Also called "water runes."

Lutyond – The Divine Mariner, god of the Fynära.

Magnus – The lord of the Fynära.

Mardon – A neighboring but unfriendly country to the west of Beaumarais. Several wars have been fought between Mardon and Beaumarais over disputed territories. Citizens from Mardon are called the Mardonne.

Mistmere – The large inland sea that brings trade and exchange to Beaumarais. Isle St. Valery is on a peninsula that extends into the Mere.

Moera – The Goddess of Fate.

Moonlight – Amaranthine. Sister of Geya. Also called Lalluna.

Pellicle – Part of the Amaranthine system of addressing points on the Continua. Pl. pellicula.

Raven – Amaranthine. Sister of Geya. Also called Keth Dirane.

Reynard, Nicholas – Former Prime Minister of Beaumarais. Murdered by Gwenn Faircrow.

Secuny – The neighboring country to the northwest of Beaumarais.

Tsmar'enth – The moon gate. Firaithi expression for death.

Skald – A storyteller or bard.

Skryvinin – Learned elders of the Fynära.

Skyre – The heavenly reward of the Fynäran raiders, an eternity of feasting and fighting.

St. Valery's Acre – The vast forest that clothes the western shores of the Mistmere.

Tane – Leader of a Firaithi Kindred. An inherited position.

Triske stones – The divination method used by the Firaithi. Consists of three octahedral bone carvings — each face is incised with a different symbol.

Yoke – The land bridge between the shores of the Mistmere and the City of Isle St. Valery. Narrow and paved with cobbles, the Yoke is gated on both ends and heavily guarded.

Yr – The continent on which Beaumarais is located.

Yrth – A watery world, with only one main landmass, the vast continent of Yr. The residents have fire and steam power, but not electricity. Several large islands exist to the west of Yr, mostly unexplored.

Appendix III

The History of the Fynära

They spoke the language of the people of the long valley, the Dalvolk of Danica, but they were in no way similar to them. The Dalvolk traded peacefully up and down the coast, providing much needed commerce to the coastal villages, and even far inland, along the broad rivers of Yr. The arrival of their ships brought joy to the settled peoples, for they came bearing spices from Shadion, silks from Cherumea and a host of other exotic commodities. They were skilled sailors, the men of Danica, but still they rarely strayed far from the shore or from their established routes. Up and down the seacoast of Yr, from Spanja to the Gulf of Angar'et, and inland, deep in the heart of Ruboralis along the Bresla River, they carried their wares, shrewdly buying and selling.

Perhaps the first ship of the Fynära might have been greeted with equal enthusiasm, when it drew up onto the beach of some unknown coastal province, though it looked nothing like the wide-bodied trading vessels of the Dalvolk. It was long and lean, built for speed, like some marauding beast of prey. Did the villagers remark on the carved dragon's head forming the prow? Did they wonder about the row of brightly painted shields hanging port and starboard? When the tall, flaxen-haired men issued forth, the villagers probably crowded around to see what they had brought to trade, not noticing right away their grim expressions or the weapons they bore. The cheerful greetings would have soon turned to screams of fear and dismay, as the Northmen drew their swords and began the slaughter.

Those villagers who fell and stained the sand bright red with their blood might have counted themselves among the fortunate, had they been able to see what fate awaited the survivors. Rounded up, tied hand and foot, the women and children herded aboard the waiting vessel were stowed along with all the other valuables of the village — the cattle and horses, silver dishes and pewter cups, golden necklaces and jeweled rings. Within an hour, the shore would be in flames, burning thatch and wood, with nothing left worth taking.

Now the dragon ships put to sea, and did not remain in the safety of the coastal waters. Back to the northwest they sailed, straight across the rough open ocean, with their cargo of sick and terrified captives. Back to Starruthe, their island home.

Far across the black waves, it was a land of mists and snow, frozen in an icy sea for half the year. Everlastingly snow-capped mountains dominated the center of the island, with glaciers carving deep valleys downwards to the sea. Quiet and dark forests of fir and pine clothed the mountain flanks, home to deer and elk. Hardly anyone lived in the interior, just a few hardy and independent farmers and huntsmen. Most of the residents of Starruthe lived in the southern coastal villages. Einar had the best natural harbor, and so grew to become the capital. The Magnus, or Lord, had an imposing residence on the hill overlooking the town. The spoil, human and material, belonged to him, for he paid for the ships, outfitted the men who sailed them, and protected the town in their absence. He would keep the best-looking women and the sturdiest children for his own use. The rest would be sold to Haba traders, who met the ships of the Fynära in ports of call far south of Starruthe. They sold them still further south and made a handsome profit.

Once their menace became known, the peoples of Yr gathered, now and again, to form short-lived defensive alliances against them. Sometimes they would chase the ships far out to sea. But the men of the Fynära possessed one unassailable advantage — they could navigate the trackless waves, and negotiate the ice-locked seas of the north. No sailor from the warmer climes and friendlier waters of Yr could touch them and they knew it. So their predations continued, for hundreds of years. The coastal villages could breathe easily in the autumn and winter, but the high tides of spring spelled danger. Once the ice broke free from the harbor in Einar, the call would go out for men and boys to man the dragonships. The Magnus found crewing such expeditions easy, despite the dangers of the open sea. They would come, huge red-bearded men and smooth-cheeked boys, from the coastal villages and inland farms, relishing the thought of battle — and desiring plunder. Because of the right of primogeniture, only the eldest son in a Fynäran household would inherit any property. Other sons had to make their own way and their own fortunes, and the spoil from several successful raids could set a young man up with a farm and a woman — or a raiding ship of his own.

Even death in combat held its own reward, for their Gods — Fyn, Lutyond and the rest — rewarded the heroes of this world with an eternity of feasting and fighting in Skyre. The Gods were as fiercely true-hearted as their human charges — and as combative. Fyn sent his swallows to lead the dragonships out of the harbors, on their voyages of death and destruction. To the peoples of Yr this incomprehensible thuggery seemed low and despicable, but the Fynära had their own code of virtue. Honor, courage and loyalty forged bonds between shipmates, an unbreakable fellowship, seeing them through battle and storm, until they returned at last in the red autumn to the sheltered bays of their island home.

About the author

Suzanne Francis believes the genesis for her inventive Song of the Arkafina series lies in her chronic travel sickness as a child and young adult. While growing up in England and on the Continent, she happily participated in many family and school trips, though riding in the back seat of a car often left her suffering from nausea for hours on end. To help pass the time, she began telling herself stories, serialized over many days and weeks, often featuring the landscapes through which she was traveling. These imaginary adventures, along with a life-long love of reading good books (but only when sitting still) sparked her interest in writing. Since then she has penned many fantasy short stories and sonnets, as well as two novels.

After earning her BA in Geography, Suzanne worked for several years as an urban planner in the USA, before retiring to have children. A series of part-time jobs followed, everything from migrant farm worker to dishwasher, retail manager to massage therapist. Her appetite for voyaging has taken her to such far-flung places as the Cook Islands, Mexico, across the deserts and Deep South of America and on many adventures through the capitals of Europe. She has drawn on these life experiences to amplify and embellish the unique characters and settings of her novels.

In addition to writing, her passions include neo-paganism and playing a perversely difficult musical instrument called the hurdy-gurdy.

She is a member of the Troth, and the Otago Writer's Guild.

Presently, Suzanne lives in rural Dunedin, New Zealand with her husband Michael and four children.

Author's Acknowledgements

Heartfelt thanks go to Mike Goodwin, my friend and talented writing buddy, for providing invaluable editing assistance and encouragement. Also to my editor, Martyn Folkes at Mushroom eBooks — without his dedication and skill, *Ketha's Daughter* would be a lesser book.

Carolyn and Fabienne helped just by being there.

My husband and children remain loving and supportive, even through the longest writing days, and are my greatest blessing.